A Fisher of Slaves

To Andy Giles
Many thanks
Dickie

A Fisher of Slaves

2nd Edition

DICK PARSONS

authorHOUSE®

AuthorHouse™ UK
1663 Liberty Drive
Bloomington, IN 47403 USA
www.authorhouse.co.uk
Phone: 0800.197.4150

Published by AuthorHouse 09/16/2015

ISBN: 978-1-5049-8998-5 (sc)
ISBN: 978-1-5049-8997-8 (hc)
ISBN: 978-1-5049-8999-2 (e)

Print information available on the last page.

To Anne and Mary

Acknowledgement

My grateful thanks to Gillian Hancock for her excellent proof reading and to Anthony New for designing the cover.

CANADA

GREAT
LAKES

AMERICAN COLONIES

NEW YORK

KANNAPOLIS

NEW FORT

CHAMERAS

ATLANTIC OCEAN

BAHAMAS
ISLANDS

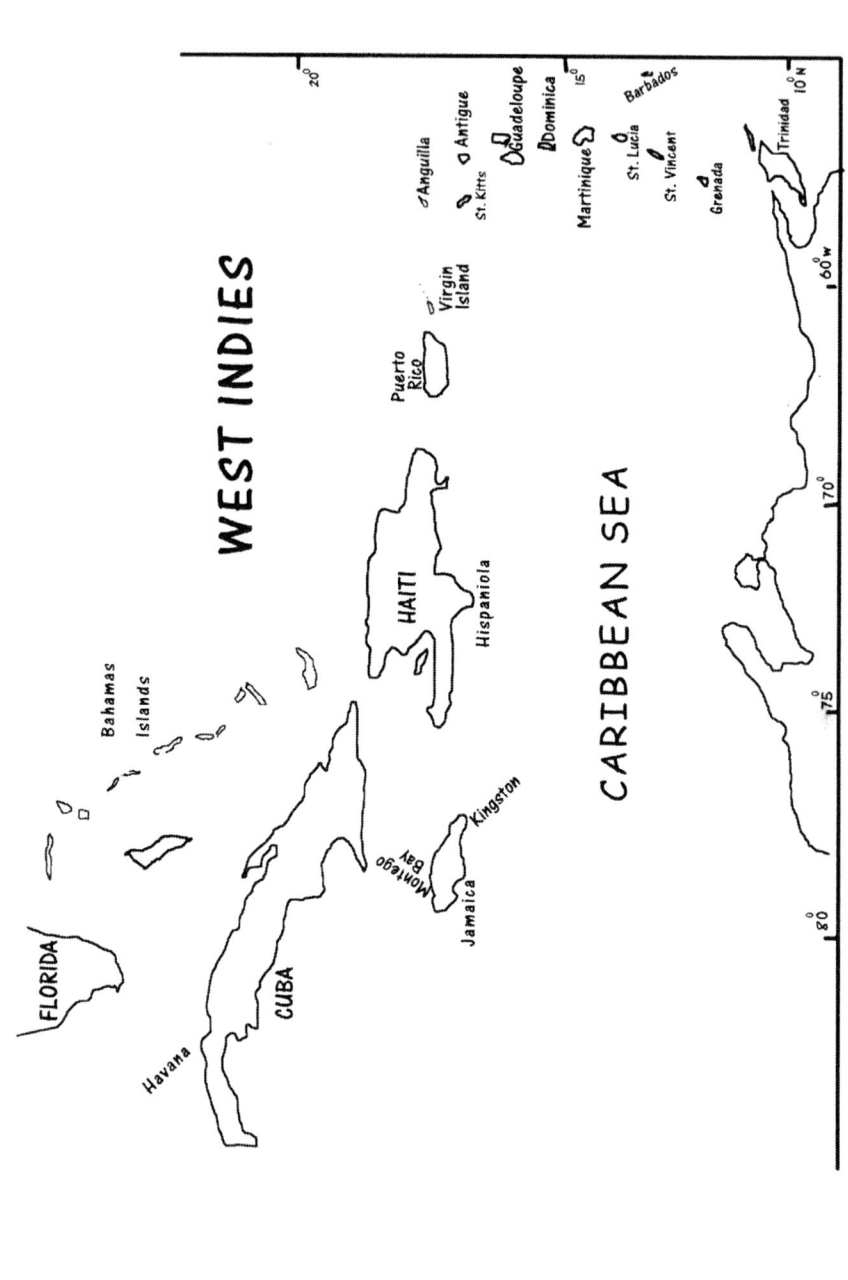

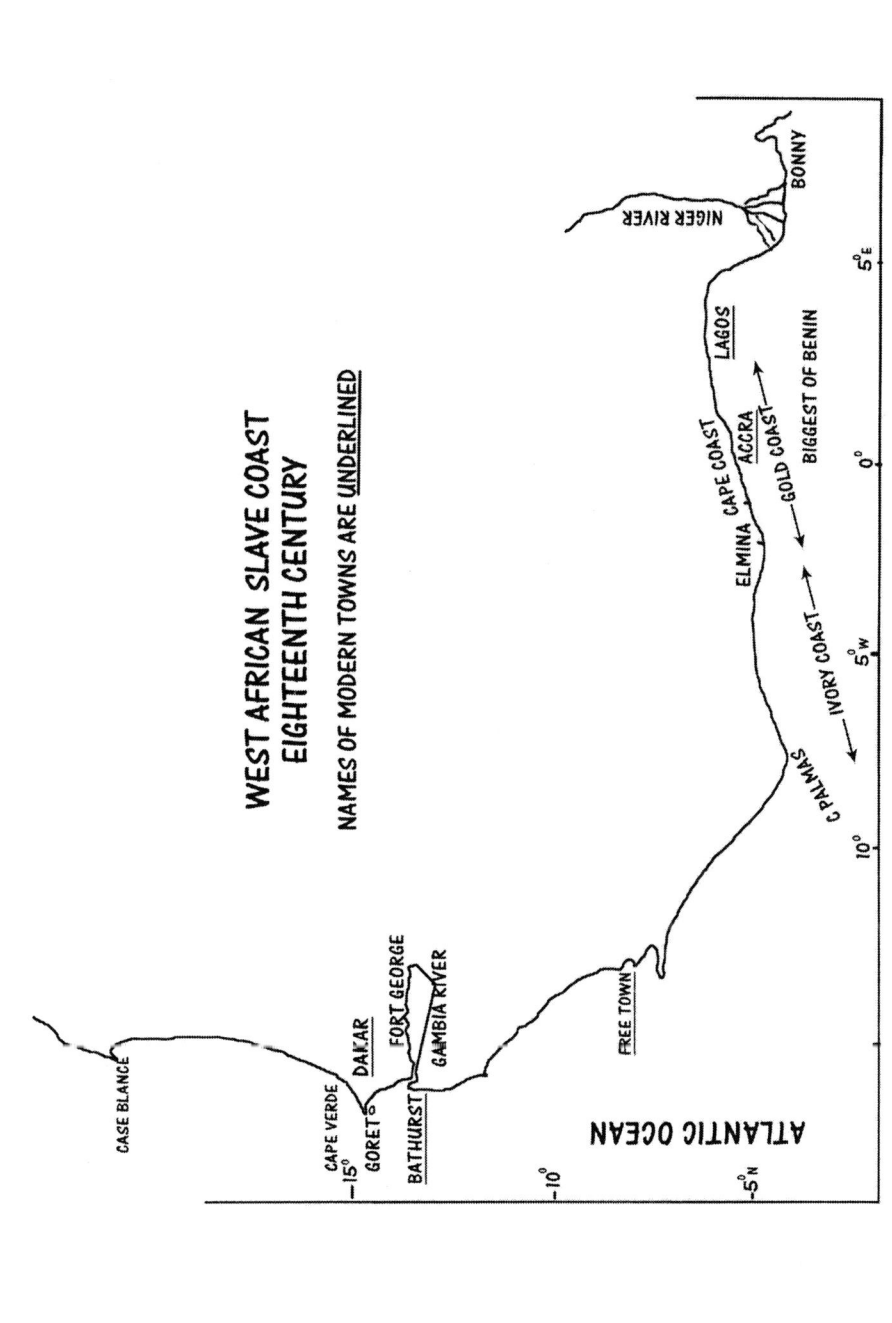

WEST AFRICAN SLAVE COAST
EIGHTEENTH CENTURY

NAMES OF MODERN TOWNS ARE UNDERLINED

CASE BLANCE

CAPE VERDE
GOREE
DAKAR
FORT GEORGE
BATHURST
GAMBIA RIVER

FREE TOWN

C PALMAS

IVORY COAST

GOLD COAST

ELMINA
CAPE COAST
ACCRA

LAGOS

BIGGEST OF BENIN

NIGER RIVER

BONNY

ATLANTIC OCEAN

Chapter 1

"Are you quite sure?" Elizabeth looked across the table at her young son. It was a question that had to be asked; though she knew his answer before he spoke.

He looked up at her, his spoon poised midway between plate and mouth. "Yes, Mama. Quite, quite sure. Why d'you keep on asking me? You know it's what I really want to do."

Elizabeth sighed. Nathaniel was right, she'd asked him the same question time and time again and he'd always given her the same answer. What was it about the sea that seemed to have such a hold over him? Didn't he know how savage it could be? Couldn't he understand the dangers? How often had she told him that it wasn't always blue and beautiful? That it could be angry. That when the wind tormented it, the sea could vent its fury on those frail ships and overcome them, or throw them contemptuously against the rocks? But he wouldn't listen; she couldn't reason with him. Whenever they saw the sea he was always fascinated by it, pointing excitedly at the distant ships and asking repeatedly about the horizon and what lay beyond. It was as if the sea had bewitched him.

"Well then Nathaniel," she said trying to hide her resignation. "Eat up your breakfast and we'll be off to the Dolphin."

She'd been to Bristol twelve months ago, when her father had seen the Archdeacon. Nathaniel, then eleven, had begged to come as well. He'd dragged her out to walk along the quayside, where the hustle and bustle of the ships unloading had been like a drug to him. It seemed he'd wanted to look at every ship in the port. When they'd returned to the inn she'd been quite exhausted, but Nathaniel had been exhilarated. Later at supper, when he'd been telling her father about their day, Nathaniel's enthusiasm had caught the attention of an old gentleman sitting nearby.

"There be a lad cut out for the sea, if ever I saw un," he'd said with a chuckle.

"D'you really think so, sir?" Nathaniel had asked. The old man had nodded, "Aye, boy. I can see there be saltwater in yer veins!"

Nathaniel had laughed and looked greatly pleased and suddenly the two of them had been engrossed in talk of ships and cargoes.

"Most of 'em 'ereabouts are slavers of course," the old fellow had said, "but some run up to the Baltic with wool or ship claret and brandy from Bordeaux. But 'tis the slavers that make a fortune, that's if Lady Luck sails with 'em. The others," he'd shrugged his shoulders. "Well, they give a livin'."

As Elizabeth heard them talking, the reality of the slave trade had burst upon her. Never before had she thought deeply about slavery, yet now she began to suspect the great wealth, which surrounded her, was founded on this inhuman trade. Suddenly she'd been quite horrified and had felt an overwhelming sense of guilt. It was as if she too was responsible for the terrible exploitation of those poor blacks. Did the colour of their skin make them less human? Did their alien features give us the right to enslave them? The plight of those innocent victims of a merciless, barbaric, savage trade had come forcibly home to her. The perpetrators of this evil business must surely be avaricious, stonyhearted brutes. Were they the merchants who lived in those finely decorated houses in King's Street just a short walk from the quay? A wave of anger had swept over her. At that moment she'd known, she must do all she could to prevent Nathaniel being corrupted by that awful trade. Never, ever would she let him serve in a slaver!

"Pray excuse me, sir," she'd broken into their conversation. "From the way you talk so knowingly about ships and trade I can tell you're a man of the sea". He'd nodded. "Were you", she'd corrected herself, "Are you a ship's master?"

The old man had given her a toothless grin. "Aye ma'am I were a master in me time. Cap'n Hawkes, that's me. Spent near all me life at sea y'know." He took the pipe from his mouth. "Last ship I 'ad as Master were the "Nancy", a fine ship, best of all of 'em. And afore that there was the "Jupiter" and the "Griselda". But Lor' bless me, that were years ago. I've seen four score summers and more y'know ma'am and me old bones ain't strong enough to stand a storm at sea no more. Only wish I was as young as this lad of yours. I tell 'ee ma'am if I were, I'd be runnin' along the quay and findin' a ship and beggin' the master to sign me on. Aye ma'am that I would! Nothin' would make me 'appier."

His love of the sea had clearly infected Nathaniel. Elizabeth had smiled; he'd seemed a gentle kindly old man. "Bless you sir," she'd said. "The sea must have been kind to you. By the look of you, you've not seen more than three score years!" A glow of satisfaction spread over his deeply lined face as she continued, "I wonder sir, might I take the liberty of seeking your advice?"

He'd smiled. "'T'would be a great pleasure ma'am, indeed an honour to advise such a graceful and elegant lady as thee self."

For a moment she'd been taken aback by his gallantry and had lowered her eyes. She'd not expected this old man of the sea to pay her compliments. Then looking at him directly, she'd said "Well, sir, you've seen for yourself how my young son Nathaniel, has lost his heart to the sea. He's set his mind on becoming a Ship's Apprentice and spending his life travelling the oceans. The Good Lord knows I've done my best to dissuade him, to make him settle for a life ashore, but it's no use. He's utterly adamant, so I've no choice but to accept his decision."

The old man had nodded gravely, as if he knew the call of the sea was irresistible. "Now sir," she'd continued, "If he must go to sea, I want to find an honest and reliable Master who will teach him well and give him a good start in this strange life he wants to follow. Pray tell me sir, do you know of such a man?"

She'd watched him put a taper to the candle and, with infinite care, relight his pipe. Only when the tobacco was glowing, had he seemed ready to consider her question. Then as if he had found the answer, he'd exhaled a great puff of blue smoke and begun. "I know many a good and honest master who'll teach your son well, ma'am, but tell me what trade do 'ee want for your boy."

Trade? His question had caught her unawares. What did he mean? She wanted her son to learn the trade of a ship's Mate. Did he think she wanted him to be a carpenter or a cook or to learn some other menial skill?

He'd been the first to break the silence. "May I be so bold ma'am as to say 'ee seems a mite perplexed." With a calloused forefinger he'd tamped the burning tobacco down into the bowl of his pipe and had taken another long draw before he spoke again. "Y'see, ma'am, before I can help 'ee choose the right master for your boy, which trade do 'ee wants him to work? Is it p'rhaps the Baltic trade, or maybe it's the wine trade to Bordeaux or," she remembered him hesitating "or is it the slave trade? Do 'ee have a preference ma'am?"

Now, as she watched her son finishing his porridge, their meeting with that old man of the sea seemed so long ago. But she remembered vividly how horrified she'd been at the thought of Nathaniel working in a slave ship. "Anything, sir, but that awful trade," she'd said. "The Baltic trade or the Bordeaux trade I don't mind which, but sir, I'll never let him serve his time in a slave ship."

Captain Hawkes had scratched his balding head. "Well, ma'am, I knows of two or maybe three excellent masters in the slave trade." His voice had trailed off as he pulled at his pipe again. "'Course that's where all the best masters end up y'know, ma'am. That's where the money is!"

Once again he'd been silent, seemingly deep in thought. Then he'd stroked his beard and winked at Nathaniel. "Well, ma'am," he'd said, "'ad to rack me poor old brain, but now come to think of it, I do know of a master in the Baltic trade, who'd do well by your son. A master of 'igh repute, a master renowned in this port for 'avin' a well-run ship and turnin' out good 'prentices. Yes 'e's a good man an' the lads that serve their time with 'im always do well."

The news had excited her. "Pray then sir, tell me his name."

"Youle, ma'am, Cap'n Youle. 'E's Master of the "Dolphin"."

"You know him personally, sir?"

"Aye ma'am. I knows 'im well enough. 'e's a good 'un, you can take m'word for it."

"And you're sure he's not a slaver?"

"Aye ma'am, quite sure. I told 'ee, 'e works the Baltic trade."

For the first time she'd felt a little happier about Nathaniel's future. This Captain Youle seemed a good choice. A master of high repute, one renowned for turning out good apprentices, what could be better? She'd decided she must see him.

"Tell me, sir, do you know if by good fortune Captain Youle is in port at the moment?"

He'd shaken his head. "Sorry to 'ave to disappoint 'ee ma'am, 'e's no longer 'ere, saw 'im sail only last week. 'Fraid 'e'll not be back for maybe a twelve month."

She'd been disappointed of course, but for Nathaniel it had been a cruel blow. And no matter how many times she had told him they'd had no intention of finding him a ship then, he'd been quite disconsolate. But he'd cheered a little when she'd asked this kind old man to be so good as to tell her the moment Captain Youle returned.

Ten months later she'd received a letter from her new acquaintance Captain Hawkes, telling her the "Dolphin" had returned and that Captain Youle had been seen. Nathaniel had been greatly excited by the news and they'd set off for Bristol the very next day, with Nathaniel beside himself with fear that the Dolphin might have sailed. But luck was with them, the "Dolphin" was in port and they had learnt where she was berthed. Nathaniel in his excitement had wanted to see Captain Youle there and then, but she'd rebuked him. "Be patient Nathaniel, we'll meet him in the morning; he won't want to see us now, so late in the day."

The morning had come, and with it a gentle breeze playing with the idle sails that hung out to dry on the ship's yards. Elizabeth took in the scene from the window and wondered what the day would bring for Nathaniel. "Help me dear Lord," she prayed, "there's no turning back now." She watched her son scrape the last morsel of porridge from the plate, then spoke bravely. "Come along, Nathaniel dear, your great moment has arrived. Pray that the Good Lord will guide us well today."

They set off just after ten o'clock with Nathaniel, in his eagerness, always one pace ahead of her. They knew the way and within fifteen minutes they were standing on the quay alongside the "Dolphin". She stole a glance at her son, now strangely quiet and looking glum. He pulled a long face. "She's not very smart," he muttered. Elizabeth studied the "Dolphin". She knew little or nothing about ships, but she had to admit the "Dolphin" didn't look at all well run. It looked thoroughly weather-beaten and neglected even to her unpracticed eye. Nor was there anyone about! The ship was deserted as if it had been struck by the plague. They waited a while on the quayside, unsure what to do. Nathaniel wanted to climb aboard and find the master, but she was more cautious. Then a head appeared through the hatchway and a scruffy, disheveled figure emerged. She heard Nathaniel shout, "Excuse me, sir. Please can you tell me if Captain Youle's on board".

"What?" came the reply.

This time Elizabeth spoke. "Can you tell me, my good man, is Captain Youle on board?"

"Cap'n Youle?" The man scratched his tousled head. "Who's 'e?"

"I'm told he's the master of the "Dolphin". This is the right ship isn't it?"

"Aye, 'tis the "Dolphin" right enough. But I dunno no Cap'n Youle."

"Would your master know him?"

"We ain't got no Master, lady, nor no mates neither. Youle you say? I'll ask the Bo's'un, 'e might know."

As the figure disappeared a wave of utter disbelief and despondency come over her. She felt near to tears. It was the right ship yet after all this time and trouble she was no nearer to finding this Captain Youle. Nathaniel was looking downcast and deflated. "Mama, d'you think we should ask at the inn if anyone knows where he is."

As she was about to reply a second figure appeared. "Cap'n Youle, lady? You'm a lookin' for 'im?"

"Yes, yes. Do you know where I can find him?"

"Ain't 'e the new master of the "Mary Anne"? She'm loadin' yonder at Broad Quay."

They thanked him and hurried off, a newfound sense of urgency speeding them on their way. Broad quay was crowded with ships of all shapes and sizes and as they hurried along, Nathaniel read out the names engraved on their transoms. By the time they were nearing the last few ships Elizabeth was feeling dispirited and had almost given up hope, but then they saw the name MARY ANNE, carved in large letters and picked out in gold. There she was at last, with men busy hoisting great wooden casks and bulging sacks on board. The ship looked smart and well cared for and the crew seemed to be working with a will.

"Gosh," said Nathaniel his eyes sparkling, "she looks a real ship!"

In his cabin away from the hustle and bustle on deck, her master, Captain James Youle had spent the last hour working on his papers. It was a job he'd grown to hate and today it seemed never ending. He sighed and turned once more to the ship's articles and re-read the time-honoured phrases.

Articles of Agreement October 26th, 1771.

The Mary Anne - Master James Youle Now fitting out at Bristol for intended voyage to Africa and the West Indies and from thence to Bristol or other English port, where the said voyage will be ended.

Well, he'd signed on most of the crew. He'd found what he hoped were three good Mates and the Bo's'un, Carpenter and Gunner all seemed men of experience. But getting a full crew to work the sails was proving difficult. He'd seen a lot of men who wanted to join. Some had reeked of rum and he'd sent them packing and one or two he'd disliked on sight. Then with the help of the Surgeon he'd weeded out those not fit enough for the rigours of deep sea sailing, but he still had to find a few more. "Better put word round the taverns again," he muttered, as he made his way up on deck to see how the loading was getting on.

"All going well, Mr. Jackson?" He asked the Second Mate.

"Aye sir, no problems so far. Reckon we'll be finished by this time tomorrow."

Jim nodded. "Good, keep the hands at it and make sure everything's properly stowed."

"Aye, aye Cap'n," Mr. Jackson paused. "I was just coming down to tell you there's a lady wanting to see you. That's her over there by the tavern." He raised his hand and pointed at the figure of a young woman with a boy standing nearby. "Says she's a Mrs. Lugger, Cap'n. D'you happen to know her?"

Jim looked across the quay and saw a slim, graceful figure in a modest grey dress and wondered who she could be. Apart from his mother and his three aunts, Jim hardly knew any women. To him they were a strange lot; they seemed to act and think in a manner he found difficult to comprehend. He'd decided quite early on in life that they were best avoided. Who could this woman be? He tried to think of any woman he'd met in the port before. He'd known the landladies of the taverns of course and he'd seen those women who wanted to sell themselves for a penny or two. Then there were his partner's wives who seemed to put on airs and graces whenever he saw them. Well thank God, she wasn't one of them. But who was she and why did she want to see him? And why did she have that young lad with her?

He caught the Second Mate looking at him with an amused expression on his face. Did he think she was some skeleton from his past? The thought irritated him, yet somehow her presence made him feel uneasy.

"No Mr. Jackson, can't say I do. She's not like the women you see round here is she? Did she tell you what she wants?"

"No, Cap'n. All she said was she wanted to see you."

Jim grunted as Mr. Jackson continued, "You're right Cap'n, she ain't like one of the local women. She's got a bit of class about her."

Jim studied her carefully. She was a complete stranger to him, so why did he feel so worried about meeting her? She had the advantage of him. She knew the object of their meeting and he didn't. What if she was a skeleton of the past, someone else's skeleton, not his? What if she thought he was that someone? He dismissed that line of thought hurriedly. It was too preposterous! What else could she want, with that young boy at her side?

"Well Mr. Jackson, we'd better see what she wants. Ask her to come aboard."

A minute or so later he found himself looking into the earnest blue eyes of Mrs. Lugger as he welcomed her aboard and led her down to his cabin. There was no doubt about it, she was no ordinary woman; she was a lady and a well-bred lady at that. He found himself admiring her dress and her bonnet and the way she moved. It wasn't until they'd reached his cabin that he remembered the boy, a lad of twelve or maybe thirteen.

"Good day ma'am. I'm the Master of this vessel and my name is Youle, James Youle. What can I do for you?" He could feel the sweat forming on the back of his neck; this strange woman was making him feel uneasy, even apprehensive!

"I know you must be busy Captain Youle. I believe you're sailing soon and it's very kind of you to spare the time to speak to me."

"No matter, ma'am." He interrupted her. "We're not off for two or three days yet. What can I do for you?"

"Well, sir, pray let me introduce myself. My name is Elizabeth Lugger, Mrs. Elizabeth Lugger and this is my son Nathaniel. He's just thirteen and for as long as I can remember he's dreamed of going to sea as his poor father did."

"Aye ma'am," he said. "I can remember how I felt when I was a lad."

"Well, Captain Youle, pray let me get to the point. I know you're looking for a crew and I'm wondering, indeed I'm hoping, sir, that you can find a berth for my son."

Now that he knew the purpose of her visit he felt strangely relieved. He looked more closely at his visitor. Yes, she was an uncommonly handsome woman and he guessed a well-read and accomplished one at that. But did she really want her son to serve in a slaver? Surely the boy would be better suited as a Midshipman in a man o' war.

"Well, ma'am". He hesitated. "I'm still wanting a few hands, but I'm only looking for men to work the sails." He saw disappointment cloud her face.

"Oh! Heaven forbid, Captain, I don't plan he should be a sailorman. I was hoping sir; you might take him on as an apprentice. I've been told of the excellent training you gave your apprentices in the "Dolphin" and I hoped you'd do the same for Nathaniel." She fell silent and looking ever more dejected, glanced at the boy at her side. "Won't you take Nathaniel? Won't you take him as an apprentice? He's very bright and enthusiastic sir and I'm sure he'd do well."

Jim shook his head in sorrow. "It grieves me ma'am to refuse you, but the plain truth is that I've no apprentices in the Mary Anne and don't plan having any. 'Tis true I had apprentices in the "Dolphin", but I inherited them from the last master. You see, ma'am, if you take on apprentices you've got to do well by 'em. 'Tis no good forgetting their training and using them as cheap labour. I remember my own time as an apprentice. The only things I learnt were those I found out for myself. Y'see ma'am having apprentices on board means extra work for me and the mates. They've got to be trained properly; leastways they have to be in any ship of mine."

She made no reply and in the silence he found himself approving her well cut dress, that clothed a trim and comely figure on which was set a fine oval face dominated by those eyes, those cornflower blue eyes. A few golden curls escaped the sharp outline of her bonnet and fell about her graceful neck. Try as he might he couldn't stop himself admiring the elegance and grace of this woman, who had so suddenly broken into his dull life. Her quietness upset him. He realised that he too felt sad for without an apprenticeship for her son, she would leave and he would never see her again. The silence seemed everlasting. Then he heard a voice, a voice he recognised as his own. "Well," it was saying, "I suppose having one apprentice on board would be no bad thing. Perhaps teaching him all we know would keep us on our toes."

He saw her face light up, she smiled and those cornflower eyes shone once more.

He turned to the boy. "Well boy, what's your schooling like? Are you any good at maths? I take it you can read and write?"

For the first time the boy spoke. He was very excited, but his voice was calm. "Oh yes sir. I can read and write and I've learnt some algebra and geometry too."

"Good." Jim was impressed by the lad's confident reply. "Tell me boy, what school did you go to?"

"Well, sir." Nathaniel's confidence had suddenly evaporated. "I haven't been to any school." He paused as if not knowing what to say next. "I was taught by my mother and grandfather."

Elizabeth felt it was time to rescue her son from this difficult question. "Captain Youle," she said. "My husband was an officer in the King's navy and while he was away at sea I continued to live with my parents. Our marriage was a happy one, but sadly short lived as my dear husband was killed in the war against the French at the Battle of Quiberon Bay." She looked sad and for a second Jim thought she might weep, then she continued, "But the Good Lord has given me Nathaniel to remember him by."

"Ma'am, it distresses me to hear of your great loss." He shook his head. "Those damned French have a lot to answer for!"

"Sir, you're most kind. Well, you'll understand, I'm sure that without a husband to provide for me and my child, I had no money to send Nathaniel to school. But my father is Rector of St Peter's in the parish of Hanbury and while I've been able to teach Nathaniel to read and write, my father has given him a good grounding in mathematics."

Well he seems bright enough, Jim thought. "Now then boy," he gave Nathaniel a friendly smile, "what makes you want to go to sea?"

"I've never wanted to do anything else sir, but go to sea just as my father did." Nathaniel spoke without hesitation. "I want to go to Africa and America and China and India, like you have sir. I want to find out what's over the horizon. Living in England's all right when you're old, but I want some adventure. I want the thrill of seeing strange and foreign parts."

The eagerness and innocence of the boy startled him. Had he been so keen and enthusiastic when he was a lad? He couldn't remember, it was so long ago. Now enthusiasm was a stranger to him, but the boy's had been strangely infectious. There was no doubt the lad had spirit. He found himself liking him, but no, he wasn't going to have apprentices aboard the Mary Anne. And yet here was this captivating widow, wanting him to take her son. Her very presence stirred his blood. Was it because of her he wanted to say yes? Could he be so easily swayed? He tried to think logically, to allow the pure fresh air of reason clear his head. Should he stand by his original decision and refuse the boy? That's what his head told him, yet his heart usually so obedient, was rebelling and saying over and over again "if you don't take the boy you'll never see her again." How could this woman he'd only just met affect him so? Women had never been important to him before. He'd barely noticed them. Why should she be so different? Why couldn't he bring himself to say no? That was the right thing to do. But what if he did have the one apprentice? Teaching him all he knew would help pass those long days at sea and he'd make sure the mates pulled their weight too. Perhaps it wasn't such a bad idea after all. Yes, he told himself, he'd thought it through carefully. He'd accept the lad; that was the right thing to do. Yet in his heart he knew he was only doing it because of her. He sighed inwardly. Well that was it; he'd made up his mind. He'd better get on with it. He opened his sea chest, withdrew the Ship's Articles and placed them on the table in front of them.

"Well Mr. Lugger if you'll sign articles, I'll have you as an apprentice aboard the "Mary Anne"."

"Yes sir, oh thank you, sir", he heard the boy gasp. But Jim wasn't looking at him. His eyes were drawn to hers. They seemed to sparkle as she smiled at him.

He gave the boy the quill and watched him sign his name carefully. When he'd finished the boy looked up at his mother, his young face glowing with happiness. "That's wonderful", he said. "That's marvellous. It's what I really want."

"Well, Nathaniel, it's done at last." Though Elizabeth still rued his choice she felt strangely pleased, a life at sea was what he'd always wanted. She turned towards the man to whom she'd entrusted her son. "Captain Youle, sir. I'm greatly indebted to you."

The pleasure on her face filled Jim's heart with joy. "Think nothing of it, ma'am. I'll get the agent to draw up an indenture for the three of us to sign. Perhaps you'd be kind enough to bring your son along to join this time tomorrow. Then we can all sign the papers." He saw her nod. "Now ma'am," he continued. "Before you leave may I suggest we drink a toast to Nathaniel and his life at sea?"

Carefully he selected a bottle of his best claret and as he pulled the cork he asked her to tell him more about Nathaniel. She talked happily and with some pride about her only son, though Jim couldn't remember what she said. The tone of her voice and the beautiful way she talked mesmerised him. He took his time pouring the wine and after they'd toasted the boy he tried to make his glass last as long as he could, just to keep her there. He offered her a second glass, but she refused him politely and told him it was time for them to go. Sadly he led them up on deck and when they'd gone he returned to an empty cabin. He felt deflated by her going, yet strangely he was excited by the thought of the boy joining. What a spirited young lad he seemed and how intelligent and well spoken he was. He'd liked his enthusiasm. Strangely it had infected him too. But then with an oath he shook himself. Silly old bugger! What had he been doing, letting a woman cloud his judgment like that; letting a woman twist him round her little finger without her even knowing it; letting a woman make him change his long held views. He shook his head. He'd never thought he'd let a woman do that!

Chapter 2

Walking down the gangway, she'd felt a great sense of relief. It was done. Nathaniel had his ship. As they reached the quayside Nathaniel shouted, "Good bye, sir." The lonely figure raised his arm "Good bye, Mr Lugger, good bye, ma'am." Elizabeth acknowledged his salutation then made for the inn.

Nathaniel was beside himself with excitement. "This is the happiest day of my life!" He stopped to gaze admiringly at the "Mary Anne". "Isn't she beautiful? Not like that old wreck the "Dolphin"!" He laughed. "Thank you mama, thank you for finding Captain Youle for me."

She found herself laughing too, though inwardly she felt sad. Those happy days with her loving son always near were over. In her mind's eye she saw the pink wrinkled mite she'd held in her arms that first day and marvelled as always, how that weak helpless thing had grown into this smiling happy boy, so full of questions, energy and life. She felt the tears welling up and struggled to stop them. He'd filled her life with joy and wonder; her very existence had centred on him. But he was a boy no longer; she had to let him go. It was time for him to make his own way in the world. His bright young voice broke into her thoughts.

"What did you think of Captain Youle mama?"

"I'm not sure I know, Nathaniel. I think I'd expected him to be quite different."

"How, mama?"

"Oh! I don't know exactly, but somehow I thought he'd be short and gaunt, even a little wizened. I had a picture of a weather-beaten old martinet, a stickler for detail, a man to be feared. He certainly wasn't that! He was polite and seemed a most kind and considerate man. What about you, Nathaniel?"

"I thought I'd be frightened of him, but I wasn't. He seemed fair and honest."

That was welcome news for Elizabeth's protective ears. "Good, Nathaniel dear. I think we've been very lucky to find such a kind man." Her own worries had begun to evaporate too, yet one thing puzzled her. At first he'd said he'd not have an apprentice. Then later he'd agreed to take Nathaniel. What was it that had made him change his mind?

They strolled along the quay, their sense of urgency now gone; Nathaniel still busy looking at ships and she lost in her thoughts.

"Look, mama, look." She turned to see what he pointed at. "Look, it's about the "Mary Anne"."

It was a paper nailed to the timbers of the "Sailor's Rest" a cheap drinking place she would normally avoid, but the notice drew her like a magnet.

"THE BARQUE MARY ANNE - MASTER CAPTAIN JAMES YOULE," she read, **"SAILING FOR AFRICA TO BUY SLAVES FOR TRANSPORT TO THE WEST INDIES IS RECRUITING ABLE, SOBER MEN."**

She could read no further. The Mary Anne a slaver? Her heart missed a beat! She was aghast! She read it again, **"to buy slaves"**. She was stunned; it was like a hammer blow. Ever since she'd realised that fortunes were made through the misery of those poor black people, she'd been adamant. Never would she allow Nathaniel to be contaminated by that vile trade. Yet now, she found the very ship her son was to join was a slaver! In her misery she asked herself, how could it be? Hadn't she gone to great lengths to find a good master in some other trade? How could fate play such a cruel trick? The Captain Youle she'd sought had been master of the Dolphin, shipping wool to the Baltic. But now he was the master of a slaver. How stupid, how gullible she'd been. Any fool would know he'd move to the slave trade if he could. "That's where the money is," she heard Captain Hawkes' voice again. A tide of anger engulfed her. "Nathaniel she's a slaver. The "Mary Anne's" a slave ship. You can't learn your trade in a slave ship. How can you?"

The joy that had shone in his face had vanished. His look of utter dejection stifled her fury.

"It's no use, darling; you can't possibly join that awful ship. I know it's disappointing, but you can't. I won't let you; I'll tell him we've changed our minds. That Captain Youle's been downright deceitful."

It was Nathaniel's turn to be angry. "How can you say that mama? He never said the Mary Anne wasn't a slaver. He never said what she did. Most ships sailing from Bristol are slavers. That's what Captain Hawkes told me and you heard him say that's where the money is. Why shouldn't I sail in her?"

His outburst startled her. He was right. Captain Youle hadn't set out to mislead her. It was her fault. She should have asked him which trade he plied, but she hadn't. Nevertheless the Mary Anne was a slaver. She would brook no argument. She would withdraw her son. She'd find another ship for him. She'd tackle that man Youle there and then. But one look at her rebellious son told her she'd have to make Nathaniel see reason first. They walked on in silence.

Persuading Nathaniel to agree with her had proved more difficult than she had thought. He'd been argumentative and petulant, but finally with great reluctance and the air of a martyr, he'd accepted her decision. It had been a difficult and exhausting evening and in the privacy of her chamber she'd prayed for guidance for the morrow. Prayer had always comforted her, but that night her prayers were confused and she felt they went unheard. Neither could she sleep. Visions of Nathaniel whipping countless slaves as he herded them on board the Mary Anne and greedily counting piles of golden guineas disturbed her broken slumbers. When fearing her nightmare would return and daring not to sleep, a picture of James Youle had formed in her mind. She saw his powerful frame and became aware of his physical strength. His face was clearly etched in her memory, the lower half hidden by that great spade beard and with large brown eyes set beneath a thick mop of black hair untarnished by the grey flecks of age. How old was he? It was difficult to tell, he could be in his late thirties or early forties. Yes, he'd been polite to her and kind to Nathaniel, but he had no polish and lacked both grace and elegance, qualities she took for granted in her few male acquaintances at Hanbury. He spoke with a West Country burr and his clothes were plain and ill fitting. Certainly he was no gentleman, but neither did he fit her picture of slaver. Masters of slave ships were surely wicked cruel sadists, outcasts from decent society. They exuded evil as others gave off the sweat of honest toil. No, somehow, James Youle wasn't like that. Never had she met a man like him. He was an enigma. He seemed kind and considerate, yet he practised that evil trade. She had to admit his close physical presence had disturbed her. Not since she'd lost Charles had she been so aware of being near a man. It had been totally unexpected, an experience both unnerving and strange, one which had sent a tingle down her spine. The sheer masculinity of him had been almost overpowering. When she left the ship the effect had remained with her, that was until Nathaniel had seen that notice at the "Sailor's Rest"!

Neither had Jim slept well. The day's events had shaken him. Hadn't he learnt not to make hasty decisions? He'd always tried to weigh the facts carefully and come to a decision based on logic not wishful thinking. Yet he'd ignored his long-held view that apprentices were a diversion and on the spur of the moment had decided to take the boy. He'd been mesmerised, there was no other explanation, mesmerised by that woman. He'd done it to please her! He must have been soft in the head! Hadn't he avoided women all his life? He'd seen the effect they could have on men and had vowed long ago to have nothing to do with them. When at last he'd dragged himself out of his cot, he'd felt jaded. Yet still that woman plagued him! He could think of nothing else! Finding it impossible to stay below he paced the deck, trying not to look along the quay. Suddenly he saw her. Yes, there she was. That woman who seemed to be taking over his life. He didn't notice the boy; all he could see was her slight, trim figure. It excited him afresh.

"Welcome aboard ma'am". He met her at the gangway and led her and the boy down to his cabin.

"Now then Ma'am if you'd kindly sit there and read the agreement before......". His voice tailed off. She made no effort to sit, but stood there with anger in her eyes, no longer cornflower blue but steely grey. Her mouth too had changed, its full generous outline now compressed into a thin determined line.

"Captain Youle, as I said yesterday I'm indebted to you for offering my son an apprenticeship on the Mary Anne." He broke in "Ma'am I'm pleased to be of service." She ignored his pleasantry and continued. "But Captain Youle, it can be no exaggeration to say that I was upset, very upset, indeed horrified when I learnt you are to embark on a slaving voyage. You cannot deny it, sir. I read your notice at the Sailor's Rest calling for men to sail with you to Africa to buy slaves for the West Indies."

Jim felt his heart harden. "Pray tell me Ma'am, what other cargo did you think ships from this port carried?"

Suddenly he'd changed, his considerate manner gone. He made her feel stupid, inept. "Wool," she said involuntarily. "Captain Hawkes had told me you were Master of the "Dolphin" and shipping wool to the Baltic." Her wrath returned. "How was I to know you were to carry slaves?"

"Ma'am, you could have asked what my intended cargo was." Now he'd made his point his pique diminished. "You're quite right, ma'am, the "Dolphin" did carry wool, but there's little call for that in this port, now it's all going from Harwich. You might have seen the "Dolphin", ma'am." He saw the boy nod. "Poor little ship, worn out and rotting away she is, without the profits to keep her going."

"Be that as it may, sir," Jim saw her eyes flash angrily again. "I abhor the very thought of slavery and I can't bear to think of my son working in such an evil trade. I tell you sir, there's no question of me signing that agreement, none whatever. Nor indeed will I allow Nathaniel to sail with you, sir."

The unexpected turn of events had stunned him and for what seemed an age he was unable to speak. He could accept her intransigence and prejudice no longer. "Well, ma'am," his voice was hard and blunt, "Mr Lugger has signed articles which bind him until the voyage is finished. If he doesn't sail in the "Mary Anne" I'll have him charged with deserting ship. And if you won't sign his indenture, I can always find him a place before the mast. He can work the sails like the rest of 'em."

As his message struck home she fell silent. Charles had told her the fate of those who deserted. How could she wish that on her son? The colour had drained from her face and her eyes had lost their grim determination. She was clearly distressed. Jim knew he'd hit her hard and a pang of anguish flowed through him.

"But, ma'am, the slave trade's been with us since God made little apples and y'know we're not all villains. Perhaps it is a cruel business, but is it worse than making little children work down the mines or the life those poor folk lead in the mills? And what about those men press-ganged by the Navy your husband was so proud to serve? And ma'am, when all's said and done it's in my own interest to look after my slaves. I can't sell a dead one y'know, not in Jamaica or any place else. So come ma'am sign. I promise you I'll look after the lad as if he was my own and I'll warrant he'll get a good training."

Now he'd fathomed why the boy had been looking so glum. It wasn't the thought of leaving his mother; it was because she wouldn't allow him to sail in the Mary Anne. That was why he looked so miserable and as if to confirm his conviction, the boy said, "Come on mama, sign it please. Please."

Elizabeth felt cornered. Those accursed articles were irrevocable. But what if she pleaded with him, what if she threw herself on his mercy as a stupid woman? Would that work? For a second she thought it worth trying but his forcefulness had unnerved her. She sighed despairingly. She had no choice but to sign. She moved to the table and picked up the quill. As she reluctantly dipped it into the ink, the horror of the slave trade struck her again.

"Captain Youle sir, to me and all right thinking people slavery is and always will be a vile, despicable and wicked trade which cannot be excused before God. I hate the thought of my son Nathaniel having anything whatever to do with it. Foolishly I thought you would be shipping wool and let him sign articles. How gullible, how stupid I've been. Now it seems my son is committed to this voyage and I have no alternative but to sign his indenture. But you must be aware sir, that I do so with the greatest reluctance and many reservations."

A long silence followed, broken only by the scratching of quill on parchment. As Nathaniel signed, Jim smiled. "Well done, Mr Lugger. Learn all you can from me and the mates and you'll be master of your own ship one day. He looked at Elizabeth. Her anger seemed to have abated. Now she looked dejected, beaten, on the verge of tears. Jim had seen her in a new light. She was no ordinary woman. She had integrity and courage too. Courage to stand up for her principles. He admired her and desperately wanted to comfort her. He coughed to break the silence that enshrouded them. "Now ma'am perhaps I can tempt you to a glass of wine. We can't part in anger and I'll look after young Nathaniel as if he was my own. You'll see. He'll come home a man."

Reluctantly she accepted the wine and they drank to Nathaniel, wishing him success in his new life. Then as Jim told her of his plans for the boy, Nathaniel suddenly interrupted them. "Mama, I must go and get my things from the inn." He dashed off full of energy and excitement.

Suddenly they were alone, thrust together, she looking a little frightened and he equally apprehensive.

"Ma'am, 'tis a rare thing for me to have a woman in my cabin and never before without a third party. No doubt ma'am it's an equally strange experience for you too."

"It is indeed, sir. My dear mother would be shocked!"

"Aye," he laughed. "Mor'n likely she would. But if I may say so ma'am, I think my old mother would be smiling proudly on her son who has so obstinately refused to commune with the fairer sex."

"You haven't a wife then, Captain Youle?"

"No, Ma'am. Y'see I've been at sea since I was a boy and wives and the sea don't mix. Never have and never will."

"You've never wanted to work ashore, on the land perhaps?"

"No, ma'am, never. I suppose the sea's in my blood, like it was for my father and his father and his too for all I know." Laughing he told her about his time as an apprentice. How he'd been second mate of the Dolphin, when she'd been chartered by the Crown for service in the war against the French. How his ship had formed part of Admiral Saunders' fleet that had taken General Wolfe and his men up the St Lawrence to Quebec for that great victory on the Plains of Abraham. He was proud of his service with the fleet, though he didn't mention how much he'd disliked the airs and graces and the fancy polished tones of the Captains of the men o' war. He knew they were men from the same background as this enchanting woman, but while he'd often found them arrogant and supercilious, he had nothing but admiration for her, despite or was it because of the reservations she had about his trade. This trim comely woman who'd so suddenly entered his life, had spirit.

As he told her about himself, she felt obliged to give him a thumbnail sketch of her family. How her father had had the living of a parish in Gloucestershire since before she could remember. How she too was an only child and about her short lived marriage. At first she found conversation with this man contaminated by the evils of slavery, unwelcome and difficult, but as the man behind the mask emerged, her prejudice slowly diminished. He spoke about a world of which she knew nothing. A world her son would come to comprehend and of which she too must learn. And as they talked that tingle in her spine returned. Once again she became aware of his powerful physique, of his well-proportioned body, of that masculinity that had disturbed her before. Inwardly she reproved herself. Foolish woman, such feelings were for starry-eyed young maidens.

The sound of feet heralded Nathaniel's return. "I've got my gear, sir," he said his eyes glowing with excitement. How Elizabeth had wished this moment would never come, this moment of parting. Would she ever see her son again? She remembered saying goodbye to Charles. When he'd gone a great world of emptiness had descended on her for what had seemed an eternity, an endless time until unforeseen he would appear laughing and joking at the Rectory door. The uncertainty of it all seemed almost as bad as not seeing him. Elizabeth prayed that unlike his father, Nathaniel would return safely. She felt the tears welling up inside her, but she must not cry. It would embarrass Nathaniel and he might cry as well. Later she could remember little of that parting. Perhaps some kindly angel had addled her brain, so that the details could not be absorbed, so that she could withstand the pain. All that remained in her memory was a picture of her only child, her dearly beloved son and the great powerful figure of James Youle standing at the top of the gangway as she turned and walked briskly away.

Chapter 3

"More damned paperwork." Jim gave a despairing sigh as the agent's clerk appeared with a crisply folded letter. He took it, dismissed the clerk with a nod of the head and carefully broke the seal.

"Instructions to Captain James Youle. November 10th, 1771." he read "When ready and loaded the Mary Anne is to sail for Africa and Jamaica and return to Bristol, where the voyage will end. The cargo we have shipped aboard you is listed in the annexed invoice and we consign it to you for sale for which you will have the usual commission of 4 in 104 on the gross sales and you and your surgeon, Mr Lawson 12 pennies per head on all slaves sold and we give you these our orders to be observed in the course of your voyage. With the first favourable winds you are to sail and on arrival on the Slave Coast we hope you will be able to purchase 300 slaves at the ports of your choosing. In addition you may have £400 to lay out on Ivory and a further £600 on Gold, which we recommend your buying at the beginning of your trade. Pray be careful in the choice of slaves. Buy no distempered or old ones, but only those which will be saleable and will stand the passage. The privilege we allow you is as follows: Yourself 10 slaves, your Chief Mate 2, your Surgeon 2, which is all we allow.
When finished on the Coast, you are to make your best way to Montego Bay, Jamaica, where you are to contact Messrs Wood and Nicholas who will advise where best to sell the slaves.

Pray mind to embrace every opportunity that offers to advise us of your proceedings for our information and insurance etc. We wish you a prosperous voyage and a safe return and are your assured friends."

The letter was signed by his four partners: Gordon Crosbie who held fifty per cent of the shares, William Brent, Charles Lomas and Robert Drew who each held fifteen per cent leaving him with just a meagre five.

He'd discussed the voyage with the senior partner Mr Crosbie at length, so he already knew what was expected of him. It was no good talking to the other partners; they were frightened of Mr Crosbie and servile too, always deferring to him without argument. Unlike them he'd been insistent and had refused to be browbeaten. He would make up his own mind where to trade. He'd decide when he reached the Coast and had heard the news. He made a mental calculation of his likely earnings. He would get 12 pennies for each of the 300 slaves that would be £15; then if the slaves sold for say £50 each he'd receive £500 for the sale of his 10. Then there would be commission on the sale of the cargo now loaded. That might bring him another £50. So with luck he might make £565 before his five percent share of the profits. How right he'd been to stand up to that old skinflint when they'd discussed privileges and commission. He re-read the letter to make quite sure that it recorded what had been agreed verbally and satisfied, he folded it neatly and placed it with his other papers in his chest. Yes, he was happy enough with his orders. He had reasonable freedom to deal with events as they occurred.

A knock on the door interrupted his thoughts and opening it he saw the now familiar features of Fred Braithwaite, the Chief Mate.

"I've got the crew on deck Cap'n, ready for you to talk to them."

"Thank you Mr Braithwaite." Jim followed him to the upper deck, where a motley crowd of chattering men was gathered. He heard the deep rounded voice of the Chief Mate, "Quiet, quiet. Be quiet for your Master, Cap'n Youle."

As the banter died away, Jim looked at this collection of men of all ages and condition. Lord, what a rabble they seemed. He peered along the ragged rows and recognised a few who'd sailed with him before. He was happy to see those familiar faces, but the rest? Well he'd recruited them, but in all conscience he knew nothing about them. You couldn't pick and choose too much in this game. For the next year or so he'd have to rely on them whatever their past. He'd have to drive them, encourage them, cajole them, lead them, and even bully them to get them working together as a crew he could trust. They'd be looking at him too and wondering whether they could count on him to do right by them, to keep them and the Mary Rose clear of danger. He knew he'd have to gain their trust; that would take time. But now was the time to start licking them into shape, to turn this mob of strangers into a crew that would pull together. He cleared his throat and stepped forward.

"We've now all signed articles to serve aboard this vessel, the "Mary Anne", for a voyage to the Slave Coast, the New World and back here to Bristol. We're a full crew and I hope a good one too. Some of you have sailed with me before and I'm pleased to have you sailing with me again. You know what to expect of me and I know I can rely on you. But many of you are strangers to me and I say this to you, I'm glad to have you with me, but I want you all to know that this will be a well-run ship, able for the sake of us all, to cope with the storms we'll meet", he paused, "and the unexpected. So that means were going to have to work hard in the next few weeks to make ourselves handy, resourceful and competent seamen. It'll be a long voyage but if we do our job well we'll return with a good profit for us all to share. But that profit has to be earned and I want you all to know I just can't abide anyone who won't pull his weight and I can't stand those who don't jump to it when given an order. Nor, God help me, those who keep moaning and whining. Do you understand? A few heads nodded. "And I should warn you," he continued "I take my responsibility for maintaining discipline in this ship very seriously and I shan't hesitate to deal with offenders even if I have to use the irons or the cat. Let there he no doubt about that. But," he wanted to end on a more conciliatory note, "if you work well, without bloody argument you'll find me a considerate master."

He paused to let the message sink in. Then as the chattering began again he shouted, "Where's the Bo's'n?"

A voice cried out "'Ere, Cap'n."

"Right Mr Green, you've got the rest of the day to make sure the hands know the rig of this vessel. I want to see the sails worked smartly and safely in this ship. I won't tolerate sloppy sail handling. Is that clear?" "Aye, Aye, Cap'n, I'll sharpen them up."

"And where's the Gunner?" Jim continued. "Over 'ere Cap'n."

"Now, Mr Hoskins, we ain't at war with those pesky frogs anymore, but there are still plenty of Frenchies out there, who'd like to take us and our cargo, given half a chance. And there are those bloody Moors too. They creep up in their fast dhows and take ships that don't keep a damned good lookout. So as soon as we're clear of the channel, I shall want you to make sure that every man in this ship, and I mean everyone knows how to fire a blunderbuss, a musket and can use a cutlass. And when we've done all that, we'll run out the cannons and make sure they damn well work and that we know how to aim and fire them. I mean to give any cursed pirate a bloody nose and a good run for his money. Is that clear?"

"Aye, Aye Cap'n. That'll be done. Don' e' worry. We'll give those frogs a bloody nose and those blasted Moors as well, if we have to."

"Thank you, Mr Hoskins." Jim raised his arm for silence once more. "Now do any of you have any questions?"

After a moment a voice piped up.

"Aye Cap'n. 'Bout these slaves. Are we going to have a few girlies to keep us happy?"

A chorus of guffaws and sniggers followed.

Jim recalled how desperately he'd sought to convince Elizabeth he'd look after his slaves, how it was in his interest to do so. Did this wretch think they were for their own personal pleasure? Jim knew if he let the crew start thinking like that there'd be trouble. They had to learn the slaves were cargo, valuable cargo to be delivered in good health so they'd fetch the best price. That was the whole point of the voyage. Any fool could deliver dead slaves. He took a deep breath to steady himself before he spoke.

"I didn't see who asked that question and I don't want to know who it was." His voice seemed to have risen a full octave, so angry did he feel. He struggled to control himself, to regain his usual voice. "The slaves are our cargo and a very valuable one at that and it's my job and your job to get them to Jamaica alive and in good health. For that reason I want to make it clear, absolutely crystal clear that I will not allow them to be maltreated nor used as whores for our personal satisfaction. And I warn you all, if any one of you disobeys me in this matter, I'll have him bound to the mainmast and flogged till I'm satisfied he's learned his lesson."

He looked angrily at his crew. They were silent and subdued. Had they learnt, marked and digested his warning? If not he knew he'd have to deal harshly with anyone who disobeyed him, who was found with a girl slave. He'd have to make a real example of him. But now there was nothing more to be said. He looked at the Chief Mate and barked, "Get 'em back to work, Mr Braithwaite."

He turned on his heel and headed for his cabin. He saw the boy. "Boy," he called him over. "Tell Mr Braithwaite I'd like to see him when he's got the men working again. And tell him to bring you along as well."

"Yes sir." Nathaniel dashed off. The way Captain Youle had spoken to the ship's company had made a deep impression on him. Was this the same kindly, polite man, who had welcomed him and his mother the day before? Now he seemed tough, uncompromising and quite terrifying. Why did the Captain wish to see him? Had he done something wrong? He racked his brains to think what it could be, but he could think of nothing. He found the Chief Mate deep in conversation with the Bo's'n. He waited timidly to give him the message then with great foreboding, he followed him to the Captain's cabin.

"Come in," the Captain greeted them. "Sit yourself down Fred and you too Mr Lugger." Jim walked towards the great window that dominated the cabin, seemingly engrossed in the view. Then turning, he spoke. "Fred, I want to get young Lugger here off to a proper start. I'll teach him his navigation, but I want him to stand watch with you, leastways for a few months. Then perhaps we might let the Second have him for a bit. But the first thing he must learn is the rigging and how to handle the sails, so he'll have to work with the hands when they're working the sails."

"Aye," said Fred. "And what about boat-handling?"

"Yes, thank you, Fred, we'll sort that out when we're on the Coast. But now I want you to find a good experienced hand to act as a Sea Daddy for Mr Lugger. I want him to teach the boy his bends and hitches and the rigging and the names of all the sails and how we handle them. I don't want to saddle the Bo's'un, he's got enough to do knocking the crew into shape. But talk to him, he'll probably know just the right man."

"Aye, Aye Cap'n, I'll have a word with him. We'll sort someone out and I'll let you know who it is in the morning. Will that be soon enough?"

"Yes, that'll do nicely. I want it arranged before we sail tomorrow. High water's at four o'clock in the morning near enough, so I've told the Harbourmaster we'll be wanting to slip at half past three. He's arranging the pilot."

"I'll have everything ready by three then Cap'n. Is that all?"

"Yes, thank you, Fred. Leave Mr Lugger with me." As the Captain turned and looked him straight in the eye Nathaniel's heart missed a beat.

"Well, boy," he heard the Captain say. "We'll be on our way this time tomorrow. So you'll soon be at sea, that's what you want, isn't it?"

Nathaniel relaxed a little, it was that kind man again; the one he'd met the day before.

"Oh yes, sir. You mean we'll have all the sails up and the wind will be pushing us along?"

"Well, perhaps not tomorrow. We've got to take the Mary Anne down river first and then we may have to wait for a favourable wind."

"Oh!" Nathaniel sounded disappointed. "What's a favourable wind?"

"It's a wind that's blowing near enough in the direction we want to go. You're going to have to learn a whole lot of strange words we sailors use. It'll all seem double-dutch at first, but you'll soon get the hang of it. But if you don't understand, ask. Don't be frightened to ask boy. If you don't ask you'll never learn." Nathaniel nodded. "Well boy, I've got a question for you. Tell me, how d'you think we're going to get the Mary Anne down to the river mouth?"

The question startled Nathaniel. Phew! He had to think fast! Well the river went through a deep gorge he knew that. He didn't think they could sail her down. There wouldn't be this favourable wind the Captain had been talking about and besides the Captain had told him they had to get the ship down river before they could start sailing.

"Well, sir." He played for time. "We can't sail her down anyway."

"Well, boy, we might if we had a favourable wind all the way, but that ain't possible, the river bends and twists and the wind would be fickle. So how are we going to do it?"

Nathaniel saw an opportunity to gain more time while he searched desperately for an answer. "Please sir, what's a fickle wind?"

Jim felt a surge of irritation. He was the one to ask the questions, but remembering he'd told the boy to ask if he didn't understand, he grinned inwardly and considered how best to explain this word that every sailor knew.

"Well, fickle means changeable, or erratic, I suppose. In other words the wind is often changing its direction or strength."

"Oh! Thank you, sir."

"Well, come on, boy, how are we going to get down river? Why d'you think we're sailing at high water on the ebb?"

"So's the tide will help us down, sir?" A relieved look spread across Nathaniel's face, but it vanished as the Captain said, "Yes. That's right, but we can't just let her drift on the tide. We have to keep her in deep water or we might end up on the mud or worse still the rocks. So how do we steer her?"

Nathaniel replied hopefully, "With the rudder, sir?" The Captain shook his head.

"No, boy. The rudder won't work until the ship is moving through the water. It won't work with the ship just drifting. So then what are we going to do?"

"Could we pull on some oars and make the ship move through the water? The rudder might work then."

"Well, you're getting the right idea." The boy's bright, Jim muttered to himself. His mother had said so and she was right. "I'll tell you, boy. We'll let the ship drift down with the tide, but we'll have lines from the bow made fast in the longboat and the yawl. Then when we want to guide the ship round a bend or keep her clear of a shallow patch or a rock, we'll tell the boats to pull our bows round and tow us in the right direction. You'll see it tomorrow and next time when you've learnt to handle an oar, you'll be in one of the boats."

Nathaniel seemed relieved.

"Now Mr Lugger," the Captain continued, "I want you to keep this journal, while you're on board my ship. You can keep it as a diary if you want, but I want you to record as much of the ship's life as you can. As your first entry I want you to describe our passage down river and explain how it's done. I shall want to see it from time to time and I'll expect to see some good drawings of the masts and the rigging and the sails and anything else you learn about, so that I know you're getting to grips with your trade."

He gave him a heavy leather bound journal and with a gruff "That'll be all, boy," dismissed him. Nathaniel thanked him and moved with alacrity towards the door. Jim watched him depart. "What a nice-looking boy he is. Pity he don't have his mother's blue eyes," he thought. "He'll do well, I'm sure of that. But why's he so frightened?" He shook his head; then he remembered how scared he'd been when he'd joined the Maid of Kent.

At half past three the next day the River Pilot came aboard and with the ebb tide and the muscles of her boat's crews, the Mary Anne made the passage downstream to the river's mouth and anchored in King's Roads to await a favourable wind. By nature impatient, Jim never enjoyed inactivity. Waiting for a fair wind, which never seemed to come, always made him feel restless and irritable. Yet he knew he had to be patient with the wind. A lifetime's experience had taught him that. Clearing the Bristol Channel needed the right wind. The prevailing South Westerlies would be of no use. They were head winds and would carry him to the North. Nor could he sail if the wind was Westerly for then he'd be close to a lee shore and the Mary Anne could at best be stranded on the sandy beaches that stretch northwards from the Yeo estuary, or worse still be driven onto the rocks in Bridgwater Bay. Like all masters he was always concerned about the dangers that lay downwind. Making ground to windward was a desperately slow business at the best of times and impossible in strong winds or a gale. Any wind from a Northerly direction would suit him, but the fresh Easterly which he sensed was about to blow, was just what he'd prayed for. With an Easterly, if he weighed anchor when the ebb began, he'd get a good start and with luck he might clear the narrows by noon and drop the Pilot at the Holms. The Pilot agreed. "Yes Cap'n that should do us well" and nodded as Jim continued, "Thought I'd anchor there for the flood tide to finish running and if the wind's still from the East sail again with the ebb. Then we ought to make Lundy and clear water on the tide."

Chapter 4

"When the wicked man turneth away from his wickedness that he hath committed, and doeth that which is lawful and right, he shall save his soul alive." Elizabeth heard her father intone the words she'd heard every Sunday morning for as long as she could remember. Today was a special Sunday, for Bishop Timothy was visiting. Not only was he to preach but there were five young children, two boys and three girls who had learnt to say the creed and to recite the Ten Commandments, waiting nervously for the Bishop to lay his hands on them and confirm their faith as Christians. While the Rector had been busy preparing his five young candidates for this important occasion in their spiritual lives, the Churchwardens and the Verger had been concentrating on more material matters. Under their direction much work had been done in the past few weeks to clean and prepare the church for this great day in the life of the parish. Villagers had trimmed the grass in the churchyard, tidied the few neglected gravestones and swept the paths in the yard. Inside everything had been cleaned and dusted and Elizabeth and her friend Alison had polished the brass candlesticks and had put out fresh altar cloths. She had also managed to find some dahlias, chrysanthemums and asters spared by the recent frost, to decorate the chancel. The church was looking beautiful.

Preparing for Bishop Timothy's visit had caused great activity at the Rectory too. He and his wife Mary had arrived the previous afternoon and after matins the church dignitaries were to have lunch with the Bishop. There would be fourteen to feed and Elizabeth had been up early that morning polishing and laying the long table in the dining room. She couldn't help worrying about it all. It was the first time she'd played hostess for her father since her mother had died some ten months ago. She'd planned the meal carefully, as her mother had always done, choosing only those dishes she knew Mrs. Jackson, the cook could manage. All had seemed to be progressing well when she had left for church, but still her worries persisted. Would that huge joint of beef be properly cooked? And the gravy, would that be good enough for the Bishop? She'd told Mrs Jackson so many times how to make smooth gravy, but she never seemed to learn. It was always lumpy! Then there was the pudding. Please dear Lord don't let it be as solid as last time. Try as she might she couldn't help being concerned about Mrs Jackson's cooking. At times it could be excellent but at others, well she struggled to find the right word, but it eluded her! She prayed that all would be well, but a voice within said, "Is that a proper thing to ask of the Lord?" "No," she admitted almost audibly. "Please, dear Lord, forgive me." Again she looked around the church. Amongst the steady stream of people making their way up the aisle she spied young Tom Tapper, freshly scrubbed and dressed in his best clothes. He was one of the five to be confirmed. His father, the blacksmith was shepherding him and his siblings into a nearby pew. Memories of Nathaniel's confirmation flooded back. Was it only twelve months ago? She remembered that day well. Her mother had been alive then and they had both watched Nathaniel kneeling before the Bishop for the act of blessing. He'd looked so young and innocent! But then they all had, yet afterwards when Nathaniel had returned to his pew he seemed so assured and confident. She remembered her mother whispering, "He's become a man". She'd been so proud of him that day. Yet now he was gone and he wasn't a man at all, he was just a child, only a few months older than Tom. She shook her head. It was now three whole weeks since she'd seen him last yet it seemed more like a year. How she longed to know how he was, how he was faring among those brutal men. She was sure they'd corrupt him that he would return coarsened, even depraved.

She looked across at Alison sitting there with her husband and her three children. How she envied her! Alison was at the centre of her family and had the joy of watching her children grow up. And when her boys were men, she'd not lose them. No, they'd stay and work the farm with their father. Oh, how lucky Alison was! Elizabeth closed her eyes in prayer; she must stop envying Alison and seek forgiveness for this corrosive sin. Tears filled her eyes. Why, oh why she found herself asking God, had life been so cruel? Her husband had been killed in the full flush of their married life and now her only child had been taken from her. For all she knew he could be dead as well. Would she ever see him again? Her misery enveloped her as she knelt and joined in the confession. "Almighty and most merciful father, we have erred and strayed from thy ways like lost sheep," the words came automatically as she thought of her son and prayed for his safe return.

She asked herself accusingly had she tried hard enough to find her son a ship in the King's Navy? Or even in an East Indiaman? Now she felt she had given in too easily! Somehow she'd persuaded herself that fate had decreed that a life at sea was not for Nathaniel; that some other calling would come. But it had been a pious hope! He'd remained as determined as ever to go to sea. And now through her own stupidity she'd delivered her son into the hands of a slaver, into the very hands of the Devil. For surely that evil trade was the Devil's work. Her guilt lay heavy on her. Would the Good Lord ever forgive her?

She tried to concentrate on the service. Her father was reading the Gospel. "From that time Jesus began to preach and to say, Repent: for the Kingdom of Heaven is at hand. And walking by the sea of Galilee, He saw two brethren, Simon called Peter and Andrew his brother, casting a net into the sea: for they were fishers. And he saith unto them, Follow me, and I will make you fishers of men." Her father paused and said, "This is the Gospel of the Lord" then raising the Bible to his lips he kissed it. The Bishop then rose, climbed the steps to the pulpit and began his sermon.

Elizabeth had felt unusually moved by the Gospel reading. It was one of her favourite passages and her father had used it as his text for a sermon on many occasions. For Peter and Andrew it had been a supreme moment of truth. They had received and obeyed God's call to do his will. It was a story she thought she knew, but today the message seemed to be directed at her. The words "Follow me" kept repeating themselves. "Follow me, follow me". She heard nothing else. Those words chased each other round her head. They came again. "Follow me". Then suddenly they were gone leaving her unnerved. Never before had she experienced such a thing. Had she been dreaming? She knew she hadn't! Could it be some trick of her imagination or, she froze at the thought, had the Lord really spoken to her? If He had, what did He want? As she agonised over what He might ask of her, she remembered that Peter and Andrew didn't know either. They had simply followed Him and had waited to be told. Perhaps she too, was meant to wait. She felt less frightened then and became aware of the Bishop preaching. She saw him fling his arms wide and say in a voice full of passion and exhortation, "So let us spread the good news of the Gospel to those poor souls who live in the shadow of darkness. Let us be compassionate as He was, He who suffered death on the cross for our redemption. Let us learn from Him and forgive those who have sinned against us. And let us go forth with courage in the sure company of the Holy Ghost and work unceasingly to overcome the Devil and his evil purposes." He crossed himself and ended, "In the name of the Father, Son and Holy Ghost, Amen."

Bishop Timothy returned to his chair and they began to sing the last hymn. As the final words of his sermon repeated themselves in her memory, Elizabeth became deeply moved and she felt she too had been called, called in some way to work for the Lord. How could she serve him? The question she knew was unnecessary. She'd be told, she was sure of that.

The two Churchwardens led the Bishop and her father down the aisle and as they drew level with her, the congregation began to sing the last verse.

O God, our help in ages past
Our hope for years to com
Be thou our guard while troubles last
And our eternal home.

At last everyone had filed past the Bishop and made their genuflections and it was time for her father to lead him and the other guests to the Rectory for lunch.

To Elizabeth's great relief the meal had gone well, the beef was tender, the Yorkshire pudding crisp and light and she'd found no lumps in the gravy. When the pudding had appeared Bishop Timothy with undisguised pleasure, had eyed the silky white crust amply dotted with raisins. "Ah! Spotted Dick," he'd said. "Quite my favourite!" She'd watched him ladle a good portion of custard over it, then with an anticipatory sigh; he'd taken a spoonful. "Excellent, my dear Elizabeth," he'd said wiping a trace of custard from his lips. "Your cook is a treasure. Please give her my compliments and tell her how much I have enjoyed my lunch."

When all had finished her father led them into the drawing room, with Mrs Jackson following with teapot and kettle. Elizabeth watched her father unlock the caddy and spoon the precious leaf into the pot, for the ritual that brought the meal to its conclusion. At last the final guest had departed and Bishop Timothy had invited her to take the fresh air with him and had asked about her son. "Let me see Elizabeth, didn't I confirm Nathaniel last year?"

"Yes, indeed you did, my Lord, may our Father in Heaven bless you."

"But where is the lad? Have you sent him off to school at last?"

"Alas no, my Lord. I haven't the wherewithal to send him to school. But I hope between us, my father and I have given him a tolerable education."

"So where is he? I was hoping to see him. I remember him as a well-mannered and likeable boy. I hope he's well?"

"He was very well when I last saw him three weeks ago, my Lord and greatly excited at the prospect of going to sea as an Apprentice."

"What good news! I hope he's with a good company. There's none better than the East India Company, I'm told."

Elizabeth tried her hardest to control her emotions. "Yes my Lord, I had hoped, indeed I did my best to find an East Indiaman for him, but," she sighed. "As he'd not been to school, none would accept him."

"I see." Bishop Timothy looked puzzled. "But nevertheless, you say you've found him a ship?"

"Yes my Lord, he'd always set his heart upon going to sea, even as a small boy." Her voice had begun to tremble. "So now he's doing what he always wanted."

"I pray he will do well, but my child, why are you so distressed?" He'd taken her arm as Elizabeth began to sob.

"Oh! My Lord, how can I tell you of my dreadful sin?" She'd paused; it was too terrible to tell. "In the gospel reading today, the Lord Jesus told Peter and Andrew to follow Him and he would make them fishers of men." Bishop Timothy had nodded in agreement. "But," she'd sobbed, "I have made Nathaniel a fisher of slaves!" The magnitude of her sin overcame her and in her misery she wept. At length she managed to compose herself and told him the whole sorry story. "When I left Nathaniel in that awful ship my Lord, I couldn't understand how a Christian country like ours could allow such an evil trade. How can it be right to sell human beings like chattels? Now I feel deeply ashamed to be English and for the past three weeks I've wanted to do something, no matter how small to help end this savage trade. But my Lord I haven't known what to do and I've done nothing at all. Nothing at all!" She looked up at the Bishop. "But today, my Lord, you exhorted us to challenge evil and hatred, when we meet it and to fight the Devil and all his works. And somehow I feel that through you my Lord, God has told me what I must do. I must find others who hate slavery as much as I do and perhaps together, with His sure help we can prevail upon our Government to outlaw this awful trade."

Bishop Timothy had taken her hands in his. "God bless you my child," he'd said. "I feel humble to have been a messenger for the Lord. I pray He will support and guide you in the task you have been given." Suddenly she'd felt assured and uplifted. She knew what she had to do.

Chapter 5

Elizabeth entered the porch and stood before the large oak doors decorated with heavy wrought iron. She hesitated wondering what he would be like. Then curiosity, which had plagued her all morning, bade her push the door open. She shivered as the cold dampness engulfed her. At first she could see nothing but a few steps later in the shafts of light from the tall lancet windows she began to see the dim interior. To her left was the chancel where a candle burnt revealing a solitary figure. Was that the Curate? Her footsteps had clearly disturbed him, for he stood up and came towards her.

"Welcome, ma'am, welcome to St Mary's. Am I right to presume you're Mrs Elizabeth Lugger?"

"Yes sir, indeed you are. And I take it that you're the Reverend David Hart?"

When Bishop Timothy had written to thank her father for his hospitality, he had enclosed a separate note for her. It had excited her greatly. So much so that she had read and re-read it and knew its contents by heart.

"My dear Elizabeth," he had written. "I was greatly moved by your confession and the great concern you have about the evil trade in slaves. I too wish to see this brought to an end, but alas it has enriched great numbers of our countrymen and to make them relinquish such a lucrative trade will be a long and difficult struggle; one which will not succeed until by the grace of God, our fellow men see that to enslave other human beings is a cruel and wicked act. Only then, when there is a public outcry will Parliament have the courage to act and outlaw slavery in all its repulsive and sickening forms. We must pray for God's guidance to help us achieve this goal. With His sure strength behind us we cannot fail. By His divine favour I know of a kindred spirit, who like you abhors this trade and also prays for its abolition. I believe you and he should meet, to draw strength from one another and to discuss the mission, which the Good Lord has given you. The Reverend David Hart is the Assistant Curate of St Mary's in the parish of Olverton. He was born in Barbados, the son of a rich planter and came to England to take Holy Orders some five years ago. He has seen slavery in the colonies at first hand and is aggrieved by the apathy felt in England about this inhuman trade. He is excited at the prospect of meeting another who shares his convictions. He will be in the parish church of St Mary's at eleven o'clock each morning and hopes that you will meet him there."

She had set off to meet him the very next day. By the light of his candle she saw that David was tall with short hair, but could see little more.

"It's cold and damp in here, ma'am", he said. "We'll be warmer outside."

In the light of day she had a better view of him. She'd been right; he was tall, over six feet she thought. He had an upright gait and his cassock hung elegantly on a slim figure. Like her, he had blue eyes, but his were set in a craggy face and a neat moustache adorned his upper lip complementing his blonde hair. She guessed he was between twenty-five and thirty years of age.

He led her to a bench warmed by the winter sun and sheltered from the wind. "It's a great pleasure to make your acquaintance, ma'am."

"And I'm delighted to meet you, sir. Bishop Timothy tells me we have the same abhorrence of slavery and said we should meet."

Her directness appealed to him. He looked at her out of the corner of his eye. He hadn't known what to expect when he'd been told about this woman who wanted to abolish slavery. Did she have it in mind to do it single-handed, he wondered. How could anyone stop a trade that had existed for thousands of years? Was she some sort of crank? Didn't she know that merchants made fortunes out of slavery? He studied her quizzically. She didn't look crazy, but then time would tell. "Ma'am, may I ask you why it is you hate slavery?"

No one had asked her that before. Everyone she knew shied away from the subject. "Why do I hate slavery?" She repeated the question to gain time. He watched her as she gathered her thoughts. By the set of her jaw he could tell she had a determined streak, yet those blue eyes of hers gave a hint of compassion and understanding.

"It's a question you may well ask me sir, a Rector's daughter buried in a little village in Gloucestershire." She paused. "Until a year ago I hardly knew that slavery existed. You see we've never seen a slave in Hanbury, no more I imagine than you have sir here in Olverton." He nodded. "But I had reason to visit Bristol with my father some time ago. Though I saw no slaves in that busy port, it soon became clear what it was that made Bristol so prosperous. It wasn't trade with France or the Low Countries that made the merchants grow rich. It was trade in human beings! When that truth struck home, I felt ashamed to be English. I was so greatly disturbed that I was glad to leave that shameful port and to shake its dust off my feet." She paused as if she wished that were the end of her story. "Then", she began again, "a few weeks ago my son joined a ship in Bristol. I thought it would be carrying wool to the Baltic, but," her voice began to quiver, "little did I know that it would be shipping slaves, carrying men, women and children from Africa to a life of bondage in the colonies." She stopped to compose herself then told him about Nathaniel and the Mary Anne. David listened intently, watching her face reflect the anger and impotence she felt as her tale unfolded. When at last she'd finished, she looked tired and dispirited. "Sir, I loathe and detest this vile trade. I cannot understand how any civilised country can condone it. I long to see it brought to an end." She looked at him directly. "What sir, can I do to help to achieve this goal?"

"Ma'am I wish I knew!" David shook his head ruefully; he'd been trying to find an answer to that question ever since Bishop Timothy had told him about this strange woman who wished to change the world. He made a wry face and went on. "The wealth of the colonies and much of England itself is founded on the slave trade. In your shameful port of Bristol, not only those who sail in its ships but those who help to victual and supply them are involved in the trade you so detest. They mightn't admit it, but they are. And it's the same in Liverpool too. And the people, who work in the mills and factories in Birmingham and Manchester, they're involved as well, for they make the muskets and the knives and the axes and the pots and pans and the cloth needed to buy the slaves. So you see ma'am, if by some magic we could stop slavery tomorrow it's not just the ship owners who'd lose their trade. Many merchants and factory owners would be ruined and a great many simple people in this land of ours would be thrown out of work. What would happen to them? Who would feed them?"

Elizabeth shook her head. "I see that and I feel for those poor souls who labour in those dreadful factories sir, but what right do we have to enrich ourselves at the expense of the poor wretched black people?"

"Enrich ourselves? I doubt if the planters feel they're enriching themselves, ma'am. They'll tell you they're carving their sugar fields out of useless jungle; that they're making a hard won profit by providing the sugar, the cotton and the tobacco we all want so much."

"But it's wicked, sir, it's thoroughly evil to enslave other human beings and use them for our own profit. Surely all right thinking people must see that."

"Must they ma'am? Our Parson in Bridgetown had no such qualms. I remember him preaching that the white man had dominion over the slaves as much as over the fish of the sea and the fowl of the air and over the cattle and over everything that creepeth upon the earth. I remember he often quoted from Leviticus," he stopped as the thumbed through his bible. "Yes here it is, Leviticus 25 Verse 44, 'both thy bondmen and thy bondmaids, which thou shalt have, shall be of the heathen that are round about you and of them shall you buy bondmen and bondmaids and of their families which they begat in your land they shall be in your possession.' It goes on 'Ye shall take them as an inheritance for your children after you. They shall be your bondmen forever'." He closed the bible and waited for her reply. But none came; she seemed stunned, taken aback. Suddenly he felt sorry for her. "That's what's written in Leviticus," he said more gently.

Elizabeth shook her head in despair. "That's just what every slave owner wants to hear, isn't it? Words from the bible that ease his troubled conscience!" Then in a quiet voice she said, "Jesus tells us to love one another as he loves us. If we all did that, slavery would end tomorrow."

"Yes, you're right, ma'am. But first we have to change the way people think about the blacks. Y'see we whites don't accept them as human. We think they're different, not real members of the human race, some don't think they're human at all! And until society admits that the blacks have similar fears, hopes and feelings as we do and accepts them as true human beings, no government will have the courage to outlaw this trade you hate so much."

She seemed lost for words, but then in a sad empty voice she spoke. "Bishop Timothy told me you were a kindred spirit that you might want to see it ended too." She got up, as if to go. "But it seems, sir, that he was wrong."

"Ma'am, don't go and pray don't misunderstand me. I do share your views; it's just that perhaps I'm more aware of the enormity of the task." He watched her sit down again. Clearly his conviction that ending slavery was impossible had distressed her. She looked downcast and despondent. Her desire to end slavery was driven by compassion; to her the economic consequences of abolition seemed to count for nothing. He found himself admiring this strange, earnest woman. He sought to break the silence which now engulfed them, a seemingly endless silence, and bring the conversation onto a more personal level. "Bishop Timothy tells me that somehow your son has been tricked into serving on a slave ship. You must be very distressed!"

In her mind's eye Elizabeth saw Captain Youle's bearded face. Tricked? No of course not. Somehow the word upset her. Captain Youle hadn't set out to trick her. He hadn't wanted to take Nathaniel. It was she; she was the one who had persuaded him to take her son. No, no he might be a slaver, but for all that, she believed he was an honest man!

"No", she corrected David firmly. "Nathaniel wasn't tricked. It was my foolishness, my stupidity that is to blame." She explained how she'd been foolish and gullible. As she finished she dropped her head. "I feel so guilty."

David broke the silence that followed by asking her if she had ever seen a slave. "No," she admitted. Her answer seemed to underline her total ignorance of slavery. "You've lived with slaves, haven't you sir? Tell me about them."

"Well, you probably know I was born in Barbados. My grandfather came to the island in 1704 and acquired some land, which he began to clear. It was very hard work and recruiting labour was all nigh impossible. The natives didn't seem interested in work, though now and then some would work for a few days, so clearing the land was painfully slow. Then a ship arrived seeking fresh water and the master offered slaves for sale and like many others, my grandfather bought some. With them he soon managed to clear about two hundred acres of good land; land that he planted with sugar cane. Now there's a great demand for sugar in England and Europe, so he and the other planters began to make a good living. By the time my father inherited, there were nearly a thousand acres under cultivation with a mill to crush the cane and a factory to refine the sugar. Now it's a big plantation with about four hundred slaves, organised and controlled by overseers."

"Overseers, sir?" Elizabeth broke in.

"Overseers," David explained, "are white men many of whom are coarse, sadistic brutes who drive the slaves without mercy. They think nothing of whipping a slave who is slow or isn't working hard enough. They treat them like animals."

"Did your father know how the overseers treated the slaves?"

"Well I suppose he probably did, but of course when he was around the overseers would be on their best behaviour. I remember seeing him reprimand one when he was whipping a slave for no apparent reason, but of course the overseers were always careful to save such cruelty until father was gone. They are repellent men."

"But sir," she interrupted him.

"Ma'am," he replied. "The time has surely come when a little less formality might not be amiss. May I be so bold as to suggest that you call me David and may I call you Elizabeth?" He saw a smile relax her earnest face.

"Please do."

"That makes me happy. Now Elizabeth, I believe you wished to question me about the overseers?"

"Yes David. I wanted to ask why are they so cruel."

"I cannot say, Elizabeth, I really can't. Except that most have fled England for some reason they wish to hide. They are the most depraved of men who are despised by the white community and the only people they themselves can despise are the slaves. So I suppose that's why they are so cruel, they take their revenge on the slaves, on the blacks that they say are little more than animals."

"Are they?" David could see anger in her eyes. "Well, Elizabeth, I must admit that sometimes I think so too. At times they scarcely look human. You've yet to see one, Elizabeth". He shook his head ruefully. "One can be forgiven Elizabeth, for thinking they're not like us."

"But aren't they, David?"

"No, no, Elizabeth they're not like us. Somehow they are different. They aren't like us." He paused as if lost for words. "But Elizabeth," he continued. "They're certainly not animals."

"So they're not animals, David, but they are different. Different, different as the French are?"

"No, Elizabeth," he laughed. "We mightn't like the French, but they are civilised."

"Is that what it is then? The slaves aren't civilised?"

"Well, yes. Now I think about it, you may right. Somehow it was hard to believe the slaves who worked the fields, were human. But y'know, we did feel very differently about our servants. I like to think we did accept them as human beings, I'm sure we did! We taught them how to behave and we dressed them in uniforms and made them look clean and tidy. Perhaps we did civilise them a little."

"Were all your servants slaves?"

"Oh! yes, Elizabeth. We had a fine big house up on the hill and had a whole army of slaves to look after us. We had a cook and several kitchen maids. Then there were parlour maids and footmen and my father and mother each had personal servants. Outside we had two gardeners and a driver for the buggy. I suppose there were a dozen servants in all. Then of course my brother and sister and I had our nanny. She was a lovely warm old soul who would fuss over us as if we were delicate garden plants. "Yes," he nodded reflectively. "It was quite an army." For a moment he was quiet as he thought of them. "It's funny really, we did love our servants, some we loved dearly; especially those near to us like Nanny. And there was Florrie too, Florrie the cook. We children loved her. She would always find titbits for us when we crept into the kitchen, though our parents forbade us to go there. I think I can honestly say the family was kind to the servants and they were faithful to us. And it was the same in most of the houses."

"So the domestic slaves weren't unhappy."

"No, Elizabeth I think they were happy enough. There's no doubt they had the best life. It was the slaves who worked in the fields or toiled in the mill and the refinery who really suffered."

He saw her turn her collar up as a gust of wind blew a bevy of dancing leaves at them and the sun slid behind the dark grey clouds. "It's getting too cold here. We'd be warmer in the vicarage." He took her hand and led her down the path by the great yew tree, out through the gate. For the first time she saw the Vicarage. She studied it with interest. Certainly no one could call it a fine building, unlike the Rectory at Hanbury. A kindly eye might call it rustic. It was certainly modest. Built of local stone with its roofs pierced by dormer windows, it seemed to sprawl in all directions. The weather-beaten door, through which they entered, led into a dark, narrow passage lit by a warm glow from a room opposite.

"My sanctum's along here," David guided her the length of the passage. "It's not much, but at least I can think in here. Please do sit down Elizabeth. I'll see if cook can produce some victuals."

When he had gone Elizabeth peered through the window. There was no sign of a lawn or a flower bed or even any shrubs; all she could see were a few cabbages waiting to be cut, a row or two of carrots and the like. It was a dreary sight after her own spacious and well-loved garden at Hanbury. She scanned this room he called his sanctum. An expensive rug covered the floor and by the window stood a large kneehole desk with well-polished brass handles and a finely tooled leather top. Adjacent was a well-proportioned bookcase in which she could see his bibles, prayer books and one or two other tomes, bound in leather and illuminated in gold. Opposite was a small circular mahogany table. Like the chair she sat in, the one by the desk was upholstered with a fine floral tapestry and on the wall nearby hung a nicely carved crucifix. The room he called his sanctum, was clearly an oasis of luxury in this plain and uninviting house.

The door opened and David appeared. "I've asked cook to bring us something." He moved to the fireplace, poked the embers and threw on some logs.

"This is the only decent room in this wretched house, y'know. It's a good job I had the foresight to bring some respectable furniture with me. You should have seen the stuff that was here when I arrived. Only fit for the bonfire!" He shook his head and sighed. "But where were we?"

Elizabeth smiled at this rich young priest, who loved beautiful things. "You were saying that the slaves who worked in the fields and the factory were the ones who suffered. You said they toiled from dawn to dusk. Did they ever have a day off'?"

"Well they didn't work on Sundays nor at Easter and Christmas."

"So Sunday was a day of rest?" She saw him nod. "Were they taught the Gospel?"

"No, Elizabeth. No they certainly weren't. Like most planters, neither my father nor his father before him ever allowed his slaves any religious instruction. Yet somehow the slaves did seem to know about Jesus. Maybe the parlour maids or the footmen taught them. The servants were always listening at doors and would have heard father reading the Bible to us and leading the family in prayers. So I'm sure it was the house servants who taught the slaves about Jesus. Often we would hear them in the evening singing their own haunting songs to Jesus. I suppose they need to believe in some Supreme Being, some God to whom they can turn to save them from their misery and suffering."

"But why David, did you stop your slaves from knowing about God? Shouldn't you have taught them the Gospel? Wasn't that your Christian duty?"

"Yes, Elizabeth, you're right we should have taught them the Gospel, but I'm sorry to say we didn't. Y'see owners don't want their slaves seeking strength and unity through any god. In fact they do all they can to destroy their tribal beliefs and traditions. They'll often thrash a slave if he's caught speaking his native tongue or worshipping his own god. You see his native language and tribal customs give him an identity and a sense of pride. Without that he feels confused and is more submissive. It's a bit like breaking in a horse, I suppose."

"So you broke them in like horses!" He could see her face redden with anger. "How could your family be so cruel?"

David stroked his face, trying to find an answer to her question. "Elizabeth, I've often asked myself such questions since I've been in England." He sighed, and continued in a low dispirited voice. "Believe me I'm not trying to make excuses for my family. They use slaves but you must understand Elizabeth none of the natives were willing to work, so they were desperate for labour and when that ship offered them slaves, it seemed the answer to their prayers, a Godsend! To buy slaves, much as one would buy oxen and horses seemed the natural thing to do."

"But David, they weren't oxen, they weren't horses; they were human beings!"

"Yes, Elizabeth, you're right, of course you're right. But when one sees slaves coming off a ship, or being auctioned or working in the fields they scarcely look human, hardly better than oxen or horses. So I'm afraid the slaves are treated like animals not like human beings, and like animals they are expected to be obedient, obedient without question."

He saw that anger in her eyes again. "Elizabeth, it's not like England you know. You must realise that planters are greatly outnumbered by the slaves. On our plantation there were only six white men to control about four hundred slaves, so the slaves have to be made subservient. They have to be kept down. Everyone worries that the slaves will rise up against the owners. It has happened, Elizabeth, believe me, and many poor white men, women and children have been slaughtered. That's what makes the white man edgy and suspicious. That's why they take harsh measures to keep the slaves dispirited, frightened and obedient."

Elizabeth was shaking her head in despair.

"I'm not trying to make excuses Elizabeth; I'm trying to tell you how slavery works."

The more Elizabeth had learnt about the fate of the slaves the more sickened she'd become. Yet she knew there was no point in venting her anger on David, he was just the messenger, the one who'd brought her the news. She made herself smile at him and thanked him. She wondered why he hadn't been corrupted like all the other white men. He'd been brought up in the midst of this terrible cruelty which had made his family rich. Why was he so different?

"David, tell me please, what is it that makes you hate slavery? Slavery made your family rich and it gave you a happy childhood. Why d'you hate it?"

"Elizabeth, you're right, slavery has made my family rich and I did have a happy childhood. We children didn't want for anything! We all had our own ponies and could ride over to the other plantations to see our friends. I had my own dog and we used to go shooting in the hills and fishing in the sea. Yes, we all had a wonderful childhood. And of course as children we didn't see the brutality the slaves had to endure, nor were we aware of their suffering. We were young and innocent."

The sound of shuffling feet interrupted him and a breathless Mrs Stewart entered and set down her tray. "There you are sir. The bread's straight from the oven."

Mrs Stewart looked at Elizabeth as she placed two bowls of soup on the table. It was a long enquiring look. Clearly, she was intrigued by the Curate's lady visitor. The lady's wretched manservant Miles had not been at all forthcoming when she'd asked him the purpose of her visit. All he'd told her was that she was the daughter of the Rector of Hanbury, was a widow and that her only son was now at sea. Could it be that she was the Curate's secret love? She'd always thought there was more than met the eye about him. He was one of the most eligible bachelors hereabouts, yet hardly ever was he seen with a young lady. Mrs Stewart surveyed the Curate's guest. "Will my lady be staying?"

"No, no thank you, Mrs Stewart," David replied with haste. "Mrs Lugger is just visiting for an hour or so."

David laughed as Mrs Stewart reluctantly left. "She thinks it's high time I was safely wed. No doubt she'll pass the word round the parish that if we're not already betrothed we soon will be!" Elizabeth could feel herself blushing, something she hadn't done since she was a girl. Her flushed cheeks lit up her face and accentuated those cornflower blue eyes of hers and for the first time David realised how beautiful she was. He averted his eyes to avoid hers.

"I'm sorry, Elizabeth. Mrs Stewart is a good cook, but sadly a very stupid woman."

He drew up a chair for her and when he'd said grace they began to eat. The soup was welcome and warmed them. Elizabeth was the first to finish. She was impatient for him to continue, but he seemed to savour every mouthful and it was an age before she could bring him back to that question he hadn't answered. "David, you were going to tell me what made you hate slavery."

He made no effort to answer but toyed with the remnant of his bread. Finally his eyes met hers. "Well it's a long story and I'm sure you'll find it distressing. Please just take my word for it. I hate slavery as much as you do."

"No David, I can't do that. You must tell me. Hearing you talk about slavery has helped me understand how much these poor people suffer. I can't let you stop now. Please David, please tell me what it was that made you hate slavery."

He gave her a questioning look. "It's not a story I'm proud of Elizabeth. Must I tell you? It'll upset you, I know."

She was quiet for a while. Then she nodded. "Please tell me."

Chapter 6

David took a deep breath. "I have a sister called Emily and a month or so before she was born, Florrie, our cook also gave birth to a daughter, whom she named Matilda. She was a bonny child, bright and happy and," he sighed, "as black as coal. Of course she lived with Florrie in the slave lines but we used to see her in the kitchen. We were all taken in by this tiny black tot. In a way she was a family pet! But we couldn't call her Matilda, it was such a mouthful for the wee thing that she was and we came to call her Tilly. Well I suppose it was inevitable that Emily would meet Tilly and soon they were crawling round the kitchen floor and playing together. They saw each other every day and when the time came for them to be separated they would scream and throw a tantrum". He chuckled, "Poor Nanny she'd have a terrible time! My parents must have known about Emily and Tilly but seemed content to let the two infants amuse each other."

Elizabeth was looking happier now. The thought of Emily and Matilda playing together pleased her. "Go on," she said.

"Well," he continued, "over the next few years Emily and Tilly's friendship ripened and they seemed lost without the other. Then Emily began going to school but Tilly had to stay behind. After school Emily would play teacher and show Tilly how to read and write and do her sums. I don't think Mother approved, but Emily was Mother's favourite and headstrong too, so her friendship with Tilly went unchecked. The two became inseparable but as they grew older they both seemed to know that they were different. Tilly accepted that Emily went to school, had her own pony and lived in the big house, while she had her slate and a rag doll and lived with Florrie in a little wooden cabin on the slave lines. When they were about eleven, Emily began finding other interests, riding with her friends, learning to dance and soon she became the centre of attraction with all the boys wanting to dance or ride with her. Elizabeth you must remember the excitement of growing up."

Elizabeth smiled and nodded.

"Well," he went on, "gradually Emily began to see less and less of Tilly. I'm sure Emily was still fond of her, but as she grew up her friendship with Tilly waned, much to mother's relief. Friendship between a white and a black toddler could be tolerated, but an alliance between adults or even adolescents was totally unacceptable."

"Poor Tilly." Elizabeth shut her eyes as if to blot out the picture of that poor black child. "She must have felt so miserable." Though in her heart Elizabeth knew the answer, she had to ask him. "There isn't a happy ending is there?"

"No Elizabeth, I'm sorry, there isn't." He seemed distressed. "No," he shook his head. "Tilly had no Fairy Godmother." The memories were flooding back now. No longer could he keep them in check. "I remember Emily's birthday. It was her thirteenth and my parents gave a big party for her and all our friends from Bridgetown and the neighbouring plantations were invited. Emily looked lovely in her new dress; somehow it accentuated her transition from a gangling child to a budding young woman. It was her night and she was the star around which we all revolved. We had a fiddler to play for us and after supper we all danced under a velvet, star-studded sky. We danced and danced and danced and drank and drank and I'm afraid I got a little tipsy. I remember going into the kitchen to find some cool water and there, there was Tilly. Tilly in her servant's garb, with her wiry black hair brushed out and looking like a big woolly hat and underneath were her large round eyes and smiling mouth. I was aware of nothing else but Tilly and that firm sensual body of hers, which her servant's clothes now seemed to embellish. Suddenly I found her enticing, alluring, irresistible, and I was holding her hand and leading her out to the stables. My heart was thumping as we climbed into the loft. I hardly knew what I was doing. But Tilly, Tilly was calm and composed and her body soft and compliant as we made love in the hay."

He stopped and looked at her. "I hope I haven't shocked you. I've never told anyone about Tilly before."

"No, no," Elizabeth heard herself reply. She'd been lost in that distant island where David had grown up and somehow his liaison with Tilly had seemed both natural and understandable.

"I was just fifteen and Tilly thirteen and after that first night we often stole away to the loft as our desire for each other grew. I knew it was wrong, that she was black and I was white but I needed her. I needed her like some men need rum. Even the thought of being caught didn't stop me seeing her, and for some reason it never occurred to me that Tilly would become pregnant."

Elizabeth nodded.

"But of course she did and as the baby inside her grew, everyone including Mother noticed her condition and there was much speculation within the family as to who the father might be. When her time came, Tilly produced a placid, beautifully formed boy whom she named Zebedee. Mother heard the news and she asked Tilly to bring her baby for us all to see. Tilly arrived looking frightened and apprehensive, with Zebedee in her arms. I can see Mother's smile even now, as she stepped forward to inspect the child, almost hidden in his shawl. It was the cold unwelcoming smile Mother used to hide anger or suspicion. I felt a tremor of fear as she reached forward to uncover Zebedee's head. When the shawl came away revealing his pale tawny, skin, the blood drained from Mother's face. But she said nothing, not a word. She seemed mesmerised by the fine shape and paleness of the baby's features. Finally in a muted voice she exclaimed, "It's a mulatto, a mulatto!" Then without another word she turned and left the room. It was such an anti-climax; I'd been convinced she'd make a scene. For a moment I foolishly thought that was the end of the matter. But soon we all knew she'd not rest until she had learnt who was the white man, who had fathered Zebedee. There were only six of us on the estate, Father, the three overseers, my brother Gerald and me. I was too terrified to admit that I was responsible and I'm positive Mother never thought it was me. From the start it was clear that she suspected Father. However as if to give him the benefit of the doubt she told him she wanted to question the overseers. At first Father refused, but Mother insisted. Finally when it seemed he would never give way, Mother threw one of her famous tantrums and the overseers were summoned one by one. Of course none of them would admit to fathering Zebedee, the very idea seemed to amuse the first two. The third became aggressive and rude, but nevertheless Mother convinced herself it wasn't him. Nor did she believe either of the other two was responsible. They had never been known to consort with the servants before. 'They've plenty of girls in the fields, to satisfy their filthy desires,' she told Father. With the overseers exonerated, Mother no longer had any doubts; it had to be Father. I happened to be by the sitting room door when Tilly came to her bidding. In a quiet determined manner Mother asked her if Massa was the father of Zebedee. Tilly remained silent. Mother repeated the question and demanded an answer. 'Tell me, you little vixen.' Tilly began to sob and in a voice scarcely audible repeated over and over again 'It ain't Massa, it ain't Massa.' As Tilly kept denying it was Father, all the pent-up doubts that had plagued Mother erupted into a towering rage. In a voice full of menace and hatred, she screamed, 'Tell me then you Jezebel, who is the father?' By now Tilly was becoming hysterical and when Mother stamped her foot and began to berate her again, she fled. But Mother never gave up and for days kept interrogating Tilly, but she would say no more. As you might imagine the tension in the house became unbearable with Mother openly accusing Father and flying into a rage at the slightest provocation. Father was constant in his denial. But nothing he said would convince her that he was not the guilty one. Of course he knew he hadn't fathered Zebedee and that left only me and Gerald. He sent for us. I'd never seen him so irate; his anger must have been fired by Mother's fury. He accused Gerald first and told me to leave the room. Father must have been certain it was Gerald, for it was a long time before Gerald emerged, indignant and rebellious. 'You're next', he scowled. 'He's trying to put the blame on us!' I was called in. Father sat there, his face as hard as stone. 'Was it you?' he demanded. For a second I hesitated. 'Out with it boy, was it you?' I knew I couldn't deny it. 'Yes, Father,' I said meekly. 'Zebedee is my son'. For a moment I thought he'd explode, but he didn't. He said nothing. He just shook his head and left."

"What happened then?"

"Father told Mother of course and when she sent for me I expected a terrible scene. But I couldn't believe it. She seemed to be extra loving towards me, as if I had to be cured of some awful ailment. 'You must put this little mistake behind you, David,' she said. 'It's all part of growing up. That little schemer laid a trap for you. It's clear she wanted to seduce you. The niggers think it smart to have a white man's child. It makes them feel important.' Mother's attitude towards Tilly sickened me, but nothing I could do would make her understand that it was all my fault. I told her again and again, that I was the one who led the way up to the loft, that Tilly hadn't set a trap for me, that I was the guilty one. I kept telling her I was the seducer, not Tilly. And I told her that since that first time in the loft I had wanted to make love to Tilly again and again. 'Love?' Mother exclaimed, a sneer distorting her face, 'Love? What love can a white man have for a nigger? Niggers are worse than animals. You can show a dog or a horse affection and there's no harm in it, but show affection to a damn nigger and in no time he'll think he's as good as you. Well, no damn nigger is, or ever will be. I shall tell your father she'll have to go. We can't have her and your bastard son on this plantation.' The news that she wanted rid of Tilly hit me like a thunderbolt. I couldn't accept it. Why should she be punished and not me? I pleaded desperately with Mother to be reasonable; to let Tilly stay, but she was adamant, she would have to go. I asked Emily to try to persuade Mother to change her mind, but she refused. Emily said Tilly had taken advantage of their friendship and to her it was obvious that Tilly had seduced me! Nor would Gerald help. The whole family was united, united against this poor black girl."

In a quiet flat voice, Elizabeth asked, "What did they do? Did they send her to the fields?"

"No, Elizabeth. Matilda and Zebedee were sold at the next slave auction in Bridgetown. They went to a planter at the other end of the island, where I was told she became a field slave. Florrie's desperate pleas to be sold with Matilda and Zebedee in order to keep the family together were ignored. She became utterly distraught and would sit sobbing in the kitchen all day long. Nobody was able to console her and if I went near her, she would scream at me and blame me for all her troubles. She was quite demented and unable to do her job. Mother kept sending for her and telling her to pull herself together, threatening if she didn't, she'd ask the Master to get a new cook and send her to the mill. But Florrie was a broken woman and the threat made no difference. Though the other servants tried to help, the kitchen became a shambles. In the end Mother could stand it no longer and at the next auction Father bought a new cook and our dear old Florrie was sent off to work in the mill."

"Oh! David, what a terrible story! I can't believe people can be so cruel. How could a Christian family treat anyone in such a pitiless, inhuman way?"

He stood up and gazed without seeing, out of the window.

"David, you said your family loved your servants!"

He turned towards her, shook his head and gave a deep sigh. "Did we love them? I don't know. I think we did love them in a strange paternal way." He stroked his forehead. "But if we ever did love them, I suppose it was only on our terms. When things were going well, if the footman had impressed a visitor or cook had made a really good pie, perhaps then we might have loved them. Loved them as one would a horse, which had jumped some impossibly high fence, or a dog that had found a bird lost in a thicket. But our love for them required them to be faithful, undemanding and honest and, and ...." he struggled for the right word. "Yes that's it, they had above all to be subservient and yes, obsequious; it was then we felt we loved them. If they weren't obsequious, if by their attitude they didn't acknowledge that they came from a lower order of life, then they threatened the whole fabric of our society; a society where the white man though greatly outnumbered is the undisputed boss. Elizabeth, you have to realise that behind the slave-owner's arrogant and confident manner lies the constant fear that one day the slaves, those sub-human animals they hold in such contempt, will take advantage of their numbers and rise against their white masters in an orgy of slaughter and destruction. How could we really love them? Love would demonstrate weakness and a lack of resolution. No, we owned them, despised them for their ignorance and expected them to conform without protest to our rules and requirements. There's no love in that!"

"Have you ever seen or heard from Tilly or Zebedee again?"

"No, Elizabeth, never. Mother and Father made sure I never knew where they were. I often think of Tilly and Zebedee and feel a great sense of shame that she has suffered so much because of what I did. She wasn't sub-human, she was a simple, happy, loving child, who happened to have a black skin and who had the misfortune to be seduced by me. I pray for her and Zebedee and beg God to forgive me."

Elizabeth reached out and took his hand. There was nothing she could say, but as their eyes met, David saw tears in hers. "Now you know why I hate slavery," he said.

Chapter 7

On the long ride back from Olverton, Elizabeth could think of nothing but Tilly and Zebedee and poor demented Florrie. When at last she and Miles reached Hanbury she could recall little of the journey. Without her guidance her mare Turnip had faithfully followed Miles as he led the way. Indeed she had noticed nothing, not even the rain and had arrived shivering and soaked to the skin. Her father had welcomed her with relief and had urged her to take to her bed. She had needed no second bidding and, when between warm sheets and her teeth had finally stopped chattering, she heard footsteps approaching.

"We were so relieved to see you safely home ma'am." Mrs. Jackson's face showed her concern as she placed a tray of hot soup and warm bread beside her. "The Rector was so worried."

Elizabeth smiled. "I was in safe hands, Mrs. Jackson. Dear Miles is a tower of strength." The smell of the soup accentuated her hunger and she ate gratefully. When she had finished she blew out the candle and settled down, but sleep eluded her. Her mind was too active. Nothing she did would allow her to forget David's story about Tilly. It had opened her eyes to the real plight of the slaves. Until yesterday only one aspect of their misery had concerned her, their capture and transport across the seas. Now she knew how they were treated in the land to which they were taken. How subservient they had to be, how they were abused and beaten by uncouth, vulgar and sadistic overseers, how families could be torn apart at the whim of their owners and how David's father had set off one morning to buy a new cook as she herself might go to market to buy a chicken! How, she asked the Almighty in her prayers, could He allow such monstrous cruelty to go unpunished? Hadn't he brought down the great flood to root out the evil in men's hearts in Noah's time? Could their sins then have been any worse than those of these terrible slave-owners of today? Why, oh why does God allow these poor black people to suffer so much? Do they really have to live a worldly life of hell to reap their reward in the next? And would these merciless slavers be condemned to eternal damnation, when they depart this world, like the rich man who begged Abraham to send Lazarus to dip his finger in water and cool his tongue because he was in agony in the flames of hell?

At last her troubled night gave way to dawn. Weary in body and spirit, she rose and drawing the curtains saw that mercifully the rain had stopped and the village was lit by the pale rays of the winter sun. "Dear Lord," she muttered, "what a blessed place this is. Folk may be poor in Hanbury, but no one starves or goes unclothed and all have that greatest of gifts, freedom! Why, oh why should we be so well endowed, when those poor slaves are denied everything?" The gross injustice of it all renewed that sense of guilt that had tormented her in Bristol. As she joined her father for breakfast she knew that what she had learnt about David's life in Barbados had disturbed her more than she had thought possible.

"Are you feeling better, my dear?" Her father enquired. "I hope you've not caught a chill. You were soaked to the skin last night. You're looking very tired Elizabeth. Are you well?"

"Yes Father, I'm well enough. I'm just feeling a little low, that's all."

Silence followed while he ate his porridge and contemplated his daughter. She was listless and appeared depressed, quite unlike her usual cheerful, energetic and practical self. What could have happened at Olverton?

"Tell me, my dear, how was the Reverend Hart?"

"He's an agreeable gentleman, Father. He made me very welcome."

Her father looked pleased, he was always hopeful she might find a good suitor. It would be good to have her safely married again. "What did you discuss?"

When she told him about Tilly and David she saw her father shake his head in disapproval, but she hurried on before he could interrupt. Despite herself, her voice began to tremble when she told how his mother had reacted when she discovered that Zebedee was David's son and how Tilly and her baby were sold to another planter and poor Florrie had become demented. Her father had listened sympathetically, but the re-telling of David's story had made her even more dispirited. "Father," she asked in a low despairing voice, "Will we ever put an end to this sickening evil?"

Never before had he seen his daughter so troubled. He tried to comfort her. "We must have patience, child. God in His own good time will bring this evil to an end".

"But Father dear, how long must poor Florrie and her family wait? A lifetime? Will they never be shown mercy in this world?"

"Elizabeth, we must have faith in God's great love. Did he not send Moses to lead the Israelites to freedom out of slavery in Egypt?"

Elizabeth sighed. "Yes Father, He did. But will He send a Moses for these slaves?"

"That I don't know," her father replied. "We must ask God for His help in our prayers. He'll find someone to lead them to freedom. Maybe He's done so already."

"Father I hope and pray you're right," she gave him a wistful smile. "Oh how I wish my faith could be as strong as yours."

When she had left Olverton, David had suggested they should meet again; he said he had more to tell her. She'd agreed, but the thought of further tales of cruelty now filled her heart with dread. How she wished she'd never asked about the fate of the slaves and how, she asked herself, could a mere woman living in a remote English parish, who had never even seen a slave, do anything to help end this evil? It was impossible. She felt so helpless; she determined to hear no more. She would not see him again. Yet as the day drew near her resolve failed. How could she ignore the plight of the Florries and the Tillies? So with a heavy heart she set off for Olverton once more.

Her doubts and fears plagued her throughout the ride, but as she dismounted and gave the reins to Miles, she put on a bold front, strode through the lichgate, made her way to the porch and pushed the door open. Almost at once she saw him coming towards her. He was delighted to see her again and was concerned for her health. Had she escaped the downpour and had she got home before the light had failed? She should leave in good time today. She must be home before the sun set. His worries about her welfare surprised and flattered Elizabeth, but she brushed them aside. "I was safe with Miles," she said with a smile. "The rain did me no harm. To tell the truth, I hardly noticed it, I was so upset about Tilly. David, I've been praying for her and Zebedee every day, and for poor Florrie too, but I'm beginning to wonder whether God really cares."

David seemed shocked. "Elizabeth, God loves and cares for all his children, you must know that!"

"But David, if He cares for us all, why does He let some suffer so much?"

David seemed lost for words. It was a question that troubled him too.

She shook her head and sighed. "I'm beginning to think it'll take a miracle to end slavery."

"Miracle or not," he said. "God does his work through us, his people. If we as Christians don't listen to him and accept his guidance, how can his will be done?"

"David I know we need to pray and listen to the Lord, but surely all right thinking Christians have been asking God to free slaves for centuries, yet men, women and children are still enslaved and exploited by the rich. Praying for guidance just isn't enough. We have to pray for a miracle."

David was nodding. "Yes you're right, we need a miracle, but maybe God can only perform such a miracle through us. If our faith is strong enough he'll find someone to do his work." He paused. "He'll find someone to perform the miracle."

"Yes, David, that's what we should pray for. We must ask God to give us someone, some decent honest person, to lead the crusade against slavery. He did it for the Israelites, didn't He? He sent Moses to lead them to freedom out of Egypt". She was looking more hopeful. "But who will be our Moses?"

"Moses," David mused. "Moses, I don't know about another Moses, but have you ever heard of Granville Sharp?"

"Granville Sharp?" Elizabeth turned the name over in her mind. "No. I've never heard of Granville Sharp. Who's he?"

"He's the son of an Archdeacon and he seems to have started an anti-slavery movement of his own. When I first arrived in England I spent some time in London, with my cousin and during that time the Gazette and the other papers kept the city agog with the story of Jonathan Strong."

"Who's Jonathan Strong?" Elizabeth interrupted him. "I thought you were going to tell me about Granville Sharp."

"Yes Elizabeth, I am. I'm coming to him, but first let me tell you about Jonathan Strong. He was a slave brought to London from Barbados by a man called David Lisle. He seems to have been a most unpleasant fellow who, for some reason known only to himself, attacked his slave. He beat Jonathan again and again with the butt of his pistol until he was senseless. Then he threw him into the street for dead."

Elizabeth's heart sank. Why had she come? She should have stayed away as she had intended. She wanted no more tales of callous brutality towards the slaves. "Was he dead?"

"No, but he was badly hurt and could scarcely see. Luckily he was found by a Good Samaritan who took him to a doctor."

"Why are you telling me this David? What about this man Granville Sharp? Where does he come in all this?"

David laughed. "You've been very patient Elizabeth. Perhaps it would help if I told you the doctor was a William Sharp." He saw her puzzlement turn to irritation and hurriedly continued, "And this fellow Granville Sharp is his brother."

"Oh I see. But what about this campaign of his?"

Her questions had unsettled him, had upset his rhythm. He tried to marshal the details, to place them in order so as to tell the story as he'd planned, but he found it difficult to concentrate. He'd begun to enjoy being in her presence, hearing her voice, savouring the shape of her body contoured so well in that modest dress and to relish the feelings so openly displayed on her face. He felt drawn to her yet he suspected she had no interest in him. She'd only come to learn more about slavery. He saw her waiting for an answer. He dragged his mind back to Granville Sharp. How had he started his campaign? He cleared his throat. "It all began with the slave Jonathan. Eventually he recovered from his injuries and was grateful to William Sharp. But Granville had become involved too. He'd managed to find a job for Jonathan and both brothers thought all was now well. But then David Lisle spotted his slave and determined to have him back."

"Oh dear", Elizabeth sighed. "I thought for once there'd be a happy ending."

"It's not the end of the story, Elizabeth. Lisle found some villains and promised them money for the recovery of his slave. Well, they found Jonathan easily enough and dragged him back to his master, but Lisle didn't keep him. He arranged to sell him to a planter, who planned to ship him to Jamaica."

"Oh, poor wretched Jonathan, he wasn't free for long".

"Wait, Elizabeth. Somehow Granville Sharp heard what had happened to Jonathan and filed a petition in the courts charging Lisle with assaulting a slave. It was a unique case. No one had ever been charged with maltreating a slave before: a paid servant yes, or even a horse, but never, ever a slave. I tell you the case became a talking point all over London and was reported in great detail in the newspapers".

"So what happened, David? Was that brute Lisle sent to prison?"

David smiled at her, as if she was a naughty child. "Where's your patience Elizabeth? I remember reading the judge's summing up in the Gazette. He could find no evidence that Jonathan had stolen from his master or had committed any other misdeed and there was no reason for him to be chastised, let alone beaten about the head with the butt of a pistol. Then to the delight of those in court he told Jonathan he was free to go."

"You mean he was a free man?" She saw David nod. "And what happened to that brute Lisle?"

"He was cautioned, as far as I remember, but I can check that for you. I still have all the reports of the case."

"But Jonathan," she looked hopefully to David. "He is still free, isn't he?"

David nodded. "Yes, he's still free." For the first time he saw her smile with joy. Before she'd always looked serious, but now her blue eyes sparkled. Suddenly she radiated happiness. He wished she could always be like that.

She broke into his thoughts. "May I see those reports David? I'd dearly like to know just what did happen to that scoundrel Lisle."

"Well, come to the Vicarage and I'll find them for you."

She followed him. On her last visit she had only seen Mrs. Stewart the housekeeper, but as they entered they were met by an elderly priest. He gave them a surprised look.

"Sir, please let me introduce Mrs. Elizabeth Lugger, she's from Hanbury. She's the Reverend Lunt's daughter. Elizabeth, this is the Reverend Parker, Vicar of St Mary's."

"Pleased to make your acquaintance ma'am." The vicar kissed her hand with a show of gallantry. "I've known your father for a very long time, but nowadays we scarcely see each other from one year's end to another. I fear we're both too old to venture far from home these days. Come my dear, come and take some nourishment with us and tell me how he's faring."

He led them into the kitchen and stood warming his hands in front of the flickering fire. "I dread the approach of winter m'dear." A resigned look spread over his face. "My old bones keep tellin' me it's going to be a hard one this year and this is the only warm room in the house." He shook his head sadly and bade them sit. He composed himself and pushed a few wisps of grey hair back from his forehead before saying grace. Then with much huffing and puffing be began to carve the cold mutton that Mrs. Stewart had placed before him.

"Tell me, m'dear," he passed her a plate laden with meat. "What brings you to Olverton? We don't get many visitors here you know. Are you and David acquainted?"

From the knowing look on Mrs. Stewart's face, Elizabeth could tell she was convinced David and she were more than casual acquaintances. The thought irritated her. David was polite and attentive to her as she would expect any gentleman to be, but it was quite ridiculous for her to think they had any affection for each other. "No, sir, we're not acquainted. The Reverend Hart and I both abominate slavery and he has been telling me about his life in Barbados and how the poor slaves are treated."

"Yes," David added. "Mrs. Lugger and I have been talking about the evils of slavery and what can be done about it."

"Aye, 'tis a great evil." The Vicar shook his head ruefully and put another forkful of mutton into his mouth. There followed a long silence as he chewed and then as if he had given the matter great consideration, he continued. "Though sometimes, m'dear, I think the plight of the slaves is greatly exaggerated. I hear they often live better in the colonies than they do in Africa." He sighed as if in despair. "But the world's full of the Devil's work and we must fight it wherever we can."

"Yes sir," Elizabeth struggled to control her anger. "It certainly is a Christian's duty to fight the Devil and I believe slavery is the greatest of all his works. That's why I've come to learn all I can about it. And though I'm only a puny woman, I'm determined to do all I can to help bring it to an end."

"Well, m'dear, that's very laudable and I shall pray that our Heavenly Father will bless and guide you in your struggles, but," he sighed and looked towards David, "there's evil enough in the parish here for the Curate and me to fight."

The remainder of the meal was eaten in silence save for the odd inconsequential comment on the happenings in the village and the prospects for a hard winter. When they had finished David sat respectfully as the vicar slowly drained his glass, then Elizabeth thanked him for his hospitality while David sought permission to take her to the drawing-room. "I've some cuttings from the Gazette I want Mrs. Lugger to see."

With the Vicar's blessing they withdrew to the drawing-room, where David led her to a chair close to the smoldering fire. He stirred the ashes vigorously and after carefully arranging some twigs and logs over the faint flame he excused himself, leaving Elizabeth with her thoughts. How could that stupid arrogant Vicar compare the evil in this sleepy village with the evil of slavery? Slavery is an outrage, a grotesque atrocity, an affront to human dignity, an evil of such magnitude that surely no sin in Olverton can stand comparison with it. She tried to be charitable, perhaps the vicar thought it had no relevance to his parish, or was he in truth indifferent to the sufferings of slaves? Was he like the church, lost in the apathy which clothes so many decent folk, whenever the subject is broached? Yet the church is a great power in the land and dear Lord if it chose to preach the evils of slavery, then surely the people would demand its abolition. Why is the church so feeble? Why won't it lead a great crusade against this awful practice?

David arrived clutching a pile of paper. "Here they are," a note of triumph rang in his voice. "For a moment I thought I'd lost them. Perhaps you'd like to take them with you." He set them down before her.

"Thank you David. I shall read them with interest and I'm greatly encouraged to find someone who cares so much for these poor people. Has Mr. Sharp done any more good work?"

"Yes, as a matter of fact, he has. Here are some more cuttings about another slave he rescued. He leant over to give them to her. Her nearness affected him, her scent filled his nostrils and a tingle of excitement surged through his body. Reluctantly he withdrew, fighting an overwhelming and frightening desire to hold her. With his heart pounding he had to breathe deeply to regain his composure. "Yes, he's helped another," he heard himself saying. "Another slave called Thomas Lewis also managed to give his owner the slip, but with a price on one's head it's nigh impossible to hide for long in London, especially if one's black. So he was soon caught and dragged onto a ship about to sail for Jamaica."

When he'd told her about Jonathan she'd looked worried and concerned, but now she was angry, her eyes hard and unforgiving. "Those ruthless slavers............." He held up a hand to stop her, he wanted to get to the happy ending. "Some Quakers who had given Lewis shelter had heard about Granville Sharp and they hurried to seek his help."

"But David, what could he do?"

"Well, somehow he got a warrant to stop the ship sailing, but she'd already left. The Harbourmaster told him she'd probably anchor at the Downs to wait for a favourable wind, so Granville returned to the judge for a writ to stop the slave being taken out of the country. The ship had indeed anchored at the Downs, the writ was served and the slave brought back to London."

Her anger had left her and she smiled. "What a wonderful man this Mr. Sharp is."

"Yes, isn't he?" David spoke without thinking. He was captivated by her. How enchanting she was when she smiled, when she was happy. Then her impatience showed; she was waiting for him to continue. He pulled himself together. "But Elizabeth, just rescuing the slave wasn't enough for Granville. He went back to court to seek a ruling that the slave Lewis was a free man and again he was successful. But even that didn't satisfy him. He wanted a ruling that all slaves in England should be declared free. Well, the whole of London thought that was a pretty tall order and this time Granville lost. Freeing a visitor's slave wasn't too much of a problem for Lord Mansfield the judge, but freeing all slaves in England would have brought the wrath of the rich and powerful on his head. And of course we have to remember that Lord Mansfield is a slave owner himself with a plantation of his own, so his judgment is bound to be biased!"

"That's dreadful." Elizabeth's eyes were hard again. "What hope is there if the judges are biased? They and the rich will do all they can to keep their slaves."

David nodded, there seemed little to say. For a moment both were lost in their own thoughts, then the silence was broken by the chiming of the clock. Elizabeth looked startled. "David, it's two o'clock. I must go now, if Miles and I are to be home by dark."

"Must you go, Elizabeth?" It was a stupid question he knew, but he didn't want her to leave. "But of course you must," he corrected himself. "It'll be dark in a couple of hours. Yes, you must go at once. I'll get Mrs Stewart to tell your man."

Elizabeth gathered her cuttings and allowed her eyes to wander round the room. Apart from a small carpet and a rug before the fire, the floorboards were bare and worn by age, as were the two chairs they had sat on. On the opposite wall stood a dusty table and by the window with its heavy curtains looking more like dusty old blankets, were two more chairs.

The room cried out for the hand of a woman to care for it. She shuddered; it was like some room in a bachelor's hall.

Suddenly David was back with her topcoat. He helped her into it and led her to the front door, where Miles was waiting with the horses. "We'd better be off quick ma'am, if we're to be in 'anbury by dark." Miles helped her mount and with a wave and a "thank you" they were off. Then he was alone. They'd gone even before he'd dared ask when he might see her again. He watched her until she had disappeared in the distance, then turning on his heel, he walked slowly back to the vicarage. He felt sad and empty.

Chapter 8

With the Easterly wind on her port quarter and a foul tide the Mary Anne was wallowing in a following sea. The sun had risen almost an hour ago, but its winter rays were too feeble to warm the watch on deck. They muttered and stamped their frozen feet as they tried to fend off the cold. It was cold below decks too. Nathaniel pulled the blanket over his head. He'd not slept well. The motion of his hammock as it swung from side to side had not induced sleep, nor had all the strange creaking and groaning noises he could hear. The irregular but repeated heavy thud on the deck above worried him. Had the ship been damaged? Was she breaking up? He told himself not to be so silly; surely he'd be called on deck if the ship was in danger. He tried to turn over, but turning over in a hammock without falling out wasn't easy. Oh! What a night it had been! He'd hardly slept a wink. Then without warning his hammock had been roughly shaken. "Show a leg Mister. Time to turn out." Turn out? He'd almost fallen out; his hammock had been rocked so violently.

As he stood there rubbing the tiredness out of his eyes he tried to remember how to lash the thing up. The Third Mate had shown him how to do it yesterday, but that was a long time ago. "Take seven turns and finish off with a clove hitch," that's what he'd said. He counted his seven turns and pulled them tight but the clove hitch defeated him. He tied some sort of knot at the end and stood back to look at his work. "It should look like a sausage as fat at the ends as it is in the middle," he heard the Third Mate's voice again. It certainly didn't look like that, it was more pear shaped! He wondered whether he should try again, but fearing he'd be late on watch he stowed it away hurriedly, yawning and rubbing his eyes as he did so.

He should have gone to bed earlier last night, but he'd helped pull the anchor up, and watched the sails being set. As they filled with wind the masts and rigging had groaned and creaked as they took the strain. At first the ship hardly moved, but then he'd heard the water rippling along the hull and the Pilot saying "Must be doing a good five knots over the ground." Those words 'over the ground' had puzzled him. Weren't they at sea? But then so many of the words were strange. The Captain had been quite right, most of them were double-dutch. Of course he knew what port and starboard was, but then there was that man up for'ard who'd kept shouting "By the mark something" or "By the deep something else." Whatever it meant it had seemed to please the Captain who kept saying "Thank you." It even gladdened the Pilot, a cheerless sort of man who seemed to find life worrisome! He'd heard many other strange words; mostly he guessed the names of sails; words like spanker, main, t'gallant and jib, and others that he'd forgotten already. He'd begun to get the hang of some of them, but the ropes the men were told to haul on well, their names had baffled him completely!

Watching the shadowy land slipping by in the moonlight and disappearing astern had enthralled him and there'd been that tiny patch of brightness ahead which had slowly grown into the lighthouse they'd been searching for. And as it came closer the dim outline of the island could be seen. It had been quite impossible to go below and he'd stayed on deck far too long. Only when they'd dropped the Pilot at five o'clock in the morning had he been able to tear himself away and sling his hammock. Then the ship had been rolling gently, but now she was pitching as well, making it difficult to stand. So difficult that he had to sit on the deck to munch the biscuit he'd saved, before he climbed the ladder onto the quarterdeck.

The coldness hit him and found its way between the layers of his clothes. He shivered and looked around but could see nothing but the cold grey sea; nothing but the sea with the gulls skimming over the wave tops as they broke and the wind snatching the spray and hurling it back. There was no sign of land, or any other ship. He watched as the great rollers built up astern and came chasing after the Mary Anne, lifting her stern high in the air and plunging her bows deep into the trough throwing up great torrents of white water. And just when he thought the bows must surely disappear under the wild waves forever, the Mary Anne lifted herself up and shook herself free. Then she rolled and sent him skidding to the bulwark. Feeling foolish and hoping the Captain hadn't been watching he picked himself up. The Captain was still there; standing close to the helmsman, as he had been when he'd gone below. Nathaniel gave him a respectful "Good morning, sir." "Morning, boy," came a terse answer. He felt the Captain had hardly noticed him.

Next to the Captain was the Chief Mate, Mr Braithwaite. "Ah! There you are Mr Lugger." Mr Braithwaite watched the boy rub his eyes and yawn. "All wide-awake for your first watch, I hope?"

"Yes, Mr Braithwaite." Nathaniel shivered. Wide-awake? He could hardly keep his eyes open and longed to be back in that warm hammock of his.

"Well Mr Lugger." The Chief Mate's voice was brisk and lively. "We're on our way now. That's the coast of Wales over there." He pointed to a faint smudge on the horizon. "The coast of Devon's over there." He pointed up sun. "There below the horizon. Make the most of it Mr Lugger; we won't be seeing land again for a while."

"Thank you, sir." Though he felt lonely and far from home, Nathaniel did his best to grin as he studied the faint grey shape on the horizon. Everything was so strange and new and the crew scared him. They looked so rough, so coarse with their beards and pigtails, their tattoos and those rings in their ears. Would he ever find a friend here? How he missed the warmth and safety of the Rectory. He pulled himself together. "When will we see land again, sir?" he asked, but Mr Braithwaite didn't reply. He was talking to the Captain.

"I think we'd be better without the spanker, Cap'n. It's not comfortable with the sea behind us."

He saw the Captain nod. "Aye Fred, brail it up" and heard the Chief Mate shout "Wheel a'port". He felt the ship lean over as she turned and saw the big sail spill the wind and start to shake and rattle like a mad thing. "Steady as you go", the Chief Mate yelled; then "Brail her up, lads." Nathaniel wondered whether he should run and help them, but felt it best to stay and watch. The Chief Mate seemed satisfied. "Wheel a'starboard," he ordered and Nathaniel saw the bows begin to swing back. It all seemed so easily done! The Chief Mate was clearly an expert; he must have spent a lifetime at sea! What would he think of a numskull like him? He remembered how the Bo's'un had cursed and belaboured the crew when they were doing their sail drill in harbour. He hoped Mr Braithwaite would be more patient.

The Captain and the Chief Mate both seemed pleased to see the land disappearing. "Should be safe in deep water this time tomorrow," the Captain said. With nothing to do but wait, Nathaniel studied the man who would teach him his duties. The Chief Mate was a great deal older than him, but then everyone was. He could be thirty or forty or even fifty, Nathaniel wasn't good at guessing ages, but however old Mr Braithwaite was, he was definitely younger than the Captain. The Chief Mate was the taller of the two, but a lot fatter. A battered tricorn sat above a round face framed with great sideburns that reached down to a large mouth, still blessed with teeth. The crow's feet about his eyes suggested he enjoyed a good laugh, Nathaniel found that encouraging. He couldn't be certain, but he felt he might get to like Mr Braithwaite.

At last the Captain seemed satisfied and with an "I'll be off then Fred. Keep the soundings going," he went below. Then the two of them were on their own and Fred Braithwaite winked. "That's better. It's more comfortable when the old man's in his cabin. They're all the same at the start, y'know; breathing down your neck the whole time. They just don't feel confident with a new crew. It's understandable I suppose, what do you think Mr Lugger?"

Nathaniel didn't know what to say, but he blurted out, "Yes, I should think so." He saw those crow's feet deepen as Mr. Braithwaite's eyes twinkled. "Sorry, Mr Lugger," he grinned. "I shouldn't be asking you damn stupid questions like that." He lifted his tricorn and scratched his balding pate. "Now then, Mr Lugger let's get down to your duties. Oh! I can't bloody well keep calling you Mr Lugger! Nathaniel's your name, isn't it?"

"Yes, sir." Nathaniel nodded.

"Do you have any other name?"

"No sir, just Nathaniel."

"Oh! Dear, it's a bit of a mouthful, isn't it?" The Chief Mate shook his head ruefully. "Can't say it's any better than Mr Lugger. Well, what's short for Nathaniel?" While Nathaniel waited silently, the Chief Mate thought for a moment. "Can't call you Nat. Might confuse you with one of those bloody midges and take a swipe at you." He paused for Nathaniel to laugh, but there was no reaction. "Tell you what, I'll call you Neil. Yes, what about Neil", he savoured the name. "Neil, that all right?"

Nathaniel felt he shouldn't argue with the Chief Mate, but it was a very strange name. But then it was better than Nat, anything would be better than that! He shrugged his shoulders and tried to look unconcerned. "Yes sir, that'll be all right."

Fred glanced at the boy; the expression on his face confirmed his suspicions. No, he knew he couldn't call him Neil. "I don't know laddie," he said. "I dare say your mother knew what she was doing, so it'll have to be Nathaniel, I suppose. Y'know my dear old mother called me Percival." He chuckled. "I ask you, what a name! But at least she had the good sense to call me Fred as well. Percival Fredrick Braithwaite, that's me!"

He saw Nathaniel grin for the first time. It was good to see him lose that worried look.

"Right then, laddie, let's get on with your duties. The most important thing is to keep your eyes skinned and report anything you see. We have to keep a good lookout all round, not just ahead. If you see something don't be afraid to sing out nice and loud so I can hear you. With your young eyes you'll see things long before I do or even the Cap'n." He saw Nathaniel nod. "Then of course I shall expect you to turn the watch glass when it's finished running. It takes half an hour for the sand to run from top to bottom, so as we're on watch for four hours, you'll have to do it eight times." He grinned. "By the time we go off watch you'll be pretty experienced at that, if nothing else!"

Nathaniel thought he should be polite and managed a laugh.

As the watch wore on Nathaniel tried hard to keep a good lookout while at the same time keeping half an eye on the watch glass, frightened he'd miss the last trickle of sand. Mr Braithwaite seemed to talk continuously, telling him he'd have to learn all the points of the compass and how to log the helmsman's course on the traverse board whenever it changed. How the log was streamed and how it was used to measure the ship's speed. Then he'd told him he'd have to learn to steer the ship. That had appealed greatly and as he turned the watch glass over for the seventh time he began to feel that life wasn't as bad as it had seemed when he came on watch. He felt even more certain when Mr Braithwaite said, "Well done laddie". Then he'd winked. "Keep that journal of yours going laddie, masters are always impressed by good journals, y'know. Come to think of it, why don't you copy the compass card and write in all the points of the compass. Eh?"

"Oh! Yes, sir. That's a good idea." Nathaniel felt much happier. He'd known he'd like Mr Braithwaite!

Chapter 9

"Lugger, your hammock's a bloody mess." The Third Mate's voice sounded hard and ominous. "Get it re-slung and I'll see you lash it up properly."

"Yes, Mr White."

Mr White looked at him coldly. "Lugger you should say Aye, Aye to acknowledge an order. We don't say yes!"

"Yes, I mean Aye, Aye, Mr White." He'd hardly come off watch and the Third Mate was after him already. He moved quickly to do his bidding. He wasn't sure how he'd get on with Peter White; he seemed a finicky officious fellow. He found his hammock and slung it.

"What's this, laddie? Turning in already?" The Chief Mate had a puzzled look on his face.

"Oh! no, sir. Mr White wants to show me how to lash my hammock up properly."

Mr Braithwaite nodded. "Well laddie, when you've finished, come and see me."

Finally the hammock had been lashed and stowed to the Third Mate's satisfaction, and Nathaniel, pleased to have an excuse to leave, ran to find the Chief Mate. He found him in deep conversation with one of the hands. Nathaniel waited respectfully.

"Ah! There you are, Mr Lugger. Meet Bert Tyacke. He's to be your Sea Daddy."

More double-dutch, Nathaniel thought. What was this man going to be? A Sea Daddy? He stretched out his hand. For a moment Bert Tyacke looked nonplussed, then with a smile he took it and they were shaking hands. "Hello, Mr Tyacke," Nathaniel said. "I'm not sure what a Sea Daddy does, but I'm very pleased to meet you." This man Tyacke seemed a friendly fellow!

"Hello, young sir." A grin spread over Bert Tyacke's face. "I'm not sure as I do either, but I think I've got to show 'ee the ropes if 'ee knows what I mean."

"Oh! well, that'll be fine", Nathaniel tried not to show his ignorance.

"Well laddie," the Chief Mate interrupted. "Usually one of the senior apprentices takes a new apprentice under his wing but as we ain't got any we're giving the job to one of the hands. Tyacke's an experienced seaman and he'll explain all the strange language we use and also teach you your seamanship."

"Well sir, I'll do the best I can, can't say better'n that." Bert stroked his beard. "Never 'ad a job like this before." He looked at Nathaniel. "Still, don't s'pose you 'ave either, eh young sir?" He saw Nathaniel shake his head and smile. "Then young sir, all we can do is try."

"That sounds like a good idea, Mr Tyacke."

"'Ere young sir, can't 'ave 'ee callin' me Mr Tyacke. I ain't no mate, y'know. Me name's Bert."

"Right Bert, so what do you want to teach me first?"

"Well young sir, 'ow's yer bends and 'itches?"

Nathaniel looked puzzled. "D'you mean clove hitches? The knot you lash your hammock with?"

Bert grinned. "Well, that's one of 'em. Can you do that one?"

Nathaniel shook his head. "Not very well I'm afraid."

Somehow Bert made the clove hitch seem simple and then he started on reef knots and bowlines. The list of bends and hitches seemed endless. There was so much to learn, but as Bert rightly said "There's time enough young sir," and soon Nathaniel was in a routine. He'd stand watch on the quarterdeck with Mr Braithwaite and then during the day when he wasn't on watch, Bert would teach him his seamanship. It seemed no time before he knew his bends and hitches and could make a bowline blindfolded and soon he had the names of the sails at his fingertips. Even the rigging and the ropes used to work the sails no longer baffled him. With Bert's help he'd drawn a picture of the compass rose in his log and had named all the points. Mr Braithwaite had been quite right. It seemed the Captain had been impressed. He'd written "good" alongside the drawing. Then with Bert's approving eye he'd filled his journal with pictures of sails and rigging and had begun working on a drawing of the ship itself. But Bert had laughed at that. He'd said "Dun look right to me, young sir, maybe you'd better wait till you'm away in a boat. Then 'ee'll get it right."

Then the time he'd been dreading came. "Come on, young sir," Bert had said. "'Tes time for 'ee to climb the mast and then when 'ee's at the top us'll go out on the yard. Ain't nothin' to it." The thought of being up there with the ship rolling and the deck so far below scared him. But he knew he'd have to do it, he couldn't let Bert down. He'd been so patient and kind and always seemed to have a joke on his lips. So he'd climbed the ratlines with his heart in his mouth, not daring to look down. When at last he'd got to the maintop, he'd wanted to stay there, but Bert was close behind and he knew he'd have to go on. "Wait till she's steady, young sir", Bert was saying. So when the ship seemed to be on an even keel, he took a deep breath, leant over the yard and stepped gingerly onto the rope that Bert called the foot rope. Then he'd begun to inch himself out to the end of the yard. It had been slow going and he'd been quite sure that when he finally got to the end of the yard he'd be too terrified to come back. Yet it hadn't been like that at all. When he'd got there, he'd hung on to the yard and for the first time he'd really felt the wind on his face. "I've done it, I've done it," he wanted to shout. It hadn't been as frightening as he'd thought. Suddenly his fear had evaporated and he was joking with Bert and enjoying every minute. Climbing the mast had been a hurdle that had scared him, but now he'd done it he could say he was no longer a landlubber; at last he felt, he'd begun to get to grips with his trade.

Soon he was trying to match Bert as he scrambled up the ratlines and out onto the yards, but Bert was like a monkey and Nathaniel knew that try as he might, he'd never be as good as him. When he voiced his doubts, Bert just laughed. "Be patient, young sir. When you'm 'alf as old as I, it'll all come natural. Just 'ee wait and see."

"Well I hope you're right Bert. But," he looked thoughtful. "If I'm not half as old as you already, it won't be long before I am, so I've not much time to learn all you know."

"Oh! I keep on tellin' 'ee there's plenty of time young sir."

"I'm not so sure Bert. Tell me how old are you?" He surprised himself with the directness of his question and Bert's puzzled look made Nathaniel wish he'd never asked.

"Fact is, young sir, I dun rightly know. But me old Mum said I were born the same year as Mr Whitefield came and preached the Gospel in Dartmouth 'aven. She always spoke to us children about 'im 'ow 'e told 'em to save their souls and repent or God's wrath would be poured on 'em as sure as fire and brimstone rained down on Sodom and Gomorrah."

He paused as if savouring the memory of his childhood then continued. "Tell me young sir, do 'ee knows where Sodom and Gomorrah be?"

Nathaniel laughed. "I think they were in the desert in the Holy Land. But, Bert, d'you know when the preacher said all that?"

"Why young sir, 'twas in 1742, leastways that's what my old Mum always said."

Well, Bert, it's 1771 now so that'd make you twenty-nine and I'm fourteen. So," Nathaniel said with triumph in his voice. "When I'm fifteen next June, you'll be thirty, and then I'll be half your age!"

Bert looked surprised and then with a guffaw said, "What, next year! Lor' 'elp us. But then young sir, with all your knowledge of arithmetic and all that learnin', well you'll catch up with me in no time, no time at all. 'Spect I'll be a'learnin' from 'ee by the time we'm back in old England."

But England was an age away as the Mary Anne sailed evermore southwards. The days began to grow warm and the evenings balmy and one night when Nathaniel came on deck at four o'clock in the morning, he was almost dazzled by the clarity of the sky with its canopy of stars and an enormous full moon. The ship seemed to be sailing herself and the gentle sound of the bows cutting through the calm sea was quite soporific. For a while he and Fred didn't talk, they were both lost in the beauty of the night. Then to his surprise, Nathaniel heard himself asking the question that had gone round and round in his mind almost since the day they'd left England.

"D'you think it right that we should have slaves?" Fred was still admiring the splendour of the heavens. "What did you say, laddie?"

It was a stupid question to ask on board a slaver and he wished he hadn't asked it. But not knowing how much Fred had heard, Nathaniel thought he'd better repeat it. "Well, sir", he spoke more timidly. What I said was, do you think it right that we should have slaves?" He hesitated, then went on. "I mean, I wouldn't like to be a slave, would you?"

Fred had no desire to discuss the rights and wrongs of slavery; it was a question no one even liked to acknowledge on board a slave ship. He remembered when he was home after his last voyage, he'd got involved in a discussion about slavery with some Quakers. Well it was really more like a bloody argument. They thought it should be abolished of course, but then they didn't seem to live in the real world. Perhaps he should tell the lad not to ask such stupid questions, but he knew he couldn't do that. He realised he'd grown fond of him. His way of asking direct questions appealed to him and his youthful innocence was refreshing after the coarse, hardened cynicism of the crew. What was it he'd said to those damn Quakers?

"Well laddie", he shrugged his shoulders. "I don't know, but one thing I do know is that slavery has been with us since the dawn of time and whether we like it or not we'll always have slavery." He paused, it seemed a good start. Gaining confidence he went on, "The Medes and Persians, you know, the ones we read about in the Bible. They had slaves and so did the Greeks and the Romans. They owned men and women and children same as they owned animals and they bought them and sold them in the same way. Even then, most of the slaves came from Africa, though in those days they were shipped from the North African ports in the Med. But they weren't all black, even the Greeks and Romans could become slaves. If you couldn't pay your debts, you could be given as a slave to settle what you owed."

Nathaniel broke in. "We don't do that now do we?"

"No, laddie, not in England anyway, but you'd probably be flung into prison till your debts are paid, so it ain't much different is it? In Greek and Roman times the slaves were used as labourers and servants and as soldiers and they manned the oars in the galleys. Some became Gladiators. Have you heard about them?"

Nathaniel shook his head. "Well they were slaves trained for combat, not as legionnaires, but to fight each other to amuse the crowds. The Romans built huge amphitheatres for spectators to see the sport, to watch the gladiators fight each other, to fight to the death."

"To kill each other?"

"Yes, laddie, to kill each other. Y'see they knew if they didn't fight they'd be killed by the Romans. The Gladiators knew the only way to stay alive was to kill their opponent!"

Nathaniel seemed shocked. "Oh!" he muttered.

"Aye, it was kill or be killed. The Romans armed them with a sword and a dagger and forced them into the arena. As they entered there'd be an expectant hush from the crowd but at the first sight of blood, they'd start baying and roaring like wild animals and screaming for them to fight harder. You see, the crowds wanted plenty of blood and gore. Then when badly wounded and near death, the gladiator at the mercy of the other would raise an arm to ask the crowd for mercy. If he'd fought well and the crowd was in a generous mood, they'd wave their scarves and he'd be saved from death and dragged off to fight another day. But if the crowd thought he'd not fought well enough, well, then they'd jeer and mock him and turn their thumbs down. That was the end, that was signal for the victor to finish him off'!"

"Oh! That's awful. Do we still make slaves kill each other?"

"No, not now. No, they're mostly used for work in the fields and the mills and as servants. And nowadays they're all Negroes. They're as black as coal and have dark curly woolly hair and broad flat noses and thick lips. Some say the niggers are a sort of sub-species of the human race, but whatever they are they're a bloody idle lot without much intelligence. When they behave I think we treat them well enough, but often they're so damned stupid they can't or perhaps won't understand what you want them to do. That's when the cat has to come out. They soon get the message then! 'Course I'd forgotten, you haven't seen any of 'em yet, have you?"

Fred was quite right, Nathaniel had never seen a Negro in his life and he wondered just what they were like. At first he thought they might look more like monkeys than men but that couldn't be right. Fred hadn't mentioned monkeys; he'd just said they were black with woolly hair and broad noses. Try as he might he couldn't really visualise a Negro, he'd have to wait till he saw one. Then he had another question. "Sir, I know we're going to the Slave Coast to load up with slaves, but how do we actually get them?"

"How do we get them?" Fred repeated this strange question. "Well, laddie, when we get to the coast you'll see. As soon as we've dropped the anchor we'll have boats coming out to the ship wanting to sell us slaves. And they'll want us to buy their gold and ivory as well. That's why we've got so much cargo on board, so that we can barter for them."

"Yes sir, I understand that but these people who are selling us the slaves, where do they get them from? I mean, do they go out into the country and catch them?"

"No, no. I suppose you could say it's like a cattle market. We go to the market to buy our slaves and the African slave traders bring them in to exchange for our goods. It's like farmers bringing their cattle to market."

"Yes sir, but farmers breed the cattle they sell. Surely the slave traders don't grow slaves!"

"That might be a good idea." Fred chortled at the thought. "No, no the Negro tribes are always at each other's throats. They're either trying to spread Islam, or like the Ashantis trying to take their neighbours' land. So they're always at war and those they don't kill they take prisoner. They don't believe in feeding their captives for nothing, so if there's no work for them to do they march them off to the coast to sell them as slaves." He paused as a memory surfaced. "I remember once seeing a column of slaves being marched to the coast. I'd been up river in the boat searching for wood to cut and I saw some blacks approaching. They didn't see us and we kept quiet and hid in the bush. There were about ten of them armed with spears and muskets and they were guarding a column of about thirty slaves. Most were men, but there were a few women and three or four were children. The women were all carrying loads on their heads and the men well their arms were lashed and they were held together in pairs by a cobble."

"A cobble? What's that?" Nathaniel interrupted.

"Well, the slave drivers use a branch of a tree with a fork in it, like a letter Y and they put the neck of one slave into the fork and close it with a leather lashing. They do the same with another slave and then they lash the stems of the two branches together so that the slaves are about six feet apart, but held together by their necks. You see that way they can walk in single file, but it's difficult for them to run off and escape."

Nathaniel shuddered. "Surely those cobbles must rub their necks raw."

"Yes laddie, they probably do." For a moment he was silent. Then he spoke again, this time almost in a whisper. "Then I saw something I'll never forget; something absolutely barbarous. Something that still makes me want to retch."

"What was it?"

Fred sighed. "There was a female slave carrying a heavy load on her head with a young child screaming at her heels. As she bent over to lift the kid up, she dropped the load. She tried to pick it up but with the child in one arm it was impossible. "She struggled with the child and the load and began to drop behind. She was wailing and crying, but no one came to help. Then the guards ran back and there was a lot of shouting and screaming. And then it happened." Fred shook his head. "I just couldn't believe what I was seeing."

"What did you see?" Nathaniel's voice was full of anxiety.

"I saw one of those black bastards pick the screaming child up by its feet, and swing it headfirst onto a rock. It was terrible, savage; utterly barbaric. Never in all my life have I seen anything like that before. I tell you as I watched that black fiend standing there with this battered, bleeding child hanging from his hand, I began to retch, I tell you I was almost sick. Then with a stream of curses he threw the little bleeding body into the scrub. By this time the mother was hysterical and tried to go after her child, but the guards beat her back to the column and they left that little child to the vultures already circling overhead."

A hush descended on the pair of them. This terrible act of cruelty had driven all other thoughts from their mind. But soon the first pink tinges of the rising sun stole over the eastern horizon and as the stars faded and the sky began to lighten, they heard the footsteps of the Captain. Their respectful "Morning Cap'n" was cut off in midstream by an angry cry.

"What the bloody hell's that?" Jim felt the anger explode within him. There was an Arab dhow, not more than a cable or two away with its sail full and the water rippling down its side as its sharp bows cut through the placid sea. It was right astern and overhauling them fast.

"Get all hands on deck to repel boarders," he shouted. As Nathaniel fled to call the crew, he saw the Captain his face red with rage, berating the Chief Mate.

"Mr bloody Braithwaite, what's going on? Why the hell didn't you call me? I suppose you've seen this blasted dhow? I told you and all the others the moors would sneak up and try to catch us unawares."

The sight of the dhow overhauling them so close astern had shaken Fred. He should have seen it as the sky lightened. He cursed himself. He'd spent too much time talking to Nathaniel. "Sorry Cap'n, I should have seen it."

"Humph," was all the reply he got from Jim, now busy examining the dhow through his telescope.

Meanwhile Nathaniel had shaken Mr Hoskins, the Gunner. He was on his feet in a trice and shouting "Wake up, lads, we've got pirates close at hand. Grab a musket and a cutlass each one of you and get to your stations." He grabbed his own and muttered "Thank Gawd, we've practised our drill!"

Men were now appearing on deck, Bert Tyacke and two others were racing up the ratlines to the main top with their muskets ready to fire on anyone who tried to climb aboard. More were lining up on the Fo'c'sle and the Quarterdeck and others were loading the swivel guns.

Jim watched the dhow carefully. It was approaching fast. "Keep your distance," he shouted in a voice that sounded like thunder. "If you come any closer I'll shoot."

The dhow was now close under the starboard quarter, a mere hundred yards off. Nathaniel could see a swarthy bearded face below a red turban on the foredeck. The figure raised his arms and shouted, "Water Cap'n, we need water please and thank you. We no bad, we good. Need water plenty bad."

Jim was scanning the dhow intently. He couldn't see much except the huge lateen sail. Then in the stern he thought he saw some bent iron. "Aye," he muttered, "they're pirates all right; they've got their grappling hooks ready." Then turning towards Fred he exclaimed, "They don't want water they want us! Steer three points to port Mr Braithwaite. We'll try and keep the bastards down wind." He was looking more confident now. "Mr Hoskins," he shouted. "Stand-by to fire a swivel across his bows. The rest of you hold your fire till I tell you."

Once again he went to the rail and cupping his hands he bellowed. "Get away, you're too damned close. If you don't move away you'll get a taste of this." He turned his head and looking at the Gunner, shouted, "Right Mr Hoskins give him a shot across the bows."

There was a sharp crack from the swivel gun and an acrid smell of smoke drifted over Nathaniel and he saw a plume of water rise from the sea about twenty yards ahead of the moors. It had the desired effect and the dhow began to move away. Again Red turban appeared. "Cap'n", he cried. "We need water bad. You give us water please."

"Bloody cock and bull story." Jim shouted in return as Fred, still subdued by the vehement rebuke he'd received, coughed respectfully. "Cap'n, he says they need water badly. Maybe they do. Could they be telling the truth?"

"What these bloody Arabs? No, not likely. You can never trust them. They all tell a pack of bloody lies. They're just looking for an excuse to come alongside. Then they'll scramble aboard and we'll have a real fight on our hands."

"You're probably right Cap'n, but just suppose they really do need water. Don't you think we could pass them a line and let them haul a cask over?"

"Humph," Jim exclaimed. He was not at all convinced. "I don't like it, they'd be too damned close." Yet how could he get rid of them? He knew they wouldn't give up easily and they were already drawing closer again. If he wasn't on guard they'd crash alongside and then they'd swarm aboard. Maybe he should open fire with his canon and drive them off or even maybe sink them? Or could Fred be right? If they really were desperate for water, he should help them. Perhaps he should call their bluff and give them a cask. Then they'd have to go and if they didn't he could open fire on them with a clear conscience.

He sent for the Bo's'n and turned to the Chief Mate. "Right Fred, we'll give them a cask of water." Fred nodded, he'd had another idea. "Cap'n", he said quietly. "D'you think we could hang a cask over the stern, from the spanker boom? We could extend it with another spar maybe, so the cask would hang well clear. Then they can come up under our stern and take it. They'd never be able to board us from there and in any case we could have all our muskets waiting for them."

Jim nodded. It was a good plan. "Bo's'n", his voice was calm and assured. "I want to give those buggers a cask of water, then if they bother us any more I'll turn the cannon on them." As he spoke Jim saw the dhow had edged a little closer. "Mr Hoskins," he shouted. "Give them another shot across the bows if they come any closer." He turned once more to the Bo's'n. "You've heard Mr Braithwaite's idea. I like it. It'd keep them astern, where they can't board us. Can you find a spar to lengthen the spanker boom?" The Bo's'n scratched his head as he thought. "Aye Cap'n we can do that, I'll sort something out." As the Bo's'n set off, the Gunner fired the swivel again. This time the plume of water was only a few yards ahead of the dhow. Red turban reappeared waving his arms angrily. "Why you fire gun Cap'n? We not pirates. Need water bad."

"Well, keep your bloody distance then," Jim shouted. "We'll give you a cask of water. We'll hang it from the stern and you can come up and cut it free."

"Me no understand, Cap'n," came the reply.

Jim could feel his hackles rising. He'd had enough of Red turban. Once more he cupped his hands and roared, "Oh! Yes you bloody do. Water cask hang from boom aft." Then he told the Bo's'n. "Show him the cask and tell a hand to walk it aft to the spanker boom." And pointing aft, he shouted once more to the dhow, "Water cask hang down over stern."

Red turban lifted an arm. Had he understood? To his delight Jim saw the dhow ease sail and start to drop astern.

"Mr Hoskins." Jim called him over from the swivel gun. "Send half a dozen men with muskets onto the quarterdeck in case those buggers try to board us. And get the rest to run out the cannons on the port side. He might try to be clever and come up to windward. If that's his idea, I'll sink the bastard."

Jim watched the Bo's'n and three hands brail up the spanker and lash a spar to the boom. Then when the cask had been hauled out and lowered to within a few feet of the water, he cupped his hands and yelled, "Water for you."

Though there was no reply, Jim could see the dhow creeping slowly nearer until she was barely ten feet away and he could hear the moors talking in their strange incomprehensible tongue. And just as he thought she would surely hit the stern, a swarthy Arab grabbed the cask and with a great stroke of his sabre cut it free. Then with consummate skill the helmsman put the tiller hard over and the dhow, showing all its grace and beauty turned sharply to port and sailed clear.

"Now go or I'll turn my cannon on you," Jim shouted with relief. He watched her recede for a time, then he turned to the Chief Mate. "Mr Braithwaite keep a good watch on her and stand the men down. They can relax, but they're to stay at their stations till I'm satisfied we've lost those buggers."

Whether the moors were genuinely in need of water or the pirates he'd believed them to be, he would never know, but as the distance between them grew he knew he'd done the right thing.

Chapter 10

It had been an uneventful week and the encounter with the Moors had begun to recede from Jim's mind. But his confidence in Fred Braithwaite had been shaken. Fred had told him he'd made four slaving voyages and his knowledge and experience of the trade had seemed impressive. He'd thought he would be an invaluable Chief Mate, one who should have known how dangerous it could be off the Moorish coast. Missing a dhow like that had been unforgivable. It could have cost them their lives. He'd vented his anger on him; he'd said the young Third couldn't have done worse! Fred had accepted his reprimand without argument and had apologised, but now Jim was beginning to think he'd over-reacted! It was twilight at the time, the sun had yet to show itself over the horizon and it would have been difficult to see the dhow much sooner. Yet it had seen them! Nevertheless he told himself he'd have to be extra careful when Fred was on watch. Fred seemed to realize this and Jim was aware that their relationship of mutual trust and respect, which had developed so well, had been threatened. Of course it was Fred who'd suggested how they should pass that cask of water to the dhow. He'd shown ingenuity and resourcefulness, qualities that Jim knew he'd need again. Maybe he had reacted too quickly and without considering all the facts. And apart from that one incident Fred had shown himself to be a good Chief Mate, who worked the hands with a firm easy manner.

He sighed. Things could be worse and young Nathaniel was coming along very well. There was no doubt about it; he had his mother's eyes. Jim smiled as he recalled her; she was an uncommonly handsome woman! He'd only met her twice and both meetings had been brief and the last one stormy! Yet, she'd made a lasting impression on him; he'd never forget her elegance, her confidence, her integrity, her cultured manner and that damned concern of hers for the slaves. He shook his head. He didn't know much about women and had never wanted to, but Elizabeth seemed to have mesmerised him from the start. He turned once more to the boy's journal with his drawing of the rig and read again his own additions and remarks. Then he began to read the boy's description of the incident with the dhow. He was impressed by its accuracy and the lucid way the narrative flowed. His account made life at sea exciting again and somehow full of adventure! He laughed. He couldn't recapture his own youthful enthusiasm, but he could enjoy sharing the boy's! He heard seven bells. It would be midday in half an hour and he wanted to show the boy how to find the noon latitude.

"Ah! There you are, boy. I think it's time you learnt how to find the ship's noon position. D'you know what latitude is?"

"Y'yes sir, it tells us how far we are from the equator," Nathaniel hesitated, "I think."

"That's not a bad answer. Not bad at all. Well, we call the equator nought degrees latitude and the North Pole ninety degrees north." Jim saw the boy nod. "So if we're on the equator d'you know where the sun would be at midday?"

That's easy, thought Nathaniel. "Right overhead, sir."

"Right." Jim was impressed. He began to wonder what the Chief Mate had been telling the boy. "Now if we were at the North Pole, we would only see the sun for a few seconds and then it would be right on the horizon, agree?" The boy nodded. "So then if we were at latitude forty five degrees north, where would we find the midday sun?"

Well it could be behind the clouds, thought Nathaniel, but perhaps it would be better not to joke! He might with the Chief Mate, but no, not with the Captain! "I suppose sir it'd be midway between the horizon and right overhead."

"You're getting there, boy! So how many degrees above the horizon then?"

"Well it would be halfway between nought and ninety, that's forty-five."

"Good. So if we measure the sun's altitude at noon, we should be able to work out our latitude. But as clocks won't work at sea, how are we going to know when it's midday?"

Nathaniel looked puzzled. "Well, boy, we find the highest altitude we can and then we know that must be midday."

"But sir, how do we measure the sun's altitude?" Nathaniel remembered at home the shadow of the church tower used to reach right across the road in the early morning but then as the morning passed it shrank back into the church yard and then in the evening it began to grow again but this time towards the fields. "At home we tell how high the sun is by the length of its shadow."

"Aye boy, that's the way the landlubbers do it. They measure the length of the shadow, but we can't measure the length of the mast's shadow at sea can we?"

Nathaniel thought for a moment. "No sir. So how do we find the sun's altitude?"

"Well, boy, we use this." He held up the back staff.

Nathaniel had seen this strange thing before and had wondered what it was. It was a long staff of nicely polished wood, with figures carved along its length. There was also a wooden arm which could be slid along the staff. He watched as the Captain kept sliding it backwards and forwards.

"Now then, boy", the Captain continued. "You must never look directly into the sun. If you do it'll burn your eyes and you'll never see properly again. So the first rule is that you must always stand with your back to the sun, like me." He made Nathaniel follow suit and gave him the back staff. "Now boy, look along the staff and point it at the sea horizon until you can observe the horizon through this little slit. Now you've got the staff level, that's at nought degrees elevation." He took the staff back. "As you use it to find the horizon, this long arm has been named the Horizon Staff." He saw the boy nod and slid the little wooden arm backwards and forward again. "This little arm," he said, "it's called the Arc and when you've got it in the right place whilst looking at the horizon, it will cast its shadow along the Horizon Staff., do you follow me boy?" Nathaniel wasn't sure he did, but he nodded "Yes, I think so, sir."

"Well, boy there's just one more bit on the horizon staff I must show you." He pointed to a little mirror at the end of the staff. "This is the Horizon Vane, and when you've got the shadow of the arc showing in it, then my boy, you've measured the sun's altitude and you can read it from the figure on the staff where the arc has come to rest. See, it's sixty two degrees. It takes a bit of practice, but you'll get the hang of it."

The Captain kept making him use the staff. At first it didn't seem to work for him, but then he began to find the horizon and the shadow, but he was delighted when the Captain said "It's getting close to midday" and took the wretched thing. Nathaniel watched as he took the sun's altitude again and again, muttering to himself as he read the marks. At last he seemed satisfied. "Well that's the highest I can get today. Near enough sixty-nine degrees". He looked at Nathaniel questioningly. "But our latitude ain't sixty-nine degrees North is it boy?"

Now getting confused, Nathaniel thought it best to agree, "No, I don't think so, sir."

"Well, then." The Captain persisted. "What is our latitude?"

Nathaniel made no reply.

"What if we subtract the altitude from ninety? What do we get then, boy?"

"Sixty-nine from ninety, um that's twenty-one. Is that it?"

"Yes, that's it, but I need to make a few corrections. I'll explain those to you another day." And with that, he disappeared below.

Satisfied with his calculations, Jim was writing the noon position in the log when the Second Mate, Sid Jackson appeared. "We've just sighted land Cap'n, on the port bow. It's a long way off, but it looks like a hill or a low mountain. Could it be Cape Blanco?"

"Aye, could be". Reaching for his telescope, he went on deck. "Better get a sounding, Mr Jackson and bring her round to East by South. Let's see if it really is the cape."

For the last few days the Mary Anne had moved sedately before the following wind, but now with the wind almost on her beam, she began to race ahead and as she threw the breaking sea aside the changed motion infected all aboard with the expectation of land ahead. By four o'clock the leadsman was reporting six fathoms, with a white sandy bottom and the shore could clearly be seen. It was low-lying, covered with palm trees and fringed by dazzling white sands. All eyes scanned the shore expectantly, the Captain and the Chief Mate with their telescopes seemingly glued to their eyes. "Over there, look, Cap'n", the Chief Mate broke the silence. "On the port bow, that low lying island. Can you see it? It looks like Goree Island to me, and look there's the fort. That must be Goree!"

"Ah! Yes, I see it. Well, let's hope they've got some slaves. Been here before, haven't you Fred?"

"Aye. The locals, the French they ain't helpful. They don't like trading with us."

"Damned French," Jim muttered. "Well, we'll anchor off tonight and see what they're like tomorrow."

While the Captain and Chief Mate made their plans for the morning, Nathaniel studied the land, now pink by the rays of the setting sun. The wind that had brought them had now died away, replaced by a gentle breeze from shore, bringing with it the smell of burning wood from the fires twinkling in the growing darkness. All was still and lulled by the rhythm of the rollers breaking on the beach.

"Enjoying the view, Lugger?" He heard the voice of the Second Mate, Sid Jackson. "Ain't it peaceful? Better make the most of it; you're going to be busy tomorrow. Cap'n wants you to man the longboat when I take him ashore."

"Oh! Mr Jackson, that'll be great. Will we land on that island? The one with the funny name. Goree it's called isn't it? Is that an African name?"

"Lor no! They'd have called it something weird and unpronounceable! Blame the Dutch, they were here first. They called it Goed Reed. In their lingo I believe it means safe anchorage. When the Frenchies kicked them out the name stuck. Well, more or less! You'd expect the Frogs to muck it about wouldn't you?"

Nathaniel laughed. "Well let's hope it is a safe anchorage, I've got the middle watch!"

Early next morning as the hands were busy lowering the longboat there was Bert grinning at him. "Mornin', young sir. All ready for a trip round the 'arbour? Ain't no charge today, 'tes on the Cap'n!"

Nathaniel laughed. "Yes I'm in the crew. Are you as well?"

"Aye, young sir. Mr Braithwaite thinks I needs extra boat practice!"

Nathaniel grinned. "It's me that needs the practice. I've never been in a boat before, so I'm bound to make a mess of it."

"Well young sir, 'taint that difficult! Just 'ee watch that oar of mine and make sure 'e keeps in time."

"Mr Mackay". Nathaniel heard the Captain call the surgeon over. "Examine the slaves carefully. I don't want any sickly ones. Nor old or pregnant ones either! They've got to be fit enough to stand the passage and it'll be a long while before we make Montego Bay."

"Aye, Mr Youle." Nathaniel had noticed Mr Mackay always called the Captain, Mr Youle. He seemed a disrespectful fellow. "I'll weed 'em out, dinny fash yersel."

The longboat was now in the water and Nathaniel scrambled down with the others. Hardly had he found his feet, than Bert yelled "Look out, young sir." He looked up to see a large canvas bag being lowered into the boat. It contained a musket, an axe, some pots and pans and other things.

"Us'll 'ave to let 'em see what we've got afore they'll do business," Bert whispered as the Captain and Mr Mackay boarded the boat and sat down in the sternsheets. Then they were rowing. To Nathaniel the oar seemed massive, but he was greatly relieved to find it balanced easily and he could control it well enough. Though now and then it took charge of him as the blade dug down into the depths and Bert would mutter, "Watch it, young sir, you'm catchin' a crab." He'd been given the bow oar, so that he could watch the others and keep in time and just as he was beginning to feel more confident, he heard the Second Mate shout "Oars."

He remembered that meant stop rowing. He glanced out of the corner of his eye and saw they were close to a stone pier. He watched it draw near. Then as the Second called "Bows" Bert whispered "Come on young sir. Get the painter and be ready to jump ashore."

Hastily he shipped his oar and had hardly done so, when he heard Bert again. "Go on, young sir" and suddenly he was ashore and holding the boat steady.

With a curt "Wait alongside, we'll be some time," Jim leapt ashore where the Factor and his clerk were waiting for them.

"Bonjour mon Capitaine," the Factor removed his hat. "Welcome to Goree. We 'ave zee veri fine slaves for you."

"G'day Monsewer." Jim lifted his tricorn in return. "Very fine slaves eh? Well, I'll be the judge of that."

The Factor studied the contents of the bag. "I see you 'ave muskets, c'est bon, you 'ave zee powder and shot aussi?"

"Aye, we've powder and shot and plenty of it." Jim replied. "And the muskets, you'll find they're well made, like all my goods." The Factor shrugged and examined the goods carefully. Then a flicker of a smile crossed his face. "Et bien, we see some slaves, eh?" He led them up one of the two staircases which curved like a horseshoe to the mansion above. "You like zee maison, Monsieur? Is veri beautiful, yes? Is veri new! I call her La Maison des Eclaves, 'ow you say in England? 'ouse of Slaves"? He gave a hearty laugh. "'ouse of Slaves, eh?" The Second laughed too. "It's an apt name. Ain't it a grand building though? Those stairs, they're impressive ain't they?"

Nathaniel nodded, it was a fine building. "Look at those huge doors!"

"The slaves will come through those," the Second replied.

Nathaniel's heart sank; he hadn't seen a slave yet. Suddenly he hoped those doors would never open. They repelled him; he turned to look at the

Mary Anne. Though she was to be a floating prison for slaves, he had to admit she was a handsome ship. He studied her intently, remembering his plan to draw her in his journal. He noted her long bowsprit set at a rakish angle, her two for'ard masts with their yards and sails, now neatly furled and the mizzen mast with the spanker now brailed up. He tried to visualize her cutting through the waves with the wind in her sails; he was sure she must be one of the prettiest ships afloat! Voices interrupted his happy musing. The Captain and the Frenchman were approaching. He heard the Frenchman's nasal tones. "Et bien, Mon Capitaine, nous avons un accord oui, 'ow you say, we 'ave zee deal, yes?" The Captain nodded. "Wee, Monsewer. I'll send the goods and we'll start taking the slaves today."

Soon they were busy loading the goods to be bartered for the slaves. "Us'll have a dozen trips, mark my words, young sir," Bert muttered. "Cap'n's bought forty-seven, so Mr Jackson says." With the boat loaded with muskets, shot and powder, knives and axes, pots and pans, bolts of cloth and boxes of beads they made many trips and they too climbed those curving stairs delivering the goods to a wrinkled, mahogany faced Frenchman. Then when at last all had been checked and noted in his ledger, the great doors slowly swung open and the first slave appeared. Just the one, escorted by two white men armed with cudgels. The slave's arms were bound tightly behind his back and his legs were hobbled so that he could only move with painfully short steps. Naked, except for a loin cloth, he had a well-developed muscular frame with skin the colour of charcoal. But unlike charcoal it glistened in the sun, which lit up the beads of sweat like precious jewels. As the guards dragged him towards the boat, he struggled wildly, but with much cursing and swearing he was forced into the boat, where the crew tied him down. Nathaniel watched, he wanted nothing to do with this barbaric practice, but the Second shouted at him with invective in his voice, telling him, "it wasn't a damned sideshow and to pull his bloody weight." So he too was struggling with the others to grab and tie down the slaves as they arrived kicking and screaming. With four sullen black men in the boat, they pulled back to the ship, where each slave was hoisted onboard to be met by the Bo's'un and his men and lowered through the hatch to the slave deck below. There the Gunner and his party manhandled him into the slave room. It was slow back-breaking work and by sunset the longboat had made ten trips and the Chief Mate had called a halt. "It's no use trying to get them on board in the dark." He'd said. "We must be able to see what we're doing otherwise we'll probably lose a slave or worse."

Nathaniel was both exhausted and dispirited. The ship felt different now. It wasn't the same "Mary Anne" that had brought him so far. The atmosphere had changed. When they had anchored last night, it had been a happy ship, with the crew joking and skylarking. But now everyone seemed tense and edgy. He felt that way too. The truth had struck home. The truth he had never wanted to face when, despite his mother's protestations, he'd signed that indenture. The truth was that the "Mary Anne's" sole purpose was to ship captive human beings over the ocean to a life of slavery in the New World. He found it difficult to sleep that night.

The next day they took the boat ashore again to collect the remaining slaves. Three male slaves were delivered one by one and then two small boys followed. They seemed very frightened and one was crying pitifully. Their plight disturbed Nathaniel more than anything he had seen earlier, but there was little he could do to comfort them, so he busied himself in his rowing. As they neared the ship he heard the Second shouting, "Just four women to come now."

After the struggles they'd had with the men, Nathaniel wondered what to expect of the women. Would they struggle as fiercely? Would they spit like the men too? But the first seemed resigned to her fate. It was as if she'd experienced more than enough cruelty already. She wept and wailed pitifully, but did as she was told. Perhaps she co-operated because of the young child clinging to her and was fearful for its safety. The next one also had a child and was equally obedient. Both were embarked without difficulty and secured. Then the final two were brought out. They were much younger, perhaps only a year or two older than him and their bodies looked soft and pliant. Like the men, they too wore only a loin cloth. Never before had he seen a woman naked to the waist. His pulse raced and his eyes were drawn to their rounded breasts, with their jet black nipples, erect and hard. Then one of them caught his eye and glared contemptuously at him. It startled him and as he looked away he felt ashamed.

Chapter 11

Chanting and the stamping of feet broke the dawn silence as the hands worked the capstan to break the anchor free and release the "Mary Anne" from the confines of Goree. Jim's intention was to make use of the off-shore breeze to find deeper water before turning south for the Gambia River. As the hills above Cape Blanco slowly fell astern they found themselves sailing along a coast lined with palm trees and sandy shores. Distant columns of smoke indicated the presence of human occupation and occasionally native canoes with big square sails could be seen close inshore.

For Nathaniel it was time to write about the events at Goree, but he couldn't settle. It was impossible to forget how the slaves had been treated and how could he honestly portray what had happened in a journal to be read by the master of a slave ship? He went forward to the eyes of the ship to think what he could concoct that might be acceptable. Passing the gratings that served to ventilate the slave deck below, the smell of urine and excreta hit his nostrils. He held his breath and peered into the darkness below, but though he heard moaning he could see nothing. Hastily he turned and continued towards the bows. There he found the women, their legs hobbled to restrict their movement. What a sorry sight they made sobbing and staring at the land that had been their home. Only one seemed resigned to her fate, the one who had glared at him the day before, the one who had made him feel ashamed. She looked composed, almost dignified. He felt a sneaking admiration for her. But her very presence made the bows untenable for him and he sought refuge by climbing the ratlines to the foretop, where he could look out at a world uncontaminated by slavery.

"Mornin' young sir." He saw the cheerful features of Bert Tyacke. "Shouldn't 'ee 'ave your 'ead down? Ain't 'ee got the forenoon watch?"

"Yes Bert, but I can't sleep."

"Can't sleep, young sir? Never did know a sailor man who can't sleep. What's up?"

"Oh I don't know, Bert. It's those slaves. I suppose I feel sorry for them. I mean," he hesitated. "What have they done to deserve this? I wouldn't want to be a slave would you?"

"Well young sir, s'pose not."

"Well then Bert, is it right that we should be treating them like this?"

"I dunno 'bout that. We don't make the rules. All we can do is do the jobs we'm giv'n, so 'taint no use thinkin' 'bout it. 'Sides, they're all at it. The Dutch, the Frogs, them dagoes from Spain and Portugal and the Danes too. I tell 'ee if the little old "Mary Anne" gave up slavin', 'twouldn't make a pen'orth of difference!"

"Well," Nathaniel sighed. "I suppose not. But Bert, is it right?"

"Lor, I dunno. But they ain't the same as us, young sir; least ways as far as I know. That's why they'm black. They'm different to us. I mean 'tes like 'orses. Some be fast and jump well and make good 'unters and some be 'eavy and slow and good for ploughin'. We'm just more clever and 'ard-workin' than they blackies. 'Sides they say they'm better livin' over there, than in the jungle with all they lions and elephants. Nothin' could be worse'n that!"

"D'you really think so?" Nathaniel brightened a little.

"Well young sir, can't say for sure. But I tell 'ee this slave business, 'taint much different from the press gang, as far as I can tell."

"Really, Bert?" Nathaniel had heard of the Press gang, but didn't know much about it. "D'you know anyone who's been press-ganged?"

"Young sir". Bert paused. He asked himself why he always called him young sir. It was a habit he'd grown into. Well for a start, he told himself, 'e's young and so damned innocent and asks so many questions. And then 'e talks like a gent, yet he ain't a toff! Aye, he was right to call him young sir. He gave Nathaniel a broad grin. "You'm looking at one right now."

"Gosh, Bert." Nathaniel looked at him in amazement. "Have you really been press-ganged? It must have been awful. How did it happen?"

Bert laughed. "Oh t'were a long time ago. S'pose I were about your age. 'Twas Whitsun and two or three of us went down to Dartmouth for some fun. None of us 'ad ever been there afore and we was all excited. There was the shops and the market and the town was full, not empty and quiet like Ditt's'm where we came from. 'Twas a great place for lads like us. And the ships and the fishin' boats drew us like bears to 'oney." His eyes twinkled.

"Then there was the taverns with men singin' and jokin' and drinkin' and the girls teasin' us country bumpkins. Soon we was drinkin' too and then I met this young maid." He stopped, he'd fancied her.

"Go on, Bert. You met this young girl?"

"Well er, yes, young sir. I found this maid. Very respec'able young lady she were. She said she were lost and like a gen'leman I 'elped her 'ome. Then I goes back to the tavern to find my friends, but they'd gone. I asked a feller if he'd seen 'em but 'e 'adn't. 'E was a friendly sort of feller and gave me a drink. Well like as not I were already a bit tipsy and that jug of ale must 'ave been one too many for the next thing I knew was wakin' up in one of the King's bloody ships with a terrible 'ead and they was all a'laughin' at me and tellin' me I'd taken the King's shillin'."

"King's shilling?" Nathaniel interrupted him. "What's that?"

"Well, young sir, if 'ee takes the King's money you 'ave to work for 'im! And takin' the King's shillin' like they said I 'ad, meant I was now a sailor in the King's Navy!"

"But couldn't you escape? Couldn't you just have run away?"

"No, young sir. Ain't much chance of that! The navy don't let the men ashore y'know, anyway not in England. Never did set foot in England again for nigh on six years. Never saw my old mother again. Poor old soul, she died while I was away and never did know what 'appened. 'Spect she thought I'd been in a fight and maybe killed or drowned, I dunno. When I did get 'ome my sister Peg told me 'ow she were always sayin' young Bert'll be back one of these days, I just know 'e will. Well she was right, but I didn't get back soon enough!"

They lapsed into silence as they scanned the shoreline and saw yet another canoe.

"Tell me about the Navy," Nathaniel said thinking about his father. "Did you hate it?"

"Well, young sir, can't say I 'ated it. We 'ad some good times I s'pose and I learnt me trade. Some good came of it. But to be 'onest I were damn glad when the war ended and pleased to be paid off. 'Twas the discipline we 'ated most. T'were 'arsh and unforgivin'. If 'ee didn't jump to it, often as not the Bo's'n would give 'ee a whack with a belayin' pin or a turk's 'ead. And if 'ee ran foul of one of the officers, God help 'ee."

"Did they ever use the cat?"

"Aye, now and then. 'T'would go in spasms. I remember one of my mates, silly bugger 'e was, 'e couldn't handle his drink and 'e was always betting with his tot. Then one day 'e won 'is bet. 'E'd drunk a couple of tots and was staggering about as drunk as a Lord. Well this Lieutenant found 'im and snarled "Drunk again? That's all your fit for, you useless scum!" Well, that was just too much for George, he'd always had a special 'atred for that officer, who 'e swore blind always picked on 'im. 'E sprang at him and 'eld him by the throat and was shakin' 'im like some old rag doll. I reckon if we 'adn't pulled him off, 'e'd 'ave strangled 'im!"

"What happened, did he get the cat?"

"Aye, young sir 'e did. 'E got forty lashes."

"Forty? That must have killed him!"

"No, young sir, didn't kill 'im. I've seen lads get mor'n that. 'Tes the ceremony of it all that gets 'ee. We was all on deck when poor George was marched on. 'E'd sobered up by then and was quite calm. There 'e was, stripped to the waist with the Marines, their muskets with fixed bayonets, lined up behind him. Then with a roll of the drums the Cap'n stepped forward and read something to us. 'Twas all about dealin' with mutineers as far as I could tell. Then he sentenced George to forty lashes. He was tied to the mast and the Bo's'n laid into him with the cat. After ten strokes the Surgeon examined George, then nodded for the Bo's'n to continue. 'E 'ad another decko at George after thirty strokes, but though poor George was 'anging limply from the mast, with 'is back cut to ribbons 'e gave the Bo's'un another nod for the last ten." Bert stopped for a moment. "We 'ad to admire George, y'know. 'E took it all with 'ardly a whimper, that was 'til they cut 'im down and the Surgeon rubbed salt onto 'is bleedin' back. That's when 'e started to scream, I s'pose 'e thought the pain was over, but it wasn't."

"Bert, why did he rub salt in?" Hadn't he suffered enough?"

"Well, young sir, salt ain't part of the punishment, though George wouldn't have believed it, if 'e'd told 'im! Salt's rubbed in to stop the wounds festerin' and if it 'adn't bin dun, mor'n likely poor George would 'ave bin dead afore the week was out."

The ringing of eight bells marking the end of the morning watch brought their talking to an end and thankfully casting all thoughts of the cat from his mind, Nathaniel scrambled down the ratlines and ran onto the Quarterdeck.

"Where've you been laddie?" The Chief Mate asked. "You're late!"

"Sorry, sir. I've been on the foretop, with Bert Tyacke."

"Have you? Did you see anything up there?"

"No nothing really sir, except a native canoe now and then."

"Well we'd better keep our eyes peeled; this is no place to run aground. If you manage to get ashore there's nothing but sand and scrub or one mangrove swamp after another. And the natives, well they ain't exactly friendly! They fancy eating a nice plump white man, y'know. You'd make a nice tender morsel." He laughed. "They'd eat you, laddie long before they tackled my tough old meat!"

Nathaniel ignored the eating habits of the natives. "Do many ships go aground here?"

"Some do, especially on a dark night, when it's hard to see the breakers. We'll see a few wrecks before we leave the coast, take my word for it."

Nathaniel shivered. "Have you ever been shipwrecked?"

"No, not so far. Lady Luck's been kind to me, but let's watch out for those breakers, just in case she's forgotten me!"

But Lady Luck was with them, and the next afternoon found the Mary Anne shaping a course to pass over the bar at the entrance to the Gambia River.

Chapter 12

To David the rain and fog which had enveloped the village for the past few days seemed a harbinger of despair. Since his last meeting with Elizabeth he had been tortured by doubts. Would she come again? But as the fog dispersed and the sun now shining in a clear blue sky, his spirits began to rise. Surely the change in the weather was a good omen. On such a glorious day Elizabeth must come!

Now more confident, he walked slowly to the church. There was plenty of time. He savoured the thought of seeing her shadowy figure coming through the porch and down the aisle towards him. He'd rise with the dignity expected of a priest and lead her out into the sunshine to sit on that bench, which had surely become their very own! Happier now, he pushed the door open, moved to his pew, opened his bible and began his morning's reading. Yet concentration eluded him. The words which usually gave him comfort and guidance seemed meaningless and empty. He stopped. It was no use reading when his mind was elsewhere; he told himself. The clock struck eleven; he bent over his bible again, though surreptitiously he watched for her. The quarter hour chimed, then the half hour. Still she hadn't come. Where was she? Had some ailment struck her low? Or could her father be unwell? Surely only her own indisposition or some family crisis would stop her coming. Besides she'd promised to return the cuttings, though he dared hope she might come because of him. Oh! How stupid he was. The clock struck twelve. He rose, she wasn't coming. He started for the vicarage; then on impulse he turned and walked the way she'd come. A faint hope still persisted, but after a while he retraced his steps; disappointment now mixed with resentment. Entering the vicarage he was met by Mrs Stewart. "Where's Mrs Lugger, Mr David? Ain't she come?" He saw that knowing look on her face again. It irritated him so. "No Mrs

Stewart. I've no idea why not, she's probably indisposed!" He hesitated. "I'm quite thankful really, I can give more time to my sermon."

He couldn't help feeling angry with Elizabeth. Why couldn't she have had the courtesy to send her man Miles to tell him she'd not be coming? Clearly he meant nothing to her. She only came because of her obsession with slavery. When the Vicar arrived and asked the same question as Mrs Stewart, he got the same reply and as soon as they'd finished eating he slipped away to his sanctum. As his bitterness slowly abated a growing determination replaced it. He would see her again. He must see her again. He'd never met a woman like her before. She was quite unlike the simpering girls in the village that were thrust upon him by their overpowering mothers. She was different, she was intelligent, a practical, mature woman, yet beautiful too. She was the sort of woman who'd make a good wife for a Rector. Yet if he went, what reason could he give? Could he ask for the return of the cuttings? No, that would be churlish. But what of the other cuttings he had, those that told the case of the slave James Somerset. He'd not told her of them. Why couldn't he take them to her? That would be a plausible reason for a visit. He rummaged hastily through his papers and found them. He scanned them quickly. The judge, the same Lord Mansfield, had ruled that the enslavement of a person in another country could not be recognised in England and some felt this surely meant that such slaves in England should be freed. It was a landmark case. She would be excited about that. Yes, he'd take the cuttings to her, he'd go on Friday. Suddenly he felt happier.

On the Friday he rose early and saw to his relief that it promised to be a fine day. Wanting to impress her father, the Rector, he dressed carefully and clutching his precious cuttings hurried down to the kitchen. The smell of bacon welcomed him. "Off to Hanbury, are you, Mr David?" Mrs Stewart gave him a questioning look as she broke the eggs in the pan.

"Yes" Mrs Stewart," He pulled a chair up to the table. He wouldn't be drawn.

She put his breakfast before him. "You'll be seeing the Rector's daughter then?"

He nodded as he put a forkful of bacon into his mouth. "It's possible, Mrs Stewart."

Mrs Stewart giggled. "I do hope so, Mr David. It'd be such a waste to go all that way without seeing her."

He wouldn't rise to the bait; she always wanted to find a wife for him. "I asked the Vicar if I should go to Hanbury to pay my respects to the Reverend Lunt. He thought I should."

"Well, you've a fine day for it." Mrs Stewart smiled sweetly. "And who knows Mr David, you might see her as well."

David didn't reply. He ignored her insinuation and eating up as fast as he could, he left for the stables.

It was a clear winter's day and his horse eager for exercise, galloped easily up the rise to the Bristol road. Then at a more leisurely pace he covered the six miles to the signpost where the road branched off for Hanbury. He'd been buoyed up at the thought of seeing her, but as the church spire came into view his confidence began to wane. Never had she given him any sign that she was fond of him. He wasn't sure she even liked him! How would she react when she saw him? He eased his pace. He needed time for his nerves to settle. Was he being foolish, going after her like this? For a moment he wanted to give up, to go back to Olverton, but he had to go on; they would all be asking after the Rector. He rounded the bend and saw the Rectory, nestling among the trees. He stopped to admire it, it was a grand house. Then he urged his horse on and rode slowly through the gates, his horse's feet crunching on the gravel. The sound alerted Miles who came to greet him. "Good morning, Your Reverence." He showed no surprise at seeing him, it was as if he'd been expected! "Let me take yer 'orse, sir. Mrs Lugger's in the kitchen."

Her very name gave his heart a lift. He walked towards the house and was met by a young servant girl.

"Good morning," he said. "Is your master at home?"

She nodded. "Yes, Your Reverence."

"Then please give him my complements and tell him the Reverend David Hart, Curate of St Mary's Olverton has come to call."

"Pray come in, sir." She curtsied and led him into the drawing room

Elizabeth looked up from her embroidery as he entered. "David! Seeing you is a surprise."

He caught her eyes, were they a little contrite? A pang of conscience had indeed struck Elizabeth as she saw him standing there. Though she hadn't promised to go to Olverton again, she knew he'd expected her to come again to hear more about Granville Sharp. But at the very last moment she'd felt she couldn't. The last visit had depressed her so! All she'd learnt about Tilly and Zebedee and the other slaves had weighed her down like a lead weight and she had come to dread what else she might learn. The cruelty of it all was sickening. And though she wanted desperately to do something to help end this awful slavery, she'd asked herself time and again, how could she? She desperately wanted to help, but she felt totally unequal to the task.

He smiled. "Good morning, Elizabeth. She looked her usual trim self, though she seemed languid and withdrawn. "I hope you're well. I was very concerned."

She gave no hint that his arrival pleased or even displeased her. "Yes, David, I'm well". She avoided his eyes. "You must think me very ungrateful, but I couldn't come. I'd heard too much about the suffering of the slaves. I couldn't bear to hear anymore. That's why I didn't come. Now I feel very ashamed."

His heart jumped. She'd not come because she disliked what she'd heard about slavery. Did that mean that she didn't dislike him? "Elizabeth, I understand, believe me. I could see how upset you were when I told you about Tilly and Florrie. But decent people like you must be told about the plight of the slaves. Ordinary folk don't know the truth. And we must also tell them about people like Granville Sharp and the good work they do. Then when the truth is known, the public will surely show its revulsion and the Government will surely have to outlaw slavery!"

His conviction comforted her. "David, please forgive me. I've been very weak. I seem have fallen at the very first fence!"

"Elizabeth there are many, many more who just pull up, who don't even try to jump."

She smiled. "I've read those cuttings." She removed them from a drawer and gave them to him. "I found them quite reassuring, but it's sad that despite all his efforts Mr Granville Sharp has only saved two poor souls."

"But it's a start, Elizabeth. Here, I've some more for you to read. These will excite you, I'm sure." He told her about how Granville Sharp had managed to free the slave James Somerset. She listened intently and when he'd finished he told her the Gazette had called it a "landmark case" and how the judgement could be interpreted as meaning that all slaves brought to England might be freed.

She was delighted. "I can't believe it, David, is it true?"

"Well, the papers seem to think it is, but there may well be an appeal." He gave her the cuttings. "But read about it yourself, Elizabeth."

He watched her as she read the first cutting, her face impassive. There was no good news, only the same story of a slave being dragged onto a ship. He saw her skim impatiently through the second. It was not until she began to read the third that her interest seemed to grow. "It's that same biased judge, Lord Mansfield." He nodded. "Yes, but read on Elizabeth."

They heard footsteps in the hall. The door opened and an elderly man in clerical dress came in. "Oh! There you are, my dear." The old man stopped and looked at David. Elizabeth rescued him. "Father, do meet the Reverend David Hart. He's the one who's been telling me the truth about slavery." She looked at David and smiled ruefully. "He's the one who's made me feel so low."

"Welcome, my dear boy, welcome to Hanbury. So you're the curate at St Mary's. Tell me how's your Vicar, my old friend Peter?"

"He's a little stiff in the joints sir, but otherwise he's as well as can be expected. He sends you his kindest regards."

The Rector seemed pleased and the conversation turned to St Mary's and David's early years in Barbados. "Well, David," the Rector shook his head and looked at his daughter, "Elizabeth has never been the same since she began seeing you. All this talk of slavery has upset her greatly, especially now young Nathaniel's away. She's taking it to heart far too much. She needs some diversion to make her forget the woes of slavery, at least for a while," He turned to his daughter. "Don't you my dear?"

"Perhaps I have been out of sorts lately Father." Elizabeth replied. "But really, I'm happy enough."

The Reverend Lunt was not easily persuaded. "But my dear, you seem so preoccupied and listless these days." He turned to David. "I'm afraid an old codger like me's no company for a young woman. Elizabeth needs the company of younger folk, people of her own age."

"Father dear, I've enough amusement. What with my harpsichord, my reading, and not forgetting my embroidery, I never want for something to occupy myself'."

"Yes Elizabeth, I'll admit you're always busy, but, my dear, you need to get out of this dreary old Rectory." He looked at his guest. "Take her riding, David. You've always loved riding, haven't you, my dear?"

She nodded involuntarily; riding had always been a great pleasure, but to ride regularly with David; that was a commitment he might misunderstand. She shook her head. "Father, Father please, you mustn't saddle poor David with a dull widow like me."

David was quick off the mark. "Nonsense, Elizabeth, it would do me the greatest honour to ride with you. I'm always free on Fridays; perhaps we could ride together then."

"That's excellent, David." Her father's face showed his pleasure. "I'm sure Elizabeth will be delighted, won't you, my dear?"

Unable to refuse, Elizabeth nodded. "Yes, David, I shall be delighted." Her father had pitch-forked her into this, yet despite the momentary irritation she felt, she knew it would be pleasant to have someone to ride with and David was a nice enough young man.

"Well, my dear, that seems to have been settled to everyone's satisfaction." Her father appeared especially pleased. "Perhaps now we might partake of a little sherry by way of celebration." He reached for the decanter and poured a glass and held it up to the light. "Ah! A glass of sherry is one of the great pleasures of this mortal life, don't you think David?"

David laughed, but before he could speak, the Reverend Lunt continued. "But of course, there's fishing too! I haven't told you my dear." He turned to Elizabeth. "I caught four excellent trout this morning. They put up a good fight I can tell you, but I managed to land them. Mrs Jackson's preparing them for lunch. You will join us, won't you, David?"

The trout were as good as the Rector had led them to believe and by the time the meal was finished it had been agreed that David would come the following Friday to ride with Elizabeth. On his journey back to Olverton, David was overjoyed. He'd see her again in seven days' time and every week thereafter. It was more than he'd hoped for, but he asked himself, would she reciprocate his feelings for her? He knew he'd have to wait patiently for an answer.

Chapter 13

They began to ride together every Friday. Elizabeth was always ready when David arrived and in no time they would be galloping full tilt over the downs. She would laugh as she raced ahead while his own poor horse, weary after the long ride from Olverton laboured after hers. When he'd caught up they'd walk the horses and exchange a few inconsequential words. This was always the moment he planned to tell her how much he admired and loved her, but as the weeks went by the right moment never came. Before he dared broach the subject, he needed some sign, however small to show she'd return his love. No such sign ever came, but he told himself he had to be patient. If he played his hand too soon he might forfeit these happy days.

As her father had said Elizabeth loved riding, but for her there was no thrill in galloping alone; to race against another added zest and excitement. So she enjoyed David's company and all talk of slaves was forgotten as they explored the countryside together. She came to see David as an ambitious but rather pretentious young man. She remembered him telling her he was stagnating at Olverton. He complained that it was an impoverished parish, without a rich patron and so poorly endowed. "We don't even have a silver chalice and paten, or even some good brass candlesticks!" he'd told her. And he'd bemoaned the lack of decoration on the chasubles he and the vicar wore. "I really don't feel I can wear my own, it would show up the vicar's!" He'd made a wry face. "I'm afraid the vicar's a poor priest." He'd chuckled. "One might say a poor priest in every sense of the word!" Another day he'd grumbled about the vicarage, how dilapidated and ramshackle it was. "It just isn't good enough for a priest," he told her with a look of hurt pride. "I'm hoping to find a good living when I've finished my curacy; a living with a good rectory, one that the Bishop will enjoy visiting!"

His obvious ambition and self-importance were not to her liking yet his interest and love of the countryside struck a chord with her. The stark beauty of the winter countryside delighted them as they cantered along the empty tracks. He would point out the great elms that spread their arms fan-wise to the sky, the bare gnarled oaks alive with starlings and the silver birches whose dense swarms of lacy twigs hung with such feminine grace. He called them the ladies of the woods! The croak of a woodcock flushed from the marshy ground, the explosive flight of a pheasant and the sight of startled rabbits fleeing aimlessly from their path always excited him. He would shout with glee and wave his arm in their direction and ask whether she'd seen them too.

Today she'd thought he'd not come. All the signs foretold a break in the weather, but he came nonetheless. He was quite sure there'd be no rain and off they'd set. Up the slope she outdistanced him as usual and on reaching the crest eased to a walk. He was pointing as he drew level. "Look," he cried. "It's still clear in the west, you can see the sea!" She looked. There was the estuary, silver in the sun. It was a view she knew well. It had been one of Nathaniel's favourites. He'd always wanted to stop here to look at the sea and the ships.

"You're looking sad, Elizabeth."

"Am I, David?"

He nodded. "Yes, Elizabeth, for a moment I thought you might weep. What's troubling you today?"

"Nothing David, really nothing." She saw he wasn't convinced. "Well," she said at last. "When Nathaniel was little we came here quite often. The sea fascinated him and he always kept asking about the horizon and what lay beyond." She sighed softly. "Well, David, he'll know now, won't he? I just pray he'll come home safely. He's been gone nearly six months and I do worry about him. He was so innocent when he left. I pray he'll not come back corrupted by that awful trade."

"Elizabeth, he won't be, he's not old enough." David tried to comfort her. "The young are always sorry for the underdog; they don't know how to be cynical. He'll come back hating slavery even more than you do, you'll see!"

"He's young enough, that's true. He'll only be fourteen in July." Elizabeth seemed a little happier. "David, do you really think he'll hate it? Hate slavery I mean?"

"Yes, I do. He'll hate it, I'm sure he will. Perhaps when he's older, when he's more accustomed to it, he might accept it as a fact of life. It's only the real hardened ones who enjoy making the slaves suffer. But tell me, what's the master like?"

"Captain Youle?" Elizabeth tried to visualise him. "Captain James Youle," she repeated his name. "Well he's not at all what one might expect a Master of a slave ship to be. He didn't seem evil or cruel or sadistic. Surely, you'd expect the Master of a slaver to be a brute, an ogre, an evil hard hearted tyrant only interested in the spoils of the trade. But he was none of that. I'd pin my faith on him being a decent man. I'm sure he's honest and upright." She stopped for a moment as if she was trying to see him more clearly. "To be sure, he treated me with courtesy and respect and he was very patient with Nathaniel. Maybe he was a trifle direct once or twice but I think he felt uncomfortable in the presence of a woman! It was as if he'd never had anything to do with a woman before!" She chuckled. "I suppose he's what one might call a rough diamond! Indeed I was very happy to leave Nathaniel in his hands; that is until I learnt that the Mary Anne was slave ship!"

David felt himself becoming jealous of this man Youle, this rough diamond she held in such high regard. "You seem to be very taken with this slave ship Master, Elizabeth."

David's reference to Captain Youle as "this slave ship Master" somehow annoyed Elizabeth. He was indeed the Master of a slave ship, she couldn't deny it, but she was sure he didn't fit David's caricature of a slave ship master.

"Well, David," she said trying to hide her irritation. "He did impress me and sometimes I feel he's too decent a man to be involved in that awful trade. But I can't deny it, he is a slaver and that makes me sad! Sometimes I wonder whether he's trapped in that awful trade and can't escape its clutches!"

"It's possible, I suppose Elizabeth," he said, but before he could add, "Though unlikely", Elizabeth was speaking again.

"Anyway, David, if Nathaniel's got to sail in a slaver, I don't think we could have found a better master. At least that's what I keep telling myself."

"I hope you're right, Elizabeth." Her praises of this man Youle had nettled him. How could she admire a ship's master, any ship's master? To a man he thought they were a crude, uncivilized lot, whose manners left much to be desired. And this man Youle was a slaver too! It irked him the more when he thought that he himself, a man of the church who had gone out of his way to help her, had not received so much as a single word of admiration let alone affection from her! Not one word! Did she not realise how he felt about her? Was she that oblivious of him? Did she think he came to see her merely to exercise his horse? The injustice of it all struck home. Anger rose within him, he would hear no more about this damned slave-ship's master. Abruptly he changed the subject. "I think it's time to start back," he said as he turned his horse.

They rode in silence. As they neared the village Elizabeth drew level and made a sorry face at him. "David, please forgive me for burdening you with my worries. You must think me a very stupid woman to fuss so much". Suddenly she looked vulnerable, no longer the practical mature woman David had come to know. His heart went out to her. "Elizabeth dear, I don't think you're stupid at all. Surely you must know that I've always admired you. I've been drawn to you ever since that day I first saw you in St Mary's. How could I of all people, think you stupid?" His outburst stopped. "Elizabeth you've come to mean so much to me. I swear I'm only happy when I'm in your presence." At last he'd told her!

Elizabeth dared not look at him. Did she hear aright? He was only happy in her presence? Never had she thought he had such feelings for her. Surely the two of them were no more than acquaintances brought together by their common hatred of slavery.

"David, I appreciate your most kind and undeserved flattery and I thank you for your company which I much enjoy." Her words clearly pleased him. "But," she continued. "You must remember I am a middle-aged widow, many years older than you. It is therefore inappropriate, my dear David for you to entertain such thoughts about me." Giving him a kindly smile she turned and spurred her horse on. Her reply had deflated him. Its directness hurt, he felt cast aside like something unwanted. Gone was the euphoria he'd felt as his admiration for her had sprung so unexpectedly from his lips. Why should a few years matter? It was not unusual for a wife to be older than her husband. Why then had she so cruelly rejected him? Wherever he went, he was used to being accepted as an eligible, indeed a desirable bachelor and mothers were always introducing their insufferable daughters to him in the hopes of marriage, yet Elizabeth who had all the right attributes and indeed connections to make a good Rector's wife had no interest in him! The self-pity welling up inside him turned to anger. Savagely he kicked his horse into a gallop and caught up with her. She acknowledged his presence with a courteous nod but did not speak and they rode on in silence.

His wrath gave way to despondency which enveloped him like the black clouds racing across the sun. Though he could see rain across the valley, it did not concern him. In his bitterness the discomfort of a soaking was of little concern. Nothing could make him more upset.

He heard Elizabeth cry out, "We must hurry or we'll be drenched". He saw her break into a gallop. For a minute or so he let her go, content to let the rain do its worst, but then with a curse he spurred his horse on. He chased her down the hill and saw her gallop through the gates and dismount and he himself was but twenty yards short, when the lightning struck. Blinded by the flash and with raindrops stinging his face, he struggled to reach the safety of the stables. As he did a great rumble of thunder rent the air. The horses began to whinny and rear up and seemed on the point of stampeding but somehow Miles and he managed to calm them both and get them safely into their stalls. Elizabeth's thanks "for being so wonderful with the horses," helped cheer him a little. He'd only done what any man would do, he'd said and praised Miles for his help.

Nevertheless after his rejection by Elizabeth, David felt little appetite for lunch, even though the Rector welcomed him warmly. Then to his great surprise her father asked him to preach in St Peter's on Rogation Sunday. "A fresh mind will give us greater insight into God's message. May I suggest you take St John 15 verses 9 to 17 as your text," he had said. "I'll write to the Revered Parker for his blessing."

The invitation to preach in such a well-endowed church as St Peter's revived David's spirits as did the Rector's obvious pleasure at his acceptance. Elizabeth's comments were very gratifying too, for she had told her father it would be most agreeable and how sure she was that his sermon would be well received. He was so diverted by this unexpected invitation, that he almost forgot the news he had for Elizabeth. Only when it was time to go, did he remember it, but then it seemed untimely to broach the subject. Though the thunder had moved further away, the lightning was still evident and the rain was as heavily as ever. The thought of riding home in that weather filled him with dread, but putting his trust in the Almighty he made a brave face and said he must go. But to his great delight Elizabeth would hear nothing of it, nor would her father.

"What nonsense you talk, David. Do you think we would let you risk life and limb riding back to Olverton in this weather? If you weren't struck down by lightning, you'd be drenched and like as not take ill. And what about your horse? He'd bolt for sure and probably throw you in some ditch or stream. No David, you must stay, mustn't he, father?"

"Of course, Elizabeth. David, you can't go in this weather." He rang the bell. "Doris," he said to the young servant girl. "The Reverend Hart will be staying the night. Tell cook and get the small visitor's room ready."

David looked pleased. "It's most kind of you to be so concerned about me sir. I greatly appreciate your hospitality and shall be thankful for a warm bed."

Now that he had been invited to stay, he felt more relaxed and putting Elizabeth's rejection behind him, remembered the news he had for her. With the Rector busy lighting his pipe and Elizabeth surveying the weather, the time seemed ripe. He broke the silence. "Sir, I've some exciting news for Elizabeth and I'd like you to hear it too sir, if you've time."

"Time you say David? I've always time to hear exciting news. Tell us pray, what has happened?"

"Well I hope Elizabeth will find it exciting." He could see Elizabeth was intrigued. "I've heard that the Reverend Thomas Clarkson is coming to Bath in a fortnight's time. Perhaps you've heard of him, sir?" Elizabeth and her father both shook their heads. David continued, "He's a deacon and a compatriot of Granville Sharp and is as committed as he is to the abolition of the slave trade. He's made it his business to visit the slave ports especially Bristol and Liverpool, to learn what he can about the trade. I hear that none of the slave ship captains will speak to him, but he's spoken to some of the sailors to learn how they and the slaves fare during the ocean passage. He has also visited many of our great cities and towns to speak about the evils of slavery and to gain support for its abolition. That's why he is coming to Bath. I very much want to hear him and I wonder Elizabeth, whether you would like to come with me. Would you, sir," he addressed himself to her father, "allow Elizabeth to come?"

"What's the fellow's name?"

"He's a deacon Papa, his name is Thomas Clarkson," Elizabeth interjected. "I'd very much like to hear what he has to say."

Her father smiled. "I can't disappoint Elizabeth. Of course she must go with you, David, but first tell me your plans for the journey?"

"Well sir, I propose we ride to Bristol and then take the stage. Of course Elizabeth would need some suitable lady to travel with her." He saw

Elizabeth nod. "And of course I would bring a manservant with me and perhaps the two ladies would do likewise."

When satisfied with the practicalities of the journey, her father turned to Elizabeth. "Well my dear, what do you say?"

"I'd very much like to hear what the Reverend Clarkson has to say. Are you really happy for me to go? I'm sure I could persuade Alison to come. You wouldn't mind being without me for a few days would you Papa?"

"No, Elizabeth my dear. I shall miss you of course but I'm happy for you to go."

"Oh! Papa, thank you, thank you. Just think, David," she mused aloud. "Perhaps we can talk to him and who knows we might even be able to help in some way."

Now that her father had given his permission, David and Elizabeth were busy making plans. His knowledge of the route and the times of the stage dispersed any doubts she had about the journey and she became ever more confident that Alison could be persuaded to come. The prospect of seeing and hearing this champion of abolition excited her greatly. The subject dominated the conversation, but by dinner, even Elizabeth's enthusiasm had begun to subside and David and her father were able to discuss the ways of the church and the life of the parish. When dinner was ready and they entered the dining room David was struck by its fine proportions and he found it most agreeable to sit at such a beautiful table in the soft light of the candelabra standing so well on its polished mahogany surface. The pheasant served on an elegant dinner service and accompanied by a splendid claret reminded him of the graceful dinners he'd enjoyed in Barbados. This was the sort of living he hoped one day he would have. Even the room he'd been given was furnished in style, with a mahogany tallboy, a graceful chair and writing table and a nicely curtained four poster bed.

In the morning he'd woken early. He found the storm had passed and dressing quickly he'd stolen across the road to St Peter's for his early morning devotions and the chance to acquaint himself with its interior. It was a splendid building that filled him with envy. The finely carved rood screen and simple stone altar had captivated him. The wooden roof impressed him too, with its delicately carved tie beams and he admired the handsome pulpit, so intricately decorated with figures of the Saints, from which he would soon be preaching.

Returning to the Rectory, he was met by Elizabeth. She seemed delighted to see him and when she said how pleased she was that he'd not ventured forth in that terrible storm, his spirits had risen. Her coolness of the day before seemed to have vanished. Once again she was that friendly companion with whom he rode. It was all very puzzling. Maybe his cousin had been right when he'd told him never to allow himself to be deterred by a woman's refusal. He'd said etiquette demanded that a woman should always refuse the first proposal. Was that what lay behind her rejection of him yesterday?

Chapter 14

The stage was ready. Their baggage had been loaded and it was time to embark. David helped Elizabeth, then Alison to climb aboard and finally took his own place. It was full; the other passengers being a gentleman, his wife and daughters also bound for Bath. Miles and the other two menservants had been told to take the horses back to Hanbury. "Make sure you're here in time on Friday, when we return," was David's last order as the driver whipped the horses and the coach began to move.

The girls' mother had begun to talk to Alison. "We'll be staying with my brother; he's an eminent lawyer. He's promised to show my daughters the sights of Bath and we're hoping they'll meet some fine gentlemen for company." The hopes and plans for the marital future of the daughters was of little interest to David, they both seemed vapid young things and like so many of their age given to endless silly chatter. He had tried to converse with their father, but he had fumbled for his hearing trumpet and when at last it had been found, his hearing seemed little better and they had lapsed into silence.

Soon the Temple toll had been passed and the pitching and swaying of the coach told them all too plainly that the road had already begun to deteriorate and not long afterwards the motion became so bad that even the girls stopped their chattering. Lost in his own thoughts, David recalled that stormy night when he had been given shelter in the Rectory. His ride back to Olverton the following morning had allowed him the opportunity to reconsider the events of the previous day. Elizabeth's reaction to his unrehearsed and spontaneous declaration of admiration had pierced his heart. Never would he forget her reply. "I am a widow, many years older than you. It is therefore inappropriate for you to entertain such thoughts about me." The phrase had revolved in his mind endlessly.

Why did the difference in their ages matter? Was age such an impregnable barrier? Did it mean that she could never return his feelings? But, could it be that his cousin was right about the etiquette ladies followed in such circumstances? The thought that he might be right, gave him fresh hope. Elizabeth always seemed happy in his company; surely in time she would forget the difference in their ages and return his affection. It was time he was married, and Elizabeth had all the qualities needed for an excellent clergyman's wife. Her father clearly liked him and doubtless would want his daughter to marry again; and who better than a clergyman? His musing cheered him. He would find another time to reveal his feelings for her. After he had preached on Rogation Sunday perhaps. That might provide a suitable opportunity. He smiled inwardly as a picture of her shyly accepting his declaration of affection, crossed his inner eye. His thoughts turned to his sermon. It had occupied his mind for days now. It was an important opportunity to impress her father. He wanted him to remember it as pithy, erudite and thought provoking.

The road surface began to improve and in no time the coach drew to a halt at the Keynsham toll. This marked the halfway point of their journey. He wanted to tell Elizabeth and call her attention to the scenery but she and Alison were in deep conversation and mother and her daughters were chatting busily, while the girl's father opposite had surrendered to slumber's embrace. Again he was left with his own thoughts. He remembered that early morning visit to St Peter's. In his mind's eye he retraced his steps round the nave and chancel and once again admired the pulpit with its elegant carving and pictured himself looking down on a spellbound congregation listening to his every word as he preached the good news. The view of the Rectory from the church crossed his mind's eye. How struck he'd been by its elegance! He'd seen it many times before, but he'd never before looked at it for its own sake! But that morning he'd seen it with new eyes, admiring its proportions, the symmetry of its windows with their delicate glazing bars and the handsome fan window which graced the imposing door. Now when he saw Olverton in the valley below, he always felt dispirited! Compared with Hanbury, it was a shabby little village and St Mary's always looked unloved and neglected. And as for the vicarage well, all he could say was that it was drab and dreary. Built of local stone, it had no cohesion, natural or otherwise. Additions had been made here and there as the need arose and now the house sprawled randomly over its allotted plot. The dormers had always irritated him. All three were different, badly formed; and looked like accidental appendages. It was a clumsy, ill-proportioned house lacking any grace and really not fit for a vicar, a man of some status! Come to that, he chuckled, it wasn't even fit for a curate! When he had his own parish he would want a Rectory like that at Hanbury and a wife as accomplished and graceful as Elizabeth. He stole a glance at her; yes she would make an excellent Rector's wife!

The coach stopped again, this time at the Bath toll. The proximity of journey's end gave a fillip to the weary travellers. The last few miles had been excruciatingly rough and they had been shaken to pieces, but now the road began to improve again and the sights of Bath diverted them from their discomfort. Its cleanliness and modernity impressed them. Everywhere men could be seen on ladders or scaffolding labouring to complete yet another fine building. It was clear that the city was growing fast, so fast that in the distance they could see it climbing triumphantly into the hills that encircled it. The road became busier and their progress slowed, but excitement mounted as they approached the newly built Pulteney Bridge which crossed the river and led into the city's centre. Entering Duke Street, the coach came to a halt outside the post house. David's hasty enquiry revealed that rooms were available and when their luggage had been unloaded the porters led them to their chambers. Alison and Elizabeth were offered a room on the second floor. The furnishings and its view of busy Duke Street below pleased them and they were soon installed. David had hoped to be on the same floor, but the porter led him towards the stairs. Nor was it on the next floor, but on reaching the fourth, the porter showed him the room that was to he his. It was small and dark, with a tiny dormer window overlooking the stables. Disappointed that it was not up to the standard he'd expected he complained, but was told all the other rooms were occupied and this was the only one available. Feeling ill-used and needing to air his dissatisfaction, he'd sought the proprietor who though servile in manner had given him no redress. In great ill humour, he returned to his room and began to unpack. All the stowage available to him was a plain pine chest of three small drawers and a tiny cupboard built into the corner of the room. "How," he asked himself angrily. "Could a person of any standing be expected to live in a garret like this?"

Having finished unpacking he carefully brushed his hair and adjusted his dress prior to calling on Elizabeth and Alison. Enquiring about their room, he found both ladies pleasantly satisfied. "And how do you find yours?" Elizabeth had asked. As he escorted them to the dining room, he told them it was no more than a garret and utterly unsuitable for anyone of any standing. "However," he adopted a martyr's air, "As a priest I must accept tribulation."

His unhappy mood stifled further conversation, but as they ate their roast beef and drank their claret his low spirits began to disperse and they discussed their plans for the morrow, the day before they would hear Mr Clarkson speak. All agreed they should see the glories of the Abbey and take the waters at the Pump Room, newly built on the very site of the ancient Roman baths. Elizabeth was well satisfied with the proposal, but Alison was keen to visit the shops. "Elizabeth, dear, we must do a little shopping. We can't come all this way without seeing the latest fashions. Besides," she giggled. "My husband, Mr Dewney's told me to buy myself something to remember our visit!"

Elizabeth smiled. "You're quite right Alison. It would never do to return to Hanbury without acquainting ourselves with the latest fashions!"

How lucky Alison was she thought, to have such a good man for a husband, a man who was constant in his love for her, a man who gave her a home and security. She knew how disappointed he'd be if Alison returned without something new to wear. She thought of her own long dead husband. What a short life they'd had together, just a few blithesome months before he went off to sea never to return. But she sighed inwardly; she'd grown to accept life as a widow. Wasn't she always telling herself she was content with her lot? But was she? Over the past two days, Alison had talked so much about her family, never ceasing to extol the virtues of her husband. "He's a good man, Elizabeth. Lor' knows what I'd do if I ever lost him," she'd said. Alison hadn't meant to be unkind, she knew that, but such talk of a husband to a widow was she felt a little insensitive. It had made her doubly aware of Alison's security and by contrast of her own vulnerability. Worries about her future always unsettled her. She had no home of her own, nor money! The house she shared with her father was the Squire's, endowed by him to the appointed incumbent and when in God's good time her father died, she knew she would have to move. Who would give her shelter then? Only a good marriage would give her security, the security that Alison enjoyed! But who would want to marry her, an impoverished middle-aged widow? Many men seemed to enjoy her company, but none had ever shown the faintest desire to burden himself with her. Yet here was David, nearly ten years her junior, blurting out his affection for her, like some tongue tied suitor! It was laughable. What was it he'd said? "I swear I'm only happy when I'm in your presence!" She hoped she'd been polite when she'd discouraged him. On impulse she'd voiced her true thoughts and perhaps had been rather curt. She hoped he hadn't been hurt. Of course she liked him; indeed she was fond of him, but was it more than mere affection and the opportunity to find a suitable wife that inspired him?

"Well, then, is that agreed, Elizabeth?" His voice cut into her thoughts.

"David, please forgive me. I'm afraid I've not been paying attention!"

Alison laughed. "Elizabeth, dear, I could see you weren't listening; that you were lost in your dreams. Perhaps you'll share them with me later. But now David must tell you what we've planned." When David had done so, Elizabeth smiled. "You two seem to have thought of everything." David looked pleased and whetted their appetites by telling how on an earlier visit he'd watched the men building Pulteney Bridge and had visited both the Abbey and the Pump Rooms.

When at last they had retired, Alison told Elizabeth how impressed she'd been by David. "He's so eloquent and has such a great fund of knowledge. He'll make a fine Rector one of these days." Then with a look of intrigue she said. "You were in a world of your own tonight when we were discussing our plans. What were you dreaming of Elizabeth, dear? Was it exciting?"

Elizabeth made no reply.

"Elizabeth dear, have I upset you? Please forgive my prying."

"No, Alison dear, you haven't upset me. It's just that, oh! I don't know. I'm afraid I must confess I was envying you; envying your good fortune in having such a good husband as Mr Dewney. I'm afraid it's my turn to ask for forgiveness. You see I was feeling sorry for myself and worrying about where and how I shall live when my dear father dies as surely one day he must."

"Oh, my poor Elizabeth."

"Alison dear," Elizabeth interrupted her. "It will happen and I confess I do worry."

"But we must find you a husband, my dear." Determination rang in Alison's voice. "Someone who will want to share his home and worldly wealth with you."

Elizabeth smiled. "Alison my dear, I'm a poor widow of mature years and past my prime. Who would want to marry me? Only some old widower seeking an unpaid servant!"

"What nonsense, Elizabeth! Why my cousin Jennifer in Berkeley was nigh on forty when she wed!"

Elizabeth laughed. "So you think there's hope for me yet, do you, Alison?"

"Oh! Elizabeth dear, I didn't mean it unkindly. We all worry about you."

"Well, Alison, perhaps I do have a suitor." Again she laughed and told her about David; how he'd sworn he was only happy in her presence.

"Surely he can't be serious, Alison; it's just a passing infatuation."

"But Elizabeth, what did you say to him?"

"I fear I was rather curt, he surprised me so. I told him it was quite inappropriate for him to entertain such thoughts about me."

She waited for Alison to react but no response came. "And truly Alison, it is. I could never contemplate being wed to a man as young as him."

"'Tis up to you, Elizabeth my dear, but pride can be a vengeful partner; one that can rob you of friends and lead you into loneliness. David may be young, but he's very courteous and attentive and he'll do well in the church I'll be bound. And," she laughed. "It seems he's rich too!"

Elizabeth nodded. "Yes, he's all that and like you, my father thinks highly of him. He'd be pleased to see me wed, I know." She paused. "But Alison, if David ever asks me to be his wife, I shall most decidedly refuse him."

The next day the weather was kind and after visiting the Baths and sampling the waters they made their way to the shops. Alison and Elizabeth were fascinated by the fashions sported so elegantly by the ladies of the city. Nor were the men outdone; they too had their own new-fangled fads which set them apart from country bumpkins such as them. At David's suggestion they partook of coffee in a tea shop, whose shelves seemed to groan with pottery, porcelain and tea caddies of every description. Refreshed, they set about their shopping in earnest and after much searching and deliberation Alison purchased a delightful gold chain and crucifix for herself and a copy of Pilgrim's Progress for Mr Dewney. Elizabeth, who had only a few shillings to spend, bought some tea for her father, but David had had no such restraints. After bearing impatiently with Alison's indecision over her purchases he'd gone off on his own. He was to tell them later that he had visited nearly all the silversmiths in town. Then he produced an elegant silver ink stand, which he had bought. "It should look well on my desk."

The following evening they had set out for the Pump Room in good time to be sure they would have good seats. This had proved a wise precaution for on arrival they found the hall already filling up, and it was with difficulty that they found three adjacent seats. As they waited patiently for the great man to appear, Elizabeth wondered how many had come to support the speaker and how many to heckle him. At last a gentleman called for quiet and two men entered from a side door. The smaller of the two then introduced "Our speaker, Mr Thomas Clarke." He was plainly dressed in clerical garb and though it was clear he was a man of intellect, Elizabeth could tell he was one who stood on no dignity. His modest reply to the praiseworthy and complimentary introduction he'd been given was interrupted by shouts and scuffles from the rear of the hall, as two hecklers were ejected. When order had been restored the speaker introduced his subject by affirming his absolute conviction that in God's eyes all men were equal and that, despite the colour of their skin or their place of birth, all men had the same potential for good or evil. But many claim a greater intellect than others and feel superior to the lower orders, he told them. Is this because they are a breed apart? No, he thundered, it's because fortune has smiled kindly on them. They are the lucky ones. Ones who've had the opportunity to learn. They've not been born intellectually superior; but have been well endowed. They have come from families where education and knowledge is valued, from families with money to buy it. But he assured his audience, change will come. It may take time, but change will inevitably come. Future generations will see children of the ignorant and uncultured reaching new heights of knowledge that would astound today's learned men. And so it will be with our backward brethren in Africa and elsewhere. They are not sub-standard people. They have the same potential as we do and in their own good time they will acquire the knowledge the white man claims his own. There can be no doubt, he declared, that some, whom we call niggers, will in the future surpass many of us in the understanding of science, art and literature. As he vehemently contradicted the slave owners assertion that slaves were little better than animals, the hall echoed with shouts of "hear, hear". Elizabeth warmed to this man, whose dedication to the cause was all too apparent. Speaking now about the trade, he brought home to his audience the sufferings of the slaves, inviting them to put themselves in their place, to feel the agony of separation from family and loved ones, to suffer their degradation at being treated no better than animals, and to envisage the sickness induced by the sea passage in such inhumane and crowded conditions and the cruelties inflicted upon them by their owners in the new world. How Elizabeth empathised with him as he spoke! To her surprise, he then began to talk about the crews of the slave-ships. He told them he had made it his business to visit all the slave ports to learn as much as he could about the conditions suffered by the slaves and the crews but though he had succeeded in meeting some ship's captains few would talk to him nor for fear of retribution, would the great majority of the men. Her fears for Nathaniel were reinforced when he spoke of cases where captains had beaten, tortured and even murdered members of their crew and he told the story of a sailor called William Lines murdered by his captain and of Peter Green, a flute player, who had been whipped to death by his. His mission he said, was to collect and record as much information as he could about the evils of the slave trade. Here he mentioned the great assistance given him by the Quakers, who were a valuable source of information. He also praised them for arranging meetings such as this one and for organising demonstrations against the slave trade. He concluded by mentioning the work of his colleague Mr Granville Sharp and assured the audience that he was convinced Parliament would eventually have to approve a bill to abolish slavery. Though, he added, this would not happen until the public were acquainted with the evils of the trade and demanded that it should end.

He sat down to thunderous applause and as he was escorted from the platform, Elizabeth pushed forward among the many to congratulate him. Listening to a man who shared her views and who had done so much for the cause had uplifted her. She longed to help him in his crusade and as she shook his hand and told him how much she admired both him and Mr Granville Sharp, she asked him how she could help. "Help me as the Quakers do," he replied. "Tell the people of England about this great evil."

Then he'd gone.

Chapter 15

In his cabin, Jim had settled down to read Nathaniel's journal. He turned to the page headed,

GOREE.

"It was late evening," he read, "when we dropped anchor off Goree, a small rocky island off the coast. At its southern end stands Fort Saint Michel, with its cannons guarding the settlement and a large tricolour flying in the breeze proclaiming it to be a French possession. Apparently the Portuguese were the first to occupy the island as a centre for the trade in slaves. However the Dutch threw them out in the early 17th century and it was they who named it Goree, which I am told means "safe anchorage". It has certainly lived up to its name for the Mary Anne lay safely at anchor here during our short visit. The English, the Dutch and the French have frequently fought over this island and only eight years ago the Union Flag flew proudly from the fort, but now the French have it once more. Besides Fort Saint Michel there is one other notable building, the Maison des Esclaves, a large building above the beach reached by two stone stairways in the shape of a horseshoe. This is the slave house from which the Captain bought forty-three men, four women and three child slaves. They have now been safely embarked. Goree is the first foreign port

I have visited and I found what little I managed to see so different from England. I had never seen palm trees before nor so many strange birds, pelicans and kites to name but two. For the first time I formed part of the longboat's crew as bowman. To begin with I found it difficult to keep time rowing with the rest of the crew, but after we had been back and forth between ship and shore many times I felt I was rowing reasonably well. We sailed early on Friday morning. Our next port of call will be the River Gambia."

Jim leant back in his chair. The boy's handwriting was neat and he wrote well, thanks no doubt to his mother. She had obviously made sure his education was not neglected. Education, he sighed, a good education, that's what makes young Nathaniel a gentleman. How he wished he had some of his polish; that he could speak and write as well as him. Then perhaps Elizabeth might one day return the growing affection he felt for her. He sighed and turned over to the next page, expecting to read about the slaves, how they had been embarked, their details recorded and where they were put, but there was nothing! He thought awhile, then wrote, "The Mary Anne is a slave ship. You need to record what you have learnt about the handling of our slaves." He put the journal down. He wondered what the boy would say about the Gambia! For him it had been a fruitless visit. He recalled that tense crossing of the bar with barely a fathom of water under the keel and the passage up river past Dog Island to anchor off Fort St George. He'd expected there'd be plenty of slaves for sale, but there weren't. But on reflection, he'd had his doubts. He remembered seeing that Dutch slaver weighing anchor just as he'd arrived. At the time he'd thought she might have taken all the slaves. How right he'd been! When that wizened, jaundiced factor, what was his name? Yes, Turner, that was it, when he'd promised there'd be more soon, he suspected he was playing for time. He was a shifty character and it had seemed pointless to wait when other slave ports beckoned. So he'd sailed on the ebb for the Gold Coast.

The next morning he'd told the Chief Mate to exercise the crew in bringing the slaves on deck to be washed, fed and watered. Nathaniel had heard him say, "Now we're clear of land, they'll be too damned frightened to jump overboard." And so Mr Braithwaite had briefed the Mates, the

Surgeon, the Bo's'un, the Gunner and the Carpenter and the hands had been organised into their parties. To Nathaniel he said, "You'll be helping next time laddie, so you'd best pay attention and see how we do it. We have to be careful; we can't afford to let 'em run riot on deck. If that happens, God forbid, we'll have blood on our hands and it mayn't all be theirs!"

Worried that wherever he went he would be in the way, Nathaniel had climbed to the maintop to watch. He saw Mr Hoskins and his two Gunner's Mates come on deck armed with muskets and pistols and after an earnest conversation with the Captain begin issuing pistols to the Mates. Then they were all beckoned over to the bulwark where one after another, they fired their weapons into the sea. "To make sure they bloody work," the Gunner had told them, "and to show them bastards we mean business."

When the firing had stopped, the Chief Mate nodded, the hatch was opened and the Bo's'un and six hands threw themselves down the ladder, cursing and promising all manner of retribution if the slaves made any attempt to resist. To add to the intimidation other men beat the hatch coamings with cudgels and screamed further obscenities. Their efforts seemed effective, for within minutes Nathaniel saw the first black head appear, its eyes wide with fear. Then driven by a curse and a prod from below, the slave climbed the last few rungs and stepped fearfully onto the deck. Close behind was the red scowling face of Hughes, who welding a cudgel drove him ever upward. On reaching the bulwark the slave was made to sit while a long chain was rove through the rings on his leg irons. When thus secured, the next black head appeared in the hatchway and the drill was repeated. It was a slow carefully controlled process, but finally all the men slaves were on deck and securely tethered to the long chain which ran from the Fo'c'sle to the Quarterdeck. How pathetic they looked now. Were they the same men Nathaniel had helped drag into the boat at Goree? Then they'd cursed and fought like wild beasts. He remembered how their fine physique and great strength had impressed him, their flashing eyes and white teeth set like ivory in their black shining skin. Now those eyes were timid and servile. Yet still one or two battled against the inevitable and lashed out at anyone within reach and spat at those beyond. Watching those recalcitrant few resist, Nathaniel felt a growing respect and admiration for them. Would he be so defiant, so fearless of retribution if he were one of them? He feared not. He was sure that like most of them, he also would resort to surliness and passive resistance.

The fresh air gave the slaves some relief and soon they began to relax; some even slept. But they weren't allowed to relax for long; it was time for washing. Pails of water were passed along by the hands. Some chose to drink it, but to the amusement of their captors, soon spat it out when they tasted the salt. Meanwhile the women, who unlike the men were not shackled, were put to work fetching food and water. While the deck party oversaw the feeding of the slaves, the remaining hands were sent below to clean the slave rooms. Nathaniel watched, dreading the time he knew would surely come, when he too would have to descend into those dark, foul smelling dungeons to clean them up. "'As to be dun," Bert had told him afterwards, "else they'll be getting' the bloody flux and they'll be dyin' like flies in their own dung and vomit. And if they slaves get it bad, it'll run through the ship in no time and strike us all down."

The next day Nathaniel had expected the worst. Surely it would be his turn to help get the slaves up and clean below. The prospect of handling the slaves in those dark confined spaces frightened him and he was sure the stench would make him ill. But to his relief, he was allocated to the deck party to receive and secure the slaves. How thankful he was! And all went well. It seemed that now when the slaves emerged from below, most knew what to expect and gave little trouble. A few still struggled however and were cudgelled into obedience. He'd been thankful to have missed the violence below, but now an inner voice told him, he too would have to join the cleaning party. Sure enough his premonition came true and soon he was descending into the darkness below and holding his breath until his lungs begged for replenishment. As he gasped for air the stench hit him like a blast from a hot furnace and in the darkness he stumbled against a bucket full of urine and excreta. He began to retch, yet somehow he managed not to vomit. His eyes had now thankfully become accustomed to the half light and he could see men bringing buckets towards the hatch. Some, like the one he had stumbled against, were full and left a trail of human waste behind them. Other men below the hatch were busy hitching the buckets to ropes from above so they could be hauled up and emptied overboard, while others full of sea water were lowered. A broom was thrust into his hands and he too was pushing the salt water over the decks. As he worked he began to see how the slave rooms were constructed. They weren't rooms at all; they were cages, cages made with strong wooden palings. There were three on the main deck, the two larger ones for the men and the other for the women and children. A fourth, by far the largest, had been built on the deck below. Like some mediaeval dungeon, it was darker and even more airless than the others. Each room had shelf-like platforms one above the other, running along the ship's side, on which slaves could lie. With only the fifty or so slaves on board, there could be a shelf for all, but he knew they planned to carry at least three hundred! How would they all fit in? Some would find a shelf, but the others? They would have to lie on the deck, where surely at sea those terrible buckets would overflow. He asked himself, how could any living being survive down here?

At last after what had seemed an eternity, the decks were declared sufficiently clean and the party emerged into the sunlight. Never had air seemed so pure, so sweet; so wonderful. It was bliss to fill his lungs again and again in an effort to purge them of that foul stench. Then he heard a familiar voice. "'ere you are young sir, 'ere's yer very own bucket to wash yourself down" and he joined in the merriment as the hands doused themselves with water. When all were thoroughly soaked and the laughter had begun to subside, the Bo's'un ordered them to man the pumps "to get rid of all that water you've been playin' with."

It had all ended in laughter, but Nathaniel knew he would never, ever forget that first time below, nor would he ever know how any human being could maintain his sanity in such a terrible place. That night he found it difficult to sleep and such sleep as he had, had been disturbed by visions of the slave deck. And that dreadful stench had haunted his nostrils. He awoke with a heavy heart, knowing that the cleaning of the slave decks would be a regular part of his daily routine.

And so it was to be and on the fourth occasion, after washing himself copiously in sea water and drying himself in the sun he had settled down to write up his journal. The Captain's remarks "The Mary Anne is a slave ship. You need to record what you have learnt about the handling our slaves" had unsettled him! He had deliberately avoided writing about them. His reader would be one who profited from their misery, so how could he in all honesty write about how the slaves were handled, without revealing his concern for them and his repugnance of their treatment? He had continued to avoid the subject and instead had written about the longboat and had illustrated it with a drawing of the boat under oars. And yesterday he had drawn a diagram of the Leadsman's line showing the various markings. But he knew he must write something about the slaves so with a heavy heart he began.

"On Thursday last we sailed up the river Gambia and anchored close to Fort George expecting to purchase more slaves the following day, but the Factor had none for sale. He said the Dutch slaver we had passed in the river had taken all he had, so early on Friday having refilled our fresh water casks and purchased yams and beans, we sailed with the offshore wind and the ebb tide. Our slaves, forty-nine of them, had been kept below in the slave rooms since we left Goree on Wednesday and the Captain ordered that they be brought on deck. This we did without harming either them or us, though it was a great struggle.

When the men slaves had been secured by their leg irons they were given sea water to wash themselves, while the women prepared food for them. Then a working party was sent below to clean out the dark and smelly slave rooms. This is to be our daily routine at sea, providing the weather allows."

He put his quill down and read what he had written. It was brief but truthful enough! Thankfully he realised it was time to go on watch.

The Chief Mate greeted him with a grimace. "Looks as if we're in for a spot of bad weather laddie! Look at the sky, see the clouds? That's what we call a mackerel sky. There's an old sailor's rhyme you should learn; 'Mackerel sky and mares' tails make tall ships carry low sails'."

Nathaniel repeated the verse. "I suppose," He spoke without conviction, "the clouds do look a little like mackerel scales. I guess the wispy bits are the mares' tails?"

"Yes laddie, that's right. Now you just remember that rhyme. I learnt it when I was about your age and y'know it's always been right. We won't get strong winds tonight though, but wait until tomorrow, then we'll see the wind getting up and we'll have to start furling our top sails."

The next morning he and Fred were on watch again. [Now that he'd begun to like him, Nathaniel always thought of Mr Braithwaite as Fred.] The day was clear and Nathaniel wondered what had happened to the strong wind that Fred had promised.

"Now then laddie," Fred looked at him quizzically. "Remember that rhyme?"

"You mean the one about the mares' tails sir?"

"Aye, that's the one. What d'you make of the sky this morning?"

Far ahead of them Nathaniel could see the mackerel sky had mostly broken up and overhead the sky was clear.

"Look astern, laddie," Fred pointed to huge clouds climbing to the heavens. "There's another rhyme you should learn. 'Clouds like rocks and towers, look for squalls and showers'."

Hardly had Nathaniel repeated this new doggerel, than the Captain appeared.

"Morning Cap'n. We've got some strong winds coming!"

Jim studied the sky to windward. "Aye looks nasty. Better furl the t'gallants before the wind backs. We'll have a squall or two before the day's out."

"Aye, Aye Cap'n. Perhaps we should furl the sprits'ls as well?"

"Yes, Mr Braithwaite do that and best keep the slaves below till the winds ease."

As the hands came on deck to reduce sail, Nathaniel joined Bert and together they climbed the ratlines to the maintop, then up by the topmast shrouds to the t'gallant yard, the highest yard of all. Taking his weight on the footrope and holding onto the yard, Nathaniel began to inch himself out towards the outer end. The men below had already eased the sheets and hove in on the buntlines and martinets to gather in the sail; now it was up to the men aloft to tame the flailing canvas and lash it to the yard. It had always sounded simple when he and Bert had discussed the drill on deck, but out on the yard with the sail fighting him with all its might it wasn't so easy. And with the wind howling in the rigging it was difficult to hear what Bert was shouting and as if that wasn't enough the motion they'd felt on deck as the ship pitched and rolled was as nothing compared with what he felt out on the end of the yard, some ten feet from the very top of the mast. It was difficult enough holding on without using his hands to deal with the sail. But he'd done it before and he knew he could do it. He remembered what Bert always said. "Take yer time, young sir, 'tain't no good 'ee rushin' at it and fallin' off. We'll want 'ee another time." The heavy canvas tore at his fingers and as he struggled he heard Bert's voice above the wind. "The more 'ee gets in, young sir, the easier it be." And slowly the unruly sail yielded to his efforts. Then it was done and Bert was shouting "Come on young sir, you'm 'ad yer fun." Relieved yet proud, he shinned down the ratlines and for the first time he felt rain on his face. He looked aft and saw huge black clouds rising to the heavens as the rain storm hit them. Now there were two men on the wheel, struggling to keep the ship on course as she wallowed in the following sea. Then for a moment the wind suddenly fell away and all was eerily quiet. Then with a shriek like a demented witch the squall hit them. With it came the deluge. Great columns of water swept across the sea like curtains, blocking out the horizon. No longer coming from the port quarter, the wind had backed and with ever increasing force now came from right astern. The Mary Anne lurched and heeled heavily to starboard, her bows swinging to port.

"Ease sheets," Fred yelled with all his strength, though his voice could scarcely be heard above the wind. "Look lively there; ease those bloody sheets before we split the sails."

Spilling the wind from the sails helped the ship onto a more even keel, but it was clear she was still carrying too much canvas. "Bo's'un," shouted Jim. "Get the tops'ls furled."

Once more Nathaniel climbed the ratlines to man the tops'l yard and with Bert began the long fight to quell the sail. Leaning over the yard he grabbed the canvas and pulled with all his might. This time it came easily and as it did he moved his weight back onto the foot rope. Suddenly it gave way! His heart froze as he hung desperately onto the sail. He looked down, but at first could see nothing. Then he saw it. The foot rope was trailing in the wind. He would never know how he found the strength to haul himself up to hang precariously over the yard. With his heart beating wildly he looked below and saw the angry sea. It seemed to beckon him! He turned his head to look for Bert. He saw him, but he was busy with the sail. He tried to scream for help, but nothing came! Then he heard Bert shouting "come on young sir,'ee'll 'ave to do better'n that."

Nathaniel found his voice. "Can't, Bert. The footrope's gone."

Bert could hear the fear in his voice and saw the broken footrope trailing in the wind. "Hold on, young sir," he yelled. "I'm a'comin'."

Hardly daring to turn his head Nathaniel caught a glimpse of Bert hauling himself spread-eagled onto the yard.

Bert paused for a moment, "'Tes me, Lord, Bert Tyacke. 'Tain't often I asks for 'elp, Lord, but I be wantin' it now. Please 'elp me get 'im back."

Though the wind seemed determined to pluck them both from their perilous perch, Bert slowly dragged himself out on along the yard.

Nathaniel convinced that he and Bert would soon lie broken on the deck below or drowned in that cruel sea could not bear to watch. But with a "Steady young sir," Bert was with him. "You'm doin' fine. Can 'ee get up on the yard like me?"

Nathaniel nodded and with Bert holding him succeeded in getting a leg over the yard so that he was facing Bert and lying spread-eagled too. Then began the terrifying slide back along the yard, until at last he could put his foot cautiously on the inner foot rope and make his way safely to the main top.

"Oh Bert," he cried fighting back his tears, "if it wasn't for you, I'd be a bundle of broken bones on the deck or food for fishes."

"Tain't nothin' young sir, 'ad to get 'ee back afore the Bo's'un got after us. I tell 'ee once 'is anger's up, 'e's more fright'nin' than any o' them squalls!"

With the footrope gone no-one could lash the sail to the yard, so it was left to the Buntlines, the Bowlines and the Clewgarnets to keep the sail furled. Yet though they were hauled as taught as possible the wind now played wilfully with the sail making it shake and crack like a whip. In the heavy seas and gale force wind the Mary Anne was clearly still carrying too much canvas and the call came to furl the main and fore courses. Finally under bare poles she was steadier and the hands were stood down, but for those who remained on deck the noise of the wind and sea and the cracking of the t'gallant sail was almost unbearable. It was little better below decks, where things were breaking loose and all that could be done was to wedge oneself into some safe corner, forget everything and try to get some sleep. Nathaniel dared not think how it was on the slave decks!

Gradually the storm eased and when finally it had blown itself out, the hands were soon busy unfurling and setting the sails. When they were all drawing again, it was time to find out how the slaves had fared. Allowing them up one by one to be secured to the chains proved difficult as they all pushed each other in their desire to escape the hell-hole below. Many were suffering the effects of seasickness and were unsteady on their feet and the smell coming from below was truly stomach-turning. When the time came for the slave decks to be cleaned, Nathaniel said a silent prayer for himself and the hands as they began their work. Seeing the state of the decks below he felt driven to add another prayer for the slaves who had endured such purgatory.

On deck, Jim was grateful to have the rigours of the storm behind him and with the ship sailing easily again he set about planning his arrival at Elmina, their next port. There he hoped to buy many slaves, though he knew he'd be unlikely to find the two hundred and sixty he still needed. In Elmina most would be victims of the Ashanti and other fierce tribes in the hill country to the north, where they constantly fought each other. In weather like they'd just had, Elmina wouldn't be a safe anchorage, so he'd have to buy as many as were available and not wait for more to be brought in. And then there was the gold he must buy and Elmina was the right place for that.

As they approached the shore, Nathaniel had been the first to sight the big fort on the hill above the little settlement. Fred told him it was Fort St Jago and that he should keep his eyes peeled for St George's Castle on the foreshore; that was where the slaves were kept. Soon this great white building could be seen and before dark they had anchored among two other ships clearly waiting to load slaves. Early the following morning Jim and Mr Mackay, the Surgeon, went ashore in the yawl. Nathaniel had manned the boat and as he was about to sit in the bows as bowman, Bert had beckoned him, handed him the tiller and had said "'Tes time 'ee learnt to sail". Though excited to be at the helm, Nathaniel had felt nervous with the Captain present, but as the sails began to fill and the yawl heeled gently and picked up speed, he felt more confident. With Bert's calloused hand ready to guide his, he was allowed to sail the boat into the very mouth of the little harbour, crowded with native fishing canoes. Thankfully Bert took the yawl alongside and when the two passengers had landed he cast off. "We'll anchor over there lads," he said. "'E'll call us when 'e's ready."

No sooner had they anchored than the crew had their lines over the side in the hopeful expectation of fresh fish. This sort of fishing had always bored Nathaniel, he was used to fishing in a fast running stream with a fly on his line, but the others were happy enough and soon with much joking and merriment they were hauling in their first catch. Like Nathaniel, Bert wasn't fishing either; he was busy filling his pipe.

"Bert, tell me about your time in the King's navy."

Bert exhaled a cloud of blue smoke. "Well dunno what to tell 'ee. The sea ain't much different no matter what ship you'm in."

"But what about the war with the French Bert? Did you fight lots of battles?"

"Bert chuckled. "Well young sir, 't'would be nice to say 't'was one long battle, but to tell 'ee the truth we spent more time lookin' for they frogs than fightin' 'em.""

Nathaniel looked disappointed. "Did you never find them?"

Bert grinned. "Aye, young sir, we found 'em alright and gave 'em a good 'idin' too."

"Where, where did you find them?"

"Right outside their own front door!" Bert took a long pull of his pipe, his eyes glowing with pleasure. "Y'see we'd been blockadin' them Frenchies, keepin' 'em locked up in Brest. Aye we 'ad 'em kickin' their 'eels in port, 'stead of attackin' our ships. That was 'till the weather turned real nasty. We 'ad a westerly gale, blowin' right onshore an' it got worse an' worse. Well, no ships and they Frenchies for sure could leave Brest in that gale, so our Admiral," he paused mid-sentence. "Sir Edward 'Awke 'e were. 'Ave 'ee ever 'eard of 'im?"

Nathaniel shook his head.

"Ah! Sir Edward 'Awke, 'e were a great Admiral." Bert exhaled another cloud of smoke. "When this gale 'it us 'e took us back to Torbay for shelter, then after the wind 'ad eased we set off at full tilt for the bay again. But y'know young sir, we was almost too late. Aye, we'd just passed Ushant not far from the bay, when we saw the French Admiral leadin' out 'is fleet. Well, 'twas just what we'd bin waitin' for all them long dreary months. I tell 'ee young sir we was just bustin' to get at them Frogs, but," He spat contemptuously over the side. "Do 'ee know what they did?"

Nathaniel shook his head again.

"They turned and ran for it, young sir, that's what they did!"

"But Bert, I heard there was a great battle at Quiberon Bay." Hadn't the father he'd never known been killed there?

"Oh there were a fight alright, when at last we caught up with 'em. I was on the wheel of the Warspite an' I 'eard the Royal George fire 'er signal gun. She'd 'oisted a flag on her maintop mast. T'was white with a red cross. T'was the one we was all waitin' for, the signal for General Chase."

"General Chase? What's that, Bert?"

Bert re-lit his pipe and between puffs told him it was the order for ships to break formation, hoist every sail they could and chase after and engage the enemy. "T'was a race, I can tell 'ee. The "Torbay", the "Resolution" and the old "Warspite", we three led the way. I ain't sure who got there first, but there wa'n't much in it, for we all opened fire about the same time."

He shook his head. "Aye, t'was a right old battle I tell 'ee! Wa'n't one of them well ordered scraps with ships in line ahead sailin' past each other and lettin' go with broadsides. No, each ship fought on 'er own with the nearest Frenchie she could find. T'was one bloody great shambles with ships blastin' at each other with all they 'ad! Then the sun began to set and there were thirty maybe forty ships knockin' 'ell out of the enemy an 'avin' to tack to miss all they rocks and shoals. T'was like a mad house with the Master getting the 'ands to work the sails and the Gunner makin' 'em man the cannon and up in the eyes of the ship was the Leadsman poor bugger, swingin' the lead and callin' out the depth! And with all the smoke, pickin' out who was French and who was English was bad enough in the light of day, but as the sun went down we couldn't tell friend from bloody foe, unless in the flash of the cannon we caught a glimpse of 'is flag or 'is side belched flames as 'e loosed a broadside at us!"

"Gosh Bert, how did it all end?"

"Well, young sir, when t'was dark we just 'ad to anchor, us and them Frogs, else we'd 'ave run up on they rocks. I remember 'twas a terrible night with the wind 'owlin' and the ship pitchin' and rollin' an all of us prayin' the anchor would 'old. But when the sky began to lighten, that's when we was really worried, wonderin' who we'd find next to us come the dawn! Well, lady luck was with us in the "Warspite". We was among friends, thank God. But not the French Admiral, Conflans was 'is name I remember. 'Is luck 'ad run out! 'E found 'iself surrounded by English ships, so 'e cut 'is anchor cable and ran."

"Oh." Nathaniel looked disappointed. "Did he escape?"

"Well, 'spose 'e did in a way. We all watched 'im goin' down wind and saw 'im tryin' to turn, but 'e'd left it too late and 'e ended up on the beach. Then we 'eard what sounded like cannon fire, but they Frenchies, they wasn't shootin'. They'd set the ship on fire and ran for it over the beaches afore the flames reached the powder! An' when the other Frogs saw their flagship on fire, they ran like rabbits too an' that was the end of the fightin'."

"What a battle Bert! How many ships did the French lose?"

"Can't rightly say, young sir. Maybe a dozen. There was the Admiral's ship wrecked on the beach and them that went aground in the river and four or five on them terrible rocks an' we took another three as prizes. But then we lost the "Essex" and the "Resolution" an' a lot of men."

"Bert, I've never told you". Nathaniel spoke quietly. "My father was killed in that battle. He was in the "Royal George"."

Bert removed his pipe; he didn't know what to say. Then the boy continued. "Thank you for telling me, Bert. It's been good to hear about it from someone who was there. I feel it's brought me closer to my father. You see, I never knew him, he died before I was born."

"Oh, 'tes terrible to 'ear that." Bert seemed greatly upset. "Aye 'tes real terrible. Yer father was in the "Royal George" did 'ee say?"

"Yes Bert that's what my mother told me."

"Well young sir, 'e must 'ave bin a fine officer. Sir Edward would only 'ave the best in 'is flagship!"

They lapsed into silence as they mused over the battle.

Then one of the hands saw the Captain beckoning. "Back to the ship then boy," the Captain said as he jumped aboard. "They'll bring the slaves in those canoes of theirs and I'll want you to deliver the goods we'll be trading for them."

And so as the slaves arrived, the yawl went back and forth delivering the pots, pans, knives, axes, muskets and shot. The Second Officer was landed with the first batch to ensure the goods were properly recorded, while the Surgeon and his mate examined and counted the slaves as they were sent down to the canoes. Everyone was at full stretch, yet still a crew had to be found for the longboat which the Captain wanted to take him and the Third Mate ashore. He had other purchases to make and returned with elephant's tusks and bags full of something, nobody quite knew what. The great tusks were manhandled down into the after store while the bags were carried to the Captain's cabin. There Jim received them and when he was alone he opened them to check their contents. The gold had been carefully weighed ashore, he using his own scales and the Merchant his. Neither had given the same reading, but after much haggling they'd agreed the weight and the price and he felt he had had a good deal. He began to stow the bags in the locker he'd had made especially for the purpose, but before doing so he searched for the little bag of gold dust he'd bought on impulse for himself. It was nestling at the very bottom of the second of the three bags. He studied the dust carefully then tightened and secured the drawstring before giving it a symbolic kiss. Then he hung it round his neck as one might an amulet. Then locking the locker and making sure the bag of dust was hidden among his clothes he went on deck.

Though by now the sun was low, the slaves were still being hoisted on board. He studied the slave ledger; forty eight slaves had been embarked. The last six were probably in the canoe heading their way. The day had gone well and early next morning the Mary Anne set sail for Cape Coast, just ten miles or so to the east.

Like Elmina, Cape Coast had been an uncomfortable anchorage, with the ship rolling in the persistent swell and many of the slaves being sick again. However the visit had been worthwhile for he had bought another sixty two slaves before setting off for the Bonny River some seven or eight days sailing further east. There he would be able to wait in the safety of the river until he had acquired the one hundred and forty slaves he still needed.

Chapter 16

It had been a kindly passage from Cape Coast and now with the sea stained by the mud from the many rivers that formed the Niger delta, Bonny could not be far away. After six days at sea, the hands were now well practised in bringing the slaves on deck in the morning and getting them below at sunset and to help keep order among the slaves it had been decided to select some of their number to act as warders. Choosing them had been difficult and at first Fred had looked for any who had some English, but the few who had, had no natural authority about them. Then the Bo's'un had had an idea. "The slaves are scared of them buggers with pointed teeth, ain't they?" he'd said. "They call 'em Lion men. They'd be too scared to argue with them! What about usin' them eh?" So they had selected four from the Quaes, that fearsome looking tribe who filed their teeth and emulated the lion. They were given the grand title of warden and provided with short cudgels as a mark of their authority and for this responsibility were given extra victuals. Their new status seemed to bring out all their latent aggression and they used their cudgels with impunity and were far more vicious towards the slaves, even those of their own tribe, than any of the hands ever were. Indeed they became so effective at controlling their fellow slaves that for their own safety they were accommodated in the slave room that had been set aside for the boys.

Pleased that the handling of the slaves seemed to be going well, Jim Youle had sat on his chair on deck and had opened Nathaniel's journal. He studied his latest drawings. One showed the arrangement of the sails and another the details of the standing and running rigging. Both were excellent, though he found two minor faults; these he circled. Then he began to read what the boy had written. To his surprise there was no mention of the mishap on the yard, when the footrope had given way.

Thankfully Tyacke had got him down safely otherwise he couldn't begin to think how he could have told his mother. And if the boy had been badly hurt or even worse, killed, he knew he would never see her again. And in his heart of hearts he knew he did want to see her again. He shook his head, trying to dismiss her from his thoughts and began to read the boy's account of their visit to the Gambia and how, when the ship was once again in deep water, the slaves had been brought on deck and the slave decks cleaned. It was a good factual account, without displaying any of the moral judgement he feared Elizabeth's son might have. After that last stormy meeting with his mother, strangely he too had begun to have some scruples about the trade, but on this his first slaving voyage he'd learnt quickly that it was best to let conscience and morals lie low. Slaving, surely the world's second oldest profession, was a fact of life and there was little he and those like him could do to stop it. All he could do was to ensure that provided they behaved, his slaves were treated as well as possible and that, when they were landed, they were as fit and healthy as they had been when he had bought them. That was the best he could do and as he had said so many times "You can't sell a dead slave." He turned the page over. It covered their visit to Elmina. He skimmed over the lines about Nathaniel sailing the yawl and his remarks about the native canoes and began to read with increasing interest the boy's description of the port.

"*El Mina,*" he had written, "*was first discovered by the Portuguese about three hundred years ago. They made a treaty with the local chieftain who allowed them to build a small fort, which they called the Castle of St George. This served as a base for their quest for gold, which they had learnt was mined many miles inland and could be exchanged for the salt produced in the salt pans on the beach. In time this became a profitable undertaking and the settlement became known as Elmina, a name derived from that given to the coastline, Da Costa de el Mina de Ouro, The Coast of Gold Mines. Lately however the production of gold has diminished as natives working in the goldfields are often captured by the Ashanti to be sold as slaves*". Was that the reason, Jim wondered, why he had found the gold more expensive than he'd been led to believe? "*About a hundred and twenty years ago*", the writing continued, "*the Dutch drove the Portuguese out and took over their trade and to protect the Castle of St George, they built a smaller fort on the hill across the harbour, called St Jago*". "Interesting," Jim wrote in the margin and muttered, "The boy writes commendably, his mother has taught him well". He sighed. His mother Elizabeth; that elegant woman, who had so impressed him! The very thought of her lifted his spirits. It seemed hardly a day passed without him recalling their meeting. She had cast her spell on him! He shook his head; it was beyond his comprehension! He began to read again, *"We arrived at Cape Coast four hours after leaving Elmina"*. A factual but dull record of events followed; anchoring, lowering boats and making contact with the traders ashore. Then again it became more readable. *"Captain Youle invited me to accompany him as he went ashore to trade"*. He remembered feeling the boy should see how the slaves were purchased. *"I was thrilled to see the Union Flag flying over the castle with its rows of canon facing out to sea. It is an imposing building built on the rocky foreshore with the sea breaking on the sands below, where rows of native dugout canoes are hauled up. Our party consisting of the Captain, the Surgeon, five hands and me, carried samples of the various goods we would use for barter. We crossed a drawbridge to enter the Castle and having been cleared by the sentry, were ushered through the main gate into a large courtyard. There we were met by another soldier who led us up a graceful stone stairway onto a balcony. To the left was the Governor's quarters and to the right the Palaver Room, where the slaves were paraded for our inspection. There seemed to be plenty, but the Surgeon being very thorough in his examination rejected many, so we only bought fifty-seven men and five women, two of whom had a child clinging to them. As the slaves were selected, a red hot iron was used to brand a number on their upper arms; then they were led away to await delivery to the Mary Anne. Now all have been received and our Slave Ledger shows that we have one hundred and sixty three slaves on board; sixteen are women and there are nine children."* "Mm," muttered Jim. "We need another hundred and sixty or thereabouts. Let's hope Bonny will provide!" He closed the journal and saw the Chief Mate approaching. "We'll be in the river tomorrow, Mr Braithwaite. You're all ready for rigging the ship once we're anchored?"

"Aye, Cap'n. And once we've got the thatch on we'll have to get the slaves up each day, otherwise in the heat below we'll start losing them."

"Yes, but we'll need to post armed sentries."

"Aye, I've told the Gunner to organise that."

"Good. Now what about the local chief here, the one we do business with?"

"Well, last time I was in the river he called himself King Pepple. He's a pompous old devil and dresses up in some sort of naval uniform. All the locals are terrified of him and if we don't scrape and bow to him he can be bloody difficult, so we'll have to watch our ps and qs. In fact many slavers fire him a gun salute as they enter the river. We did that in my last ship and it worked wonders. We soon had slaves coming while some ships that didn't were still waiting, though they'd arrived before us!"

"Right then, Fred, get that organised. Is there anything else I should know about him?"

Fred lifted his tricorn and smoothed a few wisps of hair over his balding pate. "Well, he's always on the lookout for some special gift; something that makes him feel and look important. I suppose that's how he's got all his fancy uniform! On my last visit, he took a fancy to the Master's telescope but when the Master wouldn't give it him, he was very upset and for a time the supply of slaves slowed right down!"

"So he wants some special gift eh? Well what about that old swivel gun, the Gunner's not happy with; the one with the crack in the barrel. Tell him to give it a good clean and we'll put it on the Quarterdeck near the companionway. Perhaps we could tempt the old fool with that eh?"

Fred chuckled. "Yes, that might well do the trick!"

On the next day the Mary Anne with her tops'ls furled, made her way cautiously over the bar and nearing Ju Ju creek she fired the first salvo of a nineteen gun salute. As the first canon roared and spewed forth its acrid smoke gulls rose in unison from the water, breaking the ensuing silence with their raucous cries. But from shore came no response. Was the great king deaf? Nathaniel wondered. Was their message of deference to go unheeded? Was it only the gulls who knew they'd arrived? Past the next bend the river opened out into a wide sheltered reach. From his vantage point on the main yard Nathaniel could see three ships lying there, but their appearance astonished him. They didn't look like ships at all; instead they looked like thatched cottages floating on the water. One cottage flew an English flag and he could see a Dutch and a French one. He was busy helping to furl the main course when the Captain brought the ship into the wind to drop the anchor, but when the sail was secured he was able to take in the scene around him. On the northern bank stood the Kingdom of Benin, hiding behind an impregnable barrier of mangrove trees and he could see no sign of life. The southern bank however was quite different. Close inshore the water shelved gently, leaving a grey sandy beach graced by tall coconut palms, whose fronds stirred gently in the wind. Behind, giant trees gave shadow for the thatched huts of a straggling village. Further along the beach he could see canoes drawn up onto the sand and people dragging them into the water to join others waiting a few yards offshore. A drum sounded and a huge canoe with an awning made of thatch was launched. The rhythm of the drum seemed to galvanise the other canoes and with much chanting they gathered around the big canoe and the little fleet began moving towards the Mary Anne. Hearing the Chief Mate warning the Captain of their approach, Nathaniel scrambled down the ratlines and ran on to the Quarterdeck.

The Captain was studying the fleet through his telescope, "Looks like the old bugger himself," Nathaniel heard him say. Then after a pause, "You've got to give him credit, those crews are well trained!" Nathaniel saw what he meant. Three canoes were equally spaced around the King's; one ahead and one on each beam, their paddling controlled by the beating of a drum. The other canoes followed in a well maintained line. The fleet looked impressive, purposeful and Nathaniel thought, rather frightening. When the Royal Canoe was alongside King Pepple climbed aboard and the Captain, removing his tricorn in a great sweeping gesture, welcomed him aboard. How Nathaniel managed to stifle the giggles that threatened to overpower him, he would never know! The object of all this pomp and ceremony was the most ridiculous figure he'd ever seen. He wore an ill-fitting blue tail coat, edged with yellow braid in the manner of an Admiral's gold lace. Its tarnished brass buttons were undone revealing a coal black chest. His breeches, surely once snowy white were grey with dirt and terminated below his knees leaving his shins bare like his large feet. Around his neck he wore a red neckerchief and on his head was a dusty top hat. This he now removed to return Jim's salutation. "Welcome to my Kingdom, welcome to Bonny," he said.

"Thank you, sir." Jim replaced his tricorn. "I hope we can do some profitable business together. Please come to my cabin." He led him around the foot of the mainmast in a deliberately circuitous route which led past the old swivel gun, now looking clean and purposeful. Stopping as if to admire the view, he could see the King was clearly taken with it. King Pepple stood back to admire it, then touched and stroked it. "What fine gun he is!" He exclaimed as he squinted up its barrel.

"Yes", Jim replied. "Tis very useful, especially at close quarters."

King Pepple seemed unable to take his eyes off this impressive weapon. "He make good gun for war canoe."

Jim said nothing. The king was stroking the gun, fingering the touch hole and looking up the barrel; he was like a child with a new toy. "He look good on war canoe," he said again, "Make King big, make him strong!"

Jim ignored his comments and tried to lead him away. "Come to my cabin, sir. We have much to discuss." He stood at the companionway, holding out his arm to indicate the way. But King Pepple didn't notice him. He was mesmerised by the swivel gun. Delighted that his plan appeared to be working, Jim spoke again. "This way please," but his words fell on deaf ears. Again he said "This way please." Reluctantly the king raised his eyes from the gun, looked at him and in a plaintive tone repeated. "He make good gun for war canoe!"

Jim hesitated, as if for the first time he understood what the king had been saying. "Well sir." He smiled. "If it pleases you, you are welcome to it. Mr Braithwaite, kindly load it into His Majesty's canoe."

Nathaniel saw a great smile spread over the black wrinkled face of this strange king and watched as the Captain and King Pepple shook hands and disappeared down the companionway.

Sometime later the two reappeared. Both seemed pleased and after one last handshake the King boarded his canoe and accompanied by his escorting fleet left for the village. With the canoes now clear of the ship, Jim burst into laughter. "The silly old bugger's like a dog with two tails! He's so pleased with his new toy, he says he'll send some matting right away and the first slaves for us to view should be here in a day or two."

"Good." Fred was laughing too. "You seem to have him eating out of your hand."

"Well, for the moment anyway." Jim was still grinning. "That is," he looked more serious now, "until he gets a better present!"

Fred laughed. "Our old swivel will take some beating."

"Aye, Fred. So we'd better be ready for the matting when it arrives. And best give the slaves a breath of fresh air this evening. They'll be kept below long enough, while you're rigging ship."

And indeed for the next two days the slaves were kept below, while the crew worked in the muggy heat to prepare the ship for its long wait in the river. To Nathaniel it seemed the ship was being dismantled! All sails were unbent and sent down to be folded and stored in the sail room, the yards unshipped and topmasts struck and the Mary Anne began to resemble one of those old rotting hulks Nathaniel had seen on the Avon at Bristol! Next the top masts were positioned between the masts to form ridge poles, while the yards were rigged above the bulwarks and between the fore and mainmast ratlines to serve as lintels. Then more spars were found to form rafters bridging the gap between the ridge pole and the lintels, thus completing a skeleton roof, later to be covered with the matting King Pepple had promised. With the roof completed the upper deck was transformed into the likeness of a cool airy barn. So far it had been the Bo's'un who had taken charge, but now under the direction of the Carpenter two barricades running from one side of the upper deck to the other were erected. The for'ard barrier was to stop slaves reaching the Fo'c'sle and the after to keep them from the crew, who were now to live on the quarterdeck. Each barricade was about eight feet tall and had a heavy door built in it giving access to the slave deck. On the side away from the slave deck, platforms were constructed for the crew to stand on to look over the top and if necessary to use their muskets to quell any revolt.

The slaves in their hot fetid prison below could hear strange noises above and wondered what was happening and where they were. The last time they had been on deck to breathe that sweet, cool air they had seen the village near the beach. Its huts were not so different from those in their own village and the smell of the cooking fires had been bitter reminders of the life that had been so cruelly taken from them. In the cramped, claustrophobic atmosphere below, grief for the past and anxiety for the future added to their sufferings. Some seemed to accept their plight and withdrew into a silent world of their own, resigning themselves to the will of Allah. A few constantly bemoaned their fate, while others talked of escape. But how could they? How could they overcome the white devils? Whenever they were on deck, those chains held them tight and, if with the help of Allah they ever managed to break free, there was always a white devil armed with a cudgel or a musket nearby. But if by some miracle they managed to overpower their captives, what then? No one knew how to make this great canoe move like the white men did. They had studied them climbing the masts and seen them pulling on ropes, but no one understood how they made those great sails capture the wind and even if they did, how would they find their way in the empty sea? And where would they go? They had discussed these questions endlessly, but the answers never came. The more the slaves talked about escape, the more impossible it seemed and a great inertia slowly overcame them until most came to accept their fate and to realise that the only thing to do was to survive; to survive this stinking hell, to cling to dear life and to implore Allah that when this unbearable journey ended, life might be a little kinder. Could it be worse? If it were, death would be a merciful release.

By the third morning the roofing had been completed and once more the slaves were allowed on deck. They came without struggling, eager to escape the stifling stench below and bemused by the roof over their heads, allowed themselves to be secured to their chains to enjoy with evident pleasure the shade and the cool wind which flowed through this strange hut. They were given more water too and more food, but these small mercies were soon forgotten; they were still captives and their future frightened them.

On the fourth day King Pepple's canoes arrived with the first of the new slaves, more terrified creatures, bound and hobbled and beaten into submission by their fellow blacks. Manhandled one at a time onto the quarterdeck, they were examined by the Surgeon. Those who passed Mr Mackay's rigorous inspection had their details recorded in the Slave Ledger before being sent below. Those rejected were returned to the waiting canoes. The noise and commotion unsettled the existing slaves who vented their feelings by hissing and spitting and rattling their accursed chains but the crew, busy restraining the new slaves, ignored them.

Chapter 17

For an age, life onboard the Mary Anne followed the same routine as canoe after canoe brought more wretched slaves. Nathaniel hated seeing their humiliation as they submitted to the Surgeon's examination and the violence which followed any disobedience or resistance. Whenever possible he contrived to escape and go off with the yawl to get fresh water and wood for the galley fire. Such days were magical. When the tide allowed they'd sail or pull upstream on the quiet placid water and having passed the last slaver and the village had disappeared behind the bend, he would sigh with relief. Then he felt he was entering the real Africa, a strange exciting land as yet uncontaminated by the greed of the white man. Or so it seemed, though in his heart, he knew full well it wasn't true. The river he'd begun to love played its own vital part in the cruel exploitation of the poor natives. It led into the very lands from which the slaves were snatched and was a highway for their journey to the hungry ships waiting impatiently downstream. He couldn't fool himself! Nowhere could he hide from the savagery of the trade and the torment of the slaves. Yet the beauty and peace of the river consoled him and the great profusion of birds helped lift his spirits. Cormorants would surface, then fly fast and low to a quiet perch to enjoy their catch. Swallows would skim the surface, while hovering kingfishers would drop like jewels into its depths for their next meal. And the dainty terns, contrasting so greatly with the plodding pelicans and the statuesque heron, added to his fascination of the river. He also loved helming the boat. When the wind filled the sails and the yawl picked up speed, the tiller seemed to give an excited tremble in its eagerness to guide the boat. That and the sound of her bows cutting through the still water all became part of his growing love for small boat sailing. Whenever they set off on these expeditions the crew had to carry muskets and to avoid trouble they only landed where the native chiefs would allow. Nathaniel's favourite watering place was a stream three or four miles upriver, a lonely place far from any village where the water plunged into a small pond set among huge trees in which green monkeys swung from branch to branch, screeching and baring their teeth at anyone who approached. The water was cool and inviting and the men enjoyed throwing as much of it over each other as they fed into the casks. But no one ventured far from the bank fearing what might lurk in the depths and one of the crew musket in hand, was always ready for any wild beast which might appear. Crocodiles were their chief worry, for they emerged silently from the mangrove or surfaced from the depths without warning. When collecting wood the men had to be cautious too, for there were snakes about and other creatures could easily be disturbed, but despite these dangers there was never any shortage of volunteers for this duty. And when it was time to return to the "Mary Anne", Nathaniel always felt heavy-hearted, as he neared that floating prison, crammed with desperate slaves and fast becoming a tinder box, ready to ignite at any time.

For his earlier trips up river Nathaniel had always been accompanied by one of the Mates, but lately as long as Bert was with him, he had been allowed to take the yawl on his own. It was after his last trip, when they'd returned to the "Mary Anne" and had begun passing the wood and water casks up to the hands on deck, that he'd heard a rumpus coming from the "Tamar", an English Slaver close by. At first he could see nothing unusual, but on closer inspection he saw figures on the matting roof. They seemed excited, they were shouting and gesticulating! Were they black or white? He couldn't tell, they were up sun and all he could see were their silhouettes. He climbed aboard and ran to tell the Chief Mate and almost collided with the Captain coming on deck, telescope in hand.

"Boy," he cried. "Fetch the Chief Mate and the Gunner. There's trouble in the "Tamar". It looks as if the slaves have risen. I want a dozen men with muskets. We'll go and help her."

Soon men were coming on deck and the Gunner was issuing muskets, powder and shot while the Captain and Chief Mate were discussing plans. Then they were tumbling down into the longboat, with Nathaniel clutching his musket and steering for the Tamar.

"Go alongside by the Mizzen mast, boy." The Captain's voice was calm and steady. "We'll board her by the chains."

Nearing the Tamar they listened intently, but heard nothing except the incomprehensible jabbering of the blacks. All seemed horribly ominous. Had the slaves gained the upper hand? Had the crew been slaughtered? Nathaniel heard the Captain and Chief Mate reviewing their plans, but he concentrated on helming the boat. Strangely, despite the immediacy of bloody conflict he didn't feel frightened. Later he was to reflect ruefully that there just hadn't been time to feel scared and he had found the prospect of not getting the boat alongside safely, more frightening than the blacks! Now the ship was only a few yards away. He put the tiller over to bring the boat onto a course parallel with the Tamar. "Bows," he yelled with an authority that surprised him. He saw the bowman ship his oar and reach for the painter. The longboat seemed to be racing along. "Way enough," he commanded, his voice sounding less sure, but as the oars were shipped the longboat slid easily alongside. He saw Bert give him a friendly wink, then turn and scramble up the chains after the others. "Make her fast," Nathaniel shouted to the bowman; then he too clambered aboard and found the Mary Anne's men in control of the quarterdeck, sheltered as it was from the swirling mass of slaves, by the barricade across its deck. He could see no defiant slaves here, but huddling together in a weeping group right aft were four, maybe five black women. There was no sign of the Tamar's crew, except for one old man; one drunken old man in officer's rig waving a bottle in one hand and a pistol in the other and cursing "those bloody blackbirds."

"That must be Captain Wetherill," he heard the Chief Mate whisper.

Jim nodded. "Cap'n Wetherill, what's going on? Where's the rest of your crew?"

Henry Wetherill raised a bleary eye and moved unsteadily towards him. "Who the bloody 'ell are you?"

"I'm Captain James Youle from the Mary Anne. I've come to help restore order. Tell me, where's your Chief Mate?"

Henry Wetherill belched and leant on the rail. "In there." He gestured towards the barricade. "They've killed him and a few more, for all I know."

"Well, where's the rest of your crew then?" Jim's voice showed his anger. "Pull yourself together man!"

The bottle slipped from his hand and fell to the deck as Henry Wetherill tried to straighten up. "My bloody crew? They're all drunk, mor'n likely, same as me; except for one or two frightened bastards on the roof."

"Drunken fool!" Jim exclaimed as he turned his back on the Master of the Tamar. "Mr Braithwaite, it looks as if we'll have to put the slaves down ourselves. Get the men lined up at the barricade. We may have to give them a shot or two!"

"Come on young sir, stick with me," Nathaniel heard Bert's welcome voice. At the barricade Nathaniel peered over the top. A seething mass of slaves, some armed with belaying pins met his frightened eyes. They were chanting and gesticulating to the rhythm of a stick beaten on the mast. He heard Bert suck his breath. "They'm lookin' terrible wild, young sir! 'Fraid 'tes goin' be either them or us!" Nathaniel turned to look at the Captain, what would he want the men to do? He saw him draw his pistol and point it upwards, towards the roof. There was a bright flash and Nathaniel saw smoke venting from the muzzle. Though he'd seen the pistol fire, the crack of the shot had shaken him. It shook the slaves too, for suddenly their caterwauling stopped. The effect pleased Jim who was now peering over the barricade. But after a second or two the slaves resumed their defiant chanting. Jim fired another shot. As the slaves fell silent, Jim shouted. "I've got twelve men with muskets. Go below or they'll fire." He hoped they'd understand. Surely they could see the muskets. Did they think he'd not use them? Could they be that stupid? He heard a scream and saw an arm release a missile. He ducked as a belaying pin flew past his head and landed on the deck behind him. Jim fired his pistol again and shouted his warning a third time. A few slaves seemed to understand him and slunk towards the hatch to disappear below. But their defection went unnoticed by the others, who still shouted angrily and waved their makeshift weapons. Trying to count this wild, raging mass was impossible, but he reckoned there could be eighty or even more.

"Mr Hoskins", he shouted. "I'll give them one last warning and if they don't move then, I'll want six men to fire when I give the order. They must each aim at a particular slave, do you understand?"

"Aye Cap'n". Mr Hoskins turned towards the men. "Right from 'ere to the left, get ready to fire at them 'eathens, when the Cap'n gives the order. And each of you pick out a particular 'eathen and aim to kill 'im. And when you've fired, load your musket as fast as the Good Lord will let you. Got that?" He saw the men nod and heard them mumble "Aye, Aye, Mister." "And the rest of you," he barked, "Stand by for the next volley." He turned towards the Captain. "All ready, Cap'n."

Nathaniel found he was in the group to fire first. His heart was pounding and his hands were clammy. He gripped his musket with all his might, scared that the musket would slip in his hands when he fired. He waited nervously, then the Captain fired a fourth round and gave a final warning. A few more slaves slipped silently below, but a hard core, angry and excited, remained. Nathaniel could sense the Captain's willpower as he shouted, "Right men, the first six take aim, ready, steady, fire."

Despite the Gunner's instructions, Nathaniel couldn't bring himself to aim at a particular slave. He just shut his eyes and pulled the trigger; his was the last musket to fire. For a second a stunned silence fell on the slaves as four contorted bodies lay on the blood strewn deck and two, bleeding copiously, dragged themselves painfully towards the others now hiding behind anything they could find. Then one, his face, distorted with anger broke cover and shouting defiantly hurled a missile at the hated white men. Others encouraged by his audacity followed his lead and with blood curling cries unleashed a rain of objects at their enemy.

"Reload your muskets." The voice of the Gunner jolted Nathaniel from the horror before him and he tried to pull his musket back from the barricade, but try as he might, it wouldn't move; some unseen force seemed to be pulling it from him. Struggling with all his might, he saw to his horror a black hand clutching the barrel. He held on with all the strength he could find and screamed for help, but no one heard him. They were all busy firing the next volley. But then the Chief Mate appeared and with pistol in hand leant over the barricade. Nathaniel heard the pistol discharge and as his musket came free he fell backwards onto the deck.

"All right there, laddie?" He heard the familiar voice, nodded, and scrambling to his feet hastily began to reload.

"Hold fire, hold fire," he heard the Captain's voice. "We'll give them time to think."

Nathaniel peered over the barricade. Now there were ten bodies and the baying and screaming had given way to wailing as the wounded slaves were carried or dragged towards the hatch down which, many had clearly escaped. Yet still a group, perhaps as many as twenty danced in defiance near the mainmast and waved their makeshift weapons.

Again, Nathaniel saw the Captain raise his pistol and repeat his warning. Some seeing the futility of further resistance deserted their comrades and slipped quietly below, but still what looked like a dozen slaves openly defied the guns. "Right Mr Braithwaite," the Captain shouted. "We'll have to get in there amongst them and force the rest below. I want you to take two men and guard the hatch to stop those below coming up again. I'll take the rest and go after the ones on deck."

"Come with me," the Chief Mate grabbed Nathaniel's arm as the door in the barricade was opened and they all rushed through, the Captain leading the way. Nathaniel and the Chief Mate with another hand, ran to the slave hatch. "If any of 'em tries to come up, shoot them. Understand?" Nathaniel nodded to acknowledge Fred's terrifying order, while praying none would be so foolish as to come up!

Meanwhile the others were swearing and cursing at the slaves on deck and prodding them with their muskets to drive them forward. Finally driven against the forward barricade with further retreat impossible, most were content to submit, though rather than surrender a desperate few climbed onto the rail and threw themselves into the river.

At last all the slaves had been forced below and Nathaniel surveyed the slaughter about him. Counting the bodies, he saw one lying at the base of the after barricade. One side of its face had been torn away, no doubt by the shot that had cut him down, but though now dead, his right arm still stretched out in a last agonising attempt to snatch that musket, which had so nearly been his. Nathaniel's memory of that fearful moment was interrupted by the Captain's voice. "Mr Braithwaite," he was saying. "Get your two hands to bring those fellows down from the roofing. We'll cover you with our muskets." As Nathaniel began to climb up the ratlines, he felt them shake and looking up saw the men coming down. There were six of them and all seemed unharmed. One went straight to the Captain. "I'm the Chief Mate, Alec Mitchell. I'm afraid they caught us napping. Thank God you came. I didn't think we'd last much longer up there. We're very grateful to you, sir."

"So you're the Chief Mate? Your Captain told me you'd been killed! Well it's good to have someone I can talk to. Your Captain's drunk. What's come over him?"

"Bloody old fool," Alec Mitchell looked contemptuously towards the quarterdeck. "When he hits the bottle, which he seems to do most days now, he drinks himself stupid. Says it's the only thing that can help him forget he was the only survivor of a brig that broke up on Chesil Beach. He's nearly driven me out of my mind. And I'm afraid most of the crew think if it's alright for the master to get drunk, it's alright for them too."

"Well he's certainly in his cups now," Jim glanced at the figure slumped in the scuppers. "You have my sympathy."

A search of the upper deck had now been completed and Fred came to report his findings. "We've found four of the crew dead. They're over there."

Alex Mitchell walked over to the four bodies laid out by the mainmast. All had been battered to death, their faces broken, covered with blood and hardly recognisable. "Poor sods," he muttered. "They must have had a terrible end. God rest their souls." He bent low over one of them. "That must be the young Third. I can tell him by his fancy breeches. And that's Crossley, I think, but the other two?" He shook his head. "I can't say for the moment. We'll have to find out who's missing. What about the slaves?"

"We've counted eleven dead on deck", Fred reported. "And at least three jumped overboard. They'll have drowned by now, or been taken by the crocs."

"Well, what a lesson!" Alec Mitchell shook his head ruefully. "It's a lesson we must never forget, nor must those bloody slaves either!"

But the uprising wasn't quite over. Banging and shouting could be heard coming from the slave deck. "They'll have to quieten down or I'll keep them down there for a week without food or water till they do, Alec Mitchell spoke with a determination born of desperation.

"I remember having trouble like this before," Fred said. "Alec, can you get some canvas, a sail will do, so that we can cover the gratings. That'll cut off the air. That might quieten them down."

A sail was found and secured over the gratings and all other ventilation to the slave deck blocked. At first it had no effect, the banging and shouting continued, Nathaniel thought it even increased! But all agreed that without air, the slaves must quieten down soon.

"Alec, do you have any cayenne pepper?" Fred had a mischievous air about him.

"Yes, we should have. Why?"

Fred grinned, "You'll see. We'll need plenty of it, as much as you can find." When the pepper arrived, he lined the men up. "Load your muskets with powder lads, but don't put your shot in. Use the pepper instead and tamp it well down."

The men did as they were told, though there was much muttering about whether "'e was off 'is 'ead?" and "'ow can you kill 'em with pepper?"

"Now lads," Fred said when the muskets were loaded. "Ease back the canvas and put your muskets through the gratings." Then he gave the order to fire. There was a ripple of shots and almost at once they could hear coughing and sputtering below as the acrid stench of burnt pepper attacked the slaves' nostrils.

"That'll knock the spirit out of them." Fred turned towards Jim. "What do you think, Cap'n? When they're quiet, we can let them up one at a time and get them properly secured and leave them to Alec?" Fred's plan was implemented and some hours later, when order had been restored, the "Mary Anne's" crew thankfully returned to their own ship.

Over the next few days they kept an eye on the "Tamar" and were thankful that all seemed quiet and that there was no trouble aboard the "Mary Anne" either. But concerned that the slaves had become unusually quiet and listless, Jim had told Mr Mackay, the surgeon to investigate. He found that some had lost control of their bowels and fearful that the condition might spread he ordered that these be separated from the others and kept permanently on deck. He gave them some of his special potions and within a few days most had recovered, but two got no better and gradually succumbed. When the all hands were busy removing the roofing and re-rigging the masts, further bad news came. Jack Tanner, the Sailmaker's mate was missing and a search later that day found him apparently asleep in the sail room, but all efforts to wake him proved unsuccessful. The Surgeon was called and he was pronounced dead. Jack Tanner had been a popular member of the crew and his death, just as they had been preparing to leave the hot, muggy, fly-infested coast of Africa for the open sea and the colonies beyond, was thought by many to be a portent of further troubles ahead.

Chapter 18

It was the day before Rogation Sunday. David had found his sermon more difficult to write than usual, but at last it was finished. As he perused it thoughts of the congregation spellbound with his learning and oratory, broke into his reading. He badly wanted to impress Elizabeth's father, for he would have the ear of the Archdeacon and might even have some influence with the Bishop. A good word from him might be decisive in finding him a desirable parish. No one would take notice of his own vicar. The Reverend Parker had little influence over anyone! Though devout and well meaning, he was a simple man of little consequence, without the intellect or leadership necessary for high office. On the other hand, the Reverend Lunt was a priest of some stature, a man of learning whose opinions were widely respected. His support in finding a good living would be invaluable!

Satisfied with his work, David rolled up his sermon, secured it with a piece of ribbon, put it to his lips and kissed it. "Please, Lord, let him be impressed," he muttered before placing it in his bag with his bible and prayer book. With a feeling of rising excitement he left his room, said goodbye to the Vicar and Mrs Stewart and made his way to the stables where his manservant had his horse saddled and ready. Then making his farewells he was away and galloping up the hill to the Bristol road.

It was a fine sunny day, but for once he had no interest in the wildlife, nor in the blossoming spring countryside; his future was his only interest! Of late he'd felt unsettled. Ever since returning from Bath the desire to have his own parish had been uppermost in his mind. Within a year or so he hoped he would be offered one. Visions of an elegant rectory like Hanbury had filled his mind, but such dreams only served to emphasise his need for a wife to support him in his ministry; a suitable wife to help entertain important guests such as the Archdeacon and of course the Bishop. Patrons always preferred a married priest and Elizabeth would make an ideal clergymen's wife. She'd grown up in a rectory and knew what was expected of a Rector's wife. He was sure her father would be pleased to see her married and what could be better than for her to marry a clergyman? Yes, he felt confident about asking her father, but Elizabeth? Well he must hope that his cousin had been right when he'd said that etiquette demanded that a woman should always refuse a suitor on the first occasion.

He spurred his horse on; thoughts of Elizabeth made him eager to reach Hanbury. He'd not had the chance to talk to her alone in Bath; Alison had been a good chaperone! Nor had he seen her since then. As the signpost for Hanbury came in sight, he realised he was in good time. He eased his horse to a walk and recalled the events at Bath. She'd been impressed by the new buildings and the shops and though she'd bought little herself, he was sure she'd enjoyed that first day. Hearing Thomas Clarke speak had clearly made a great impression on her and on the journey home it seemed she had talked of nothing but him and his work. The visit had clearly stimulated her and when they had parted she had thanked him profusely for arranging it. Could it be that having done so much to open her eyes to the evils of the trade she abhorred, she'd now accept him? He prayed they would have a moment alone so that he could ask her to be his wife, to tell her she must marry him.

At the Rectory, Elizabeth and Mrs Jackson had prepared his room. It was the one he'd had before, but now he was expected, a fire had been lit, the bed aired and Elizabeth had placed a vase of daffodils on the table by the window. Mrs Jackson always loved daffodils. "Ah! Tis a lovely time of the year ma'am, full of hope and promise." Elizabeth had smiled. "Yes, Mrs Jackson, summer will be with us soon."

"What a nice young man that Reverend is ma'am and so polite and considerate too. His wife must think herself very fortunate."

Elizabeth looked puzzled. "Pray tell me, Mrs Jackson, to whom do you refer?"

It was Mrs Jackson's turn to look confused. "Why the Reverend Hart, who else ma'am?"

"Oh!" Elizabeth laughed. "He's not married. He's too young."

"Really, ma'am?" Mrs Jackson seemed taken aback. "Not married, well bless my soul." She gave Elizabeth a knowing look. "Should've thought some clever girl would've caught him by now!"

"Oh! There's many a young lady in Olverton longing to marry him I'm sure. He'll find a wife when he's ready." Elizabeth tried hard not to show her irritation, the innuendo had not been lost on her. She changed the subject hurriedly. "There'll be seven of us for lunch tomorrow, Mrs Jackson, the three of us, Squire Thomas, Mr Waring, the churchwarden and their good ladies."

She stayed a little longer while they discussed the menu, then hearing the noise of hooves on the gravel she went down the stairs. That would be David, she knew. She hadn't seen him since their return from Bath. He'd been the perfect gentleman and had made no further mention of this fondness he seemed to have for her. She hoped he'd taken her rather curt reply to heart and would be content to remain a friend, a friend whose company she valued, not a suitor but a friend. Turning the corner on the stairs, she saw him in the hall below. Her father had been summoned to greet him and was shaking his hand. "Good to see you my boy, come in, come in."

Elizabeth stopped to watch them. It was quite apparent that her father liked David and David was looking like a dog with two tails, shaking her father's hand and smiling and saying, "How kind you are sir, to offer me a bed."

Her father would have nothing of his thanks and led him into the drawing room. "Take the Reverend Hart's bag up to his room," he told Doris, the young servant girl. "And tell Mrs Lugger our guest has arrived."

They both stood up as she entered. David was plainly pleased to see her. "Elizabeth, I'm glad to see you looking so well. I feared the strain of the journey might have pulled you down."

His needless worry about her health nettled her. "Thank you for being so concerned, David, but I assure you the journey caused me no distress and I am well, perfectly well."

"But my dear," her father interjected. "You did seem a little dispirited on your return."

"If I was dispirited, Father, it was most certainly not the journey that was the cause. Both Alison and I enjoyed that to the full. If I was out of spirits, it was because of what I'd learnt of the barbaric conditions which the slaves endure on the sea crossing. And, Father dear, it's not just the slaves who are maltreated, the crews often suffer great cruelty too at the hands of their captains. And," now she did look dispirited. "It made me worry about Nathaniel." She hesitated as she composed herself. "But the

Reverend Clarke cheered us by telling us about the growing movement up and down the country pressing for the end of slavery. He is convinced their demonstrations will sooner of later make Parliament enact a bill for its abolition. But what can we do here in Hanbury? It seems all we can do is to be patient and ask for God's help."

"Yes, Elizabeth, I'm afraid that's all we can do. Buried as we are in the depths of Gloucestershire, we can only pray and be patient." As David turned to her father, he hoped he looked wise and discerning. "Isn't that so sir?"

The Reverend Lunt nodded, but before he could speak Mrs Jackson appeared laden with a tray. "Ah! Mrs Jackson, a very timely entrance," the Rector said as he produced the key to the caddy. "David, you must try the tea Elizabeth gave me. It's quite excellent!"

Elizabeth watched her father spoon the precious leaf into the pot. She was saddened that the tea which pleased her father so was the only positive thing she had to show for her visit to Bath. She had learnt more about the slave trade indeed, but she couldn't help feeling dissatisfied. She'd hoped that the visit would point to some role, however small, for her. But all Reverend Clarke had said when she'd asked him how she could help was, "Help me as the Quakers do. Tell the people of England about this great evil." At the time she'd felt uplifted but as she'd pondered what he'd said, her motivation had waned. How, she had asked the Lord, how in this village, where no one has ever seen a black man let alone a slave, could she tell of the evils of slavery? It was so very frustrating, and here was David telling her in that grave and pompous manner "to pray and be patient." Inwardly she shook her head. Patience had never been one of her strengths! She had wanted an active role!

Bath continued to dominate the conversation as her father encouraged David to air his considerable knowledge of the city. With such an avid listener as him, David showed how knowledgeable he was about the new buildings and especially about Pulteney Bridge and the Abbey. He also voiced his enthusiasm for the excellent craftsmanship of the artisans whose work filled the shops.

Elizabeth interrupted him. "Your silver ink stand must look exceeding well on your desk!"

She saw a look of sheer delight cross his face. "Oh! Elizabeth, it does, it looks superb. Did I tell you about the gold one? It was magnificent, the decoration was exquisite. How I wanted that one!" He laughed. "Sadly it was beyond my pocket. So," he sighed. "I had to make do with the silver!"

Talk of their visit engrossed them; then when tea was over she showed him to his room. As she led the way he repeated his profuse thanks for her hospitality and told her of his growing fondness for her father. "Not only is he greatly respected as a priest, but he's so kind too. And believe me, Elizabeth, you're so like him!"

"Am I?" Elizabeth laughed. "I'm told I'm more like my dear departed mother. She was kind too, but given to stubbornness! Never would she do anything she didn't believe was right. Though father loved her I'm sure he found her difficult at times!" Reaching the door of his room, Elizabeth told him she hoped he would be comfortable, that dinner was at 8 o'clock but bade him come down whenever he was ready.

There were just the three of them for dinner. Her father had shot the pheasant and was delighted to see his guest enjoying it with such relish. "Do you shoot, David?" David pulled a face. "As boys my brother and I had guns of course, but there was no game to shoot. I'm afraid we just shot whatever we could! And now in England while I am sure I would find the sport most agreeable I have yet to find an opportunity to try it. Maybe one day sir I might prevail on your generosity and ask you to introduce me to its secrets."

The Rector smiled. "It'd be a great pleasure David. Perhaps when the season starts again we might have a day's shooting."

The arts of shooting and fishing and hunting monopolized the conversation as they tackled their pheasant. It was followed by jam roly poly, one of the Rector's favourite puddings, with stilton and more claret to cleanse their palates. When they had finished Elizabeth rose and thanking Mrs Jackson for the excellent meal withdrew to the drawing room. Her father, promising to join her shortly, reached for the port and they drank the King's health. David savoured the port and having complimented his host on its excellence waited patiently for him to charge his pipe. When at last the time seemed suitable, he broke the silence.

"Sir, I have a private matter I wish to discuss with you."

His host turned, the burning taper poised expectantly over the tobacco. "A private matter?"

"Yes, sir." David hesitated. "A matter of the greatest importance to me."

The Rector, his pipe still unlit, sighed sympathetically. "Tell me, my boy, what is it?"

David had rehearsed his speech all week but now, with his host waiting expectantly, the carefully chosen words eluded him. He faltered, but then words came. "It concerns your daughter sir."

"My daughter, Elizabeth?"

"Yes sir. I'd like her to be my wife." He hesitated; this was not the way he'd rehearsed it! Feeling disconcerted he struggled on. "That is sir, if I may have your permission." Suddenly he felt relieved. It was said now, not as eloquently as he'd planned, but the message was clear enough!

The Reverend Lunt relit his taper and was soon exhaling great clouds of blue smoke. Satisfied that the tobacco was well alight, he leant back in his chair and gave David a paternal smile. "Tell me, David, has she accepted you?"

"No sir. Not yet. I haven't asked her, but I'm hopeful she will."

"Well, David, nothing would give me greater pleasure than to see Elizabeth wed. She needs a husband to provide for her and give her home when I'm gone. And I'd be very pleased to have you as a son-in-law."

"Oh! Thank you, thank you sir."

"Well then, David, now you have my permission. When are you going to ask her?"

"Tonight sir, if I can find the right moment."

"Good. I'll retire early David, and leave the two of you together."

David smiled, "That would be most considerate sir."

The two collaborators drained their glasses and with a whispered "Good luck" in his ear, David followed his host into the drawing room. Elizabeth busy with her embroidery watched them enter. They had a conspiratorial look about them, she wondered what was afoot! Her father hadn't been over generous with the port, she hoped.

Her father was the first to speak. "My dear, I'm afraid we've kept you waiting far too long."

"Yes, Elizabeth," David smiled. "Please accept our apologies."

She thought she saw her father give David the smallest of winks as he added "We had an important matter to discuss." It seemed they were bound by some new-found affinity!

"Well, father, whatever it was; I trust it's been resolved to your mutual satisfaction. But there is no call for an apology I assure you. Truly you were not absent longer than I had expected."

Though their deliberations had clearly pleased them, she noticed that neither made any attempt to enlighten her. Feeling excluded from their secret thoughts, Elizabeth decided to forget the matter and, moving to the harpsichord, allowed her fingers to console her with the comforting touch of the keyboard. The two men quiet now, were looking more composed. She knew her father would be lost in the music, but something told her David was impatient for her to finish. She began with one of her father's favourites but when the last note faded, surprisingly he made no request for her to play on. Instead he rose and thanking her for playing so beautifully, confessed he was ready for his bed and, bidding them good night departed.

His abrupt and uncharacteristic departure intrigued Elizabeth. Why had he retired so early? Did he mean to leave her alone with David? That was quite improper. She decided she would retire too and stood ready to go. "David, it's been a busy day for me and my bed is calling too." David looked upset. "Must you go so soon Elizabeth, I'd hoped we could talk a little?"

"David, I'm very tired and we have all tomorrow for talking. And I must confess I'm a little concerned at my father's departure. It's so unusual for him to be early abed. I hope he's not unwell."

Unable to detain her, David escorted her to her father's door and then bidding her good night he left. The plans her father and he had so carefully made had been confounded!

Chapter 19

As Elizabeth tidied herself for church she couldn't help laughing. David's face had been a picture of astonishment when she'd told him he must stir his porridge in a clockwise direction.

"Stir it clockwise? Why should I do that?"

"We always do in this house," she'd said. Her father had laughed. "David, you must do as Elizabeth asks. It's a family tradition started by my dear departed wife's mother! She always told her children that stirring their porridge that way would keep the Devil at bay! She was exceedingly superstitious, but it's a practice we've followed for years. Haven't we, Elizabeth?"

David had grimaced but did what he was bid. Then reluctantly he'd smiled. "Well, it's certainly unusual." She remembered she'd laughed and had told him, "Stirring it that way may well help you with your sermon!"

The rain the land needed so badly had finally come and with it a strong gusting wind making for a wet and chilly walk to church. But the faithful villagers, obedient to the call of the bells, were struggling in and to Elizabeth's joy she found the church almost full. As the bells gave their final peal an expectant silence fell, broken only by her father's melodious voice. "Rend your heart and not your garments, and turn unto the Lord your God and repenteth of evil: for He is gracious and merciful and slow to anger." Elizabeth glanced at her father. As he stood there in his chasuble reciting those timeless words he had a truly saintly air about him. David was standing at her father's elbow; she studied him. He wore a chasuble too, but unlike her father's plain and simple one, his was elaborately decorated and embellished with gold. She found David's ostentation irritating. Wasn't it arrogant to flaunt his opulence here in her father's church? And how could a young curate afford such expensive vestments? Everything about him displayed his wealth, from his elegant cassock to that expensive saddle and tack of his. And there was that silver ink stand too! A disturbing question came to her. From whom would a son get such riches if not from his father? And if David's father was his benefactor, then surely the riches would come from that plantation in Barbados; from the profits of slave labour! A coldness came over her; it was a sickening probability!

She closed her eyes, trying to forget the chasuble and concentrate on the service. Her father was reading the Gospel. It was a passage from St John she knew well. Its message was incorporated in those oft repeated words, "This is my commandment, that ye love one another, as I have loved you". To her it was the essence of Christian life and today it was the capstone of David's sermon; how God's people must clothe themselves with humility, freely forgive their transgressors and hold out the hand of love to their fellow men. "When we speak against others", David cautioned the congregation. "We implicitly sit in judgement, bringing to bear our worldly standards and usurping the authority of God! Such judgement is without mercy and love and is an anathema to God's loving grace." He spoke with an unexpected authority yet with evident compassion. It was a compelling sermon!

In the Rectory afterwards as they took sherry, Elizabeth saw her father pat David affectionately on the shoulder. "That was a fine sermon David, a very fine sermon. I've preached on that text so many times and I've tried to draw the lesson, but you made it seem so clear and relevant".

"Yes, David, if I may call you that." Squire Thomas interjected.

"It would be a great honour if you did, sir". Elizabeth saw him gave a fawning smile.

"Well, David, it was a good sermon," Squire Thomas continued. "You had the congregation hanging on your every word. Why," he laughed. "You even kept Colonel Travers awake!"

"That, David, is quite an achievement," her father chuckled. "He usually snores happily through mine!"

"Nonsense, father dear." Elizabeth wouldn't let her father belittle himself so. "I recall him getting quite agitated during one of your sermons. It was when you reminded us all that we should love one another as God loves us. D'you remember saying that now we are at peace with France, we should try to love the French too and remember that they too have lost many men in the war?"

"Oh! Yes." Her father was laughing now. "I kept him awake then didn't I? He was very upset. He spoke to me afterwards and asked if I was in the pay of the frogs, or was I becoming a papist? He even accused me of being a traitor and said people like me were undermining the will of our countrymen to stand up to the French! I think he'd quite forgotten that the Treaty of Paris had brought the war to an end! I can tell you, it was a long time before he could bring himself to shake my hand again!"

As they moved towards the dining room, Elizabeth heard the churchwarden's wife telling David she'd been deeply moved. "Thank you, Mrs Waring, you're most kind." David replied. It was only too clear that he was revelling in the acclaim bestowed upon him.

During lunch David remained the centre of attention and was kept busy answering the many questions about his family, his decision to come to England and his parish. Finally the meal was over and the guests offering their thanks before departing were keeping her father busy in the hall saying goodbye to them. As on the previous evening, Elizabeth found herself alone with David again. Having reflected on the events of that occasion, she had become convinced her father's early departure had been contrived! The reason seemed plain enough. Surely it was to allow David to propose! And now he had the same look about him! She decided she must seize the initiative.

"What a sermon that was, David. You've had us talking of nothing else. Surely you must have excelled yourself, or do you usually preach so well?"

David smiled. He was thrilled to hear such applause from her. He felt he must be modest. "Thank you Elizabeth, everyone's being far too generous! It happened to be a very good text and perhaps stirring that porridge as you told me to, really did help!"

Elizabeth laughed. "I doubt it, David. It's a sermon I shall remember for a long time."

David found himself looking into the very depths of her eyes. "If you were to remember it Elizabeth, it would make me very happy."

His look unsettled her. He seemed about to ask that question! She had to keep talking! "I tell you David, if you were to preach such a convincing, such a moving sermon on the evils of slavery, then I'm sure the whole diocese would sit up and take note. Couldn't you do that?"

David's face had changed. He looked out of sorts. "Must we always talk about slavery, Elizabeth?"

"I'm sorry," she said. "But try as I might, David, I can't forget the suffering of those poor people." She hesitated. "Could you not preach about the evils of slavery? Could you not support Mr Clarke? To please me?"

David cursed inwardly. This had been an opportunity he'd been hoping for, but once again he'd been thwarted! It was all too infuriating! And now she had this ridiculous request. What could he say? Somehow he'd have to prevaricate! He smiled encouragingly at her. "Well of course I'd like to, Elizabeth, but of course I'd have to seek my Vicar's approval. And it might be that he'd want Bishop Timothy's blessing before he'd agree!"

"Well, David dear, you must ask him. The church needs to show where it stands on this terrible evil!"

"Yes Elizabeth, you're right, it should, but it may be that the Bishop doesn't see its evil with quite the same clarity as you!"

"How d'you mean, David? Surely the church must see the wickedness of slavery! How can it tolerate the enslavement of black people for the enrichment of a few, a few who profess to be Christians?"

"Elizabeth, I agree with all you've said. I've discussed slavery with my vicar and when Bishop Timothy visited us a few weeks ago he asked about you and we talked about it then. Of course the Bishop and the Vicar agree it's an abominable evil. Bishop Timothy calls it a canker in our society. But when I suggested that the Church should make a stand against it the Bishop didn't seem keen. He said in any case it wasn't a problem relevant to the parish."

As he spoke, David could see the anger in Elizabeth's face. "Not relevant David! How can the Bishop say such a thing? Doesn't he know he has a huge slaving port in his diocese?" She shook her head ruefully. "He seemed so sympathetic when I told him about Nathaniel. I can't understand it!"

Her father's return interrupted their discussion. His cheerful expectant look vanished quickly as he saw the obvious tension between the two, which despite his efforts remained unabated; even his offer of more tea fell on deaf ears. Then Elizabeth fearing the return of rain and seeing the sun beginning to shine suggested that David should take the opportunity to leave. "David, you should hurry," Elizabeth said. "You've a long ride ahead of you and we'll have more rain later. I'll tell Miles to saddle your horse."

Seeing an opportunity to leave them alone once more, her father hastily interjected. "Don't ring for young Doris. She'll be busy helping Cook. I'll find Miles."

As her father disappeared Elizabeth began to regret her outburst! David had looked so upset! She had been fiercely critical of him and the church! "David, I'm sorry I've been so outspoken. If I've hurt you please forgive me."

"Elizabeth, there's nothing to forgive; I'm not hurt. But I do realise how deep and strong your hatred of slavery is." He paused. "I fear mine by comparison, is feeble and shallow. No, what you said didn't hurt me. It's made me admire and respect you all the more."

"David it's kind of you to say that."

"Elizabeth," he paused for a second. "Do you remember a few weeks ago when we were riding together I told you I'm only happy when in your presence?"

The memory of that day disturbed her; she'd been very curt. "Yes, David."

"You told me I was so much younger than you and that such thoughts were inappropriate."

"David, please forgive me, I seem to excel in saying hurtful things to you."

"Elizabeth dear, your friendship is important to me, very important and I'd never do anything to jeopardize it, but Elizabeth, for me friendship can never be enough. The truth is that as my respect and admiration for you has grown, so has my affection and devotion." He waited to see how she would react, but she gave no sign.

"Elizabeth dearest," he continued. "I've been a curate for nearly six years and soon I hope to have a living of my own. Like your father did, I shall need a wife to help me in my ministry, to support me in difficult times and share my joys. Elizabeth, everything about you tells me as a clergyman that you would make an ideal wife for me. Will you be mine? I would count myself among the luckiest and happiest of men if you were to marry me."

He stopped. He felt relieved, as if a heavy weight had been lifted from him. At last he'd asked her! But as he waited for her response anxiety began to return. Why was she so silent? Would she refuse him yet again? He reached for her hand. "Elizabeth dear, say you'll marry me!"

Still she said nothing. Then she smiled. "David dear, you flatter me greatly by telling me that I am the object of your admiration. I cannot think what I have done to warrant such esteem! You say you would never do anything to jeopardize our friendship and indeed nor would I." Desperately she searched for the right words to express her feelings. What she'd said so far was certainly true, but how should she continue? How could she tell him she couldn't love a man like him? A man of vanity, who surrounded himself with beautiful things, with expensive possessions, paid for by the sweat and suffering of his father's slaves. A man who, like the church could be hypocritical about slavery. She could never marry such a man, yet he was a friend, a friend who'd patiently opened her eyes to the horrors of slavery. How could she refuse him without hurting him?

"David I do value our friendship and have enjoyed your company but friendship cannot be the only basis for marriage. Oh! How can I refuse you, as refuse you I must, without hurting you? You've been patient and understanding and a truly good friend, but David dear I cannot be your wife. A wife must love her husband, but love requires a desire to submit one's own will if need be, to that of the one you love. David, I am driven by different desires from those that motivate you and my will cannot be submissive to yours. David, my feelings for you are those of friendship, not love and that is why I cannot marry you."

It was an age before he spoke. He looked disheartened, as if unable to believe what she'd said. He just stood there eyes downcast, looking like something discarded. Then he turned. "I'd better be going, if I'm to make Olverton by dark. Shall we be riding together on Friday?"

"Of course David, it would give me the greatest pleasure."

Then he was gone.

Chapter 20

A gentle Atlantic swell met the Mary Anne as she crossed the bar. After a long period in port, Jim always enjoyed that special moment when the ship was reunited with the open sea. On the Bonny she'd been a dead hulk but now she was alive again and the gentle creaking of her timbers seemed to express her joy at being free once more, free to wander the lonely sea, free to lead the life for which she'd been built. Jim welcomed the fresh salt air too; it would clear that all pervading smell that had enveloped them in that bug-infested river. Even the rain couldn't dampen his pleasure. Wouldn't it wash away the dust of that cursed place? The crew were in high spirits too. Only the slaves despaired. Crammed in the overcrowded slave decks, life was made even more unbearable by the motion and the sickness it induced.

But Jim's euphoria was short-lived for soon the wind began to fade and the sea took on that smooth oily look that becalmed sailors hate. He scanned the horizon and more in hope than conviction thought he could see patches of disturbed water ahead. Was that a zephyr? He knew he was mistaken. The Mary Anne slowly lost way and her sails hung limp.

"She won't answer the wheel, Cap'n; can't hold the course." Jim acknowledged the helmsman's report. He always felt irritated and frustrated when the wind died and left the ship helpless, but they were quite safe. They'd negotiated the bar and what current there was would take them along the coast clear of danger for the moment. He sighed. Things could be worse!

"Better take soundings every half hour," He told the young Third. Though they weren't going anywhere fast, it was as well to know if the bottom was shelving. Besides it was something to do, something to help pass the time until the wind came.

He struggled to control his impatience. All his life he'd had to submit to the wind. He'd had to understand it. If a Master knew what he was doing, the wind could be an ally and a friend. But you had to know its moods. Sometimes it could be a little too lively and at other times downright angry. Then it would rage and rant and would have to be treated with every respect until its anger had abated. But without the wind a mariner was impotent, a mere pawn at the mercy of the ceaseless tides. He fretted and bemoaned his luck. Knowing he had to do something to assuage his frustration he sat down and opened the boy's journal. There were two new drawings. The first showed the ship as she had been prepared for her long stay in Bonny with her yards removed and the matting roof covering her deck. It was entitled:

"Thatched Cottage at Bonny".

It made him grin. The next showed the Mary Anne cutting through the sea under full canvas. He studied it with increasing pleasure. It was full of detail and the proportions were good. He liked it. It would serve well as a sketch for a painting, a painting which would look good in his cabin. "I wonder if the boy can paint," he muttered. He was sure Elizabeth could, surely it was a thing all ladies like her could do. Well he couldn't ask her, but he might ask the boy sometime. He smiled to himself; the mere thought of Elizabeth made him feel happy. He saw the boy appear and hastily began to read his account of their arrival at Bonny, of the comical yet powerful figure of King Pepple and how the ship had been transformed by that thatched roof. Next he read about the events in the Tamar. It was a forthright and accurate account. He liked it; it could be useful when he compiled his own end of voyage report. The next page was headed:

"The burial of Jack Tanner"

He read – *"We were all shocked and greatly upset by the death of Jack Tanner. He had shown no signs of being unwell and when we found him dead in the sail room, even Mr Mackay could not tell us why he had died. He was the Sailmaker's mate and so it was fitting that the Sailmaker should make his canvas shroud and sew him up in it, putting the needle with the last thread through Jack's nose. This I learnt is a mariner's custom to make sure the man is really dead. The next morning we set off in the longboat with Jack's body to bury him on Yeji Island in Ju Ju Creek, where other Christians are buried. After a long pull we rounded the point and a low sandy island came into view. We beached the boat and set off with Jack's body to dig his grave. There were many crosses marking the graves of other men and when the Captain had selected a suitable spot we began to dig Jack's. The ground was very sandy so though it was easy work, we could only dig a shallow one. When all was ready the Captain read the Burial Service and after lowering poor Jack into the ground we shovelled the sand over him. We placed a wooden cross at the head of his grave and after saying our own goodbyes we left. I studied some of the other crosses as I walked back to the boat. One was very new, hardly older than poor Jack's. I went to see whose it was. It read "Captain Henry Wetherill Master of the Barque Tamar". I must admit I feel little sympathy for him, for surely he was responsible for everything that led to the uprising and all that killing. On the long pull back everyone seemed lost in his own thoughts and I felt a great sense of injustice, for while Jack had been given a proper Christian burial, the bodies of our two dead slaves had been quietly dropped overboard."*

Jim read the last sentence again. It could be his mother writing! It was the first time the boy had shown any emotion when writing about the slaves. To his surprise he found himself admiring him for it! While he himself accepted the miseries suffered by the slaves as an inevitable part of the trade he now plied, the memory of the uprising in the Tamar had made a deep impression on him. Never before had he been involved in such violence! While he secretly marvelled at the way he'd taken charge and quashed the rebellion, he could hear Elizabeth's voice as she sternly reminded him that those slaves weren't animals, that they were human beings! Had she known what had happened he was certain she'd accuse him of being too ready to kill! Yet if he had done nothing, the entire crew of the Tamar could now be dead! His hand involuntarily groped beneath his shirt for the bag of dust that hung around his neck. As always it comforted him. He hoped it would be a talisman; that it would bring her closer to him.

His thoughts were interrupted by the droning of the leadsman. He'd been calling "By the mark seven" for some time. But now and then he would call "By the deep six." The bottom was shelving but for the time being the ship was safe. "If only the wind would come," he muttered. But he'd had to wait until the first flush of pink in the western sky, before he could feel that unmistakable coolness on his cheek and see the t'gallants begin to tremble.

"Boy, look at them," he pointed happily at the sails. "They're eager to be off! We'll soon have the trade wind with us and then we can get clear of this damned coast."

As Jim had promised, the sails soon began to draw and the Mary Anne slowly picked up speed and settled onto her course. This part of the voyage, the Captain told Nathaniel, was called the middle passage; the middle of the three passages that made up the triangular trade, the first had taken them to the coast of Africa and the third would bring them home to Bristol. And on this, the middle passage the Captain went on "We shan't see any land until we reach the Caribbean, so we shall be using this to find our way." He held up the back staff. "Aye, we'll be taking the sun's altitude at noon each day." He laughed. "You should be quite good at it boy, by the time we see land again!"

"Thank you, sir." Nathaniel hated the wretched thing. Getting the arc's shadow in line with the sea horizon seen through the through the slit on the horizon vane was difficult enough on a calm day, but if there was a sea running and the ship was rolling it seemed almost impossible!

"Now, boy, you remember the noon sun sight gives us our latitude?" Nathaniel nodded. "Well," Jim went on, "Bonny is a little south of latitude five degrees North and our destination Montego Bay is at latitude seventeen degrees north or near enough. So for the time being we'll steer West by North to make ground to the North. Then, when our noon sight tells us our latitude is seventeen degrees north, we'll steer west. Then if we stay as best we can on latitude seventeen we should find Jamaica and Montego Bay without trouble. D'you understand?"

"Yes sir, I think so." Nathaniel hoped he did!

"Right then, boy, perhaps you should write something in your journal about how we plan to find Montego Bay."

Nathaniel had politely agreed, but he thought it would be difficult. Thankfully however it was time to go on watch and he put all thoughts of his journal behind him. The Chief Mate welcomed him with a grin. "Didn't I tell you, laddie, we'd soon be off? When I said His bloody Majesty would be back with the fifty slaves we wanted, you didn't believe me, did you?"

Though he'd said nothing at the time, Fred had been quite right. Nathaniel hadn't believed him. But it was true, for only a few days after that great flotilla of canoes had set off up river he'd seen them returning with King Pepple's canoe in the van. When they passed the Mary Anne, Nathaniel had seen that each canoe was full! And as they neared the beach, the air was rent by the sounding of horns and the beating of drums. The whole village, every man, woman and child, or so it appeared, was there to welcome their King and his canoes. At the time he had wondered whether the canoes had gone up river to collect a friendly tribe for some great feast. But Fred had assured him that the passengers were slaves. He'd been convinced that Fred was wrong! Surely the villagers wouldn't welcome slaves in such a rowdy way! But it became abundantly clear that it was he, not Fred, who'd been wrong, when the very next day canoes full of men and women bound hand and foot, began arriving alongside. Seeing those poor wretches made him wonder what violence had been inflicted on the villages upstream as King Pepple and his men came to seize all those fit enough to be sold as slaves. How, Nathaniel asked himself would the very young and the very old survive without them. But King Pepple's raid had provided all the slaves the Mary Anne needed and at last they had started on what he'd been told was the middle passage.

As the land slid below the horizon, the crew slipped into their routine. At daybreak the slaves would be released from their cramped quarters below and the males secured on deck. Only the women were left unshackled to prepare and distribute the food and water. Then Mr Mackay would conduct his cursory examination of them and enter his findings in the slave ledger. Then it was time to empty the latrine buckets and clean out the slave rooms. After the events in the Tamar neither Jim nor Fred felt at ease when the slaves were on deck. And besides stationing three or four hands armed with muskets on the quarter deck close to the mate on watch whenever the slaves were on deck, Jim insisted that no mate stood his watch alone. So it was decided that the Bo's'un would to keep watch with the Second Mate, the Gunner with the Third Mate and Nathaniel would continue to stand watch with the Chief Mate. And each armed sentry was to fire his musket every now and then to impress the slaves.

On the fourth day out it was Nathaniel's turn to supervise the hated task of cleaning the slave decks. He was armed with a pistol and his three men with cudgels as they went below taking the six young boy slaves with them. The young boys had by now been trained to do this filthy work. Jim and

Fred had reckoned they were easier to handle in the dark confined spaces, where Nathaniel and his compatriots could more easily be overpowered by the stronger, more determined adults. The boy slaves being keen to regain the precious fresh air above worked with a will and soon the latrine buckets had been hoisted through the narrow hatchway and returned full of sea water for scrubbing the decks. In the upper slave deck, their eyes quickly became accustomed to the half-light, but in the room below they could see nothing except by the feeble light of the lantern. As he climbed down into the blackness Nathaniel held his lantern high to give as much light as possible. The thick heavy stench hit him and he tried not to retch as he watched the young slaves cleaning up the mess where the latrine buckets had stood. At last the job was done but as he thankfully turned to follow the others towards the welcoming shaft of light, he heard a strange noise, a weird, eerie noise. What was it? It wasn't a rat. What could it be? There it was again! It was some sort of creature, he was certain! His flesh began to creep and he desperately wanted to flee to that shaft of light, but somehow he managed to control himself. He called one of the hands. "What's up Mister?" Came the reply. "Quiet," Nathaniel whispered. "Can you hear anything?" Neither spoke. Then it came again! Now he recognised it! It was a weak helpless moan. Nathaniel felt his hair bristle. "It's over there," he whispered. The moaning began again, weaker this time. "Send two slaves down with another lantern," he shouted up the hatch. The extra lantern gave him courage and gingerly he led his party towards the sound, but the faint glow of the lanterns revealed nothing. He heard the pitiful moan again, now very close. The dim outline of a shelf came into view, a shelf where the slaves would sleep. There was nothing there. He searched the one above with his hand there was nothing there either. Standing on the bottom shelf and steadying himself with the middle one he reached into the top one. The ship was rolling gently and as it did he sought a better grip, but to his horror his hand found hot, sweaty flesh. Hastily he snatched his hand away. Shaken, he pulled himself up again. There in the dim light of his lantern he saw a body!

"He's up here, he's sick, maybe he's dying," he cried. "We must get him on deck."

The slaves made no response. Clearly this unknown thing that made these awful noises frightened them.

"It's not a ghost. It's a man," Nathaniel shouted. Their stupidity and reluctance to help filled him with anger.

"It's a sick man, you wretches. He needs help." How he managed to rally them he never knew, but he did and the limp, stinking body was manhandled up through the hatches and into the sweet fresh air. The Surgeon was sent for, but when he came he said he could do nothing. The slave was one of the much feared lion men. He with the pointed teeth had lost his fight to live and that night they dropped his body into the hungry sea.

The demise of the lion man was the forerunner of a wave of deaths as the dreaded flux visited the "Mary Anne". Within three days, the flux had the ship firmly in its grip. Five more slaves had died, four men and a woman. And as soon as their bodies had been committed to the deep, new victims seemed eager to take their place. More ominously, one of the crew, Ted Williams, had also breathed his last and fear began to spread through the ship's company as they wondered who would be next. Bonny was only seven days behind them, yet already eight slaves had died and one of the crew had been struck down. The suddenness of its onslaught had shaken Jim; if the disease could not be contained soon the future seemed bleak. He had sent for Mr Mackay in the hope of hearing better news, but the reassurance he had hoped for had not been forthcoming. However they had agreed that any slave or any of the hands struck down by the flux would be kept on deck away from the others and be dosed with Mr Mackay's own special remedy.

He mulled over his calamity, his thoughts turning to Elizabeth. What would she say about these deaths? Would she hold him responsible? He was certain she would; and of course she was right. It was his ship and he was master. He thought of his last ship the Dolphin, and wished he was still working the Baltic trade. Wool and wine had never died on him! What would Elizabeth do in his position, he asked himself. He knew without even thinking! She would pray, she would ask her God to deliver them from this pestilence. And she would be certain he would answer! Should he do the same he wondered? But if he did would God listen to him? He wasn't sure that God had even heard of James Youle! He'd never been a religious man; never had he acknowledged God's existence! Well he said to himself, perhaps it's time I did. Perhaps it's time for me to admit that there is a God, the God who created this world and everything in it. He searched for the prayer book he had somehow always carried with him and thumbed through. But finding a suitable prayer was beyond him. How he wished Elizabeth was near to help him. He tried again. This time he found something that might be suitable. He read it through a second time and as he did so felt the presence of Elizabeth encouraging him! Now he knew what to do. He would assemble the crew at sunset each day and ask God to deliver them all from the flux.

Nathaniel remembered the call for the hands to lay aft. They came in their ragged clothes, looking more like desperadoes than men come to worship God, but they bared their heads and listened quietly as the Captain led them in prayer.

"In the time of King David," Jim read from the Prayer Book. "In thy wrath thou didst slay with the plague of pestilence three score and ten thousand and yet remembering thy mercy did spare the rest. Have pity on us miserable sinners, who are now visited with great sickness and mortality; that as thou didst then accept an atonement and didst command the destroying Angel to cease from punishing, so may it now please thee to withdraw from us this plague and grievous sickness, through Jesus Christ our Lord." The Amens rippled round the assembly. Then he recited the Lord's Prayer, closed his Prayer Book and dispersed the hands.

But their prayers went unanswered. Two more slaves died that night. But undeterred, Jim continued his prayers at sunset each day and mercifully two days later the flux seemed to lose its hold and there were no more deaths. Though relieved that the sick were showing signs of recovery, some asked if it really was God's doing. Others said their luck had changed because that Jonah, Ted Williams, who no one had liked, had died. But whatever the reason, all were thankful. Perhaps Mr Mackay had indeed found the right remedy. "Och! Aye," he'd been saying repeatedly of late. "Wash their mouths out with vinegar, twice a day and stop their victuals. That's the best cure."

With the North East trade wind blowing steadily the Mary Anne began to make good progress, often as much as a hundred miles a day and the crew now more relaxed, had settled into the daily routine. But the last time Nathaniel had stood watch, the Chief Officer hadn't been his normal cheerful self. He'd been quiet and listless. And when they'd seen that mackerel sky and those mare's tails he hadn't laughed or berated him when he'd said jokingly, "I see we've got some stallions' tales up there." Fred had merely grunted and in a quiet subdued voice had said, "We'll have strong winds tomorrow." As usual his forecast had been right and by noon the hands were up aloft furling the t'gallants as the wind backed westerly and blew with ever increasing force. Soon black rain clouds were climbing into the heavens "like rocks and towers" and threatening them with "squalls and showers." Again Nathaniel climbed the ratlines as the order came to furl the tops'ls. When the job was done and he was on the deck again, he saw the Chief Mate gesticulating at the slaves. He was leaning weakly against the mast, his lips moving though no one seemed to hear him. "What is it? What d'you want?" Nathaniel shouted as he went to him. Drawing closer he could see Fred's lips moving, but could hardly hear what he was saying. The Chief Mate repeated his order. This time Nathaniel caught his message. "Get the slaves below, before the squall hits us."

"You heard the Chief Mate," he shouted at the hands with an authority that surprised him. "Get the slaves below before the squall hits us." To his relief, he saw the Bo's'un and his men begin to hustle and bustle them below. When the deck was almost clear he went back to the Chief Mate. He looked exhausted, his head hanging low and his face a deathly grey, yet no one else seemed to have noticed how ill he looked! The Captain was busy choosing the best course for the helmsman to steer in the change of wind and everyone else was busy with the slaves.

"What's happened to him?" Nathaniel asked himself desperately. "Why is he so weak? Please, God," he prayed, "Please tell the destroying Angel not to punish Fred. He's a kind honest man, truly he is. Please don't take him from us." He touched the Chief Mate on the arm. "Fred", as he spoke he realised for the first time he'd called him Fred to his face! "We'd better get you down to your cabin." He saw Fred's eyes open and heard him whisper "Thank you, laddie."

Nathaniel rushed to tell the Captain what was happening and with a couple of the hands helped Fred below. Mr Mackay arrived. "Och!" he exclaimed. "He's got a nasty colour". He shook his head slowly from side to side. "A nasty colour indeed." He put his hand on Jim's forehead. "Aye and he's running a temperature too." He paused as if to underline the seriousness of it. "Mr Lugger, you'd better tell Mr Youle that his Chief Mate is not so well and that I'll be keeping him in his cot."

Not so well? The phrase repeated itself endlessly in his head as Nathaniel ran to tell the Captain. What did he mean? Did he have the flux or didn't he? Please God make it anything but the flux!

The Captain was clearly worried by the news. "Oh my God, not Mr Braithwaite." He'd said. "Ask Mr Mackay to come and see me as soon as he can. And while the Chief Mate's sick I'll stand his watch."

When the time came for Nathaniel to go on watch again, the storm was still raging and in the strong westerly wind the Mary Anne was laid over to starboard as she struggled to make headway through the heavy seas. Such conditions however no longer frightened Nathaniel. Indeed when standing watch with Fred in weather like this, he'd always enjoyed it. It was fun hanging onto the mast as the ship pitched and rolled and they dodged the spray that the wind hurled so contemptuously at them! When the spray caught one of them, the other would laugh. It was a stupid game, but it helped pass the watch! But now it was different! He stood his watch with the Captain and was uneasy in his presence. The Captain seldom spoke except to correct him or teach him something and though Nathaniel was thankful for all he'd taught him, there was no rapport between them. He felt the Captain saw him as an apprentice, not as a person, not as someone who needed friendship and understanding. And he always called him boy! How he hated that name. Didn't he realise he was no longer a boy? He worked as well, if not better than many of the hands, he'd taken charge of the yawl and the longboat, had helped restore order in the Tamar and took his turn cleaning the slave deck. Why couldn't he be given credit for that and be treated like a man? Why couldn't the Captain be more like Fred? Fred was fun to be with and he'd taught him so much just by talking with him. And Fred didn't call him boy! But Nathaniel laughed; you can't call a man laddie either! But laddie is a friendly name, boy isn't!

At midnight his watch over, Nathaniel went below and slipping out of his soaking clothes went to Fred's cabin. It was a little box of a place off the flat where they ate their meals and opposite where he slung his hammock. He tapped gently on the door, but there was no response. He waited a second or two and then slowly slid it back. "It's me, Nathaniel." He whispered. "How are you feeling? Are you any better?" Fred turned his head towards him, his face ashen and drawn. "Oh! Laddie it's you. I'm so thirsty, so thirsty." His voice trailed away.

"Haven't you any water?" Fred shook his head feebly. "Hasn't Mr Mackay left you any?" Nathaniel asked angrily. A wave of fury came over him as he searched hurriedly for a bowl and returned with it full of water.

"Here you are." He said as cheerfully as he could. "This'll help." Fred looked grateful, but was so weak that Nathaniel had to support his head while he drank. Swallowing seemed a great effort for him and when Fred had finished, he seemed utterly spent. "Thank you, laddie," he struggled for breath. "That damned Surgeon won't let me have water. All he does is give me that foul", he stopped mid-sentence and began to retch. Then in a scarcely audible voice he continued, "That foul vinegar". His whole frame shook as he spoke. "Vinegar, it makes me vomit." Exhausted, he lay back, his eyes closed. He was still.

Seeing Fred so ill had shaken Nathaniel. When he'd got him down to his cabin, he'd told himself that Fred only had a touch of the colic he used to have when he was a boy, but in his heart of hearts he'd known it was the bloody flux! But hadn't he asked God to spare Fred? Hadn't he told God Fred was a kind and honest man? He'd implored God not to take Fred away, to give him the strength to fight and conquer his sickness. But Fred was no better; in fact he was much worse! Like the Lion man, Fred seemed utterly worn out and waiting to slip quietly away!

Fred's sickness haunted Nathaniel and he couldn't sleep that night. In the morning, sick with tiredness he went on watch to find the weather had improved, the towering clouds had gone leaving a grey overcast sky and a kinder wind.

"Looks better this morning, boy." The Captain greeted him. "We'll soon have the tops'ls spread and we should be able to get the slaves up this afternoon".

And he had been right for after a few hours the sky had cleared and the sun was shining. During the storm it would have been foolhardy to open the hatch to the slave deck so the slaves had been kept below without food and water and Jim knew that conditions below would be atrocious. It was therefore vital that the slaves be brought up, watered and fed as soon as the weather allowed. And hardly had Nathaniel swallowed some warm soup after the end of his watch than the Captain decided now was the time. Since they were well out of sight of land Jim was sure the slaves would accept the futility of any desperate action, so while the armed sentries were to be posted as normal, he decided that there was no need to secure the slaves in their chains. When the hatch was finally opened the slaves pushed and elbowed their way up the ladder in their desperation to escape the fetid air below. They seemed not to notice the lack of chains but sank gratefully onto the deck gasping like landed fish as they sucked in the cool sweet air. It was clear they had suffered badly and a party of hands were sent to search for any still below. Three close to death were found and brought up. Mr Mackay examined them with all the others. Jim waited patiently his Surgeon to finish his inspection, conscious of having lost eight slaves already though they had barely left the coast of Africa! When he came to report his findings Mr Mackay brought bad news. Two of the three brought up would die, he had no doubt about that, and there were four others in a bad way. "So what do you propose to do to stop this bloody disease, Mr Mackay?" Mr Mackay gave a non-committal reply couched with as much optimism as he could manage.

"And what about the Chief Mate?" Jim asked in despair. Mr Mackay, unwilling to incur the Captain's wrath with more bad news, hesitated. "He was well enough when I last saw him."

"And when was that?" Jim enquired angrily.

"T'was last night, I must admit. I've been too busy with the slaves today."

"Humph," Jim growled. "Well you'd better go and see him now."

Mr Mackay looked offended, but did as he was bid. When he'd seen Mr Braithwaite the previous evening he'd thought he wouldn't last the night and his visit proved him right. He returned to the Captain and in a solemn voice said, "I have to inform you Mr Youle that Mr Braithwaite has given up the struggle, God rest his soul."

Though he'd expected bad news, Jim found it hard to believe that Fred was dead too! "Not Fred as well", he muttered. "Dear God, what have we done to deserve this?"

Mr Mackay waited a moment then spoke in deferential tone. "I've arranged for the Sailmaker to sew him up."

"Thank you, Mr Mackay." Jim shook his head sadly. "We'll bury him this evening."

Fred's death had come as a great shock to Jim. He'd never expected the flux to kill any of his mates, let alone his Chief Mate. How would he manage without him? He'd grown to value and respect him. And it had been abundantly clear the crew respected him too, even liked him. He'd worked the hands with that patient easy manner of his, which had contrasted with his own blunt, direct approach. How could Fred of all people let the flux beat him? He sighed. Poor fellow, was that the end of Fred Braithwaite? Or could St Peter be waiting for him as Elizabeth would have him believe?

At sunset with the ship's company gathered round him, Jim read the prayer he'd found asking God to free them from this pestilence. Then they cast Fred's body into the deep. With the loss of the Chief Mate an air of gloom and uncertainty had spread throughout the crew. They had grown to accept him as fair and trustworthy, one who they had liked better than "any of them others". It had been him, more than any other who had controlled their life and though they had had to obey him, he had been approachable, had been willing to listen to them and had understood their needs. Things would surely change without him, probably for the worse!

Nathaniel was bewildered by Fred's death. He remembered he'd been devastated at the loss of his Grandmother a few years ago, but strangely he'd never felt so close to her as he had to Fred. Fred had been like an understanding and indulgent uncle, an uncle who always had a chuckle or a smile on his face and one who had taught him so much! He felt lonely and vulnerable. He'd seen many slaves die and burying Jack Tanner on Yeji Island had upset him, but he knew he'd never forget the sight of that canvas shroud containing Fred's body disappearing into the sea. The finality of it was so awful. In that fleeting moment the enormity of his loss had struck him like a hammer blow! Fred was no more! Never again would he see him! He tried to recall the face of the man with whom he'd shared those long watches, but the picture was dim and blurred. Suddenly he was frightened his memory of Fred would fade. Would it? How could he forget the face of the man who'd made him laugh; who'd held him enthralled with stories of life at sea, who'd opened his eyes to the world around him? No, he'd never forget Fred. He fought back his tears. Never again would he hear that word "laddie" said in such a way that without thinking he'd known whether to expect a joke or words of encouragement or, on rare occasions a well-deserved rebuke. He would miss him more than anything and an aching void filled his heart. He was utterly miserable.

Chapter 21

After the death of the Chief Mate the weather relented. It seemed that Poseidon had exacted sufficient tribute and was now content for the Mary Anne to resume her westward passage, but there were many repairs to be made. The main t'gallant had been torn and had to be brought down for the Sailmaker's attention. The Bos'un had problems too. The sliding collar that attached the yard for the main tops'l to the mast was starting to break and more worryingly the starboard main shroud, which kept the mast vertical, was seen to be fraying. So as to transfer the tension onto the port shroud the ship had to be put about while it was repaired. And those hands not thus employed were put to the pumps, to shift the water that had found its way between the hull's creaking planks. Without the encouraging and patient leadership of their dead Chief Mate, Jim could see that there was muddle and a lack of co-ordination as young Jackson who he'd promoted from Second to Chief Mate tried to make his mark. Inwardly he sighed; he just had to hope that Jackson would manage. And he'd had to make young White, his new Second Mate. Now that he had no Third Mate, he'd told young White to transfer all his Third Mate's duties other than his watch-keeping to the boy. The boy had seemed greatly thrilled when he had told him and strangely he'd felt he'd make a better fist of his new duties than either of the other two.

Nathaniel was delighted that though in reality still an apprentice and required to go aloft to work the sails, he now had some of the responsibilities of a Third Mate. For nearly a week now he had been keeping watch with the Captain and had become used to the long periods of silence, punctuated only by a brief order, or some instruction on the duties of a mate. How he missed the anecdotes that had made his previous watches pass so quickly. Now life seemed so very different! And indeed so it was for the ship.

With the passing of the storm the deaths had miraculously stopped. Even those who had seemed certain to die were gradually restored to health and Mr Mackay's confidence in his "special treatment" grew by the day. But Nathaniel remembering Fred pleading so desperately for water and hating the vinegar wasn't so sure! He felt it was the Captain's decision to keep the slaves on deck both by day and night, when the weather allowed, that had made the difference. Good fresh air to replace the fetid conditions below, Jim had reasoned, would surely help.

The weather became ever more favourable and good fortune seemed to smile on the Mary Anne. As the sailing became easier, even the Captain seemed more relaxed. One evening as he and Nathaniel watched the sun dipping slowly in a scarlet sky, it was clear it would be a beautiful night. Nathaniel captivated by the changing sky, hardly heard the Captain when he spoke. "Sorry, sir, I didn't catch what you said."

"I said we'll need all the sail we can carry tonight. The wind will ease shortly." In his eagerness to please, Nathaniel strained his eyes in the twilight to check the sails. They all had a full belly. The Captain agreed, but added, "Nip for'ard and check the sprits'l, boy."

In the faint light of a pale crescent moon Nathaniel made his way for'ard, carefully stepping between the male slaves, who lay in long lines on the deck. For'ard of them were the female slaves. As usual they had been left unsecured and they spread over the deck haphazardly. Avoiding them was more of a problem, but reaching the Fo'c'sle he stood at the cathead to sight the sprits'l spread on the yard below the bowsprit. He saw it was filling well and stayed awhile to admire the curve of the sail and to listen to the sound of the bows thrusting through the gentle sea. Reluctantly he turned to go aft, but as he started he heard a strange sound. It sounded like a howl from an injured dog, but it couldn't be a dog and they'd killed the last pig two days ago. He crept quietly towards the lee bulwark. As he did the noise became louder. Was it a woman, a woman whimpering? Then he saw her, crushed beneath a man, whose white buttocks rose and fell in the moonlight.

What was he doing? Why was he hurting her? In his innocence he cried out, "What's going on?"

The white buttocks stopped and a savage-looking man tore himself from the woman and stood glaring at him. "F... off", he said. His voice was angry and even in the dim light he could see the anger in his face. As the figure approached Nathaniel took a step backwards. It was Taffy, Taffy

Hughes. Nathaniel heard himself saying "Sorry." Then Hughes laughed, his anger apparently gone. "Can't a fellow 'ave a little bit of girlie now and then? 'Ere go on 'elp yourself. I ain't one as wants to keep it all to 'iself!"

"No, no thank you. It's kind of you, but no thanks." Nathaniel stuttered. The poor black girl was sobbing quietly, though Nathaniel couldn't see how she'd been hurt, or even how he could help. But it was clear that his presence had saved her from Hughes. He felt he should stay near.

"Must go and check the sprits'l," he announced for Hughes' benefit.

"Aye Mr Lugger." Hughes spoke in a mocking tone. "You'll find it more interestin' than this black wench! Then he left, laughing. Nathaniel stayed for a moment or two to let his fear subside and then seeing that the girl had stopped crying and was being comforted by another woman, he quickly made his way aft. What he'd seen had disturbed him. He asked himself what more he could have done for the girl. He was still thinking about her when he reached the quarterdeck. At first the Captain was silent. Then his patience exhausted, he spoke. "What's up with you, boy. Tell me. How's the sail?"

"Fine", Nathaniel stammered. "Fine, sir."

For some reason the boy's reluctance to tell him about the sail made Jim suspicious. What's he mean fine? Is that all he can say? And why's he frightened?

"Fine," Jim repeated. "What d'you mean, boy?"

Nathaniel pulled himself together. "Well, it's filling nicely sir, very nicely."

"Humph," Jim grunted. "Well, what took you so long?"

"Nothing sir, nothing."

Jim was getting more suspicious. Something had happened and he wanted to know what it was. "What d'you mean nothing, boy?"

"Nothing sir, nothing honestly." Jim could sense he was trying to hide something.

"You were a long time, boy. Tell me what kept you?"

For a moment Nathaniel was silent. Then trying to sound confident he said, "Well sir, it was so peaceful up for'ard watching the sails, I'm afraid I lost all count of time."

The Captain didn't believe him. Nathaniel knew that. He ought to tell him all he'd seen, but he was too scared of the consequences. Hughes was a giant of a man and a bully. How could he tell him what he'd seen? And what had he'd seen? He wasn't sure he knew. Except that whatever it was that Hughes had done had made the slave girl whimper and sob.

"Well, boy", Jim realised the conversation was getting nowhere. "I hope you haven't been up to any mischief because if you have I'll find out."

Now frightened Nathaniel blurted out, "Oh! No sir. It wasn't me". No sooner had he said it than he knew it was a stupid thing to say.

"What d'you mean it wasn't you?" Jim's voice was more kindly now. "You'd better tell me all about it."

Nathaniel tried to remember how it all happened. "Well sir, I'd seen the sprits'l filling nicely and was coming back when I heard a strange noise. A noise like an injured dog. Well, I knew it couldn't be a dog so I went to see what it was. Then I found this girl slave with a man on top of her. He was.....", he paused.

"Go on, boy", Jim was eager to know who this man was and what he was doing.

"He was having a bit of girlie," Nathaniel continued. He'd worried that perhaps the Captain like him wouldn't know what this strange phrase meant, but it was quite clear he did!

"What! D'you mean he was f...ing the slave?"

"Well yes sir, I suppose so, sir." Nathaniel had heard that word so many times before; the hands seemed to use it all the time, but he'd never known it meant the same as having a bit of girlie, whatever that was!

"Who was it? No", Jim hesitated; it would be dangerous to involve the boy. "Don't tell me, I'll find out."

For the rest of the watch their conversation was stilted. Nathaniel, surprised that his interrogation had come to such an abrupt end, had no wish to disturb the Captain, now apparently deep in thought.

The next morning Jim sent in turn for the Bo's'un, the Carpenter, the Gunner and the Sailmaker to enquire whether they knew if any of the men had been getting at the women slaves. All four denied knowledge of such happenings, but on further questioning the Carpenter and the Sailmaker each said they had overheard one of the hands boasting that he'd laid one of the slaves. Both had said it was Taffy Hughes, the Welshman. Wasting no time, Jim had immediately sent for the Gunner.

"Mr Hoskins, it's that Welshman Hughes. He's the one who's been at the slaves." Jim told him. "Fetch him."

"Stand still 'ughes and show respect'." the Gunner ordered

"Hughes", the Captain said fiercely, "I've good reason to believe you've been gratifying yourself with the women slaves. What've you got to say for yourself"?"

"Gratifying meself? Gratifying meself"?" Hughes had an innocent look on his face. "Can't say as I 'ave or 'aven't since I dunno what you mean, Cap'n."

A flash of anger crossed Jim's face. "You know what I bloody well mean Hughes! You've been using them as whores. Admit it!"

"I ain't admittin' nothin'. But what if I 'ave? They'm only nigger wenches."

"I told you all before we left Bristol that I wouldn't allow the women slaves to be used for our personal satisfaction. The slaves are our cargo and we have to get them to Jamaica alive and well, so as to make a good profit. And you know as well as I do that we've already lost ten and I don't want to lose any more. They're our cargo and I won't have them used as whores." He paused; he wanted his warning to be understood. He also needed to simmer down, to control his breathing, he was so angry.

"I'm going to make an example of you, Hughes, and give you thirty lashes."

Hughes gave a contemptuous look but made no reply.

"Take him away, Mr Hoskins." He turned to his new Chief Mate. "Mr Jackson, he's to be flogged at the mainmast before all the ship's company and the slaves too. Let me know when you're ready."

With the crew and slaves assembled Hughes was brought forward, stripped to the waist and bound to the mast. The slaves seemed mystified but the crew were quiet and thoughtful; they knew what was about to happen. Seeing all was ready, Jim stepped forward and cleared his throat. "This man Hughes has been using one of the women slaves as a whore." A muffled titter came from one or two of the hands, but quickly died as Jim continued. "I warned you all before we left Bristol that I'd not tolerate such behaviour and I told you if I found any of the crew with a woman slave I'd have him flogged." He paused and turned his face towards the half-naked figure. "Hughes, by the authority invested in me in the Articles of Agreement to maintain order and discipline in this ship, I sentence you to receive thirty lashes from the cat o' nine tails." For a brief moment there was total silence, then it was broken by a curse and shout from Hughes. "I'll get that little bastard Lugger."

"Quiet, Hughes," Jim barked. Then he nodded to the Gunner. "Get on with it."

Nathaniel heard the leather thongs bite into the flesh and saw the blood flow. How he wondered, could Hughes stand such pain without so much as a groan? If it were him he'd screaming and pleading for mercy, but not Hughes! Nathaniel had to admire his courage, though Hughes deserved all he got. After all he'd caused that poor black girl great pain and distress.

After the last stroke had cut into Hughes' bleeding back Jim barked, "Cut him down" and turning on his heel, he left. Nathaniel watched as the Surgeon approached the limp body sprawled on the deck and began to wipe the blood from the lacerated back. Hughes began cursing again, but as the salt was rubbed into his wounds his swearing turned to screams of agony. Nathaniel turned to go and heard a quiet "Young sir". It was Bert. "You'll 'ave to watch Taffy. 'E's sworn to kill 'ee. Make sure you ain't alone with him ever!"

The Captain seemed worried that Taffy might attack him too, for when Nathaniel saw him next he called him over. "Boy, I didn't want you to be seen as a witness. That's why I didn't press you for an answer last night. I got all I needed from the Carpenter and the Sailmaker, but Hughes may think otherwise. So be on your guard with Hughes and don't ever be alone with him."

"Thank you, sir, I'll try." Nathaniel's voice betrayed his fears; he felt a marked man and Hughes' threat haunted him. He was very frightened and found it difficult to sleep and when he did his dreams revolved around the angry Welshman.

The crew seemed affected by Hughes' desire for vengeance too and even the weather seemed unforgiving as once again malevolent clouds began to gather. In no time the storm was upon them, but not before the slaves had been sent below and the sprits'l, t'gallants and tops'ls furled. The wind blew with ever increasing force

"She's still carrying too much canvas," Jim shouted. "Bo's'un can you hear me?" He saw the Bo's'un nod but the words he spoke were torn from his mouth by the howling wind. "Furl the main course," Jim yelled. He saw the Bo's'un nod again and begin to organise the hands.

In the failing light Nathaniel climbed to the main yard, the lowest of the three yards, from which the largest of all the sails, the main course was set. With his feet on the footrope and clinging to the yard, he felt his way slowly towards the outboard end. At last he was there ready to gather in the sail and waiting for familiar cry "Ready young sir?" But his heart froze; he heard a different voice, a Welsh voice, "'ello Mr young bloody sir, enjoyin' the view?" Nathaniel felt his throat run dry. It was Hughes! That giant of a man was on the main top, waving his knife and shouting "I'll teach you to keep your bloody mouth shut, you little bastard."

Dear God, he's going to knife me. Nathaniel was mesmerised by the blade that would rip into his tingling flesh. He daren't take his eyes off it. As he watched it he saw it was moving towards the foot rope. A message, a message clear and urgent flashed through his mind. "He's going to cut the foot rope so you'll fall overboard." Terrified he watched the knife slice through the rope and reacting automatically found himself spread-eagled on the yard, his eyes glued to the man who was going to kill him. In his frustration, Hughes cursed. Then with an ingratiating voice he shouted, "My, ain't the sea temptin'? I tell 'ee, young bloody sir, 'tain't long afore you'm 'avin a nice long swim!" He gave a murderous laugh. "That's if 'ee can." Hughes, now also spread-eagled on the yard, began pulling himself towards him. Nathaniel retreated as far as he could as Hughes inched ever closer. "Not long now eh! Young bloody sir," Hughes leered. Then raising the knife he struck. Nathaniel his senses at fever pitch reacted quickly and ducked. The knife flew past Nathaniel's ear and Hughes cursed savagely. Somehow Nathaniel managed to regain his balance before Hughes struck a second time. Again he missed! "Third time lucky eh, young bloody sir?" Sure his last moment had come Nathaniel braced himself for the fatal blow. Once again he saw Hughes raise his chest from the yard as he prepared to strike. Nathaniel shut his eyes as he submitted to the inevitable. The cold steel was about to pierce his body. But strangely he felt nothing, No searing pain ran through him. What had happened? Could death be so painless? Was he dead? If so, why could he hear that blood-curdling shriek? In abject terror he opened his eyes. Where was Hughes? Where was this fiend who wanted to kill him? Then he saw him, hanging upside down by a leg. Scarcely believing that he was still alive, Nathaniel watched him as he struggled to regain the yard. Then he saw the leg slip free and heard a scream followed by a dull, sickening thud as Hughes hit the bulwark and bounced into the water. For a moment he saw Hughes floundering in the water and as he disappeared beneath the surface a feeling of deliverance overcame him. The brute who had determined to kill him was gone, gone forever! He steadied himself and laughing and crying began to inch himself back to the mast. Never could he remember how he reached the safety of the maintop, but he would never forget that contorted, evil face with its wild eyes and broken teeth. That would haunt him for the rest of his life; this sweet life, which had so nearly been taken from him.

Chapter 22

For two days the Mary Anne ran before the wind with bare poles. All sails had been properly furled except the main course, but without a footrope no one had been able to go out onto the yard to furl it properly and once more as the wind tormented it the noise on deck was deafening. It was quieter below but even in the mate's quarters the air was stale and it was difficult to move about. And with the constant rolling and pitching it was too dangerous to keep the galley fire alight so the ship's company had to make do with hard tack. As for the slaves they'd not been fed since the storm hit them. Not that many of them would have wanted food anyway on those fetid slave decks. They would all be sick!

Nathaniel had found it impossible to write up the ship's log on deck. He'd brought it below and made his entries when he was off watch. Not that there was much to record. They'd not seen the sun for a couple of days now, so the Captain had been unable to find the noon latitude. Nor were they too sure what course they were making good, though to Nathaniel's surprise the log when they managed to stream it, showed that even with no sails set, the Mary Anne was averaging about three knots. Only the state of the weather had any factual basis, yet one entry was unarguably true. He remembered the relief he felt when on Thursday, May 27th he wrote, *"At about half past six in the evening William Gareth Hughes fell from the main course yard and was lost overboard"*. In the darkness no one had seen what had really happened and the Captain had accepted his story that without the footrope Hughes had fallen.

Almost as quickly as the storm had hit them it subsided leaving the Mary Anne becalmed with her sails hanging limp. Without a single cloud in the sky the burning golden disc overhead began to torment them as they searched for any sign of life in their hot and airless world; but they saw nothing, nothing on the sea, nothing in the sea and nothing above the sea. The Mary Anne was alone and at the mercy of that cruel sun. For five days they lay becalmed and though makeshift awnings were rigged and they drenched the slaves and themselves with pails of sea water, the daytime heat was unbearable.

Jim sent for the Chief Mate. "Mr Jackson, how's the water going?"

"Well sir, in this heat everyone's clamouring for water. I checked the casks this morning, only just over a quarter are full."

Jim shook his head ruefully "That's not looking good, Mr Jackson. We're not half way across yet!"

Mr Jackson nodded. "Aye, it's going to be tight sir. I've had the Carpenter fix a lock on the water store. I'll keep it locked and keep the key myself."

"Good! Keep the ration as it is now. We'll have to pray for rain and, Mr Jackson make sure you're ready to collect it when it comes."

Despite their prayers, no rain came, but on the evening of the fifth day Jim was sure he'd felt a zephyr and by midnight a light breeze from the North East had the Mary Anne moving westwards again. Eager now to sight land the crew were speculating about the day's run. Often it was depressingly small; the best lately had only been seventy-six miles. Such meagre figures did little to encourage the crew and they became depressed and dispirited.

It was the Bo's'un who thought of a way to lift their spirits. He'd always enjoyed a bet and it was he who suggested that they should wager their rum ration on the day's run. Knowing the Cap'n wouldn't tolerate gambling with their rum, the crew were sworn to secrecy and the Bo's'un's suggestion was accepted with enthusiasm. The betting began. The Captain became intrigued by the eagerness of the men waiting for the daily run to be entered in the log, but he supposed like him they were eager to sight land!

By the agreed rules the daily prize would be won by the one who correctly forecast the day's run as recorded in the ship's log or was within five miles of it. He would claim his winnings from the man whose bet was furthest from the winning number. For the first five days no one was near enough to win, but then Josh Matthews came within the magic five miles and won the first tot of the competition. When another hand won a day later, the Bo's'un was sure his luck had deserted him. His was the furthest of all from the correct figure so not only did he not win, but he had to give his tot away. Though he never had to forfeit his tot again, he resented the others winning. It had been his idea after all and he felt he had to win if only to show his greater experience. The next day after carefully considering the wind, he was sure the Mary Anne would do well. He placed his bet on a run of ninety-eight miles. None of the others were anywhere near his forecast and fearing he might lose his tot again, he decided to place another bet. In fact he placed a further two; one on ninety-three miles and another on one hundred and two.

It was a clear day and the Captain and Nathaniel had little difficulty shooting the sun. Nathaniel had become reasonably proficient and was pleased that his observed latitude was very close to the Captain's. Working out the "westing" was more difficult. The half-hourly log readings gave an estimate of the ship's speed through the water and resolving the course steered into its westerly and northerly components gave them a first estimate of their track. Then they had to allow for any current. That was difficult! The Captain had told him the Sailing Directions would indicate the direction of the current in this part of the ocean. Nathaniel had accepted that, but how fast it was going seemed to be anyone's guess. "We have to make our best estimate, boy." That was what the Captain had said as he ruminated over the problem. Finally he had made his decision and the noon position was entered in the log. "Boy," Jim shook his head ruefully, "that's only ninety-eight miles in the last twenty four hours. Well, he continued in a more cheerful tone, "I suppose it could be worse."

The news of the day's run reached the crew in no time. "Ninety-eight miles", they whispered to each other. When the Bo's'un heard it, he could hardly believe his ears. Ninety eight miles? He'd hit the jackpot. And not only had he bet the exact mileage, but he had two other bets within five miles of it! He'd won three times over! He'd won three men's rations and still had his own, four gills of that golden brown spirit, which took your breath away and burnt your throat as it went down. As a man of the sea he'd drunk plenty of rum in his time; he could carry his liquor well, but four gills of that raw spirit; well that was something!

Bert sounded a note of caution. "Bo, I'd leave a couple of tots for another day." But the Bo's'n only laughed. "I've drunk mor'n that afore now, Bert me boy," he grinned as the losers handed over his winnings. He gulped the first tot down and the second followed almost as quickly. They all drank their rum that way. It really didn't taste so good; it was the effect they wanted, even needed! It was that warm glowing feeling that started in the gut and spread through all the body that they needed! Then for a moment they'd feel relaxed without a care in the world!

The Bo's'un looked at the third tot and swung the pot to his lips, spilling a little on the way. He took a swig, followed by a deep breath; then with a bleary wink he tossed the rest into his mouth. They watched him as he struggled for breath. A voice rang out "Cor, Bo, I couldn't drink it that fast!" The Bo's'n half-smiled, half-leered at him and reached unsteadily for the fourth tot. "Steady Bo", another said quietly. "I'd leave that 'un till the dog watches if I was you."

"Bollocks!" The Bo's 'n's voice was slurred. "I could drink another bloody four." He grabbed the last tot, waved it at his audience and slopping some on the deck, gulped it down. Then with a great belch he staggered off.

"'ow did 'e get them figures, eh?" one of the hands asked. "Dunno 'ow 'e does it," another replied. "Must 'ave Lucifer 'iself on 'is side I reckon!"

Somehow, perhaps with Lucifer's help, the Bo's'un reached the tiny box that served as his cabin. Soon he was sprawled on his back, snoring heavily, but later when it was time to return to work, no one dared to shake him. All agreed, "Tes best to leave the old bugger alone!"

Worries about the shortage of water had pestered Jim as he ate his midday meal. If it didn't rain soon, he'd have to cut the ration again. But the previous night the sun had set in a pale sky and he'd remembered that old sailor's jingle. "If the sun goes pale to bed rain tomorrow it is said." Well it hadn't rained yet, but he had spotted clouds in the west and there could be rain.

"Mr Jackson," he called his new Chief Mate over. "I've a notion we might get some rain before the day is out. Have a word with the Bo's'n and get some canvas rigged to catch it."

Mr Jackson duly sent for the Bo's'n. But no Bo's'n appeared. Later the Sailmaker came aft. "Where's the Bo's'n?" Jim asked. The Sailmaker appeared uneasy. "He ain't well, Cap'n."

"Not well? What's wrong with him? He looked well enough this morning."

"Well, Cap'n, we just can't wake him."

Not liking what he was hearing, Jim sent for Mr Mackay and told him to look at the Bo's'n.

Later he appeared. "Mr Youle," he began in that mournful voice he kept for bad news. "I have to tell you that Mr Green is dead."

"Dead!" Jim repeated. "How can he be dead? I was speaking to him only an hour or two ago. What's happened?"

"Och! Tis the drink. He's smellin' of rum somethin' awful. Choked on his own vomit, that's what did for 'im. He's a terrible sight, terrible, terrible!" Mr Mackay shook his head. "Tis the devil's work."

Devil's work or not, Jim was determined to find out what had happened. The Bo's'n must have had a skinful. One tot of rum wouldn't have made a man of his experience so drunk. He sent for the Chief Mate, the Gunner, the Carpenter and the Cook in turn. But no one could throw any light on the Bo's 'n's death. Yes, they all agreed it was probably the rum that made him spew up and choke, but no one could understand why his tot should have made him so drunk. No, as far as anyone knew, he'd only drunk his own tot. His death was as much a mystery to them as it was to him. No one mentioned the betting and the use of their rum as a wager, but the betting stopped and soon it became apparent that the hands had lost interest in the ship's daily run!

The loss of the Bo's'n, with his knowledge of the rigging and his ability to get the crew working even in the most atrocious conditions was a great blow. After his body had been committed to the deep, Jim asked Mr Jackson who he thought should replace Mr Green as Bo's'n. "I've no hesitation in suggesting Bert Tyacke", he replied. Jim agreed. He would have made Tyacke the Bo's'un anyway, but it was always good to let the mates think he was taking their advice! "He's the obvious man. He's a good seaman and knows his job. The hands will respect him too. Tell him I want to see him."

Later that day Jim told the assembled ship's company that Mr Tyacke was to be Bo's'n, and the hands seemed to accept the news well. Nathaniel was overjoyed. "Mr Tyacke", he said. "I'm so pleased. I'm sure you'll do a marvellous job."

"I hopes you'm right young sir," Bert replied. "Never saw meself as anythin' other than a deck'and. That's what I've bin all me life and never wanted to be anythin' else. But the Cap'n said no one else could do the job and I 'ad to take it. So 'ere I am Mr bloody Bo's'n Tyacke." He laughed self-consciously. "Fancy you a'callin' me Mister!"

Nathaniel laughed too. "The Captain's right, you know Bert. You're by far the best seaman on board. And now I have to call you Mr Tyacke!"

"If 'ee does that, Mr Lugger", Bert said with a grin, "I'll be sendin' 'ee out on them yards to mend all they broken foot ropes!"

Chapter 23

"Look sir, look, over there", Nathaniel cried. "Can you see those birds?" He could see a wavering black line a few feet above the water racing towards them. As it drew near individual birds could be seen, about twenty of them. Suddenly they broke formation and climbed into the sky.

"Ah!" Jim had his telescope on them. "They're boobies. That's a good sign. Land can't be far now."

These were the first birds they'd seen for weeks. Nathaniel was captivated by them. He pointed them out to the men nearby and soon everyone, slaves and all, were peering skywards to watch these welcome visitors. Nathaniel studied them intently, admiring their effortless yet purposeful flight. He saw one of them fold its wings and drop like a stone into the sea, piercing the surface like an arrow. Soon others followed throwing up great plumes of water as they plummeted into the depths. He waited expectantly for them to surface with their catch but he only saw them flying away low and fast until once more they climbed into the heights for yet more spectacular dives.

A masthead lookout was soon posted and all waited impatiently for the traditional cry that ended a long ocean passage. It wasn't long coming. "Land ho!" shouted the lookout. "Land fine on the port bow."

"That's good, boy." The Captain looked pleased. "We'd best get up there and have a look ourselves." Climbing the ratlines together, Nathaniel was impressed by the Captain's agility and in a moment they were at the foretop studying a faint grey conical shape.

"It's land right enough boy. About twelve miles off, I'd say. Could be Barbados." He surveyed the land carefully through his telescope. "Yes, it must be Barbados," he muttered. "Well, we'll soon know."

As they neared the land and it grew larger, Jim became more certain it was Barbados, the most easterly of all the West Indian islands. Now he could relax. No longer need he worry about his position and whether the water would last. Soon he could put in at Barbados, or indeed whatever the island was, for water and victuals. He sighed inwardly. What a treat it'll be to have plenty of fresh water and some good meat and vegetables.

Later that day the "Mary Anne" anchored in Carlisle Bay, a short distance from the beach and Nathaniel was making endless trips in the longboat refilling the water casks, while boats from the shore, laden with pigs and chicken, bananas, coconuts, yams and weird green vegetables were besieging the ship in an effort to sell their wares.

Well laden with victuals and water the Mary Anne weighed anchor two days later and set course for the channel between the islands of St Lucia and St Vincent which led into the Caribbean Sea. With a following wind she made good progress along the coast of Hispaniola and when Cape Les Irois was abeam she bore away to port to sail along the northern coast of Jamaica, and finally to her destination, Montego Bay.

It was in the Caribbean that Nathaniel saw a change coming over the Captain. With easy winds and plenty of landmarks to guide them, all the cares and worries of the past few months seemed to have slipped from his shoulders and he became more approachable. He spoke about his time as an apprentice and in the Dolphin and took great pains to involve him in the navigation, pointing out everything of interest. As their rapport grew Nathaniel began to feel an unexpected sympathy for this gruff, silent man who had that uncanny ability to foresee dangers and hazards before they arose. He realised he hardly knew his Captain and was sure none of the mates did either. Yet it was to this silent gruff man that they all looked for guidance when perils beset them. Now their watches no longer passed in silence and on one glorious day, when the sun shone on a lazy blue sea and the wind was driving them along the tree-clad coast of Jamaica, Nathaniel asked him what would happen to the slaves, when they got to Montego Bay?

"Well, boy, I have to visit the local agent for further instructions."

"What sort of instructions?" The answer hadn't satisfied Nathaniel.

"Well, we left Bonny later than I'd hoped and we've had a slow passage. So it's likely we'll arrive after the sugar harvest is over. That'll mean there won't be much of demand for slaves."

"D'you mean they won't want our slaves?" Nathaniel couldn't believe what he was hearing.

"Oh! They'll want some that's for sure."

"But we mightn't sell them all?"

"Well perhaps not all, boy. But one thing's certain we won't get the best prices."

"Well sir, what'll happen to the ones we can't sell? Will we have to wait for the next harvest? We might have to wait for months, mightn't we?"

"Oh! I expect we'll sell most of them, but we'll probably have to take the rest to another port."

"What other port?"

"It's hard to say. Cuba maybe, they always need labour for their silver mines and then there's the American Colonies. We'll have to wait and see. The Agent'll have some ideas."

The steady purposeful passage among the islands was restful and indeed enjoyable to all and for most of the day Jim sat on deck enjoying the view and taking the opportunity to read the boy's journal, a task he'd overlooked during his recent trials and tribulations. He turned the pages and came to the heading:

The Bloody Flux

This silent killer is haunting us. No one can see it coming, nor knows why it kills nor how it chooses its victims. Though we, the crew of the "Mary Anne", all pretend that only the slaves will die, we are all frightened. I am and I can tell the others are too, from the look on their faces and their unguarded talk. I think we were all pleased when the Captain began to pray each day at sunset to God to ask for deliverance. I know I was! He asked God to command the destroying Angel to cease from punishing us and it seemed that He did since the plague left us. Oh how we thanked God, or did we? But some days later the silent killer struck again killing more slaves and this time our respected Chief Officer, Mr Fred Braithwaite who had become like an uncle to me, became sick of the flux and he too died. Why, why

*did God allow him to die? Was he chosen because we are
slavers? Or was it because we hadn't thanked him for our
deliverance? Mr Braithwaite was a kind, honest man,
who didn't deserve to die. If he had to die, what hope is
there for us?*

Jim put the journal down. It was a powerful piece of writing. Maybe
the boy had a point! He too had wondered why Fred had been singled out.
He sighed. He'd never known much about God, never had much time for
him, yet when the flux had them in its grip he'd called on him for help
and his prayer had been answered! He like all of them, had been greatly
relieved, but had he really thanked God? Well, perhaps he hadn't and
perhaps that was why the flux had returned! Was that God's doing too? Was
he punishing them because they traded in slaves? Was the slave trade really
sinful? Well if it was men had been buying and selling slaves for centuries,
as far as he knew ever since God had created this world! Yet somehow he
knew he couldn't defend the trade before God – that was of course if he
believed in him, which he assured himself he didn't. Yet he couldn't deny
it, the boy's writing had unsettled him. It was almost as if Elizabeth herself
had written it! He shook his head to clear his mind determined to forget
the boy's comments. Picking up the journal he read on. But his reading
was automatic and he remembered none of it. The message he believed
Elizabeth had sent him through her son's writing troubled him. Hastily
he scratched his signature on the last page. It was time to clear this myth
about God from his mind. He got up and busied himself checking the ship's
position.

Nathaniel had been worried that his writing about the flux might have
drawn a caustic comment from the Captain and was relieved to find that
he had made no such remark. He had merely signed it! Knowing that he
would be busy once they had anchored in Montego Bay he went below to
make a further entry in his journal.

Wednesday May 11ᵗʰ, 1772
*For the last two days we have been sailing in gentle
winds along the north coast of Jamaica and tomorrow
we expect to arrive at Montego Bay, where we hope to
land and sell all our slaves. To make them look fit and*

healthy for the auction Mr Mackay has ordered that they be given extra water and victuals, and made to take exercise. One of the hands has been playing the fiddle for them and they seem to have been happy dancing in their strange way. The slaves have also been rubbed down with oil, so that their black skins shine like ebony!

I must admit to being somewhat anxious when we left the coast of Africa seventy- two days ago and sailed into the unknown! The Captain says this has been a very slow passage with two storms and a becalming and we were all grateful when we sighted Barbados. Since then our sailing has been easy. Now that we have almost reached our destination, I feel a great sense of achievement in being part of the crew of the Mary Anne and making a safe passage across the ocean. It has fulfilled my long-held wish to go to sea! Yet, on reflection it has been a sombre experience. When I joined I had little idea of what lay ahead of me and I certainly never thought anyone would die. But having checked the ship's log I find that five of the crew, including Mr Braithwaite our Chief Mate, and Mr Green, the Bo's'un, have died as have seventeen of the slaves. He put his quill down. He could write no more. The memory of Fred's death still upset him.

The next day as Jim had predicted, the "Mary Anne" arrived in Montego Bay and as soon as she had anchored Jim was in the longboat heading for shore. Landing at the quay he walked along the track leading to the little township. The town seemed deserted, but he found a black man who pointed him towards a single storey wooden building bleached by the sun. Above its covered veranda was a painted board, "Messrs Wood and Nicholas - Attorneys". He climbed the steps and using the brightly polished brass knocker knocked on the door. A young black girl appeared. She smiled respectfully, enquired the purpose of his visit and ushered him into the presence of a wizened, balding old man, whose straggly grey sideburns met in a moustache above pale thin lips.

"Good morning. I'm Captain James Youle, Master of the "Mary Anne"."

"Ah! The "Mary Anne"." We've been expecting you this last month. I'm Ebenezer Wood. Please sit down, Cap'n. Would you like some tea?"

Over tea and cakes they got down to business. Yes, Mr Wood would arrange the sale, perhaps in two lots over three weeks; he'd take advice from the auctioneers. No, they hadn't had a shipment for about five weeks and the last lot had sold well. Yes, the sugar harvest was almost finished and that might affect prices, but the planters had been short of labour this year and he thought they'd buy most if not all.

"Good." Jim looked happier. "So Mr Wood, you think they'll sell alright?"

"Cap'n, I can't promise they'll all sell. We'll have to wait and see."

"Well, if they don't all sell, where's the best place for me to take them?"

Ebenezer Wood sighed. "That's a difficult question. Perhaps Annapolis in the Colonies would be best. But there's also Cuba. I hear they're short of slaves. But let's cross that bridge when we come to it eh? We'll do our best to sell them here!"

The subject changed to victuals and water for the ship and the cargo they would load for the homeward passage. Then Jim rose. "Well thank you for your help, Mr Wood. I'd like to be sailing for Bristol in three or four weeks' time!" Ebenezer Wood nodded. "Well, we'll do what we can Cap'n. I'll ask the auctioneer to come and see you tomorrow."

Jim moved towards the door. Then he turned. "One last question before I go, Mr Wood. I'm wondering is there a goldsmith in the town?" Ebenezer Wood gave him a quizzical look. "Yes Cap'n. I'll get my boy to take you to his workshop."

"Toby," he shouted. "Show Cap'n Youle where the goldsmith has his shop."

Jim thanked him and followed the black man until he saw a small wooden house with a board over the door. It read "Thos Bishop Jeweller and Goldsmith." He thanked his guide and pushing open the door saw a bent, bespectacled man wearing a leather apron appear from a back room.

"Mr Bishop?" He enquired.

"Aye. Bishop's the name sir. Pray what can I do for you?"

Jim hesitated, he'd never set foot in a jeweller's shop before. He felt nervous!

"D'you make rings, Mr Bishop? Gold ones?"

The jeweller looked surprised. "Yes, sir, that I do. Been making gold rings and jewellery all my life. That's my business, sir." He smiled reassuringly at his strange, nervous visitor. "Pray sir, what did you have in mind? A ring for your little finger with the family crest on it perhaps?"

"No, no. It's not for me!" Jim felt the blood rushing to his face. He coughed and put his hand to his mouth to hide his embarrassment. "It's a... it's a wedding ring I'm wanting."

"Getting married are you, sir?" Mr Bishop smiled respectfully.

Now embarrassed, Jim grunted his assent.

"May I offer you my congratulations, sir?" Mr Bishop gave a deferential cough "Is she by any chance a local lady?"

"No, no, Mr Bishop. You wouldn't know her," Jim muttered hastily. "Now I've got some dust here, from the Gold Coast." He pulled at the string round his neck and produced a little bag. Placing it on the table he undid its fastenings. The goldsmith looked intrigued!

"There's four ounces of best quality gold there," Jim said proudly. "I'd like you to make it from that."

As he studied the dust Mr Bishop massaged his chin.

"Well sir," he said eyeing his customer closely. "I've never been asked such a thing before. It's the custom for me to supply the gold!"

"Well, I dare say I'll find someone else to make it for me." Vexed, Jim turned to go.

"Wait, wait sir! You must excuse me. It's a request I've never had before. I was taken aback, you must understand."

"Right then," Jim's anger began to leave him. "Will you make it for me?"

"Yes, yes of course sir."

Now more relaxed Jim asked him if four ounces would be enough.

Mr Bishop, now thoroughly intrigued, smiled. "That depends, sir on the size and shape you want." He reached for his jeweller's scales. "Perhaps as a start we should weigh the dust."

Jim watched the goldsmith carefully pour the dust into the dish and build up the weights on the other arm. He tried the same weight two or maybe three times before shaking his head. "Sir, please excuse me." Mr Bishop hesitated. "I don't know your name."

"It's Youle, Mr Bishop. Captain James Youle."

"Well Captain Youle, if you look at the scales you'll see there aren't quite four ounces of dust."

Jim nodded. "Those pesky factors on the Gold Coast have cheated me, eh? How much is there then?" Mr Bishop adjusted the weights to get a balance, then counted them. "That's three and a half ounces, sir and nine pennyweights."

"Well, what's that mean, sir?"

"Well Captain Youle you're one pennyweight short of four ounces."

Jim grunted "Damned thieves."

"But don't worry, sir, you've plenty enough for a ring."

After much discussion it was finally agreed that Mr Bishop would make the ring from two ounces and nine pennyweights and would keep the remaining ten pennyweights for his labours.

Jim seemed happy with the bargain, but had one last question.

"When will it be ready?"

"I shall have it ready for you in a week's time, Captain Youle. I trust you're not sailing before then?"

"That'll be fine, Mr Bishop. I shan't be sailing for about a fortnight. I'll see you a week today."

"Right then, Captain Youle but before you go, may I ask, do you wish the ring to be engraved at all?"

Jim looked puzzled. "Surely", he thought, "Wedding rings are just plain gold bands."

Mr Bishop rescued him. "Captain Youle, some husbands like to have their initials and that of their lady wife engraved on the inside of the ring. Had you considered that sir? Perhaps you'd like to think about it."

"Oh thank you, Mr Bishop, thank you for reminding me," Jim wished to hide his ignorance about marital affairs. "I'd quite forgotten about that. Yes, yes I'd like that. My initials are JY and those of my betrothed are EL."

"Well, thank you, Captain Youle. JY and EL eh! They'll look very nice, very nice indeed!"

"Well Mr Bishop," Jim gave a sigh of relief. "I'll leave it to you." Thankfully he donned his hat and left. Never had he thought it would be so difficult to buy a wedding ring, but he'd done it. A glow of happiness and satisfaction spread over him as he stepped out for the longboat. He felt quite light-headed.

At Mr Wood's behest, the agent and one of the auctioneers boarded the Mary Anne the next day to inspect her cargo of slaves. They had all been fed and washed and their skins, having been freshly rubbed with palm oil, shone like jet. Jim had been delighted to see them looking so well, but the auctioneer, a self-important little man, seemed unimpressed. "I've seen worse", he said as he was leaving, "I suppose one might say they're in tolerable shape." He waited for his verdict to be received. Then with a sigh he continued, "Slaves don't come like they did when I first started selling. Great big strong niggers they were then." He shook his head sadly. "The best get shipped to the American colonies these days. But now we have to make do with what we can get." He shrugged his shoulders. "Take my advice Cap'n feed 'em up and have the men shaved and trim their hair, you know same as you'd groom a horse you want to sell. The customers like 'em looking clean and neat."

This pompous little man irritated Jim, but he would be selling the slaves, so he knew he had to tolerate him. "When d'you expect to be having the sale?"

"The first will be a week on Wednesday. We'll have the second a week later. Two auctions should do the trick."

"And the price? How d'you think we'll do?"

The auctioneer shook his head. "'Fraid it's late in the season. The harvest's finished. Prices will be low. Can't say mor'n that, Cap'n."

Later Jim received a copy of the handbill:

FOR SALE AT PUBLIC AUCTION ON WEDNESDAY MAY 25th 1772

At ten o'clock in our fine new sale room in the square

One hundred and forty strong, healthy male slaves and ten young females of child-bearing age. All newly arrived from the Slave Coast in the "Mary Anne", now anchored in the bay. Also for sale at eleven o'clock the well known mare "Highflyer" and her new colt "Black Star" and four geldings and at 12 o'clock or thereabouts fine rice, paddy, items of good furniture, books, bales of cotton cloth, muslins, ribbons, needles &c, &c.

Chapter 24

For days after David had left, her father had been fulsome in his praise for him, what an excellent sermon he'd preached, how he was wasted in a small country parish, what fine prospects he had and what a thoroughly nice young man he was! At breakfast on the Friday, he'd enquired whether she and David would be riding together that afternoon. When she'd replied in the affirmative, he'd seemed delighted, almost relieved!

"Father," she'd chided him, "you've been talking about David all week. It's almost as if he were your son!"

"Have I, Elizabeth?"

"Tell me, Father, why has David become so important to you?"

He shrugged his shoulders. "Important? Well I suppose I've grown fond of him and of course I'd like him to do well in the church and have a happy life."

She saw again that almost imperceptible wink her father had given David as they'd joined her after dinner the previous Saturday. They'd been discussing her, hadn't they?

"Father, you know David has asked me to marry him?"

"Yes, my dear." Her father's face brightened. "He asked my permission to do so and I readily agreed. He'll make a good husband and he'll give you a home and security." He waited for her to reply, but she remained silent. "Tell me, my dear, what was your answer?"

"I refused him."

"Oh my dear, that saddens me. I do worry about you and what will happen to you when I die, as die I must. Nothing would give me greater pleasure that to see you married to a good man, who'll provide for you when I'm gone. Perhaps, when you've known him a little longer and have thought about your future, you'll think again? In the meantime, I suppose I must be thankful that you haven't broken with him."

"No, Father, we're still friends."

And indeed David and Elizabeth did continue to ride together, but as the weeks passed he never repeated his desire to make her his wife, though her father continued to worry about her future and would often ask whether she'd changed her mind. However her answer was always the same. Like her hatred of slavery, it would never change!

Though the euphoria of meeting Thomas Clarke had begun to fade, she never forgot what he'd said. Yet, as she asked herself so often, what could she do to help his campaign here in Hanbury, where no one had ever seen a slave! How could she tell them about the evils of slavery? If only David would, from the pulpit! They would surely listen to him! In her frustration she had busied herself in the parish. Helping others had always helped her to forget her own troubles.

It was the anniversary of her mother's death and she had gone to tidy up the grave and lay a fresh posy of flowers beneath the inscription she knew so well.

> "SACRED TO THE MEMORY OF ANNE MARION LUNT
> WHO DEPARTED THIS LIFE OCTOBER IX, A.D. M.DCC.LXX
> BELOVED WIFE OF GEORGE AND MOTHER OF ELIZABETH
> MAY SHE REST IN PEACE"

Having arranged the flowers, she tackled the undergrowth in the long-neglected grave next door that threatened to engulf her mother's. It had been difficult enough to clear the brambles, but a hawthorn sapling had taken root at the very base of the headstone and as she struggled to pull it up, she heard a strange whisper. At first she couldn't make out from whence it came, or what it said. Then it came again, "Excuse me, ma'am." Turning she found herself looking into the large brown eyes of a young woman. She had a small black child at her side and was holding out a hand. "Please ma'am, could you spare a little food and water for us? We've had nothing all day."

"Oh! You poor things," Elizabeth exclaimed as she took the child in her arms. "Come with me and I'll find you something." As she led the way, she sat the little tot on her hip and felt it nestle against her body. She hadn't carried a child like that for years, not since Nathaniel was a little boy. It felt so good and the little one seemed to trust her implicitly! "Poor little thing, it's absolutely dog-tired," she murmured. She looked again at its little face framed by those dark tight curls. "Goodness, it's asleep already," she said to the child's mother. They hurried to the Rectory and soon were in the kitchen. "Mrs Jackson, Mrs Jackson," she cried. "Fetch some bread and milk. This poor girl and her child are starving. Oh! And butter and cheese too, there's a dear. She looked at the little mite's mother. "Or would you prefer jam? Bring some jam too, Mrs Jackson," she shouted at the retiring figure. "Bring the raspberry or rhubarb or whatever you can find, but hurry."

Suddenly she felt foolish; the girl hadn't come to tea. She was clearly so hungry she'd eat anything! She must be in some sort of trouble, she thought, why else would she be on the road? She studied the girl more closely. She wasn't white, but nonetheless she had a fair skin, perhaps a little tawny. Yet the child with her was as black as coal! It was very odd! Then she noticed the red weal below the girl's left eye. It looked raw and angry. She wondered what had happened. Then a thought struck her. Could she be an escaped slave? Had she run away from her master? Was that why she was so reticent? She'd not spoken a word since that first plea for food! She'd just followed her into the Rectory and now sat there looking frightened.

At last the girl spoke. "You won't send us back, will you, ma'am?" The fear in her voice was unmistakable. "No, my dear, you're safe with us," she heard herself saying. Then she too felt frightened. All of a sudden she knew she'd come face to face with slavery! She must be calm, she told herself. She must gain the girl's confidence. She had to find out how she could help, yet instinctively she knew this was not the time for questions. She rocked the dear mite sleeping so peacefully on her lap and looked anxiously at its mother and asked her what she called the child, but she made no reply. She gave the girl an encouraging smile, but as she did she saw the girl's head fall forward. She too was asleep!

The rattle of the larder door told her Mrs Jackson was returning. "I've brought......," she started to say, but Elizabeth cut her off. "Sh! They're both dead to the world," she whispered. "Be a dear and get a bed ready in the little spare room. I'll bring them up in a minute or two."

Mrs Jackson scurried off, calling for Molly to help her, while Elizabeth was left to contemplate her unexpected guests. The child looked so peaceful. Was it a boy or a girl? She really couldn't tell. It had a round face with full lips and such woolly, crinkly black hair! She glanced at the girl. She supposed she was its mother! Unlike the child she had a fair complexion and her hair, drawn loosely into a bun at the nape of her neck, was straight and silky. She wore a dark blue gown open to the waist revealing a lighter blue underskirt. Though her clothes were creased and dusty and the hem of her gown was torn, they were well made and of good quality! They were certainly not the clothes one would expect a slave to wear! Perhaps she wasn't a slave after all. Could she just be a servant girl employed by some rich merchant? But the child? It was so black; surely it must be the child of a slave!

She saw the girl lift her head and her eyes opened. They were full of fear! The girl gave an involuntary cry, then seeing her child, her face relaxed.

Elizabeth did her best to reassure her. "You're safe now. There's no need to worry!"

The girl gave a hesitant smile, but said nothing.

"Tell me, my dear, what's the boy's name?"

"She's a girl, ma'am," she gave a little chuckle. "I call her Alice."

"Oh Alice," Elizabeth looked down at the sleeping child she held in her arms. "So you're a lovely little girl. And you're her mother?"

The girl smiled, she seemed less frightened now. "Yes, I'm her mother. She's all I have."

The sound of footsteps in the hall announced the return of Mrs Jackson. "The bed's all ready, ma'am."

"Thank you Mrs Jackson. I'll send Molly down to bring up the tray." Then turning to the girl she said, "My dear, you look absolutely exhausted. The best place for you and Alice is bed. Can you manage to come with me? I'll carry Alice, if you'll let me."

"Oh thank you, ma'am. You're so very kind". As the girl stood up, Elizabeth could see how small she was. She smiled at her. "And what are you called, my dear?"

"My name is Martha, ma'am."

"Well, Martha, come and have a good sleep. Then we'll see what we can do." Carefully she placed Alice on her hip and led the way, worried that the little tot might wake. How far had Martha and Alice travelled, she wondered and how long would they have survived without shelter?

Molly opened the door as they approached. "The bed's made," she said eyeing the two strangers. "Is there anything else, ma'am?"

"Yes, Molly dear, please go and see cook and bring up the food she's prepared." As Elizabeth laid Alice on the bed and Molly reluctantly left, Martha arrived, walking clumsily into the doorframe.

"Are you all right?" she asked the girl. "Yes, ma'am," the girl exclaimed. "I'm sorry, I didn't see it."

"Never mind, Martha." Elizabeth gave her an encouraging smile. "You're half asleep already!"

Martha put her hand over her eye. "Yes, ma'am, I'm very sleepy!"

Martha's eye worried Elizabeth. It really was a nasty weal. It must be bathed, but not now. Martha must rest first. "Now, Martha", she adopted a cheerful air, hoping to reassure her, "there's no need to be frightened any more, you're perfectly safe here. So, settle down and have a good sleep. Molly is bringing some food and then when you've eaten and rested, we can discuss what can be done."

Martha made no reply, but reaching for Elizabeth's hand, she kissed it and kissed it again. Elizabeth could feel warm tears on her skin and struggled to control her own emotions. To be thanked so deeply for such simple hospitality, was quite heart breaking! To her it was convincing evidence that Martha must have been cruelly treated. Staying until Molly arrived with the tray, she helped undress Alice and settle her between the sheets. Then, telling Martha to sleep well, she left.

The strange happenings had excited Molly. In a whisper she asked Elizabeth, "What's up, ma'am?" Her question, she knew, was one of the many the servants, and indeed the whole village, would soon be asking. "I can't tell you anything at the moment Molly, but I beg you to keep silent about our unexpected guests and I'll ask Mrs Jackson, Doris and Miles to do the same."

Molly looked crestfallen. "I'm only curious, ma'am, that's all."

"Yes, Molly dear, I can see that, but I must tell the Rector first. Then we'll have to decide what's to be done."

As Elizabeth walked over to the churchyard to retrieve her tools, she could think of nothing but Martha and her child. To keep them safe, they would have to defend them from prying eyes. How could she do that? In her heart she knew it would be impossible. The presence in the Rectory of a tawny skinned young mother and her black child would be common knowledge in no time! Yet it was obvious that Martha and Alice had to be kept safe from some unknown, but dreadful threat! But what if Martha was a common criminal, who had stolen, or even worse attacked her master, even killed him? A list of awful possibilities raced through her mind, all too frightful to contemplate. She longed for her father to return, so that she could share this heavy responsibility with him and in the morning, after Martha had rested, she'd have to tell them the whole truth. Only then would it be possible to decide what should be done.

Chapter 25

Her father had returned in time for tea. "How's Mrs. Thomas?" Elizabeth enquired. The Squire's wife was unwell and her father had gone to pay his respects and pray for her recovery.

"She's well enough, though she thinks she's gravely ill, but," he chuckled. "We must bear with her, she is the patron's wife!"

Elizabeth watched him lean back in his chair and sip his tea contentedly. How could she tell him about Martha and her child? Helping a passer-by was one thing, but sheltering a runaway slave was quite another.

Her father broke into her thoughts. "Elizabeth you look worried. Is anything wrong?"

His question didn't surprise her. He'd always been able to read her thoughts, ever since she was a child! She took a deep breath. "Father dear, you know how much I hate slavery." She saw him nod. "Ever since Nathaniel joined the Mary Anne I've wanted to be part of the fight against that evil trade. I've wanted to do something, anything no matter how small to help. When I went to Bath and met the Reverend Clarkson I was full of hope, but since my return I've come to realise there's nothing I can do, at least not here in Hanbury. Father I feel discouraged and oh! So useless!"

"My dear", he took her hand. "You must put your trust in God and be patient. In His own good time He'll find a way for you to help, a way that will use the talents He's given you. Have faith Elizabeth!"

"Oh! Father, how I wish my faith was strong as yours. But how right you are! You see I believe the Lord has at last found a way for me to help!"

"Do you want to tell me about it, Elizabeth?"

"Yes, Father dear and if I'm to do His will I shall need your help."

He'd promised to help her immediately and encouraged by his support she'd told him all she knew about Martha and Alice and how she was sure that Martha was an escaped slave.

He'd listened patiently. "A slave eh?"

"Well, she didn't say she was a slave. The poor girl was so exhausted I couldn't question her, but Father, I just know she is. She's run away from some cruel master. I'm sure of that! Father she needs our help, we must give her sanctuary."

He nodded again. "Well, my dear, she can certainly stay for a day or two, but," he hesitated. "We'll have to find out why she's on the run. For all we know she may be wanted for theft or even worse!"

"Oh thank you Father dear. I knew you'd help. I'll find out all about her when she wakes up."

Her father dismissed her thanks. "Did any of the villagers see them, d'you know?"

"No, I don't think so, but I can't be sure. Mrs Jackson, Molly and Miles and young Doris know about them of course, but I've sworn them to silence."

"Good, you did well Elizabeth."

As she left to question Martha, she felt happier. Her father had been as sympathetic as she'd hoped. For the moment Martha and Alice were safe.

"Please Martha," she muttered as she climbed the stairs. "Tell me you haven't stolen from your master or done anything wicked." Approaching the door, she tapped gently on it and pushed it gently ajar. "May I come in?" Martha stood up with Alice in her arms. "Please do ma'am. You've been so very kind."

Elizabeth was pleased to see that the food had been eaten, but her eyes were drawn Martha's swollen eye and the long angry weal below it.

"Did you sleep well, Martha?"

"Yes thank you ma'am, we've both slept well. I don't know what I've done to deserve such kindness."

Elizabeth could see tears welling up in her eyes. "Well my dear, it's clear you need help. Tell me why were you on the road?"

Martha hesitated, then having decided to put her trust in this strange but sympathetic lady, she began. "I'm a slave ma'am and I've run away from my master."

"Oh dear! Martha that's what I thought! Where does your master live?"

"In Bristol ma'am." Martha began to sob. "You won't send us back, will you ma'am? Please promise you won't do that. I'd rather die than go back to that brute!"

Elizabeth reached out and took her hand. "Martha dear, I promise we won't send you back. I've told you, you're safe here, you and little Alice."

Seemingly re-assured, Martha wiped the tears from her eyes.

Elizabeth waited a moment before she asked. "What made you run away?"

"I had to get away ma'am. I couldn't stay any longer, the master was so horrible." Martha shuddered. "He's vile and depraved and whenever he can he leers at me and touches me. He'd always told me he wanted me to be his woman, but when my mistress was alive I always managed to avoid him. But then," she began to sob again, "The other night when I was in bed I heard the door of my room being forced open. Then he was by my bed. I was terrified! At first he just talked, calling me his little black plaything and telling me how he missed his wife. Then he began to handle me, to stroke my arms and legs. I begged him to stop, but he grew angry, called me a little slut and hit me in the face. Then he tore off my clothes and then," for a second she seemed unable to find the right words, "then he had his way with me." She hid her face in her hands.

Elizabeth felt helpless, unable to comfort this poor sobbing girl who had been so shamefully abused. "Oh! You poor child," she whispered. Now she understood why she had that ugly weal below her eye.

After Martha had composed herself she continued. "He used me like an animal and only when he was satisfied did he go. He said nothing, he just left. I felt sick and was terrified he'd come back. If he did, I knew there was nothing I could do to stop him. It was then that I knew I had to run away. When I was sure he was asleep I crept quietly downstairs with Alice in my arms and stole away. It was pitch black outside but though I've always been frightened of the dark I was thankful for the cover it gave me."

"Where were you going, Martha?"

Martha shook her head. "I didn't know ma'am, I had no plans! All I knew was that come what may, I had to get away from him. At first I ran with Alice in my arms, but in the darkness I nearly tripped. Then I forced myself to walk. The narrow streets seemed never ending, but as the sky lightened I could see there weren't so many houses and the roads seemed wider. As the sun rose I saw we were in the country, but there were people about so I left the road and hid among trees. Alice was hungry and crying and I managed to find some blackberries and nuts and when we'd eaten all we could find, we hid among the leaves and fell asleep. We must have slept for hours for when we woke the sun was beginning to set. When it was dark we began to walk again. We walked all through the night and at daybreak I found another place to hide, but we were so hungry we couldn't sleep. I had to find something to eat and began to search for more berries. That's when I saw a church and then dear lady," her eyes began to fill with tears once more. "We found you."

"Well, Martha dear, you're both safe now. That brute won't find you here. Was he always like that?"

"Well, ma'am, he always said he wanted me to be his woman and I often found him leering at me, but my mistress always made sure he never touched me. She was kind to me. When I was twelve I was bought to become her personal maid. Oh! How lucky I was." Her face took on a happier look. "She was a lovely mistress. She treated me almost like a daughter. It was she who taught me how to speak proper English. Can't abide slave talk in my house, she'd say as she corrected me. Through her I learnt to read and write, to do my sums, to sew and make dresses. I loved her dearly." Martha wiped her eyes.

"What happened to your kind mistress, Martha?"

"She became ill and died."

"Oh!"

"I'd been devoted to her for six years, ma'am."

"Where were you before that?"

"In Jamaica, ma'am. My mother was the maid-servant to a planter's wife. When the master and mistress came to England they brought their personal slaves and my mother was allowed to bring me."

"Is your mother still in England?"

"No ma'am. She went back with the master a long time ago, but I didn't see her go. You see I'd been sold before they left."

"Oh! You poor child. Have you ever seen your mother again?" Martha shook her head.

"Oh! Martha dear, I'm so sorry." Elizabeth waited for the girl to compose herself once more.

"Martha, I have to ask you one more question and I need a truthful answer."

"Yes of course ma'am. I always try to tell the truth."

"That's good Martha. Now then tell me please, have you ever stolen anything from this master of yours?"

"Lord, no ma'am. Never."

"That's the truth Martha?"

"Yes ma'am. I'll swear to it on the bible if you want."

"Martha dear, I believe you. Now," she said masking her relief with a business-like tone. "We'd better go down to the kitchen and take a look at that eye of yours and Mrs Jackson can give you both some supper. What do you think of that Alice?" She picked her up and gave her a little hug. "You are a little dear, aren't you?"

Moving to the door, she heard something fall and turning saw Martha picking up a chair. "Ma'am I'm sorry to be so clumsy. I didn't see it. I hope it's not broken."

"No, no, Martha." Elizabeth hastened to reply. "It's not broken and you're not clumsy." She was becoming very worried! Earlier Martha had walked into the door and now she'd knocked over a chair. Had that eye of hers suffered more than superficial damage? It was a disturbing thought!

In the kitchen she found Mrs Jackson busy at the range. Molly was there too, getting in the way and clearly determined not to miss a thing. Both she and Mrs Jackson seemed much taken with Alice who was soon being offered titbits. With Alice the centre of attraction, Elizabeth sat Martha down to bathe the angry weal.

"What happened Martha?" She asked.

"He hit me," Martha replied. "He hit me in the eye."

Elizabeth felt sickened. How could she and Alice be allowed back into the hands of such a savage beast?

Having cleaned the wound, she asked Martha to cover her uninjured eye, then she moved her hand sharply towards her swollen eye as if to hit her. There was no reaction! Martha neither blinked nor moved her head! Could she not see with that eye, she wondered? Was that why Martha kept walking into things? Had that beast done so much damage to her eye?

"Martha," her voice was sad. "Tell me dear, can you see with your left eye?"

"Well enough ma'am." Martha spoke in a matter of fact voice. "It's a little misty, but it'll mend I'm sure."

"Oh! My poor girl." Elizabeth's voice betrayed her fears. "We'll have to bathe it twice a day and pray that in his great mercy the Good Lord will restore your sight."

Leaving the two of them in the capable hands of Mrs Jackson, Elizabeth stood quietly in the hall for a moment as she rehearsed what she should say to her father. He was in the sitting room dozing in his chair, unaware of the problem that so troubled her. She closed the door quietly so as not to disturb him, but he awoke. He asked her what she'd discovered about the girl. Elizabeth told him all she knew, how she'd learnt that Martha had been raped and beaten by her evil master and how worried Martha was that men would be scouring Bristol and the countryside looking for them already.

"They'll be easy to find," Elizabeth said. "Though Martha's almost white, the child's as black as coal. The two of them must stand out like sore thumbs!"

Her father nodded. "Yes, and no doubt there'll be a reward. That will loosen a few tongues!"

"What can we do, Father? We can't throw them out."

"No. We can't do that. We've enough room for them."

"Yes, Father dear. There's plenty and she can help in the house. She can sew and mend and she tells me she can make dresses too and…….."

"But, Elizabeth," her father cut her off in mid-sentence. "What about the Squire and the villagers? They'll find out in no time!"

Reluctantly Elizabeth agreed. "We need a plausible reason for them being here. What can we tell them? Could we say Martha's our new parlour maid?"

"Mm." Her father was not enamoured with the suggestion. "Elizabeth, we'd have to explain how we found her! And wouldn't the village girls resent her taking work from them? Mrs Jackson tells me little Daisy Cooper's been asking if there's a job at the Rectory for some time now. No, Elizabeth. We can't say that."

For a moment they were silent as they sought a solution. Then having relit his pipe, he said it was no good telling a lie. "If we are honest" he said. "The Lord would surely help us. We'll have to tell the Squire and the villagers the truth and that we are doing what the church has always done. That is giving sanctuary to those who flee from injustice and persecution."

"Father, we can't do that! Won't someone go for the reward and betray them?"

"Perhaps they might, if they hear of a reward, but Elizabeth." He moved to the window as if already on the lookout for men coming to seize their unexpected guests. "We'll have to rely on the loyalty of our good villagers. We'll have to pray that they'll accept Martha and Alice in our midst. Besides if there is a reward, what makes you think we'll hear about it in our remote little village?"

Elizabeth was full of doubts. "Do you really think they'll be safe when the villagers know they're runaway slaves?"

"I can't say, Elizabeth. We must pray that they will be. We have to put our trust in our Heavenly Father." He turned to face her. "What else can we do? We can't keep them hidden for ever!"

Chapter 26

Riding back to the Rectory, the Reverend Lunt had known he and Elizabeth would have to be content with the Squire's grudging approval of their plan. There was much to be done. The biggest problem had been to convince Martha. When Elizabeth explained what had been planned, Martha's eyes grew large with fear. Lifting Alice onto her lap, she shrank back into her chair as if it would hide them from the villagers. She asked how she could trust them. They were white people and the white man had brought nothing but suffering to her people. And she was certain that by now notices offering a handsome reward for their capture would be appearing in all the taverns and lodging houses in Bristol. News of a reward would soon reach the village and she was certain that one of the villagers would be tempted. Nothing that Elizabeth could say would persuade her to trust them. The very idea of telling them that she was an escaped slave filled her with terror.

Elizabeth understood her fears. "Not all white people are cruel, Martha."

"Yes Ma'am, I know. You've been so good to me and so has everyone in this blessed house, but are none of the villagers cruel? Are they all as kind as you?"

Those were questions Elizabeth could not answer and despite all her efforts to allay her fear, Martha remained convinced that she would be betrayed. In desperation Elizabeth struggled to assure her that the villagers knew nothing about slaves, that she was sure they would welcome her and none would wish her harm. Martha listened dutifully, but the very idea made her nervous and edgy and her doubts began to infect Elizabeth. Martha could be right! Men might come searching for her and Alice and some of the villagers could be tempted by a large reward. Could there be another way? Could she persuade her cousin in Peterchurch to give them refuge? Surely they'd be safe in the depths of Herefordshire. But would Martha agree to go? Elizabeth would be upset to see them go. She'd grown fond of Martha and would sorely miss little Alice, but their safety was what mattered! The more she thought of it, the more she became convinced that sending them to Herefordshire would be the best thing to do. She suggested it to Martha, but she looked even more worried.

"I don't want to leave you Ma'am." The plaintive tone in Martha's voice rent Elizabeth's heartstrings. "Everyone has been so kind to us here. Don't send us away please."

"Of course we won't send you away Martha dear." She told her she'd be sad, very sad to see them go. "But Martha dear if you stay you can't remain hidden forever! Someone from the village will see you sooner or later". Martha nodded forlornly. "That's why", Elizabeth continued. "We have to tell all of them about you and Alice and ask them for help. It's the only thing we can do, if you're to stay."

Martha liked neither solution, but after much discussion she admitted that it would be impossible to keep her and Alice hidden forever. Finally to Elizabeth's great relief she accepted the Rector's plan.

Elizabeth held Martha's hand. "You're being very brave Martha, but it's the only thing we can do."

"Yes ma'am." Martha nodded hesitantly. "It's all we can do."

Relieved by Martha's agreement Elizabeth hastened to tell he father. She found him working on his sermon. "Elizabeth, sit down, sit down my dear and tell me how's Martha's eye?"

"No better Father, she's still bumping into things. She says everything looks fuzzy."

"Good, good," he broke in. "Well, Elizabeth, that's not what I mean of course. Like you I'm horrified for the poor girl. But," Elizabeth saw that gleam that always shone in his eyes when he was excited. "I've been searching the bible, reminding myself of the treatment of slaves. And the book of Exodus is quite clear. See here in chapter 21 verse 26 it says unequivocally - and if a man smite the eye of his servant, or the eye of his maid, that it perish: he shall let him go free for his eye's sake."

"Father, does that mean in God's eyes, Martha's free?"

"Yes, Elizabeth, that's what the bible says! And here in the Book of Deuteronomy." He turned the pages hurriedly. "Ah! Here it is Chapter 23 verses 15 and 16." He began to read, "Thou shalt not deliver unto his master the slave, which is escaped from his master unto thee. He shall dwell with thee, even among you, in that place which he shall choose in one of thy gates, where it liketh him best: thou shalt not oppress him." His eyes were twinkling now. "So you see my dear, if we give them refuge, we're doing God's will."

She was smiling, almost laughing. "Oh Father, the villagers will have to support us now."

"Yes, I must make them understand that according to God's law, Martha is free and his law puts a duty on us to give her refuge."

Sunday came, dry, sunny and autumnal. With no rain to excuse the dilatory, the church was full when Elizabeth entered with Mrs. Jackson, Miles, Molly, young Doris and Martha and Alice. Elizabeth had given Martha one of her own dresses and Martha had worked hard cutting it down to size. Being black and very plain, Elizabeth had thought it most suitable for Martha's introduction to the villagers. Martha's own would have seemed far too elegant and some of the women could have been envious! To her great surprise, Elizabeth saw that the Squire was accompanied by Mrs. Thomas. She had made a truly remarkable recovery for one so ill; no doubt the notion of seeing the slave and her child had been greatly therapeutic. Apart from the Squire, only the Churchwardens had been forewarned of the plan, the rest of the congregation being unaware of what was to come. Elizabeth and Martha were equally fearful. Would her father's scheme work? Would the village accept this strange girl and her black child? Would they heed her father's sermon? Would some Judas Iscariot betray Martha for a few pieces of silver? Her worries distracted her from the service and it was only when the Churchwarden collected the Bible for the first lesson that she was able to concentrate on the liturgy. In his usual clear and succinct manner Mr. Waring began to read from the Book of Deuteronomy. Its message was clear and uncompromising. Then her father read the Gospel after which he mounted the pulpit.

"My text." His voice was quiet, yet strangely powerful. "Is taken from St John's gospel. Jesus said this is my commandment, that ye love one another as I have loved you. Greater love hath no man than this; that a man lay down his own life for his friends." He paused. It seemed he looked directly at each person assembled in the congregation before continuing. "Dear friends on this day, this very special day in the life of our village, our Heavenly Father has set us a test, a challenge to obey our Saviour when he told us to love one another. But before I tell you about this test, I must say something about slavery, no, not the slavery of sin, but about

the enslavement of men, women and children by others to do their will."
He told them how men owned other human beings as men owned horses,
oxen and sheep, of the misery suffered by those sold into slavery, how
they were treated as animals, how men were beaten and women raped and
how families were broken up at the whim of their master. "Dear friends,
we've never experienced slavery in this blessed parish," he went on. "But
what if our sons and daughters were torn from us and sold as slaves, what
if they were beaten and raped, what if we never saw them again? What
anguish we would suffer, how we would grieve and how deep would be
our despair! My friends would we not pray for them to escape the clutches
of their cruel masters? And if somehow they did manage to escape, would
we not fall onto our knees and beg the Lord to give them shelter? Would
we not beseech Him to find refuge for them somewhere, anywhere safe
from those who seek to recapture them? Let me read the law again, the law
written in the fifth book of Moses that we call Deuteronomy." He read the
verses he had quoted to Elizabeth about not delivering an escaped slave to
his master. "And there's another law I want to tell you about. It concerns
a man who uses violence against his servant. It's in Exodus, the second
book of Moses." He turned the pages over. "Here it is - if a man smite the
eye of a servant, or the eye of his maid, that it perish: he shall let him go
free for his eye's sake." He rested his hands on the pulpit rail and studied
the congregation. Then he leaned forward. "Tell us you ask, why is this
a special day and why am I talking about slavery"? He stood back and
opened wide his arms as if expecting an answer. Then in a whisper he said
"I will tell you." In a voice once more powerful he spoke again. "Today
is a special day because the Lord has put us to the test. He has sent us an
escaped slave and her child to seek refuge amongst us and He expects us
to obey his commandments. Remember always, Jesus told us to love one
another as he loves us My dear brothers and sisters as we love our fellow
villagers, God expects us to love this escaped slave and her child too.
Remember what is written in Deuteronomy - thou shalt not oppress nor
deliver to her master a slave who has escaped unto thee. So my dear people
this is the test God has set us. It is to welcome an escaped slave, raped and
beaten by her Master so that her sight is damaged and with her, her young
child. It is to welcome them into our midst and offer them refuge so they
can live in peace and freedom. We must be obedient to the Lord. We must
not fail the test." Again he studied his congregation; his eyes seeming to
find each one of them. "I hear you saying, where is this slave? I tell you

she's here; she and her daughter are with us. Let me show her to you." He nodded to Elizabeth, who led Martha and Alice to the chancel steps. As the congregation began to whisper and ask themselves who this slave and her child could be, Martha stood there silent and frightened with Alice clutching her mother's knees.

"I'll tell you who they are." The Rector spoke kindly now. "This is Martha and her daughter Alice. My dear friends, just think for a moment. Had your daughters been taken into slavery and been raped and abused, could they not be seeking sanctuary too, like Martha? But in His great mercy the Lord has delivered our village from the evils of slavery. For this we must be truly thankful and welcome Martha and Alice into our midst. Amen, Amen, Amen."

Chapter 27

It had been an uneventful passage home and Jim had had plenty of time to write his report to the partners. Nathaniel's journal had helped him with his own writing, but his had of necessity been confined to facts and it made dull reading compared with Nathaniel's script. His compositions had often brought home the bloodshed, cruelty and mortality of the trade and one of his last entries had encapsulated the suffering and degradation of the slaves.

The Sale of our Slaves

On Wednesday May 25th after having fed and oiled our slaves we ferried the first eighty ashore and having chained them together we marched them to the auction rooms. The Captain said I should come with him so that I could see the result of our voyage. He was pleased to see so many potential buyers; indeed there were a lot of well-dressed gentlemen present, smoking their pipes and joking with their compatriots as if it were a great social occasion. When the auctioneer was satisfied that all was ready the first batch of slaves, men and women together were brought in to be examined carefully by those wishing to buy, some checking their teeth and eyes and feeling biceps and thighs to gauge the power of their muscles. I recognised many of those poor wretches as they stood huddled together in their nakedness. Not knowing what the future held for them, they made a *pitiful sight. Each was put up for sale separately and at first the bidding was brisk and most were sold at £50. £65 was the highest price achieved, this being for a shapely young female slave. When the richer plantation owners were satisfied, prices began to tumble and the highest bid was £30 and that was for a big male. It was then that the auctioneer said there would be a scramble. I had no idea what this meant but the remaining buyers clearly did for his announcement raised a cheer! The remaining dozen or so unsold slaves were then herded in and the auctioneer declared they would be sold at £25 each. When all was ready he rang his bell and the buyers pushed and struggled as they rushed to grab the slaves they wanted. I could now understand why it was called a "scramble"! It was indeed aptly named! But my heart went out to those poor terrified creatures who were the subject of such belligerent and argumentative treatment. Then the auctioneer sold the horses! It was just one animal sale! I could not help feeling ashamed to be English.*

James could see Elizabeth with her cornflower blue eyes smiling proudly at Nathaniel, her son who so resolutely refused to be corrupted by that "evil" trade. He wondered what she would think of him, the slave-ship Captain into whose care she had so reluctantly surrendered her son. He would only know if they ever met again. As his fingers caressed the ring hanging from his neck he knew he'd have to engineer a meeting somehow!

Two days later he brought the Mary Anne safely to anchor in the King's Roads to await the River Pilot. With the voyage at an end he put the finishing touches to his report and prepared himself to meet the senior partner. He knew the loss of seventeen slaves; almost a fifth of those he'd bought, would upset Mr Crosbie, not of course on humanitarian grounds, but for the profit lost. The avaricious old skinflint would probably censure him for buying sickly slaves and even question his ability as Master. One expected such undeserved criticism from him. Crosbie knew nothing about the sea and the problems of the middle passage. His time was spent in Bristol in his comfortable house. Figures, prices, money, profit were his only concerns. And the loss of the Chief Mate, the Bo's'un and three hands wouldn't trouble him either. "In fact," he muttered savagely to himself. "The old skinflint will probably be pleased. He'll think they won't have to be paid!" He cast his eyes once more over his report and satisfied went on deck. The ebb tide was easing and soon the flood tide would be upon them to help them up river.

"Any sign of the Pilot, Mr Lugger?"

The boy shook his head. "No, not yet sir."

"What a change Elizabeth will see in her son," he thought as he glanced at the boy still wearing the clothes he'd worn when he'd joined. How he'd outgrown them and now they were faded and frayed. He was pleased he'd taken him to that tailor in Montego Bay and had bought him a new coat, breeches and shirts. "I can't have you going home in rags", he remembered telling him. He wanted Elizabeth to see him looking like a gentlemen. And he'd take with him his letter telling Elizabeth how well the boy had done. And he had done well, so well indeed that two weeks ago he'd told him he could stand day watches on his own. "It'll give you a chance to earn your acting rank of Third Mate," he'd added. And the previous evening as they stood their last night watch together, he'd said, "I hope, Mr Lugger, [he'd determined to stop calling him boy] you'll be signing on for the next voyage to complete your apprenticeship." The boy had seemed delighted. "I'll sign on sir, if you'll have me." Jim wished he could be as enthusiastic about the next voyage too. Could he be enthusiastic about another as master of a slave-ship? Could he? Elizabeth would never marry a slaver, he knew that for certain and the temptation to give up slaving was compelling! If he did, if he did give up the trade, she might agree to marry him. His spirits rose at the thought. But his euphoria soon vanished; he knew he was contracted to serve as Master of the "Mary Anne" for two voyages, with an option for two more. He sighed in despair; he'd have to complete one more slaving voyage. But, he determined that would be his last. Then she might marry him; that was all he could hope for.

The next day saw the Mary Anne berthed alongside Broad Quay unloading her cargo of rum and sugar and the great elephant's tusks. Weight for weight, except for the gold which would be unloaded when all was quiet, the tusks were the most valuable cargo. Indeed some of his partners had come to see and admire them. All were sure they would make a good profit!

Once her cargo had been unloaded the Mary Anne was warped to a quiet mooring away from the commercial harbour. Here the ship's company were to be discharged, the gold quietly sent ashore and a small party retained to complete her repairs. As each man was paid off, Jim in the company of the clerk gave him the balance of his wages and his share of the profits. Nathaniel was the last to report. As an Apprentice he knew he could expect nothing. The Captain explained this to him but when they shook hands he told him he'd done well and added, "Come and see me at the end of January and I'll tell you when we're sailing."

"Thank you sir, I will," Nathaniel happily replied.

"Well, Mr Lugger, you'll be off in the morning, I suppose."

Nathaniel nodded. "Yes, sir as soon as it's light."

"Right, but make sure you see me before you go. I'll have a letter for your mother. And here's something for you." Jim handed him a little bag with a string neckband. "Can't have you going empty handed!"

Nathaniel took the bag and loosening the drawstring looked inside. There were two coins, gold coins.

"They're guineas, Mr Lugger. Keep them in the bag and slip it over your head and hide it under your shirt. And don't tell anyone about it till you get home, else you'll be robbed." Nathaniel thanked him profusely, but Jim waved his hand. "Don't forget to see me before you go."

When the boy had gone, he took out the letter and read it one last time. This was the fifth and last version he'd written to her. Despite all his efforts, it still didn't express his feelings as well as he'd hoped! Letter writing was an art that eluded him. Normally he only wrote letters when he had to and then only to the owners or an agent or some contractor. He hardly ever wrote private letters and never before a letter to express his innermost feelings! Well, it was the best he could do! He folded it with great care and pressing it to his lips he kissed it. "Bring me luck," he whispered. Then re-charging his quill with ink he wrote 'Mrs Elizabeth Lugger' on it before sealing it. As the hot wax ran onto the paper, he searched for something to use as a seal. He had no fancy signet ring! The wax was beginning to harden; soon it would be too late. On an impulse he took his knife and pressed the tip into the warm wax. He left it there for a moment or two, then removed it. "Oh my God," he said. "It's left a triangle, a bloody triangle." He couldn't help laughing; it seemed an appropriate mark for a Master working the Triangular Trade! Then dismay struck him. Would she also see it as a symbol of the trade she hated so much? If she did, it would probably upset her! He daren't risk that! He lit the taper again and ran more wax onto the seal to obliterate the mark.

He found it difficult to sleep that night as he worried about the letter. When at last a fitful sleep came, he dreamed the boy had lost it; that Elizabeth never read its contents. As the sun filtered into his cabin, he awoke feeling dismal and disheartened and was barely up when a knock on the door announced the boy's arrival. "Come in, come in," he shouted.

"You wanted to see me before I went, sir?"

"Yes, yes, Mr Lugger." The boy stood there in his old, tattered clothes. "Here's the letter for your mother." He gave it to him with a silent prayer. "It contains a report on your progress as an apprentice, so don't lose it. And give your mother my best regards."

"Thank you sir, I will." The boy seemed anxious to go.

"I see you're not wearing your new clothes, Mr Lugger. Very sensible. You'll be much safer dressed as you are. And make sure you don't let anyone see those guineas."

"No, sir I won't and I didn't want to get mud and dirt on those clothes you gave me. I've left them behind. I'll be back for them in a few days."

"Good. Make sure you see me when you come back." He reached in his pocket and pulled out some coins. "Here, Mr Lugger. Here are three pennies. You'll need to buy food and something to drink on the way home no doubt. I don't want you showing those guineas to anyone on the road, remember?"

"Oh! Thank you, sir." Nathaniel stood there not sure what to say, nor when he should go.

"Well, be off with you now boy and don't forget to give that letter to your mother."

With the boy gone, Jim sat back in his chair. There was nothing more he could do, except hope and pray that Elizabeth would put her hatred of the trade to one side and see him for the man he really was.

Nathaniel had made his way on deck to bid farewell to this, his first ship. It had been his home for almost a year and had taken him safely across the ocean and back. He knew he should feel excited at the thought of going home but now, having to leave the "Mary Anne", he suddenly felt sad. When he went to say goodbye to Bert, a lump filled his throat and as he walked down the gangplank he heard Bert saying "Don't 'ee forget to sign on next time, young sir." He'd always liked Bert's special name for him and as he remembered his other name "laddie", a picture of Fred's friendly, laughing face brought tears to his eyes. He pulled himself together with a curse. Cursing like that made him feel more like a man; men didn't bloody cry! He turned, looked back at the ship, waved farewell and set off. The quayside was unfamiliar and he wasn't sure which way to go, but he followed the river round to Broad Quay and then struck off up the hill. Ahead of him he could see a tall church spire and on an impulse he headed for it. Soon he was in a street full of people pushing and shoving while others chatted or haggled with the stall holders. He saw a barrow laden with fresh crusty bread and feeling for one of his pennies he bought a small loaf. Another stall sold cheese and after buying some he asked for directions to Hanbury. "Take the Gloucester Road," the wizened old hag had said as she turned to serve another customer. He wrapped his purchases in his neckerchief and set off. "Which is the road to Gloucester?" he kept asking until finally a kind old lady in black pointed him in the right direction.

Once he was sure he was on the right road he stepped out briskly and soon the houses gave way to lonely cottages. It was a cold crisp October day with the countryside dressed in the soft russet colours of autumn. It was so much more beautiful than the harsh colours of the Jamaican landscape. The bare trees flaunted their fine tracery against the clear blue sky, while copper-coloured leaves danced at his feet. Here and there he saw a lonely cow or a goat but they showed no interest in him, unlike the dogs guarding the cottages he passed. They heard him coming and warned of his presence with fierce barking. Sometimes this went unnoticed, but now and then a bent figure would look up from his toils and nod, bidding him "Mornin'" or "G'day to you", but he never stopped. The pale wintery sun did nothing to allay the coldness of the wind, and though his walking kept him warm enough he was thankful when the road entered the forest and he was sheltered from the breeze. Soon he came to a clearing where men were making hurdles, but passing by unnoticed, he entered the forest again. Thankfully he found a mossy bank where he sat and as he ate his bread and cheese he saw the first pack horse. Others plodded gently behind him. Some carried bulging bags, others great boxes. He watched them pass, all forty three of them. He wondered what they carried. The bags were full of wool, he guessed, but the boxes? Maybe they were packed with pots and pans, knives and muskets like those they'd used to buy their slaves! It seemed the slave trade pervaded even this lonely forest! As the last horse plodded wearily by he began walking again and reckoning that he must now be half way home he stepped out with renewed vigour. Clearing the forest he scanned the distant slopes, hoping to see the turning. Nothing would make him slacken his pace now, not even the long hill ahead. Then he saw the signpost and as he grew nearer he read the word Hanbury! He was almost there; just a mile or so and he'd be home! Would his mother recognise him after all this time? He tried to recall her face, but after a year the picture was faint. Not that his love for her had waned, it was a strong as ever. Was she was still upset, he wondered, because he'd joined a slaver? And what would she say when he told her he wanted to sign on for the next voyage? Would she forbid him? What would he do then? The Captain had promised to make him Third Mate after one more trip, so he must go. He'd have to persuade her somehow. And he knew she'd ask him hundreds of questions. What should he do if the answers were likely to upset her? He sighed. Well, he'd tell her as much as he could; he wouldn't lie to her, but he mightn't tell her everything!

The church steeple came into view and then the Rectory. As he revelled in the thought of living in the luxury of that huge house, a sudden disturbing thought struck him. Would his grandfather still be alive? He was troubled now, for when his grandfather died, as some day he must, he knew his mother would have to leave the Rectory to make way for the new incumbent. "Dear God, let grandfather still be alive," he said out loud. "If he's not, where will I find Mama?" He thrust the thought hastily from his mind and running up the pathway reached for the familiar brass doorknocker and beat loudly on the door. For an age nothing happened, then the door swung open and he saw a strange swarthy-looking girl with long shiny black hair. A child clung to her leg, a black child, as black as any slave he'd seen. It even had the same woolly hair! The girl stood expectantly. "Can I help you, sir?"

"I've come to see Mrs Lugger," he replied. "She does still live here, doesn't she?"

"Yes, Mrs Lugger lives here. Who, sir, shall I say it is?"

Greatly relieved he told her he was her son. The appearance of this strange olive-skinned girl worried him. He'd seen swarthy slaves in Jamaica. Was this girl one too? He couldn't believe his mother would own a slave!

He heard footsteps in the hall and then his mother's voice as she ran towards him and wrapped him in her arms.

"Nathaniel, dearest Nathaniel. How wonderful it is to have you back. It's been such a long time!" She held him away from her to look at him. "My! You've grown! Your poor tattered clothes are far too small, and my Dear I do believe you've got the makings of a beard! Come, come let Grandpa see you. We've been so worried about you." She took his hand and led him away. "Martha dear," she said to the strange girl. "Tell Mrs Jackson Master Nathaniel is back at last and ask her to bring some tea and scones and some of her best raspberry jam for the poor lad" and, turning once more to her son, she exclaimed "Poor dear. I expect you're starving."

He followed her into the sitting room where Grandpa, still his sprightly old self welcomed him, telling him he looked like a weather beaten old salt! Laughing with delight Nathaniel told him it was good to see him looking so well.

"Thank you, thank you, Nathaniel." He smiled at his grandson. "Have you enjoyed being at sea?"

Then it was the turn of Mrs Jackson, laden with a great tray of scones and cakes to exclaim how he'd grown. "But he needs feeding up ma'am. He's all skin and bones!"

Elizabeth laughed. "And he needs new clothes. Fie Nathaniel, I've never seen such rags!"

"It's the wind and sea, mama. But I've new clothes on board. Captain Youle took me ashore in Jamaica and had some made for me."

"Did he now? That was kind of him, very kind indeed."

"And he gave me these." He pulled the little bag from his neck and undoing the draw strings proudly showed her the two golden guineas. "I knew that as an apprentice I wouldn't get paid, but Captain Youle gave them to me. He said he couldn't let me go home empty-handed!"

"My! He gave you two whole guineas?" His mother seemed taken aback. "That's a small fortune, Nathaniel!"

"And he gave me three pennies to buy something to eat on the way home. He told me on no account was I to let anyone see I had guineas. If I did, he said I might be robbed."

"Indeed you might have been. It's evident Captain Youle is not only generous, but wise too!"

Tucking into the fresh scones and cakes, Nathaniel found himself telling them about his time at sea and as he had foreseen, his mother kept asking questions, the questions he'd known she'd ask! Some were difficult to answer, without upsetting her so whenever possible he was vague with his answers. Thankfully she didn't ask about conditions on the slave deck and before she did he felt he should change the subject. He produced the letter.

"Oh! Mama. I've forgotten I've a letter for you." She seemed surprised. "It's from Captain Youle. It's probably not important. I think it just tells you how I've done. I'm sure it can wait till tomorrow."

"No, no." She shook her head. "If it's to tell me how you've done, I'd like to see it now!"

Nathaniel reached into his pocket. When he'd been given it, it had been carefully folded. Now it was crumpled. He tried without much success to smooth out the creases and was relieved to see that though cracked, the seal was still intact. Elizabeth gave the letter a searching look and going to the window unfolded it carefully and glanced at the first few lines. "You're right, Nathaniel. It's all about you." She began to read:

Dear Ma'am, I am writing to you for two reasons".

Two reasons, she asked herself, why two? Mystified she hastened to read on.

"The first is to tell you how pleased I have been with Nathaniel".

She looked up. "He says he's been pleased with you, Nathaniel dear. I knew you'd do well." She began to read aloud.

"He is willing and obedient, has been quick to learn and has made good progress. He shows great promise with his seamanship and navigation."

She looked quickly at Nathaniel, he was clearly pleased. "Sounds as if you've made a very good start, Nathaniel." Her father interrupted. "Does he say any more Elizabeth?"

"Yes, yes. Let me continue. Ah! Here we are".

"When sadly the Chief Mate died of the flux ....

Oh! Poor man", she interrupted herself. "Was that your nice Mr Braithwaite?" Nathaniel nodded as she began to read again.

"When sadly the Chief Mate died of the flux on passage to Jamaica, I had to give his job to the Second Mate and his to the Third and though your son, ma'am was still only an apprentice I was happy to give him the Third Mate's job, which he did well. You have every reason ma'am to feel proud of him and I hope you will allow him to sign on for our next voyage so that he can complete his apprenticeship. He will make a good Mate, of that I am convinced ma'am,"

She stopped. "That's a very good report, isn't it father?"

"Yes my dear. It most certainly is." He turned to his grandson. "It's evident that Captain Youle thinks highly of you, Nathaniel."

"He must, I suppose, though I never thought he did." Nathaniel was smiling with delight. "It is a good report, isn't it? He told me he'd have me as Third Mate after the next voyage. Does he say any more? Do read on Mama."

She scanned the letter to find her place. "Ah! Yes, here we are." She saw it went on *"The second reason ma'am is a more personal one"* Startled, she took a deep breath.

"What is it, Mama?"

"Nothing, dear, that's the end of your report. He just sends his regards, that's all!" And folding the letter quickly she tucked it into her bodice. She'd skimmed quickly through the next paragraph. He'd written of her integrity and concern about slaving and how he'd thought of her throughout the voyage! She'd not read any more. How could she in front of the others? The letter, whatever it said, would have to wait until later, until the privacy of her room.

Nathaniel and her father seemed mystified, but neither spoke. And wishing to change the subject she said how tired Nathaniel must be. "I'll ask Mrs Jackson to bring you some hot water so you can have a bath. And you need some clean clothes too! Your old ones are still in your room, but," she shook her head in disbelief. "I doubt if they'll fit you, now you've grown so much!"

Elizabeth looked admiringly at her son. Suddenly he'd grown up and how handsome he was! Just like his father. An idea struck her. "I wonder whether your father's clothes would fit you. You said you had more on board?"

"Yes, Mama. They're packed in my chest. I told Captain Youle I'd come back for them in a few days' time. Will you come with me? Then you could have another look at the "Mary Anne". I'd like you to see her; she's such a handsome ship."

"I'm sure she is, Nathaniel dear. We could go on Thursday." His face brightened. "Then you can show off your new clothes in church." She laughed as he pulled a face.

"For Heaven's sake, Nathaniel." The Reverend Lunt interrupted. "I do hope you're not going to show us all up with your fine new clothes. You must remember we're all just country bumpkins here!" He groaned. "Can't he go as he is, Elizabeth? He looks a real old sea dog."

Elizabeth shook her head, laughing. "Come along Nathaniel, we can't have sea dogs in the Rectory! We'll find some clean clothes for you one way or another!"

When at last she'd got her poor dear, weary son up to his room, made sure the bath was hot and that he had some clean clothes she slipped into her own room. Settling herself in the chair by the window she pulled out the letter and began to read the neat careful writing.

"The second reason, ma'am, is a more personal one. It is a matter to which I have given long and repeated thought. It was indeed a happy day for me, that Tuesday the seventh day of October last year, when you came to ask whether your son could serve as an apprentice aboard the Mary Anne. I was struck by your evident desire to do the best for him and your manifest concern for the slaves left a lasting impression on me. Such an impression indeed that I determined to treat those we were to carry in the "Mary Anne" as humanely as possible. That became an important principle for me throughout the voyage and indeed one which I can truthfully say has guided my actions. Dare I mention also that I was struck by your great integrity, your beauty and the genteel and dignified way in which you bore yourself at our last meeting?"

The memories of that last meeting flooded back. How horrified she'd been to discover the ship she'd found for Nathaniel was a slave-ship! And how she hated herself when she found that he'd been trapped by the articles she'd unwittingly let him sign. She shook her head. She'd been so certain her son would be corrupted by that evil trade; that he'd return coarsened, yet it was the same happy, cheerful, honest Nathaniel who'd returned so unexpectedly. She read on.

"I have had you in my thoughts throughout the voyage and a picture of your charming face has never been far from my eyes. I am, ma'am, infatuated and bewitched by you and can never be happy until you are my wife".

His wife! The idea shocked her1. He wants me to be his wife! How could she possibly marry the master of a slave-ship? Never could she marry such a man, not even one who professes to treat his slaves humanely. Disturbed by this unexpected admiration, she read on.

"I am not a rich man, neither am I poor. I have sufficient to purchase a modest cottage for us and to provide for you, ma'am, and I should be the happiest of men if you would agree to marry me. I am on tenterhooks as I await your reply and pray that you will be agreeable to my proposal. I am, dear Elizabeth, your most humble and devoted servant, James Arthur Youle."

Shaken, she put the letter aside. Though he was a slaver, it was a very agreeable letter and she felt strangely moved by his proposal. It had come out of the blue! He had only met her twice and at that last meeting she'd been angry and over-bearing, even arrogant in her condemnation of his trade. Yet she remembered that though his reply had been somewhat blunt, he had never been anything other than polite. Furthermore it was clear that he had kept his word when he'd promised "to look after the lad as if he were my own." She couldn't help but admit that she'd developed a sneaking regard for him; a regard that had been amply confirmed by his kindness and concern for Nathaniel. She read the letter again. His sincerity shone through like a flame on a dark winter's night. He was an enigma. She had seen him as a tough, resolute master of a ship plying an evil trade, yet it was evident that he was a kind and honest man, who was dependable. A man who kept his own counsel unswayed by the opinions of others. That rough, uncompromising exterior concealed a deeper kinder nature.

Yet though in many ways she admired him, she could never marry him. Never, ever! How could she become the wife of a man associated with that abhorrent, repugnant, despicable trade? No, it was quite out of the question! Yet she laughed; here she was, a widow of thirty-three, old enough to be a grandmother with two men wanting to marry her! It was all too ridiculous! But how would she respond to James? She'd refused David! David who looked like a Greek God with his blue eyes, golden hair and tall athletic frame had also told her of his love for her and had proposed marriage. But charming, polite and attentive as David was she could never marry him! But how would she reply to James? She would have to give it great thought. She had been a widow for thirteen years, since Nathaniel was at her breast and she would remain one for the rest of her life.

Chapter 28

"Good morning darling." Elizabeth lent forward to receive Nathaniel's kiss. "We were wondering if you'd ever wake up, weren't we Mrs Jackson?" Mrs Jackson smiled "Yes to be sure we were Master Nathaniel, but I thought the smell of home cooking would make you get up sooner or later. Would you like me to fry you some eggs and nice piece of bacon?"

Nathaniel smiled "Yes please Mrs Jackson."

As he began to drink the milk his mother had set before him, he saw the little black child contemplating him with her great round eyes. The silent inspection unsettled him, but his mother and Mrs Jackson were laughing and then he was too.

"This is little Alice, isn't she sweet?" His mother picked the child up. "And this, Alice, is Master Nathaniel. He's a sailor home from the sea. You have to be very good when he's around. As good as you are with Gampy."

As his mother put the child on her lap, the strange olive-skinned girl with the long black shiny hair appeared. "Alice! I've been looking for you everywhere. I hope she hasn't been a nuisance, ma'am."

"No, no, Martha. Alice has been very good. She and Master Nathaniel have been getting to know each other, haven't you Nathaniel dear?"

"Yes Mama." he laughed. "Though we haven't said much yet!"

Elizabeth told him Martha was the mother of Alice. Nathaniel smiled at her. "We met yesterday, when you let me in. I was expecting Mrs Jackson or Miles. Seeing you was quite a shock. For a moment I thought maybe Grandpa had died and you were the new Rector's maid."

"Oh, Nathaniel dear. I thought you seemed very concerned about Grandpa's health! He's been fine; really he's as fit as a fiddle!"

As Martha took Alice away, Elizabeth pulled some breeches out of a basket, shook them and held them up. "I've found some of your father's clothes. He said they were too tight for him." She looked a little sad. "I've kept them ever since. Perhaps now they'll be of use. Will they fit you, I wonder?"

They climbed the stairs together carrying the basket between them and entering his room, she emptied its contents onto the bed. There was a blue tail coat, two pairs of white breeches, two doublets, some stockings and some shoes. Sitting quickly on the bed, he tried on the shoes. Perhaps they were a little large, but they were much more comfortable than his own and he was very taken with the stylish buckles. Elizabeth was delighted. "At least they fit, Nathaniel dear. I'll wait in my room while you try the rest." Having reached the privacy of her chamber she removed the letter from her bodice and began to read its contents once more. Its simplicity and directness appealed to her and she found herself admiring the neat script. She tried to picture him in her mind's eye. His great spade beard came quickly into view, as did his thick mop of hair. But other details of his face eluded her. She endeavoured to list his features. His eyes, were they brown or blue? And his brow, deep or shallow? And his nose? The harder she tried to recall his features, the more difficult it became. Evidently he was not handsome; else his countenance would be easily recalled. Nevertheless, she remembered an honest face! A knock disturbed her thoughts. It was Nathaniel standing there wearing his father's clothes. She gave an involuntary gasp of delight. He looked like a young prince, his face framed by sun-bleached curls and his eyes alight with excitement. He looked just like his father, that young Adonis who'd swept her off her feet; the husband she'd hardly known. The resemblance was uncanny! "Well, mama, what do you think?"

She pulled herself together. "They fit you well. You look as handsome as your dear father."

Nathaniel laughed. "I'll try the other breeches, then." As he disappeared, memories of her life with Charles flooded back. How tall and handsome he was and what an intoxicating smile he'd had. Charles was her father's second cousin once removed. They'd met at his sister's wedding and when they were introduced she had lost her heart to him. He'd been a Midshipman in the "Lion", a battleship in the Channel Fleet and was waiting to join the "Royal George" as a Lieutenant. It had been a whirlwind romance between two young people who'd scarcely grown up. Two months later they'd been wed and after seven weeks of married life, the Navy called and he'd had to go. When he'd gone nothing could console her, not even the first stirrings of life within her. As her belly grew and sickness followed, she needed Charles more than ever! Yet as time passed his features had begun to fade from her memory, as if he was slipping from her and when her time approached something seemed to tell her she would never see him again. She remembered wishing to die in childbirth, but it wasn't to be! Instead she was blessed with a son, a fine healthy boy who helped fill the aching void in her heart. But her premonition that she'd never see Charles again was to be fulfilled. She recalled that other letter. "Ma'am," it said. "It is with the deepest regret that I have to inform you that Mister Charles Archibald Lugger, Lieutenant of His Majesty's Ship "Royal George", was killed in action against the French Fleet in Quiberon Bay on the 20th day of November last. He died in the midst of battle and comported himself to the end with conspicuous bravery." Though her foreboding had helped prepare her for that cruel news, she had never been able to accept the finality of it. Only the need to nurture the tiny speck of life which they had created gave her reason to live. Slowly as the child grew he replaced Charles as the centre of her life, but now she was losing him too! How she hated the sea! If only Nathaniel would give up his apprenticeship! For a moment she considered trying to persuade him. Then perhaps she might keep him home. That was what her heart demanded. But she knew if she did she might forfeit his love. She sighed inwardly. She had to let him go.

"They're fine too Mama." A cheerful Nathaniel presented himself wearing the second pair of breeches. "There's only one thing mama. There's a nasty tear here." He pointed to the cause of his dissatisfaction.

"Is the old sea dog complaining about such a trifle?"

He grinned. "No mama. It's nothing really. I just thought I'd mention it." And settling himself down at her feet he asked her to tell him about Martha.

Elizabeth told him how she had appeared from nowhere asking for food, that she and Alice had been on the road for two days, how exhausted they were and how she'd taken them in.

"Where was Martha going?"

"She wasn't going anywhere. She was running away." She told him all that Martha had told her, though she found it difficult to talk about her being raped. However Nathaniel's questions drew the whole story out of her. Finally she had to tell him that Martha's master had had his way with her.

"Had his way with her?" Nathaniel had interrupted her. "You mean he wanted to have a bit of girlie?"

Elizabeth felt herself blushing. This was some sailor man's saying, she presumed. Nevertheless it was clear these two quaint phrases had the same meaning. "Yes, Nathaniel," she said. "You could put it that way!"

Thankfully Nathaniel didn't question her further and she was able to compose herself. She'd been getting out of her depth!

Nathaniel broke the silence. "The Captain got terribly angry when he heard that one of the hands was having a bit of girlie with a woman slave."

"Did he? What did he do?"

"Oh! He gave him thirty lashes."

"What do you mean?" Suddenly it was her turn to be naive!

"Mama, you know, thirty lashes with the cat of nine tails. The Captain had him tied to the mast and flogged in front of everyone, slaves and all." Nathaniel didn't mention that it was he who'd found Hughes with the slave-girl, nor that later Hughes had so nearly killed him. He would never tell her about that, nor for that matter how Hughes had died.

"Oh! Poor man." She said involuntarily.

"He got what he deserved, mama! You should have seen that poor slave-girl; she was sobbing her heart out."

"Yes." Elizabeth agreed. "I'm sure he deserved it. Captain Youle must be a good man to care so much for his slaves."

Nathaniel shrugged his shoulders "So Martha's an escaped slave! What will happen d'you think if they find her?"

The possibility haunted Elizabeth. "I really don't know, Nathaniel. I can't bear to think about it. I just pray she won't be found!"

Nathaniel saw his mother looking apprehensive and sought to change the subject. "We're off to the "Mary Anne" to get my gear on Thursday aren't we?"

"Yes, if the weather's fine." The thought of seeing this man who wanted to marry her tempted her!

"Mama, Thursday will be fine, I know it will! And I'll show you round the ship too."

They'd made an early start on the Thursday morning. Mrs Jackson had given them a huge breakfast and Miles had all three horses saddled and ready. It had been sometime since Nathaniel had ridden but despite his fears he soon felt happy on his grandfather's gelding, a gentle old fellow. His mother rode her mare Turnip and Miles followed on trusty old

Bracken. Nathaniel glanced admiringly at his mother. He was so proud of her! She made a striking figure in her dusty pink habit and he especially liked her matching hat with its pheasant's feather. It gave her a youthful, devil-may-care look!

Apart from an odd word now and then about their route, they rode in silence lost in their own thoughts. Elizabeth's sleep had been strangely beset by dreams. She'd been in a barn with hundreds of others. Naked and in leg irons she had struggled towards the light which promised freedom, but she was surrounded by lecherous men who barred her way. She fought them as best she could. Then she saw James. How strong he was! He pushed her tormentors aside and reaching her threw his coat over her. "Come," he said and led her towards the great doors. But the promised freedom was a delusion. She found herself on a stage surrounded by licentious men. A voice cried "Who'll start the bidding for this shapely wench?" She heard David's voice, "Five guineas." Then James', "Six." The bidding was fast and furious. Then with a mighty crash the auctioneer's hammer fell. She'd woken up terrified! The curtains were billowing in the wind that streamed through the window that had fallen open with such an ear splitting crash. But who had bought her? Charming, polite, handsome David or James, the resolute slaver? Not David surely! She'd never marry him! Then she'd smiled. Perhaps James had bought her!

Chapter 29

Jim paced the deck as he had done the previous afternoon, watching for Nathaniel to arrive and hoping that Elizabeth would be with him. He'd half expected him yesterday, but that had been foolish. He really couldn't expect Elizabeth to let Nathaniel return on his very first day home. Like all mothers, she'd have spent the day fussing over him, not letting him out of her sight! He tried to convince himself they'd come today, yet he knew he might have to wait a week or more. He felt cold and dispirited. He looked along the quay again; still there was no sign of them. He could concentrate on nothing but the thought of seeing her and as the tension built up inside him, he'd become ever more irritable. He'd been short with the Bo's'un earlier over some minor matter, something so trivial he couldn't now remember what it was! He gave a wry laugh. Patience had never been one of his best attributes and not knowing if she'd come today, tomorrow or even if she'd come at all was tormenting him! He kept wondering how she'd reacted to that clumsy letter of his. Had she been appalled that a rough, common, uneducated Master of a slave ship should have had the temerity to suggest she should be his wife! He pictured her reading it with a laugh of derision on her lips; showing it to her friends for a cheap giggle, before feeding it to the candle. Yet it could be that she'd keep it for what he'd said about the boy. But what of the second part! The words came back to him! 'I'm infatuated and bewitched by you and can never be happy until you are my wife.' He could see her and her cronies laughing over that!

But was that really the way she'd behave? Would this woman he admired so much really be so cold and arrogant? No, he couldn't believe that! If she did reject him as he feared she might, he was sure she'd do it with grace and compassion. He sighed. It all hinged on that letter of his! But had it been delivered? Surely the boy wouldn't have forgotten. He'd thought at the time it was a good idea to tell him it was his report. He'd hoped the boy would want to know how he'd done. Now he wasn't so sure! What if he thought it was a bad report? Surely he wouldn't throw it away. No, he was certain he wouldn't do that. He was a trustworthy lad. But then of course if the boy thought it wasn't a good report he might wait a few days before he gave it her. He cursed his stupidity! He could do nothing now, except wait, wait, wait!

He turned forlornly and strode aft. He'd give her a little longer then he'd accept she wasn't coming today. He reached the after rail, paused and fingered the ring hanging from his neck. It comforted him. He found it helped him think more clearly about her. Did she still feel so strongly about slavery? Could she have mellowed? No. He was sure her views wouldn't have changed. He shook his head ruefully. If they hadn't there was no hope for him! How could he persuade her that he was a decent man, making a living in the only way he knew? He turned again and strode for'ard. But was it the only way? He didn't have to work the slave trade! Well he had to for one more voyage, but then, well then he could look for a ship in another trade! He felt the tension ease. He could see a way forward! He stepped out again, this time with more of a spring in his step, his mind a-whirl with this new idea. But his step soon faltered. There was that wretched be-spectacled clerk approaching with his infuriating ledger. "Damn," he exclaimed. "More bloody queries. He won't be content until he's checked every last detail!" How he'd love to have him and all his like on board in a gale. He'd have them up there furling and setting the t'gallants all day! The thought cheered him. He laughed and putting on a good face ushered the clerk below.

As he had expected, it was a pettifogging query that had brought the clerk onboard. What exactly had been bartered for the slaves at Goree? He'd found his papers and they buried themselves in the figures. But still he couldn't satisfy his questioner. As his blood began to boil, he heard a knock on the door. "There's a lady come to see you, Cap'n, she's with Mr Lugger."

It must be her, it can only Elizabeth! His heart raced. "You'll have to go now," he told the startled clerk."

"But Captain Youle, sir," he heard him complain.

"Go, go, damn you. I've got more important work to do than playing with these damn figures. I'll send for you tomorrow or maybe the day after" and so saying he bundled the startled clerk and his damned ledger out through the door.

At first he couldn't see her, though he saw the boy. Then he spotted her! She'd come, she was here! For a while he was content to let his eyes feast on her. She looked so feminine, so elegant, quite out of place on the deck of a weather-beaten vessel. He started towards her, but she hadn't seen him. She was talking to the Bo's'un! He heard her say "I'm very glad to meet you, Mr Tyacke. Nathaniel's told me so much about you! I hear you've been very kind and helpful to him." He stood and watched them chatter for what seemed an age. He fumed impatiently. They were quite oblivious of him! He'd always thought highly of the Bo's'un, but now he felt angry. Get on with your work, damn you, he wanted to tell him. But he couldn't say that, it would upset her! Still they chatted, with him laughing and turning on the charm like some young gallant!

He could bear it no longer. He stepped forward and greeted them with as much nonchalance as he could muster. "Morning, Mr Lugger, you've come for your possessions?" As soon as he'd spoken, he knew it was a stupid thing to say. Why else would he come? But Nathaniel seemed not to notice. He seemed too pleased to be back! "Yes, sir, I said I'd come in a day or two."

Well, that's fine". He doffed his hat at Elizabeth. "And it's good of you, ma'am, to come with him."

Elizabeth glanced at him and he found himself looking into those cornflower blue eyes he remembered so well. She smiled and her eyes took on a friendly look.

"Not at all," he heard her saying. "I wanted to come. Nathaniel's told me so much about you and the "Mary Anne". For a moment he daren't speak. She seemed so warm, so friendly! The hope he'd clung to for all those long months came surging back.

"Well, ma'am, welcome aboard. I'm afraid the ship's not as smart and tidy as she was the last time you saw her. But come along to my cabin ma'am. I'm sure you'll remember it." At the top of the companionway he turned. "Bo's'un," he called as he extended a hand to help her down the ladder. "Send a hand to Mrs Wright at the Anchor and ask her to bring along the victuals I ordered." He turned to her. "I was sure you'd both be hungry after your early start, so I've taken the liberty of ordering some victuals."

"That's most considerate of you, sir. We did leave uncommonly early and the icy wind has certainly put an edge on my appetite. How about you, Nathaniel?"

Nathaniel grinned. "I'm starving!"

Jim offered her his chair and cleared his throat to say what he'd planned. But her presence mesmerised him, it filled the cabin like an exquisite flower and he found himself lost for words. Elizabeth smiled. "It was a very good report you wrote for Nathaniel. It was most encouraging and I enjoyed reading it to him."

"Yes," suddenly Jim felt at ease. "Nathaniel's done very well. You've every reason to be proud of him, Elizabeth." Her name had slipped so easily from his lips. He used it so often when he thought of her, but never before had he called her Elizabeth to her face. He looked for her reaction. She seemed unmoved, neither offended nor pleased! Had she not heard him? Maybe she'd chosen to ignore it! Women had always mystified him! If only he knew how their minds worked!

He realised she was talking again, but he hadn't heard a word.

"I'm sorry, ma'am. I didn't catch what you were saying."

Elizabeth was intrigued, he seemed so apprehensive! This man who could bring a ship safely into port through storm and tempest was looking like a nervous youth! She smiled and began again. "Captain Youle, if I let Nathaniel sail with you again, as I know he wants to….."

"Yes, Mama, I really do," Nathaniel broke in.

Elizabeth went on. "If he does sail with you, what plans do you have for him?"

If he does? If? Her reservations had him worried. If the boy didn't sail with him for a second voyage, he knew he'd never see her again!

"Well ma'am." He felt he, not the boy, was under examination! "Nathaniel must continue with his instructions and duties as an apprentice but after the next voyage, providing he continues to do well I'll be willing to sign him on as Third Mate."

"So, he'll finish his apprenticeship at the end of his next voyage?"

"Yes, ma'am, providing he continues to do well, as I'm sure he will."

"So when do you expect your next voyage to end?"

"Well, I expect to sail in February and if the winds are kind I should be back in the spring of seventy-four."

"Good. Now, Captain Youle, if at that time he wishes to work in another trade, would you recommend him as a Third Mate to another Master?"

"Aye, ma'am. If he's good enough to serve as a Third Mate with me, of course I'd recommend him. I don't want any mate sailing with me who'd rather serve another Master. You can't run a ship properly least I can't, if the mates aren't on your side!"

"Well, Captain Youle, as I'm sure you must appreciate I want him to work in the slave trade no longer than absolutely necessary." A quizzical smile brightened her face. "No doubt you remember how unhappy I was, when I learnt what your cargo was to be."

"Yes, ma'am, I do indeed." He sighed. It all seemed to be going wrong. She'd brought up the one subject he'd wished to avoid!

"Well, sir. If you're as good as your word and I do believe you're a man of integrity, I am willing for Nathaniel to sail with you on your next voyage."

Integrity, integrity! She'd said he had integrity, the very quality he admired so much in her! That had to be a good sign. Suddenly he saw a ray of hope!

"Well that's capital, ma'am, just excellent." He could feel himself grinning. "I hoped you'd agree!" He looked across at Nathaniel. "That's settled then, Mr Lugger. We'll sail together again eh?"

"Oh! Yes sir. That'll be splendid." The worried expression on Nathaniel's face had vanished. Now he was all smiles. "Thank you, mama. I'll be a Third Mate next time I come home."

She returned his smile. "Yes, Nathaniel, I've no doubt you will."

Though his obvious happiness pleased her, her guilt returned. Once again she'd abandoned her principles. Yet what else could she have done? Having started articles it would be foolish to take him away before he'd finished. She hoped the Good Lord would forgive her! Captain Youle was clearly pleased, yet the conversation faltered. Her search for a congenial topic was interrupted by the sound of footsteps, the clatter of pans and the chatter of voices. The door sprang open and a large woman appeared. She was short of breath and carrying a huge platter on which sat a great joint of beef.

"'Ere tes, Cap'n." Mrs Wright puffed her way into the cabin. A serving girl followed with a tray of vegetables and then a lad carrying tankards and a jug of ale. Having laid the table, Mrs Wright handed Jim a carving knife and with a well-practised wink, led her team out. But the door had hardly closed when she reappeared. "Apple pie's to follow, Cap'n. I'll send it over later." The smell of roast beef filled the cabin as Jim carved and Elizabeth dispensed the vegetables. Nathaniel was quite ravenous, but as he reached for his knife and fork his mother caught his eye and hurriedly he replaced them. Jim was puzzled by his apparent reluctance to eat, but then he saw Elizabeth lower her head and speak in a quiet voice. "For this good food and all his many gifts, may the Good Lord make us truly thankful." He heard Nathaniel say "Amen" and he hastily followed suit and taking a lead from Elizabeth he began to eat. But Elizabeth stopped. "Oh dear!" She exclaimed. "I've forgotten poor Miles!"

"There's no need to worry, ma'am. I've told the Bo's'un to take him to the Anchor and get him fed." Jim laughed. "Mor'n likely, he's eating beef, same as us."

"Oh! Thank you, Captain. You've thought of everything. You're most kind!"

"Ma'am I'm just delighted to have you on board." He felt happy. Then with a start he remembered the ale. He poured the amber liquid into the tankards and passed them round. "We should drink a toast."

"Who are we to toast sir?" Nathaniel asked.

"You my boy!" Jim raised his tankard. "Ma'am perhaps you'd drink a toast with me to the long life and great success of Nathaniel. May he be a wise navigator and a considerate Master!"

"To Nathaniel." They said in unison. Nathaniel laughed and muttered "Yes. I'll be a Master one day."

The apple pie had duly arrived and had been consumed and when the table had been cleared, Elizabeth thanked him. "That was a tasty meal, sir, and all the better for being unexpected." She turned to her son, "Now Nathaniel you must get your belongings. We must be off soon."

Nathaniel grinned. "I won't be long. I'll be back in a minute."

"Don't hurry Nathaniel dear. Captain Youle and I have another matter to discuss. When you've finished go and talk to that nice Mr Tyacke."

When they were alone, she was the first to speak. "Now, James, if I can call you James?"

She saw his face light up. "Please do, ma'am. May I call you Elizabeth?"

"Yes, James you may. You already have and I was delighted!" She saw him smile. "That was a most touching letter you wrote. It moved me greatly. I've never had its like before!"

Jim laughed. "Elizabeth, believe me, it's the first I've ever written!"

She'd never seen him laugh. It suited him. Those twinkling eyes and that chuckle made him look young and carefree.

"Elizabeth, I meant every word!" He was looking serious again.

"James, I know you did. Your sincerity was all too apparent. But," suddenly she seemed lost for words.

He knew, he knew it! The word 'but' was all too ominous. It had seemed to be going so well, but he'd been fooling himself! It was clear she was going to reject him!

Elizabeth had seen his face fall. She reached for his hand, his hard calloused hand. "James, you're a kind and considerate man and you'll make some woman a fine husband. But James dear I'm sorry to say, that woman cannot be me."

His heart almost stopped. Yet it was what he'd expected! She wouldn't have him! All his long held hopes had been crushed in an instant. Why, why couldn't she be his wife? He broke the silence that engulfed them.

"Elizabeth, I've been captivated by you ever since the first time I saw you standing on the quay with your son. Scarcely a day's gone by when I've not thought of you and dreamt of having you as my wife. I love you, Elizabeth, and always will." He sighed and opened his hands in a gesture of despair. "You say I'll make a fine husband for some woman. But why, why can't that woman be you? Tell me I beg you."

She'd known this would be difficult. She had given his unexpected proposal great thought and she knew she'd made the right decision. If he'd been a cleric, a farmer or a merchant, she might have agreed to marry him, but nothing would induce her to marry anyone connected in any way with the slave trade. How could she? With her hatred of slavery, it would be quite immoral! No matter how much he appealed to her, no matter how much she had come to admire him, even to hold him in her affection, he was the master of a slave ship! That was why she couldn't and wouldn't be his wife. She realised she was still holding his hand. She gave it a gentle squeeze and looked into his eyes.

"James, surely you must realise how much I abhor slavery. To tear people from their homes and families and ship them across the ocean into a life of slavery is an evil, wicked act, a despicable crime. It is for that reason I cannot and will not marry any man who is associated with such an evil trade." She paused. "No matter how much I might admire him!"

He looked forlorn. "So there's no hope?"

His wretchedness touched her. "James, dear can you not see how I feel? Can't you give up this awful trade?"

"I'd give it up gladly, if you'd marry me Elizabeth, but." It was his turn to use that wretched word! "But, I must make one more voyage."

He thought she looked disappointed. "Why? Why must you?"

"Well, you see, Elizabeth, I'm one of six partners who own the Mary Anne and when I invested my share of the capital I insisted that I be guaranteed command of her for at least two voyages with an option for a third. I made sure it was written into the contract. So Elizabeth I have to complete a second voyage before I can renounce my option."

"But James could you not refuse to work this terrible trade as a matter of principle? That would be the honourable thing to do!" Those blue eyes of hers had that earnest look about them.

"I could refuse a second voyage Elizabeth, but if I did my partners would sue me for breach of contract and I'd have to make a costly settlement. I'm afraid doing what you call the honourable thing would lead to poverty and poverty leads to misery and unhappiness!"

She was silent.

"Elizabeth, dear, I love you and I want to you to be my wife, but I have to be realistic and accept my obligations." He'd hoped she would agree, but she said nothing.

He took a deep breath. "Elizabeth, I promise you faithfully I'll give up the slave trade after my next voyage. Will you marry me then?"

She shook her head slowly. "James dear, if I won't marry a slaver, how can I be betrothed to one?"

He was devastated. "So will you never marry me?"

"James, dear, I never said that. Perhaps you should ask me again once you've given up slaving."

She saw the tension ease in his eyes.

"Elizabeth dear, when I ask you then, what will you say?"

She laughed. "I might say yes."

Chapter 30

She'd been gone for three long weeks; her presence now a distant memory Life without her had become a mere existence, a meaningless passing of the days! He longed to see her again. He must see her before he sailed. His only hope was that she'd come with Nathaniel when he joined. But would she? Why, he asked himself, was life so cruel? Why did fate decree that the woman he loved should live so far away? Why couldn't her father be a priest in some church here in Bristol? Why did it have to be in a distant village? A village whose name, try as he might, eluded him. Somehow with Nathaniel departing in such haste he'd not had the chance to ask him where he lived! Since then he'd searched his memory time and time again, but the name never came! Yet of all the names that came to mind, Hexberry repeated itself more than any other! Could there be such a village? He just didn't know. He put the thought behind him; it was time he ate.

"Evenin' Cap'n." A cheery Mrs Wright welcomed him. "Find yourself a warm seat by the fire and I'll bring along some ale."

"Thank you Mrs Wright. D'you have any roast beef tonight?"

"You mean like I gave you when you 'ad yer lady love aboard?" She winked and gave a raucous laugh. Jim nodded sheepishly. He'd found that wink of hers unsettling and her laugh made him feel conspicuous. Soon the whole inn would know about Elizabeth!

"I'm sure we 'ave, Cap'n, but if we ain't, there's some tasty pork." She gave him another wink. "Will that do?"

"Yes Mrs Wright. Either will do." Jim sat on the settle and warmed himself before the fire.

"She a local lady?" Mrs Wright was back with his ale.

"No, no." He shook his head. Pleased she'd asked no further questions, he sipped the warm ale and surveyed the room. A noisy party filled the long table by the stairs and three old cronies sat sucking their pipes by the other fire. The food was good here, but he wasn't enamoured with the Anchor. Mrs Wright's hail-fellow-well-met manner irritated him. Normally he avoided the place, but the Sailor's Rest had been crowded.

Mrs Wright was approaching. He had to be wary of her. She seemed to know everyone's business and clearly loved to gossip!

She placed a well laden plate before him. It smelt good!

"You'll not find better beef anywhere round 'ere, Cap'n."

Jim took a mouthful. "Aye. Maybe not."

"Where d'you go for yer victuals then Cap'n? We ain't seen much of you in 'ere."

"Oh! Here and there. Mostly the Sailor's Rest I suppose." He wished she'd go away and let him eat his meal in peace. He watched in horror as she drew up a stool.

"Sailor's Rest eh? What's up with you Cap'n? I'd 'ave thought a man of the world like you who's fond of the girls would want good food an' all." She winked again and gave him a nudge. "You won't get that at the Sailor's Rest!"

"It's good enough, ma'am."

"How's the careenin' goin'?"

The sudden change of subject startled him. "Careening? We haven't started yet."

"'Ave you thought where you'll stay when your ship's hauled over on her side? We can make you comfy 'ere y'know! We've had many a Master sleepin' 'ere when his ship's been lying on her beam ends."

"Have you, Mrs Wright?"

"Aye. That we 'ave!" She nodded. "Why don't you stay 'ere then, Cap'n? We'll give you the best room in the 'ouse." She winked again. "And I'll get you a special price, what d'you say?"

He didn't say anything.

"The room I 'ave in mind has the biggest bed of all. You could sleep four in it if you wanted, but I don't s'pose a gent like you would want to share his bed with more than one, eh?" She nudged him and shrieked with laughter.

"All right, all right, Mrs Wright. I'll look at it after I've eaten." He had to say something, anything to get rid of her!

"Right then, Cap'n, I'll leave you to enjoy your meal."

He knew he shouldn't have said he'd see the room. He couldn't stay here with that damn woman around. She'd drive him crazy with all that winking and nudging. He hoped maybe he could settle his bill with the landlord quietly and sneak out. But that had been wishful thinking; he'd hardly finished his pudding, when she was back again.

"We ain't busy tonight. You're in luck." She chortled. "You've got me all to yourself!"

He felt a sudden urge to escape. "Perhaps I can settle up?"

"The landlord'll have yer bill. 'E's told me to show you the room."

He knew he'd been trapped. Obediently he rose and followed her up the stairs. The room was on the first floor, looking out over the quay. By the light of the moon he could see the Mary Anne opposite and away to the left, where the river curved was the careening berth. He could make out the shape of a ship hauled over on her side! It'd be quite convenient, he had to admit. She was right about the bed too. It was huge. Alongside it he saw a commode and by the window a table and two chairs.

"When d'you say you're careening her?"

He sighed. "I didn't say Mrs Wright, but it'll be next Monday."

"Next Monday? Right, you can 'ave it. I'll keep it for you."

Clearly fate had decreed he should stay at the Anchor and be tormented by this overpowering woman. "Well, how much is it?"

She winked again! "It's a special price, Cap'n."

"Yes. You've told me that already. But how much is it?"

"Lordy, I dunno! You'll 'ave to see the landlord!"

He'd sought the landlord to pay for his supper and after some haggling had finally agreed to move in on the Sunday. Though he'd been talked into taking the room, he found it to be all he needed. It was close to the ship and had a good view of the careening berth.

He settled in easily, but he did all he could to avoid Mrs Wright. He found her irrepressible!

On the Monday she appeared with his breakfast. "Seen yer lady love lately?"

"No, Mrs Wright." His heart sank.

"Ain't seen 'er for a while now 'ave you?"

"No, Mrs Wright, not since the day you brought us that roast beef'."

"Well, what's up, Cap'n? She's a real lady that one. I knew it as soon as I clapped eyes on 'er. You ain't fallen out with 'er, I 'ope?"

"No, no, Mrs Wright. It's just that she lives a long way away."

"Oh dear! Well where's she live then?"

"In the country, Mrs Wright".

"She's a country lady is she? I thought as much! Tell me then, where's she live?"

"Well, Mrs Wright, that's the terrible thing, I'm not sure."

"Not sure, Cap'n! How can a grown man be so stupid as not to know where his lady love lives?"

It seemed for once he'd taken her breath away. She shook her head as if she was looking at some half-witted youth.

"Sorry, Cap'n," she said at last. "Didn't mean to be rude, but some might say not to know where yer lady love lives is mighty careless!"

"Yes, Mrs Wright." He sighed. "It's stupid, careless; downright bloody foolish. All I know is that her father is Rector of St Peter's in a village called something like Hexberry or it could be Hamworthy or even Hanbury. I just don't know!"

"'amworthy, 'anbury or 'exberry that right? Well I ain't no good with places, but I do know two old fellers who might know. They come in for a jug of ale and keep talking about the time they spent as boys in the country. Perhaps one of them names'll jog their memory. You leave it to me, Cap'n. I'll see what I can do."

"That's very kind of you." He said weakly. "But, Mrs Wright please be discreet."

"Discreet, Cap'n?" She winked again. "I'll be the very soul of discretion. Trust me, Cap'n."

When she'd gone he cursed himself for confiding in her. What an idiot he'd been! Soon the whole port would be laughing at this lovesick fool who didn't know where the woman he wanted to marry lived!

The next day he'd slunk into the inn hoping not to be seen. He was sure they'd all be pointing at him and sniggering. But to his great relief he'd gone unnoticed, except of course for Mrs Wright. She'd hurried over. "Cap'n, I've got good news. 'Ad a word with old 'Arry. Thought 'e might know and 'e did! 'E says it must be 'anbury. Says 'e remembers the church. St Peter's 'e said it was."

"If he says it's St Peter's it must be the right village! Hanbury eh!" He savoured the name. "Hanbury. Oh! Mrs Wright you're a marvel."

She gave a great cackle. "Old 'Arry says it's maybe nine or ten miles from 'ere, out on the Gloucester road."

"The Gloucester road, you say." She nodded.

"Hanbury eh? Oh! That's marvellous!"

"So when," she gave him a nudge. "When are you going to see 'er Cap'n? Poor lady, she'll be pining for you!"

"Well, Mrs Wright, I'm not sure she'd want me coming to Hanbury. I don't think the Rector would want his daughter associating with the master of a slave ship!"

"Well, Cap'n, you know what they say, 'faint heart never won fair lady'. Surely you'll be wantin' to see yer lady love now you knows where to find 'er. Go out there, Cap'n, and sweep 'er off 'er feet!" She gave him a nudge and left.

Knowing where to find her was like stumbling across hidden fruit. And she was only ten miles away! Now Mrs Wright nagged him without mercy. "When're you going to see yer lady love?" and "What a surprise it'd be!" and telling him how easy it would be to find him a horse! When he told her he hadn't sat on a horse for years it did nothing to dampen her enthusiasm. "Oh! Mr Reed 'as all sorts of 'orses," she'd said. "'E'd find one tame enough for a three year old to ride! 'E'll sort you out."

Mrs Wright's cheerfulness and enthusiasm affected him and with her encouragement a plan began to form. He'd get a horse and arrive in Hanbury early on Christmas morning. He'd go to St Peter's for matins. He'd be bound to find her there!"

"Well if you can wait that long, it'd be a lovely Christmas surprise for her," she'd said.

He nodded. "And as it's the season of good will, I might get a better reception from the Rector, eh?"

"Cap'n, you worry too much! Now what'll you take as a present for 'er?"

Straight away she started making suggestions, it seemed she had a fresh idea every time she saw him, but none seemed right to him. Then one afternoon he'd passed a goldsmith and on an impulse had gone inside. When he'd shown Mrs Wright what he'd bought, she'd been overcome with delight. "Cap'n that's beautiful, really beautiful, she exclaimed as she fingered the gold chain and crucifix. Then she winked. "And very suitable for a Rector's daughter!"

With Christmas so near, he could think of nothing but the journey to Hanbury. Careening the Mary Anne had gone well and by the end of the week she'd be safely alongside the wall again and he could leave her for a few days. He'd had a satisfactory meeting with the shipwright to discuss outstanding repairs and was returning to the Anchor. Hearing horses behind him, he'd turned and had seen a pair coming directly towards him, one being ridden side saddle. It was Elizabeth! She was calling "James, James I thought I'd never find you!" He ran towards her and held the horse's head as she dismounted. "James, you must help me!"

He saw she was upset; close to tears. "Whatever's happened, Elizabeth?"

"Martha and Alice, they've been taken."

Martha and Alice? The names meant nothing to him but she told him they were two slaves she'd rescued. He looked at her with renewed admiration. How typical of her to be rescuing slaves! He held her hands to comfort her. "Elizabeth dear, come to the inn and tell me all about it. Nathaniel, can you deal with the horses and meet us in the Anchor?"

She let him take her arm as they walked to the inn. Now she'd found him, her story flowed as if a dam had burst! It had happened yesterday afternoon, she told him. She'd been riding and as she returned home Mrs Jackson had rushed to tell her Martha and Alice had been seized. There had been a knock on the door. Martha had gone to see who it was and Alice had followed her. Mrs Jackson had heard Martha screaming and had run to the door, but she'd been too late. They'd been taken. She'd seen two men galloping away with them.

A worried Mrs Wright met them at the door of the inn. "You found the Cap'n, then, ma'am."

"Yes," Elizabeth composed herself. "Thanks to you."

"Come, Elizabeth, we must think what we can do." Jim turned to Mrs Wright. "I'm taking Mrs Lugger up to my room. She's very distressed!"

"Right Cap'n. I'll bring you some tea."

He turned to thank her and noticed that for once she hadn't winked! She really is a kind soul, he thought as he led Elizabeth to his room. He gave her the chair by the window and asked her whether anything was known about the two men.

"No. Nothing." She looked at him in despair. "James, what can we do to get Martha and Alice back?"

He shook his head; it seemed an impossible task, but he daren't say so. She was on the verge of tears again. "Well," he said. "There's no doubt those two men were employed by Martha's owner and offered a good reward!"

She nodded. "So," he continued. "We must assume that Martha and little Alice have now been returned to their owner."

"Yes, that possibility haunts me. She'll be at the mercy of that savage beast."

He took her hand. She looked so wretched, so forlorn. "Elizabeth, d'you by any chance know his name or where he lives?"

"No, James, I don't. All I know is that he lives in Bristol but where I've no idea." She sighed wearily.

"Bristol's a huge place, but, Elizabeth, there can't be too many people with slaves!" He had to say something to comfort her! "If only we knew his name."

"Martha did tell me once, but it didn't mean much to me then. I've been trying to remember ever since! It could be Crossley, or something like that! Oh! Why didn't I write it down?"

"Crossley?" He'd repeated the name. Did he know anyone by that name, she'd asked him. No, no one, he'd told her sadly. Crossley eh! He'd repeated the name again. Then it struck him! Could it be Crosbie, his partner? He had a slave or two!

She saw him smile. "I know a Crosbie, a Mr Gordon Crosbie. He has slaves!"

He saw a flicker of hope cross her face. "James, d'you think it could be him?"

"Well, it's a possibility."

"But how d'you know him?"

"Well, Gordon Crosbie is one of the six of us who own the "Mary Anne"!"

"D'you think it really could be him, James?"

"Well, he's a difficult, selfish man and cruel too! I've seen him whip his horse without mercy." He hesitated as a thought dawned on him. "You say Martha's mistress died recently?"

"Yes, yes. About eight or nine months ago."

"Y'know, it could be Gordon Crosbie. He lost his wife last year!"

"Oh! James. The Good Lord must be with us! D'you know where this man Crosbie lives?"

"Yes, yes. I've been to his house twice. It's a big house on Hotwells Road."

"Well, we must go at once! I shall plead with him to give them back to me."

As she stood and reached for her hat, a knock on the door heralded the approach of Nathaniel followed closely by Mrs Wright with a tray of tea. "There you are, m'lady. That'll make you feel better."

"Before you go, Mrs Wright, Mrs Lugger will be staying for a night or two in my room." He saw her smile and half expected to hear one of her terrible laughs, but she said nothing. "Mr Lugger here will also be staying and he and I would like separate rooms, if that is possible."

"Right Cap'n I'll 'ave a word with the landlord. We'll 'ave two rooms free, I'm sure."

As she left, Jim gently relieved Elizabeth of her hat and persuaded her to sit down and pour the tea. "It's no good rushing up to Hotwells Road, Elizabeth. Before we do that we have decide how to tackle him."

She nodded. "Yes, James, you're right. Finding Martha and Alice is one thing, getting them back is another."

"Mm, that's right. Now, Elizabeth, whether we like it or not, we have to accept that he has a legal right to hold the girl and her child, since by the law of the land they're his property. He might even feel that he has the right to charge you with their theft!"

Elizabeth looked shocked. "James, I hadn't thought of that!"

He wasted no time developing his plan. He feared she might launch into her usual condemnation of the slave trade and all those who participated in it, but instead she listened quietly.

"Elizabeth, if we do find them, our best plan is to buy them."

She didn't reply. The thought of owning another human being filled her with horror!

"It's our only hope Elizabeth. Once Martha and the child belong to you, no one can take them away from you."

"But James," she said with evident dismay. "I don't want to own them! I want them to be free like you and me."

"It's the only way Elizabeth. Later when you're sure they're safe you can think about giving them their liberty, but not till then!"

His suggestion seemed to make her a little happier. "James if we do find them and if he's willing to sell, how much will he ask for them?"

"That's a difficult question Elizabeth. He might have paid anything between thirty and forty pounds when he bought Martha. Then he'll expect to recover the money he gave those two blackguards."

Jim stroked his beard. "That might be ten pounds. Then, there's little Alice."

"James, surely he can't charge for her. She's not old enough to work."

"Elizabeth, she's not old enough now, but she will be one day. Then as a young desirable slave girl he'll get a good price for her."

"Oh James, how hateful mankind can be! Is Alice really just an object to be bought and sold to alleviate man's basic desires? Dear Lord help us! We must get Martha and Alice back."

"Yes, Elizabeth, but first we must find them!"

"Yes, James." Elizabeth was looking distressed. "But how will I ever find so much money?"

"Elizabeth, dear, don't fret. I've plenty on account in the partnership."

Through her tears she looked lovingly at him. "Oh! Thank you James. Whatever would I do without you?"

Her gratitude set his pulse racing. He longed to embrace her, but this was not the time!

"Don't thank me yet, Elizabeth. We haven't even found them!"

"When shall we go to see this Mr Crosbie, James?"

"Elizabeth, I think it would be better if I saw him on my own. If you show him how upset you are and he agrees to sell them, he'll more than double the price. That is of course if he has them!"

She looked disappointed. "I suppose you're right, but James how will you know it's Martha? You've never seen her!"

"Yes, but you've told me how pale she is, how straight her hair is and that she has a black child! There can't be many slaves like her in Bristol! Besides I'll insist the clerk draws up a deed of sale and that the exchange takes place in his office. Then I'll take you along and you can make sure they really are Martha and Alice."

Reassured and persuaded that it was sensible to wait till morning; Elizabeth agreed to remain in the Anchor while James went to execute his plan. Delighted to be with Elizabeth, he comforted her as best he could, but the evening was a sombre one. Nothing he could do or say would make those eyes of hers smile. They remained obstinately anxious and downcast!

Chapter 31

In the airless little cell of a room he'd been given, Jim could think of nothing but Elizabeth and her two lost slaves. Could it really be that Gordon Crosbie had them? And if so could he be persuaded to sell them? Crosbie was a heartless, domineering man motivated by power and greed. Persuading him to sell them could be all nigh impossible. Yet he'd have to. He couldn't fail Elizabeth. His worries kept sleep at bay and it seemed he'd only just closed his eyes when the pale light of dawn awoke him.

"How's your lady love?" Mrs Wright greeted him as he sat down for breakfast. "She seemed terrible upset last night."

He nodded, not knowing what to say. Then he told her how she'd rescued an escaped slave and her child, how she'd given them shelter and how they'd been recaptured.

"Oh! Poor lady. She looks as if she's lost one of her own!"

"Yes. She loved them dearly."

When she left him he cursed himself for telling her. After that sleepless night he hadn't thought of the consequences.

"Mrs Wright," he began as she offered him his porridge, "You've been very kind and helpful and I know I can trust you. But if we're to rescue that slave girl and her child you won't repeat anything I've said, will you?"

"Don't worry Cap'n. I shan't mention it to a livin' soul! I just hopes and prays she'll get 'em back."

What a change he'd seen in her. The winks and nudges and even her cackle of a laugh had disappeared in her concern for him and Elizabeth. What a motherly old soul lay hidden beneath that coarse exterior. He finished his breakfast hurriedly and set off for Hotwells Road. Surprisingly he felt encouraged. Something told him he'd find Martha and Alice there, yet how he'd broach the subject of the slaves still eluded him. If you got off on the wrong tack with Gordon Crosbie, he could be very difficult! But as he came over the crest of the hill and the elegant terrace of houses came into view an idea occurred to him. The more he thought about it the better he liked it! Yes, he'd enquire about that excellent slave girl Mrs Crosbie had had and ask what had happened to the girl when Mrs Crosbie so sadly died. He'd tell him he was wanting such a lady's servant for his intended. He began to feel more confident. It was a plausible approach. It would have to do, he could think of no other! Walking past the terrace where so many rich merchants lived, he wondered what sort of house he could afford for Elizabeth and him. Nothing as grand as these, he knew! At last he reached number nine and beseeching the help of Elizabeth's God he climbed the steps and knocked on the door. There was no response, the door remained obstinately shut! He knocked again, but still there was no answer. He waited impatiently, then tried a third time. Almost at once the door swung open and a pale coloured servant girl with straight black shiny hair appeared. "Sorry, sir. I don't know what's happened to the footman."

"Don't worry Martha", he whispered. "I'm a friend of Mrs Lugger. I've come to do what I can to get you back for her." A look of disbelief crossed the girl's face.

"Oh sir! I'd do anything to be back with her. Alice and I were safe there."

"Well, take me to Mr Crosbie and trust me Martha."

She led him into the sitting-room. "There's a gentleman to see you, sir."

Gordon Crosbie rose from his chair. "You idle, stupid bitch, how many times do I have to tell you to ask visitors their name? Will you never learn? Get out of my sight before I hit you."

Jim watched the girl tense, readying herself for the blow. Then she turned hurriedly and left the room.

"G'morning James." Gordon came towards him with out-stretched hands and feigned bonhomie. Jim had seen him like this before. "Sit yourself down and tell me why I have the pleasure of your company this fine morning."

"Good morning, Gordon," Jim replied. "Well we haven't seen each other for a while and I thought you'd like to know how we're getting on with the refit of the "Mary Anne"."

Gordon nodded. "Yes. I've been thinking it's time you told me when you'll be ready to sail."

"Well, Gordon, we've almost finished caulking the hull and if all goes well, she should be afloat again early next week. Then we've got work to do on the masts and rigging, before we can bend on the sails."

"Good. You've had a lot of work done on her by all accounts. I hope it's all necessary!"

Jim controlled his irritation. Only when you've survived a storm at sea can you understand why a ship has to be properly maintained. But Gordon Crosbie had never been further than the mouth of the river. He was content for others to face the peril of the sea!

"Gordon, if you want me to ship cargo across the ocean, I must have a seaworthy ship, one that won't break up and founder."

Gordon nodded again, the conversation wasn't to his liking. He could smell more costs in the offing! "Well then James, tell me when d'you expect to sail?"

"I'll be signing on the crew at the end of January. Then we'll have to load victuals and cargo and if we have a fair wind, we should be off about two weeks later. About the middle of February, I'd say."

"By February 14th at the latest eh?"

"If all goes as planned and the wind's favourable."

"Good. I'll arrange a meeting of the partners to agree your sailing orders. We made a reasonable profit on your last voyage, but next time we'll do better eh? And James, we can't afford to lose so many slaves!"

The number of slaves lost on the last crossing had been a sore point between them. Jim was sure the only thing that had comforted Gordon was that so many of the ships company had died too. Not having to pay their wages had helped offset the profit lost on the slaves that had perished.

"Well, Gordon." Jim tried not to show how much he loathed his miserly partner. "We can only do our best."

"Aye and I hope you always do! Now, James, is that all or do you have anything else to discuss?"

Jim said a silent prayer as the moment came. "Yes Gordon, as a matter of fact I do. It's a personal matter."

Gordon raised his eyebrows. "Well, get on with it, man. You ain't wantin' a loan I hope!"

"No, no, of course not, Gordon. I've got plenty enough on account with the partnership."

"Oh!" Gordon looked relieved. "Well then, what is it?"

"Gordon, I haven't told anyone else yet, but I'm planning to get married."

"Gettin' married eh?" He broke into laugh. "Who's the girl?"

"She's a widow I've met. No one you'd know. But the point is Gordon, before I sail I want to give her a good slave girl as a personal maid."

"James, what you do is your affair! Why are you telling me?"

"Well, you see, Gordon I remember your good lady wife, Mrs Crosbie, had a lady's slave. Didn't she? I remember she always seemed pleased with her."

"Yes she did. Priscilla spoiled her you know, treated her almost like a daughter. I never held with it! Slaves must know their place and have plenty of discipline, otherwise they argue."

"But she was a good slave I believe?"

"I never liked her, she was an impertinent little harlot who didn't know her place, but strangely Priscilla seemed pleased with her and so I let sleeping dogs lie."

"Well Gordon, now that Mrs Crosbie has passed on, God rest her soul," he paused respectfully. "And doesn't need a slave now she's with the Lord." Gordon's face showed no reaction. "I wondered if you know what happened to her slave. A slave like hers is just what I'm looking for. I don't suppose you know where she is?"

"You mean Martha?"

"I never knew her name, Gordon."

"No James. I suppose you didn't. Well as it happens she's still with me and that brat of hers too. She might have pleased Priscilla, but since she died Martha's shown her true colours. She's a sullen calculating little hussy and always has been. But mind you Jim, [the thought he might be able to sell the girl suddenly struck him], mind you, she'd make a good lady's maid. She's been well trained and I'm the first to admit she always got on well with Priscilla. Come to think of it I suppose she's always been good with the ladies. She just don't fit in here now though, and that's a fact. Seems she dislikes me and goes out of her way to be awkward."

"Well, Gordon, I had thought that if I could find the girl I might try to buy her, but if you say she's sullen", he stopped as if reconsidering the purchase of this difficult slave.

"Well perhaps sullen's too strong a word." Gordon Crosbie stroked his chin. "As I said she made a perfect lady's slave. I think she just ain't suitable for men," he gave James a friendly wink. "Y'know what I mean

Jim? Anyway, she don't like me, that's for sure, no matter how kind and considerate I try to be!"

"She's alright with the ladies then?"

"Yes Jim, take my word for it, she'll do your lady well. Do I understand you're wanting to buy her?"

"Well I wasn't expecting to find her so easily, but since you mention it, I might be interested. But Gordon I'd have to have a good look at her."

"That's no problem Jim, but you'd have to buy the brat as well. I can't be left with the worry of selling that separately."

"Well perhaps I'd better see the child as well!"

"I'll get her in." He went to the door and shouted "Martha, Martha come here and bring that brat of yours."

Jim heard her coming along the passage, then hesitantly she entered the room.

"You wanted me and Alice, sir?"

"Yes, this gentleman wants to have a look at you and the child. Seems he's wantin' a lady's maid."

Jim tried to not to show his excitement. "It's Martha, isn't it and the child's Alice?"

"Yes sir." Martha's heart was beating rapidly as she studied the man who knew her name though they'd never met! And he knew about Alice and Mrs Lugger too! He'd said he'd come to rescue her! Dare she believe it? Her mind had been in a whirl ever since he'd come. That's why she'd forgotten to ask his name and had announced him as a 'gentleman'.

"Martha, I understand you were a good servant to your late mistress."

"I did my best for her, sir. She was kind and gentle and I loved her."

"Well Martha, I'm seeking a personal servant for a lady I know." He saw her eyes fill with hope. "Turn around and let me look at you."

"Mm. She seems fit enough, Gordon. Can she sew and mend and brush ladies' hair?"

"Yes, yes." Gordon seemed irritated by such a stupid question. "I told you she's been well trained."

"And how old's the girl, Gordon?"

"Don't ask me James, ask her." Gordon's irritation was visibly growing.

"She's nearly four, sir."

"So she'll be useful in a few years eh?"

Martha nodded. "You won't buy me without her, sir, will you?"

"No, Martha. Not if the price is right."

They sent Martha and Alice away while they haggled.

"You're asking too much, Gordon. This is a private sale with no agent's commission," Jim kept telling him.

"Yes Jim, but she's the very slave you've been searching for," Gordon would reply.

"Ah! But you've said she's no use to you." Jim would counter.

Then there was the child to consider. He had to make Gordon believe she was a liability, though he daren't emphasise that too much. He had to have them both! But now in Gordon's eyes she was no longer a brat, she was an asset with a growing value. "Jim, in ten years or less," he kept saying, "you'll get a good price for her."

It was an exhausting battle of wits, between one who wanted to buy, whatever the cost and the other whose very nature demanded the highest possible price. But at last the bargaining was done and a price agreed.

"Martha." Gordon had opened the door. "Captain Youle has bought you and the child. Get your things ready, we'll be leaving in ten minutes."

"Well, it's a fine bargain for you." Gordon Crosbie had adopted an effusive manner. "But Jim, I don't mind letting a partner of mine having them cheap. Look after your partners that's always been a guiding principle for me."

"Well Gordon, I'm satisfied. Now all we need do is to see the Clerk."

"Aye, Jim. That's all that remains to be done. I'll get him to draw up a bill of sale and transfer the money from your account to mine. Then you're welcome to 'em."

Chapter 32

Though heartened by James' welcome support, the trauma of Martha and Alice's sudden disappearance had left Elizabeth quite distraught. While she feared his suggestion that his partner had them was too good to be true, she prayed that James was right. But if he had them, how would they get them back? Her worries were interrupted by a tap on the door. She rushed to open it.

"James, James, have you've found them?"

He nodded. "Yes, yes, Elizabeth. And I've arranged to buy them both!" He was laughing and she saw that youthful carefree look again. "Come, I want you to see them to make sure it is them!"

"Oh! Thank God." She hugged him. "James dearest, how wonderful! Tell me I'm not dreaming. Tell me you really have found them!"

"Elizabeth dear, you're not dreaming. I really have found them!" He saw her eyes smiling. It made him want to shout for joy. But a voice inside warned him, "What if by some awful trick of chance they aren't Martha and Alice?"

As he led her to the Clerk's office he told her all that had happened. Listening intently she nodded vigorously as he described the slave who'd let him in and the little black child who had appeared later. Feeling more confident but fearful that any signs of joy on her part would make Crosbie suspicious and thereby jeopardise the deal, he warned her not to show she recognised them. "Just ask Martha the sort of questions any lady wanting a maid would ask."

Gordon Crosbie made no effort to welcome them as they entered the office. He seemed engrossed in the ledgers. Seeing his opportunity James looked hard at Martha and putting his finger to his lips indicated that she should keep silent. It was important she should not recognise Elizabeth.

Alice, he was pleased to note, was clearly frightened by the sudden turn of events and stood with her head hidden in her mother's skirt. He prayed she would remain quiet.

"Good morning, ma'am." Gordon Crosbie raised his eyes from the ledger and turned towards Elizabeth. "May I say how fortunate Captain Youle is, that you have agreed to be his wife." He smirked at Jim. "You are indeed a lucky fellow sir!"

As Elizabeth thanked him for his compliment, a blush coloured her face, but she quickly regained her composure and in a business-like manner enquired how long the slave had been in his wife's service.

"Four years, ma'am. She found her to be an excellent servant."

Elizabeth turned to Martha. "And can you sew, girl, and mend and help me dress and brush my hair?"

"Yes, ma'am. That's what I did for my last lady, God rest her soul."

"And the child, is she well behaved?"

"Yes ma'am. She'll give you no trouble."

"Well, what do you say my dear?" James caught Elizabeth's eye. "Will you accept them both as a betrothal present?"

Elizabeth gave a slight nod and thanked him graciously. Then feigning boredom she sat quietly fanning herself while trying to hide her growing impatience as she waited for the two of them to place their signatures on the bill of sale.

When all was complete and they were ready to leave, Gordon Crosbie put on an affected air. "Ma'am I would not have sold them had I not been sure they would be given the same affection that I and the dear departed Mrs Crosbie lavished on them. But I have to admit to being satisfied that you will treat them well and it is for that reason that I am content to have sold them to Captain Youle for such a trifling sum!"

His effrontery and hypocrisy infuriated Elizabeth, but she bit her lip. She knew it wouldn't help if she showed her anger. James however merely smiled! "Sir, it seems both parties are satisfied with the bargain. Pray excuse us. I am sure we have taken up too much of your valuable time already."

Gordon smiled superciliously. "It's been a pleasure to meet you, ma'am."

"Come, Elizabeth my dear." James took her arm. "Martha," he gave the slave a stern look. "Bring Alice and follow us." And with a "G'day, sir", he led the party out and along the quay to the Anchor.

How he'd managed to refrain from laughing he'd never know! He'd really pulled the wool over that miserly, money-grubbing, mercenary, self-centred partner of his! If Gordon Crosbie had only known that it had been Elizabeth who had given Martha and Alice sanctuary and how eager she was to recover them he'd have held out for a huge price. "'Ain't no use trying to sell your slaves in a port that's awash with 'em." Gordon Crosbie had told him before the last voyage. "Find a port where they're in short supply. When they're really wanted, you'll get a worthwhile price." Well thankfully Gordon hadn't known how desperately Elizabeth had wanted Martha and Alice. He laughed; it had been a good deal, a very good deal! He'd had to lie of course and tell Gordon that Elizabeth was his intended and he remembered how she had blushed when Gordon had told him what a lucky fellow he was! Sadly it wasn't true. They weren't betrothed, it had just been a subterfuge. She hadn't accepted him yet, but after the next voyage when he'd given up slaving he hoped she would. He'd not give up till she was his! He stole a quick glance at Elizabeth. She was looking radiant; her beauty made him gasp. He always wanted her look like that!

"Martha, keep close," he heard her say. Then turning to him, "James you've been wonderful, however would I have got them back without you?"

He relished her praise, but strove to decry his efforts. "Lady Luck was with us," he said modestly.

"Nonsense, James. It was your clever plan that did the trick." She chuckled. "And you handled him so well! Oh! What an odious, malevolent creature he is. Just being near him made my flesh creep. But you had the better of him and it's all because of you that I've got Martha and Alice back."

He revelled in her gratitude, but his modesty forbade him accept full credit for their recovery and he was still humbly praising Lady Luck when on reaching the inn, Martha reached for his arm.

"I don't know how you managed to find us, sir. It's been a miracle. I can hardly believe we've been restored to my kind lady Mrs Lugger. Thank you, thank you." Her thanks were cut short by Mrs Wright as she rushed out to greet them. "Lordy ma'am you've got 'em back! I knew your nice Cap'n Youle would find 'em for you. You can count on 'im, ma'am. 'E's a real gen'leman. I tell you ma'am 'e's the sort who'll go through fire and water to get what 'e wants." She gave Jim a wink.

"Thank you, Mrs Wright." Elizabeth was laughing now. "I can see you hold the Captain in high esteem and you're right. He's a truly remarkable man! I can hardly believe that Martha and Alice are back! I'm so very happy." She turned towards the two slaves. "This is Martha and here is little Alice."

As Mrs Wright cooed and clucked at Alice, Jim caught her eye and gave her a wink. It startled her and she gave one of her characteristic guffaws.

"Mrs Wright," he couldn't help grinning. "We'll be needing an extra room for Martha and Alice."

"Aye, Cap'n, I was thinkin' you might!"

"And, Mrs Wright, we'd like to have supper for all of us in my old room. Can you arrange that?"

"Aye, I'll 'ave a word with the landlord."

Supper that night gave them the chance to celebrate. Mrs Wright had excelled herself and had arranged a huge meal served on the table in the window. As they took their seats, Jim remembered to wait for Elizabeth to say grace. "Let us give our heartfelt thanks to the Good Lord for his everlasting mercy, for providing us with the meal we are about to enjoy and above all for the safe deliverance of Martha and Alice. Amen."

"Elizabeth dear," James interjected. "We should also thank God for your enduring kindness. What would have happened to Martha and Alice if you hadn't given them refuge in the first place?"

"Yes ma'am. You've been our guardian angel! I don't know what would have become of us if I hadn't found you!"

Though overjoyed at being rescued, Martha felt out of place. Never before had she eaten at the same table as her owner. It was a strange, unnatural experience, one that broke every law that governed her life. Being treated as if she was white, as if she was like them, as if the blood running through her veins was no different from theirs. And she wasn't used to such food and when the meal was over she thanked them and politely asked to be excused. "Good night ma'am and thank you sir for rescuing us. Now we belong to Mrs Lugger, I know we're safe at last. Thank you, sir." He felt her tears on his hand as she bent over and kissed it. "The Lord must have sent you!"

When Martha had gone Jim poured the brandy. As he sipped it his eyes feasted on Elizabeth still radiant and elated. He felt happy and relaxed. He glanced at Nathaniel. He was looking out of sorts! Nathaniel was indeed nettled. He'd played second fiddle to Martha long enough. Throughout the meal he'd been no more than a bystander, watching his mother fussing over her and Alice and hearing her talk endlessly to Jim. And during his lonely meal he'd noticed for the first time just how attentive Jim was towards his mother. Naturally he would expect any gentlemen to be polite and courteous to her, but Jim had seemed to hang on his mother's every word. He seemed to be mesmerized by her! Like him, Jim seemed to need her love. It unsettled him! Strangely he felt jealous! He'd had to console himself with the claret, but the departure of Martha and Alice gave him a chance to break into their conversation.

"Mama, how does it feel to be a slave owner?"

His mother's face stiffened. "Nathaniel! Whatever do you mean?"

He wanted to tease her, to shock her, to get his own back for being neglected so much during dinner.

"Well, you own Martha and Alice now don't you?"

"Nathaniel, we've rescued them from that awful man."

"Yes, Mama. But don't you have a bill of sale to show they're your property?"

Elizabeth looked hurt. "Nathaniel, haven't I saved them from a terrible fate?"

Her discomfort upset him, but nothing would stop him now. "Yes, Mama, you have. But who did you turn to for help?"

"Nathaniel dearest, I don't know what it is you wish to imply, but you know as well as I do that I sought help from Captain Youle."

"Yes, Mama, you asked the master of a slave ship to help you." He paused as if wanting to emphasise the point. "You turned to someone working in the trade you profess to abhor!"

"Nathaniel, why are you being so cruel to your mother?" Jim could let him bait her no longer. "Of course your mother is a slave owner now. She has to be! If she's to keep Martha and Alice safe from Mr Crosbie, she's no choice in the matter!" He stopped to let his anger abate. "And, Nathaniel, you know as well as I do that she'll treat them well and set them free when it's safe to do so."

"Of course I'll set them free just as soon as I can. When that happy day comes and slavery is outlawed I promise you they'll be a free as you and I. Don't you believe me?"

"Yes, Mama, of course I do." Now he felt ashamed. "I'm sorry, Mama. It was the irony of it all that made me talk such nonsense. It's just seems so inconceivable, so inexplicable that you of all people should ask a slave ship Master to buy you some slaves!"

"Yes, Nathaniel dear." His accusation of hypocrisy had struck home. She nodded her head slowly. "Yes, I see exactly what you mean! But I'm sure the Good Lord knows I've done it for the right reason!"

"Well, Mama." He was grinning now. "It's good to know that you're one of us now! We're all tarred with the same brush, all tarred with the evils of slavery!"

As she tossed and turned in her bed that night, Nathaniel's words persisted. 'You're one of us now. We're all tarred with the same brush!' The words would not be silenced! Had she indeed condoned the very trade she professed to hate?

Martha broke into Elizabeth's disturbed night. "Morning, ma'am. Captain Youle says he's arranged horses and wants to leave for Hanbury at nine o'clock that is if you're ready."

So began the long journey back with Alice sitting before Nathaniel on his horse and Martha mounted on the quietest mare that could be found. Martha could recall few landmarks, but at last Elizabeth drew her attention to the steeple of St Peter's rising through the trees and she cried, "Alice, we're home."

Chapter 33

It had been a wretched journey back to Bristol. He should have left earlier, but it had been so hard to part. With Martha's horse in hand progress had been painfully slow and he'd been thankful to see lights in the cottages before darkness overtook him and to return the horses without mishap.

Mrs Wright met him at the door of the Anchor. "How's your lady love, Cap'n?"

"She's back home safely with Martha and Alice."

"Pity she don't live in Bristol eh?" She gave him a friendly nudge. "She's a real lady that 'un. Mind you treat 'er right. She'll make a good wife."

"Yes. You're right as usual! Elizabeth would be his wife, he knew that now. He just had to be patient!

For the next few days he lost himself in the work of the ship. Hauling her upright and refloating her was a tricky business and then she had to be warped back to the quay. Now everything that had been removed from her, for fear of breaking loose when the ship was hauled over on her side, had to be replaced. Then work could begin on the masts, spars and rigging.

With the Mary Anne once more alongside, Jim had moved back on board. He was sad to leave Mrs Wright. She was a warm-hearted soul and he'd grown fond of her, winks and all! When he'd said goodbye, he'd given her a shilling and had promised he would still come for supper each night. Though the work kept him busy he found the days dragging as he waited for Christmas. Never before had it excited him so, but then never before had he spent Christmas in the company of the woman he loved.

One night at supper when Mrs Wright began talking of Christmas, he asked her. "Should I give her father a present? What d'you think?"

"Well, Cap'n, ain't you 'opin' to marry 'is daughter? 'Ain't no 'arm in keepin' 'im sweet!"

"Aye, Mrs Wright." He nodded. "You're right, as usual!"

She gave him a beaming smile. "So Cap'n, what're you going to give 'im?"

"I've no idea. I'm not good at buying presents!"

"Well." She gave a conspirator's wink. "When I was a girl and went to church, my old grampy used to say they clergy, they like their tipple! So how's about givin' 'im some French brandy, eh?" She gave him a nudge. "I can get you a bottle." She tapped the side of her nose and added, "At a special price!"

"You're always full of good ideas Mrs Wright! You should set up in business, you know, and have a great banner taken round the town. 'Bring your problems to Mrs Wright. Best solutions offered at special prices'." He smiled as she laughed.

After he'd eaten he took the brandy back to the Mary Anne. His cabin was cold and full of that damp musty smell that came in autumn and stayed like an unwelcome guest till the blessed rays of the summer sun swept it away. It was silent too, silent as a grave. The Mary Anne seemed dead, a great inactive skeleton without flesh or being. She was only happy when she felt the power and rhythm of the sea. Then she became a living thing, her timbers creaking and her rigging singing in the wind. That was her own language, which he'd come to know and understand. For the past three years she'd been his constant companion and together they'd made their way safely across the ocean through many a storm. His was the guiding hand that lead the way. She had been his faithful, long suffering servant who had gone wherever he led without complaint or rancour. It was a relationship he understood and indeed relished. In a strange sort of way he knew he loved the Mary Anne, though not as he loved Elizabeth. His love for the Mary Anne was a blend of respect, loyalty, gratitude for keeping him safe and a feeling of belonging. She didn't tug at his heart strings, as Elizabeth did, nor was he upset when they were separated, but he knew he'd feel sad even a little heartbroken, when the time came for him to say goodbye to her. He'd have to do that when Elizabeth and he were married. He'd promised to give up slaving. Surprisingly the idea pleased him. Some of Elizabeth's revulsion of the trade seemed to have rubbed off on him and rescuing Martha and Alice from the hands of that brute Crosbie had reinforced his newfound distaste for the trade. Before Elizabeth had come into his life he'd scarcely thought about its rights and wrongs. On the rare occasions when such thoughts had entered his mind, he'd done his best to ignore them. And when they'd persisted, like all slavers he'd sought to overcome his scruples by convincing himself that the Africans he bought were sub-human, that they lacked the capacity to think and reason. That they were different. But being with Martha and Alice had convinced him that such assertions were erroneous. But, while his new feelings about slavery made him happy to give up the trade, he would be reluctant to relinquish his calling as a ship's master. He'd been at sea since he was a boy. For twenty-seven years it had been his life; he knew no other. The sea was part of him, it dictated the very way he thought; it had made him the man he was. He knew and had grown to understand, even love its many changing moods. That was its seductive fascination. It would be difficult to live without it. Yet that was what Elizabeth might want him to do. "How can we have a married life together if you're always at sea", he could hear her say! And "How will the children ever know their father?" Yet how could he live without her? But if he gave up the sea how could he earn a living? Elizabeth and he had to be practical. He had to provide for her and their children! He'd promised her he'd try for a ship in the Baltic trade. Their voyages were short, no more than six months! That seemed the best solution.

Such worries left him when he set off for Hanbury at Christmas time. In his excitement he noticed little of the winter scenery until the signpost showing the Hanbury road greeted him. Gratefully he rode down the hill towards the church spire rising through the bare trees. Then he saw the Rectory and Miles ready to greet him.

"Welcome, Cap'n. Miss Elizabeth's expectin' you."

He dismounted, thanked him and there she was; her blue eyes sparkling with that bewitching smile lighting up her face. She held his hands and offered him her cheek. He kissed her gently. "Elizabeth, how I've missed you!"

"I've missed you too, James dear! But now we have two whole days together. We must relish every minute."

"Yes, Elizabeth dear. Every minute has to last an hour!"

She laughed. "Or even two, but now, James, I must introduce you to father. He's looking forward to meeting you." He followed her into the sitting room.

"Father dear, this is James. Captain James Youle of the "Mary Anne"."

"Good afternoon, sir." James offered his hand to the frail old man struggling out of his chair. "Please, please sir, don't get up."

"Can't welcome you to the Rectory sitting down, sir," the old man retorted. He was on his feet now, a tall, distinguished man, with his daughter's blue eyes and silver hair thinning at the temples.

"Pleased to meet you, sir." He gripped James' hand and despite his apparent frailty shook it firmly. "I've heard so much about you from Nathaniel and," he turned to Elizabeth, "my daughter has never ceased to tell me how clever you were to rescue Martha and Alice."

As they talked the Reverend Lunt studied his visitor carefully. So this was the man Elizabeth had told him she wanted to marry. He was tall and strongly built, with an air of authority about him. Though it appeared he had had no formal education he seemed articulate and by all accounts was courageous and resourceful too. And he was pleasant enough though he had none of David's natural charm. The Reverend Lunt sighed inwardly. He'd hoped for many months now that Elizabeth would marry David. David was a man of intellect, a man who would go far in the church, who would provide for Elizabeth and give her a secure, comfortable and well-ordered life as he had for his dear Mary. He shook his head involuntarily. Elizabeth had already married one man of the sea who'd been killed fighting the French. Why couldn't she learn her lesson and find a husband able to resist foolish ideas of adventure, a man impervious to the call of the sea? Elizabeth needed a husband who was content to remain at home; a land-lubber, a man like David!

"Father," Elizabeth interrupted them. "I must show James his room. You'll have plenty of time to talk to him at dinner."

James followed her out of the room and into the hall. There he took her hand and turned her to face him. "Oh! Elizabeth. Let me look at you. Just to be near you fills my heart with joy."

She gazed lovingly into his eyes. "Dearest, it's been so long!"

She moved as if to break away.

"No, no, Elizabeth." He held her firmly. "Let me feast my eyes on you. Let me fill my memory with every detail of your lovely face. Then when I'm away I shall see you still. If I can't do that I shall worry I've lost you, that you'll never be my wife!"

"James dear, I shall be here chafing for your return!"

"Elizabeth. Tell me you'll marry me then!"

"Dearest my heart tells me I must, but my head, my stubborn head tells me I must wait until you've given up that trade!"

He sighed. "I must be patient then?"

She smiled tenderly. "Yes, dearest. We both have to be patient!"

She saw his eyes twinkle. "Mrs Wright tells me you'll marry me one day." He grinned. "She's always right you know!"

She laughed too. "Perhaps! But James dear, I must show you your room."

She led him up the stairs and along a corridor. "Here we are, James. I hope you'll be comfortable."

The room was spacious with fine furniture, the like of which he had only seen in Gordon Crosbie's expensive new house. And through the window he had a view of the surrounding hills.

"How could I not be comfortable in a room like this, Elizabeth?" He shook his head ruefully. "How will I endure that cabin of mine after such luxury?"

She smiled at him. "I thought your cabin was quite beautiful. It seemed to exude a spirit of adventure. I felt it could take me round the world and show me life in faraway places. I wondered what strange sights I might see through that great window. When you gave us luncheon on board I began to understand what it was that took my poor departed husband to sea and made my son want to follow in his footsteps."

He found himself asking her. "Would you have gone to sea then Elizabeth, if you had been a man?"

"If I had been a man?" She laughed at the improbability of it. "Would I have had the courage to go to sea? I wonder! I hope I would. I hope I would have wanted to break free from the humdrum life here at Hanbury, to find out what's over the horizon! Yes. If I had been a man I'm sure I would have wanted to do the same as you and Nathaniel."

She broke off and laughed again. "What a silly question that was!"

He took her hand. "Yes. Wasn't it! But don't ever be a man, Elizabeth. Stay as feminine as you are!" He pulled her towards him and embraced her. Then they kissed. All day he'd been worrying how he might kiss her, but it had happened so naturally and she had responded so easily! Mrs Wright was right again, he worried too much!

After a moment she gently pushed him away. "We must be patient, James dear."

He groaned and squeezed her hand. "Must we? How long must we wait?"

"Until we're married in the sight of God, James dear."

"But you will marry me Elizabeth?"

He saw her eyes dancing with delight. She took his hand and led him out of the room. "I might." She laughed. "I just might!"

She ran ahead of him down the stairs and when he had caught up with her she took him to the kitchen. "You must meet Mrs Jackson. She's been asking about you."

The kitchen was a hive of activity with Mrs Jackson busy plucking the fowl ready for Christmas. Martha and little Alice was there too. He took a long surreptitious look at Martha. Was this the same girl he'd seen at Gordon Crosbie's house? Then she was cowed and tense. Now she was relaxed and happy. Indeed everyone looked happy and seemed delighted to meet him and overwhelm him with kind comments about the rescue of Martha and Alice. Embarrassed he patted the dogs and fondled their ears. "You're all so busy," he told them lamely as he sought some excuse to retire. Then thankfully Nathaniel appeared. "Sorry I wasn't here to greet you, sir. I've been fishing." He opened his basket and put four brown trout on the table.

"How's the "Mary Anne"?"

Elizabeth had sensed that James was seeking some excuse to escape and bade Nathaniel to take "his Captain away to discuss their maritime affairs" and as he did she could hear James reply, "Fine. Now we've caulked her bottom I hope she won't leak like she did."

James was happy to talk with the boy. It pleased him to see he'd not lost his enthusiasm and was delighted when he asked when he should re-join. He told him of his plans and said sometime in the last week of January.

That night the four of them sat down to dinner. While Elizabeth's father bent though he was, cut an elegant figure, Jim felt overdressed in the new tail coat and breeches he'd had made in Montego Bay. However he was delighted to see that the coat and breeches he'd bought for Nathaniel fitted him so well. When Elizabeth had appeared he couldn't keep his eyes off her. She looked wonderful in a simple yet graceful gown. When he had expressed his admiration to her she had reciprocated by saying he had looked very stylish himself! After her supportive comment he had felt less self-conscious though he remained diffident amid all the grand furniture and polished silver. In the Mary Anne he never dressed for dinner, not that he could call the meal he ate alone, dinner! For him meal times were for filling your stomach! Making polite conversation while you ate was an art he'd never acquired!

He surveyed the handsome mahogany table with the candlelight reflected in its polished surface and wondered what topic he could discuss with his learned host. They had so little in common. Each loved Elizabeth in their different ways of course and then there was Nathaniel, beloved grandson to one and trainee to the other. What else was there? He wondered what the Rector thought of him. Did he accept him as a suitable companion, let alone husband for his only daughter? Or did he consider him a coarse seafarer, to whom hospitality was due only for rescuing Martha and Alice? What would he say if he told him his heart was set on marrying Elizabeth? But then he smiled to himself. Mrs Wright was quite right, he worried too much! In the event his dearest Elizabeth came to his rescue and soon had them laughing as she teased Nathaniel about the trout he'd caught and the many he'd missed. And she related the story of how when they rode home with Martha, they had borrowed breeches for her so that she could ride like a man! And what trouble they'd had getting her into the saddle! She even teased Jim about his fast-growing friendship with Mrs Wright and his new found ability to wink!

After the pudding, Elizabeth withdrew. "Enjoy your brandy, gentlemen, but don't be too long, I shall be lonely all by myself." They stood as she left, then in obedience to her father's bidding they moved closer as they sat down again. An anticipatory smile spread across the Reverend Lunt's face as removed the stopper and passed the decanter to his grandson. Nathaniel hesitated. This was not the first time he'd had brandy, but never before had he been offered any in the Rectory. "You're old enough now, Nathaniel," his grandfather said. The boy grinned and poured a little into his glass before passing the decanter to James. "It's a fine brandy, a present from the Squire." The Reverend Lunt laughed. "Probably smuggled over some Cornish beach, I shouldn't wonder." He watched Jim fill his glass and then poured the golden liquid into his own and raising it he turned to Jim. "Welcome, James", he said. "Welcome to Hanbury." Jim drank the smooth silky spirit, so different from the harsh raw rum he drank on board. "It's an excellent brandy", he said. His host nodded. "Yes, you won't find better, not hereabouts anyway." For a moment there was silence as they savoured the warm glow that spread through their bodies. Then the Reverend Lunt spoke. "You know, James, I've always been be surrounded by seafaring men. Always! Had two brothers in the navy, both now dead. George lost with Torrington when they put the Spanish to flight off Messina and my younger brother Neville drowned when the "Galatea" foundered." He sighed and took another sip of brandy. "And Nathaniel's poor father killed at Quiberon Bay!" He shook his head. "Can't for the life of me understand what draws men to the sea. It seems a harsh and hazardous life!"

"It's the adventure of it all, grandpa, and the thrill of seeing foreign parts, isn't it sir?"

"I suppose so, Nathaniel." Jim often wondered why it was that after all these years the sea still beckoned. "Can I tell you, sir, what draws men to the sea?" He shook his head. "I don't know that I can." He was beginning to warm to this wise old man of the church. "You may think it's a strange life and many will agree with you but it's the only life that men like me have ever known." He paused while he marshalled his thoughts. "You may not believe me, sir, but I still feel good when I've found my way across the ocean, when I've made a good landfall, when I've harnessed the wind and survived the storms to bring my ship safely into port." His host saw him grin as he himself might have done when he landed his first salmon. "Surely sir, there can't be anything more satisfying than that. Leastways," he laughed. "Not for me!"

"No, James, not for you, that's plain. But so many of your brethren don't arrive safely in port!"

"Aye. You're right there, sir. Many do get lost." He looked serious for a moment. "Maybe the sea will take me too one day, but be that as it may, I couldn't give it up."

The Reverend Lunt smiled. "Tell me, James, are you a religious man?"

Jim sipped his brandy. "Well sir, my mother, May she rest in peace, made sure I was baptised. But I'm afraid I don't go to church too often, if that's what you mean." He laughed again. "There aren't many churches at sea, but that don't mean I'm not aware of God! I may not know my bible, nor be much good at saying my prayers, but I tell you this sir. Out there in His great cathedral of the sea you often see the hand of God. We simple seafaring folk may not understand him, nor often hear his word, but we feel his presence and can see his work. We see his anguish as he rents the sky with lightning and hear his anger in the thunder. Sometimes as the wind rages He leaves us clinging to our poor frail ships and praying for deliverance and sometimes he forgives us and calms the sea. And when we have sickness onboard we pray to him too." He remembered leading the crew in prayers for deliverance from the flux and asked himself as he so often had, had God really saved them and if so why had he allowed Fred to be taken?

The Reverend Lunt looked pensive. "D'you not feel His presence ashore?"

"Well, sir." Jim shook his head and smiled. "I can't say I do sir, but then I'm not a religious man."

"You surprise me, James." The Reverend Lunt gave a wry grin. "Perhaps we should insist that all curates go to sea before they're ordained. Maybe they'd learn more of God in His great cathedrals of the sea than in our safe churches."

When the decanter had completed its second round, the Reverend Lunt refilled his glass and looked at Nathaniel. "Are you bitten by the bug as well then, Nathaniel?" They listened to the boy as he told them how he loved sailing the yawl, how he'd loved going up river to get wood and water, how peaceful it had been and how different life was at sea compared with the hustle and bustle of the port. His enthusiasm amused his grandfather but gladdened Jim! "I can see you're a lost cause, Nathaniel," his grandfather said. "Come, we'd better join your mother."

As they filed into the sitting room, Jim looked eagerly at Elizabeth. She seemed a trifle petulant. "I wondered if you'd ever come," she said.

"I'm sorry, my dear. We had a most illuminating conversation about the sea and how the Lord shows himself to those who venture forth into its great spaces. It made me think sailors may see him more clearly than we landlubbers do." He laughed. "You know, Nathaniel, I'm beginning to think we should all go to sea. But not just now, I'm afraid my bed is calling." He kissed his daughter and made his farewells.

Nathaniel had always loved the sight of a glowing fire and he busied himself coaxing the embers into life.

At last when it was burning brightly again he stifled a yawn, told them how dog-tired he was after his fishing and asked to be excused. "Of course, Nathaniel dear. Tomorrow is Christmas. It'll be a long day."

Now they were alone. Since he'd arrived Jim had shared her with others, others who unlike him had the pleasure of her company all day and every day! To have Elizabeth to himself had seemed a prize beyond reach. Now that prize was his! He looked at the woman who'd turned his life on its head and took her hand. He told her how inexcusable it had been to tarry so long over the brandy, how he had hated the thought of her being lonely and how he had longed to be with her. He reached for her other hand and silence engulfed them as their eyes met. Elizabeth could feel the strength of his desire and her resistance began to weaken, but that insistent inner voice of hers made her draw back. She kissed him lightly on the cheek and squeezing his hands tried to break the spell. "Tell me what the three of you were talking about."

He sighed, the magic moment had passed. Obediently he replied. "Your father told me the sea had taken both his brothers and your late husband. He said it was cruel and he couldn't understand why anyone would want to go to sea."

Elizabeth nodded. "Father has never come to terms with the loss of his brothers and he hated the thought of my marrying a Lieutenant in the navy. He'd always hoped I'd marry a priest!"

"Perhaps you should have married into the church. Then you could live in the comfort and style you're accustomed to."

"James dearest, if I'd married a clergyman, I wouldn't have met you!"

"I suppose that's true," he said in a low voice.

"James dear, why are you suddenly so sad?"

He sighed. "Am I sad? I don't know."

She reached for his hand. "Tell me, James dear. What's upsetting you?"

He didn't answer for a moment. "Well Elizabeth, the truth is we've had a lovely dinner in a gracious dining room in a beautiful house." He fell silent again.

She looked mystified. "Go on, James, tell me why does that upset you?"

"I'm not upset, Elizabeth. It's just that ….." His voice trailed away.

"What is it, James dear?"

"Well, you see, Elizabeth, I've never lived like this before, in elegant surroundings with good food and fine wine. It's been a strange experience for me, one that I shall remember for a long time. But," he hesitated.

"But what, James dear? What are you trying to tell me?"

He sighed. "I don't know! It's just that I'll never be able to provide an elegant house like this for you. Never, ever."

Elizabeth laughed. "Oh dear! Is that all that's worrying you? I thought for a moment you were frightened of being tied down by marriage. I thought you might regret losing your freedom. You don't, do you, James?"

"No, no, of course not, Elizabeth. I want to marry you, but I worry whether you'll be happy in a tiny cottage without all this fine furniture and all that goes with it. That's what's been worrying me!"

She pulled him to her and kissed him. "My love, it's you I want not a grand house. It's how we feel about each other, how we care for one another, that's what makes a happy marriage. Our happy marriage will flourish in your little cottage. We don't need a huge rectory!"

He laughed. He felt light-hearted again.

Chapter 34

She hadn't seen James for four whole weeks. Elizabeth sighed as she went to bed. Life was so empty without him. How she longed for the time to come when she would go with Nathaniel as he joined the Mary Anne. Then she and James would enjoy one last evening together in the Anchor, before he sailed. Part of her waited impatiently for that day, yet as a mother she never wanted it to come. How could she long for the day when Nathaniel must go? But that was what she was doing, wanting the days to pass quickly so she could see James. She felt a pang of remorse. Was her father right to caution her against marrying James? He'd said "The sea only brings loneliness and suffering to the wives. Haven't you suffered enough losing Charles, losing him even before he could see your son? Surely you don't want to go through all that sadness and misery again?" His questioning had been difficult to counter and she'd tried to ignore it. But that hadn't stopped her father saying a few days later, "Elizabeth my dear you need a husband who'll live with you. Not one who's always at sea. Why don't you marry David? He'd make you a fine husband and give you a secure life. A life you're used to in a decent house with a servant or two." His argument had logic, but to her marriage wasn't founded on logic, at least not hers! She'd told him so many times before that she was fond of David and valued his friendship, but she'd remain a widow rather than marry him. Nevertheless she had to admit that marrying James would indeed mean constant separation and heartbreak! She was experiencing that right now, but that didn't stop her from loving him and wanting to be his wife! Once again memories were becoming increasingly important. Before James had entered her life she had learnt to dismiss them as so many were sad. When trying to come to terms with Charles' death, her memories of their time together had given little consolation and in her heartache she had swept recollections of their youthful romance from her mind. They had only served to accentuate her grief! Only the preoccupations of a new baby and the companionship of her mother had eased her misery. Now she felt guilty of burying her memories of Charles! Though at the time it had upset her, dear Aunt Agatha had meant well when she said "You can't live in the past my dear." Yet Aunt Agatha never took her own advice! She was always reminiscing about life in Calcutta. But then her memories were happy ones! And the memories Elizabeth wanted to retain were happy ones too! Cherished memories of James and the precious few hours they'd shared. Her diary would help. She pulled it out and turned the pages to December 25th. *"To matins with James and Nathaniel,"* the entry began. She remembered it had been a cold morning with the wind driving the sleet in great curtains before it. They'd hurried across to St Peter's and like the villagers had arrived cold and damp. But the church was full and as the servers carrying their flickering candles led her father into the chancel a hush had descended. When he'd recited the well-remembered collect "Almighty God, who hast given us thy only-begotten son to be born of a virgin......." she had, in a silent prayer, acknowledged her happiness in having both Nathaniel and James with her. It had been the start of a truly blissful Christmas! After the service they'd returned to the Rectory with their guests to drink warming punch and when they'd gone, they'd exchanged presents. She had knitted a scarf for her father and had made a shirt for Nathaniel. Choosing a present for James had been difficult, but an idea had come. What better way to show him her love than to give him the Lord's book? She'd opened her own bible. On the flyleaf was the inscription, **'Elizabeth July 15th 1749'**. It had been her tenth birthday and the bible had been a gift from her mother. Now that her dear mother had departed this mortal life, she had her bible too. So with great care she had put a line through her own name and below it had written ***James December 25th 1772. May the Good Lord protect you. Elizabeth.*** When she had given it to him she'd watched him read the inscription. He'd clearly been moved and had promised he would treasure it and had added "It will always remind me of this happy day." Then he'd asked to be excused and she'd heard him running up the stairs. Within seconds he was back with a beaming smile on his face holding three parcels in his arms. "This is for you, sir, with my best wishes", he'd said as he gave her father his present. Then he'd turned to Nathaniel. "You need one of these. I hope it will give you long service." When her father had unwrapped the brandy and Nathaniel his jack knife he'd turned to her "And this, Elizabeth my dear, is for you." He'd handed her a carefully wrapped parcel. It was tiny, the smallest of the three and it had been tied up so well it was difficult for her to open. "I'm sorry Elizabeth," he'd laughed. "I've tied those knots too well! I'm afraid I'm more used to lashing up sails! Perhaps Nathaniel could help with his knife!"

Nathaniel had eagerly obliged. "There you are Mama," he'd chided her. "Can you manage the rest?"

She'd thanked him and finally removing the last wrapping had seen a golden crucifix and chain. It was so beautiful! It had quite taken her breath away! James had helped her put it on and as he did so she'd felt his fingers linger on her neck and had heard him whisper quietly "I love you, Elizabeth." Oh! It was such a lovely Christmas!

She fingered the cross as she so often did these
days and turned the page in her diary.
'December 26ᵗʰ 1772' she read. *"Riding with James"*

The morning after Christmas had been fine, the sleet had gone and the wind had dropped. They'd ridden through the village, past the little cottages with their thatch steaming in the warming sun and beyond. As James wasn't an experienced rider, they'd only walked the horses but this had allowed them to talk. He'd told her of his early life, of his father who'd been a master before him. Of his mother who'd borne ten children, of the six who had died as infants and of the little cottage overlooking the river at Pill in which he'd been born. How he too had served his apprenticeship in a slaver before joining the Dolphin as a mate. How the Dolphin had been used to transport men and supplies in the war against France and how he'd bought himself a share in the Mary Anne and had been made Master. He'd asked about Nathaniel and she'd told him of her marriage to Charles and her life as the daughter of a clergyman. She remembered how sad he was when she told him she had no brothers or sisters. "Oh! You must have been so lonely. I was always surrounded by brothers and sisters." Perhaps she had been lonely, though she'd never been conscious of it as a child. She'd made friends in the village and her mother had been her constant companion, teaching her how to sew and embroider, to ride, and to play the harpsichord and even paint a little. Their talk had confirmed her perception that they had such different backgrounds. That was why her father wanted her to marry David, rather than James. To her father, David was safe. He'd been brought up as a gentleman and her father felt at home with him. James was different, he'd been raised in a poor household and denied the finer things in life. James had never held a trout rod or a sporting gun and hardly knew how to ride! He'd been denied the education David and her father had had. He'd had to make his way in life by his own determination and effort. That was why her father was reluctant to bless their union. But while James lacked David's education and sophistication, he was honest and dependable, open-hearted and kind. He might be called a rough diamond, but to her he was a diamond whose sparkle outshone David's.

Her fingers caressed the crucifix. She reached for the quill, turned the page and wrote

January 26th 1773.

As she underlined the date she sighed. What should she write today, that she'd sent her father to bed to nurse his cold? That the weather had been unseasonable? That she'd finished another pair of hose for Nathaniel? That she'd seen some snowdrops? She shut the book. Life was so dreary and dull. She pushed the diary away, rose, undressed and retired to bed. "Just three more days now before I see him," she muttered as she blew out the candle.

The weather had changed when she awoke. Dark storm clouds were racing across the sky and rain beat against her window. She dressed hurriedly and went to the kitchen to prepare her father's breakfast tray; warming porridge and tea would be good for his cold. She reached her father's door and pushed it open. "Good morning Father dear. I hope your cold is better." She heard only a low grown by way of reply. The bed was empty! Where was he? She heard another groan and placing the tray on the chest searched the far side of the bed. There she found him. He was lying face down on the floor! "What's happened?" She cried. There was no reply. She tried to lift him, but he was too heavy! All she could do was turn him onto his back. His breathing concerned her. It was laboured and his face was ashen! She ran downstairs for help, "Miles, Mrs Jackson come quickly. The Rector's fallen. I need your help." As they ran up the stairs she told them what had happened and with their help managed to move him on to the bed. He was trying to speak, but no one could understand him! Nathaniel was hastily summoned and sent for Doctor Wilkinson who arrived after what seemed an age. Having examined his patient he announced that the Rector had had a stroke. "He's lost the use of his left arm and leg and can't speak. His heartbeat is rather irregular too. He must stay in bed. Keep him warm and make him rest. I'll come and see him again tomorrow."

"He will he get better, won't he?" She had asked him anxiously. Dr Wilkinson had shaken his head ruefully. "Elizabeth, it's difficult to say at this stage. I've known some get their speech back after a while, but I'm not so hopeful about his arm and leg! We'll have to be patient and ask the Good Lord for His help."

She'd sat with her poor crippled father for the rest of the day. At times he slept peacefully and at others he made those queer incomprehensible noises that worried her so. When night came she'd crept exhausted into her own bed and prayed he would soon be restored to health. With one ear cocked ready to catch any sound and a candle lit ready to light the way to his room, she'd slept badly. Twice she had been woken by his strange mumblings and had gone to comfort him. When morning came she took him some warm milk and tried to encourage him, but the sight of her articulate and intellectual father unable to talk or use his left arm and leg frightened her. Looking at the poor disabled father she loved, she realised he needed her now more than he'd ever done. She dare not leave him now, not even to go to James! How cruel life could be! Why had her father, who'd done nothing but good, been struck down in such a terrible way? And why had it happened at this time when she wanted so desperately to say goodbye to James? How could she tell him that fate had denied them their last few hours together before he vanished for an eternity? She knew she should not be feeling sorry for herself, but she was close to tears. She shook herself sternly, she must be practical. Her duty now was to the parish. She must inform the Squire and Nathaniel was sent with a note to tell him about her father's ill health. An hour or so later Squire Thomas arrived full of outward compassion, but seemingly more concerned about his own problems.

"Oh! Elizabeth, my dear, this couldn't have happened at a worse time. As you know I'm deeply worried about my dear wife's health and I'm very pressed with my own affairs." He sighed mournfully. "But I'll call a meeting of the church council to discuss what's to be done." He looked at the figure in the bed and shook his head. "It'll be a long time I'm afraid before we have him in the pulpit again. We'll have to find a parson who can come and visit us now and then." For a moment he appeared deep in thought. "What about that young curate who preached so well a few months back?" He scratched his head. "Let me see now, what was his name?"

"You mean the Reverend David Hart?"

"Ah! Yes, Ma'am. That's the fellow." He sounded more cheerful. "He comes from the next parish, don't 'e?"

"Yes, Squire. He's the curate at St Mary's, Olverton. Perhaps you should talk to the Vicar, the Reverend Parker."

"Good, I will." He turned to go. "We must pray for your father."

"Before you go Squire, I need some help." He was already in the passageway and turned with a look of irritation on his face.

"It's just that......" she began as she explained how she had planned to go with Nathaniel when he re-joined the "Mary Anne". She planned to take Miles with her to help bring back Nathaniel's horse and the pack horse that would carry Nathaniel's gear. Now she couldn't possibly leave her sick father and was worried about Miles returning with two other horses on his own. "Is there any possibility that you could lend me a reliable man to go with Miles?" Squire Thomas grunted. For a moment she thought he'd refuse, he looked so prickly! Then he'd nodded. "I'll send young Henry over." She had thanked him profusely and it was agreed that young Henry would come by eight o'clock on Friday morning. "If they leave early, they should be back by dark," she'd said as he left.

That night she prayed for a miracle, that her father could be restored to health, "by Thursday evening, dear Lord," she had added though in her heart she knew her selfish prayer would not be answered. Thursday came with her father no better. As she helped her son pack she felt more and more despondent. Nathaniel would be gone tomorrow and her hopes of seeing James one last time had been dashed. As she bid good night to her stricken father and retired to her own room, she unburdened her misery in her diary. Why should this last chance of seeing James be so brutally denied? It was so cruel! All she could do was to write to James and tell him about her father and how bitterly disappointed she was not to see him before he sailed.

She had another disturbed night and in her misery had hardly slept and was up early, checking on her father, fussing over Nathaniel and worrying whether the horses and young Henry would be ready by eight. Though it was cold she was thankful it was a fine day with a clear sky and no wind. Trying to hide her tears she told Nathaniel he had a good day for the journey. He nodded. "Yes, Mama. I'm sorry you can't come too. What shall I say to Captain Youle?"

"Just tell him how ill grandpa is." She spoke in a flat voice. "And give him this." She handed him the letter as Miles and young Henry appeared. Now that it was time for Nathaniel to go she thought she would sob, but she collected herself and gave him one last kiss. She followed him to the stables, where the horses were saddled and ready. She watched him adjust a strap, then mount Bracken and with a final wave he was off.

Though Nathaniel was sad to leave his mother, the excitement of another voyage in the Mary Anne cheered him and he was determined to enjoy this, his last ride for many months. Barely two hours later he reached the Mary Anne and bidding Miles farewell and a safe journey back with Henry and the horses, he climbed the gangplank. "Come aboard to sign on please sir," he said to the Captain.

"Right, Mr Lugger," Jim tried hard not to look upset. Get your gear on board and see me in my cabin. The boy dashed off. "Wait, wait, Mr Lugger. Where's your mother? What's happened? I thought she would be with you."

"Oh! Sorry sir. I, I forgot. Grandpa's ill and she can't leave him. She asked me to give you this."

Thanking him, Jim took the letter. Perturbed by the unexpected turn of events Jim walked as slowly as he could towards his cabin. When he had closed the door, he sank into his chair. For a moment he was reluctant to open the letter. What might it say? Was it some excuse not to see him? Had she changed her mind? He gave a deep sigh and gently broke the seal. *"Dearest James,"* he read. *"I am utterly heartbroken not to be with you today. Over the last few weeks the thought of seeing you one more time before you sail has sustained me, but fate has dealt us a bitter blow! Nathaniel will have told you about my father. I found him on the floor in his room three days ago. He has been struck down and cannot talk neither can he use his left arm and leg. He is so gravely ill I fear I cannot leave him except for the shortest of moments. So, James dearest that is why I cannot be with you. The thought of not seeing you before you sail has made me feel utterly wretched. But I am trying hard to put a brave face on my disappointment and shall pray constantly for your safe return and the happy day when I see you again. We had such a happy Christmas together and so we must both try to be content with our memories of those blissful days. I wear that beautiful crucifix you gave me constantly and whenever I touch it I feel you are near. I am inconsolable not to be with you, dearest James. Elizabeth."*

He felt stunned; he had so wanted to see her again. For a while he sat there contemplating her letter and thinking of the dismal months that must pass before they were reunited. It was an eternity! As he began to read the letter again, there was a knock on the door. It was the boy.

"Sorry about Mama," Nathaniel said. "Grandpa's very ill. I don't know what's happened; he can't talk. All he does is grunt and make odd noises. Only Mama seems to understand him."

"Well, Mr Lugger, I'm sorry not to see your mother, but I can understand why she can't come. Now, let's get you signed on." He dipped his quill into the ink and wrote carefully, Mr Nathaniel Lugger, Apprentice. He passed the articles to Nathaniel and watched him sign. He grunted "Next time, Mr Lugger, I hope you'll be signing on as Third Mate!" Nathaniel grinned and nodded. "Thank you, sir." He turned to go.

"Mr Jackson's still the Second Mate." He saw the boy nod. "Go and find him and tell him I want him to introduce you to the new Chief Mate. And when you've met him, give him my compliments and ask him to come and see me."

When Nathaniel had gone he read the letter again. He felt angry that fate should treat them so! "Damn, damn, damn," he said aloud. "If she can't come to me, I'll damn well go to her!" Suddenly he felt better. He heard a knock on the door. "Come in, come in, Mr Murray. Tell me how are things going?" He was too excited by his sudden plan to pay attention to what the other was saying. In any case he knew as well as the Chief Mate, that the ship was as ready to sail as it would ever be!

"Good, good, good, Mr Murray", he said when the other had finished speaking. "It looks as if we've got a spare day then before we sail." Mr Murray nodded. "Yes. Just a few odds and ends to tidy up, Cap'n."

"That's fine. Perhaps tomorrow the Bo's'un can give the hands some sail drill. Make sure they know the rig eh? I've some urgent business to attend to before we go down river. I'll be off first thing in the morning."

They chatted for a few more minutes, then the Chief Mate took the hint. "Is that all, Cap'n?"

"Yes, Mr Murray. I'll leave you in charge tomorrow then."

He woke up early the following morning and walked briskly to the stables to collect the horse he'd arranged the previous night. It was the same staid old fellow he'd had before.

"Come on boy," he said as he urged him forward. "You know the way to Hanbury as well as I do!"

Chapter 35

Elizabeth had been with her father all morning, but at last he'd dropped off. Thankfully she left to see Mrs Jackson. On the stairs she heard Martha's excited voice and a squeal from Alice. She hastened her step, then in amazement she stopped. Were her eyes deceiving her? Was it some cruel trick? Could that really be James standing there saying "Elizabeth dearest, I couldn't sail without seeing you one last time!" It was like a dream. Seeing James left her spell-bound, unable to believe it really was him. Neither had known what to say and for a moment they had stood in silence staring at each other. Then she'd thrown herself at him and he was holding her in his arms and kissing her. Never before had she felt such a passionate desire to be held and loved. As he'd kissed her again and whispered "I had to see you," she'd heard a cough. Instantly she'd pulled away from him and turning had seen Mrs Jackson. "Shall I get the Cap'n some tea, Ma'am?" Elizabeth had nodded. "Thank you Mrs Jackson. I'll take the Captain into the drawing room."

She led him away, their spell broken. When he tried to kiss her again, she whispered "Dearest. We have to be patient!" So they had sat there, holding hands and revelling in each other's presence. When the tea came, he asked about her father. When she told him how incapacitated he was and how she feared he would never be restored to health, he was full of sympathy and compassion for her! She in her turn enquired about the ship and he told her they were ready to sail the next day. Seeking some privacy they'd walked in the garden and had conversed in a fitful, stilted manner as both willed those few unexpected hours to last forever. Mrs Jackson had called them in for lunch, served on their own in the splendour of the dining room, but by three o'clock she'd begun to worry about his return journey to Bristol. "You must be going soon dearest. You must reach Bristol before dark." He'd lingered for a while and then he'd kissed her and telling her he'd always love her, he'd gone. The whole unexpected, joyful visit seemed to have lasted barely a fleeting moment!

For the next few days she felt numb, her being frozen at that moment of parting. Life seemed empty and pointless. She'd not see or hear from him for at least a year! How, she asked herself could she endure such separation? Then in the midst of her misery she felt a pang of guilt. What about her son? He was gone too! How could she forget Nathaniel?

Her practical nature came to her aid as she lost herself caring for her father. Slowly he began to improve and to say a few isolated words, though he was unable to form them into sentences. Strangely Alice was helpful and a great comfort to him. When she climbed onto his lap and talked to him in the simple direct way children do, Elizabeth could see the pleasure it gave him. Alice seemed to understand what he said too, often better than she! As the bond grew between the little black girl and the handicapped old man Elizabeth kept assuring herself he would recover. There was no doubt about his walking! Though he dragged his left leg, now with the aid of a stick he could take a few hesitant steps. She admired the way he suffered his afflictions so bravely and she could see that trapped inside that twisted, useless body, her same dear father lived on. Why she kept asking herself, had God allowed this kind and dedicated man of the church to be so cruelly struck down? Hadn't he been His loyal and faithful servant all his life? It seemed so unjust, so unfair! But no such thoughts seemed to enter her father's head for still he opened his prayer book each day to worship God, often pointing at the prayer of thanksgiving! For him it seemed that each little improvement became another milestone on the road to recovery, a road that to Elizabeth seemed as endless as the one that would lead her back to James! As the weeks passed however her father's equanimity began to infect her. She too began to learn to be patient and even to accept her long separation from James.

The life of the church was affected too. No celebrant being available, the monthly service of Holy Communion had now been abandoned. On Sundays the Church Wardens took it in turns to lead worship, when prayers were offered for the Rector's recovery, but the parish knew many a Sunday would pass before the Reverend Lunt led his flock in prayer again. Squire Thomas and the Wardens regularly contemplated the problem as it became evident that without their priest the life of the church was slowly withering. A letter was sent to the Bishop to apprise him of the situation.

This elicited a sympathetic reply and the promise of prayers for the Rector's speedy recovery, but the practical help for which they had hoped was not forthcoming! A second letter received a few weeks later, conveyed a more helpful response. The Bishop had "requested the Reverend Parker, Vicar of St Mary's, Olverton, or his Curate to say matins once a fortnight in St Peter's, Hanbury and to celebrate the sacrament of the Lord's Supper once a month until such times as the Reverend Lunt was restored to health."

Squire Thomas came to see the Rector to tell him what had been arranged by the Bishop and asked Elizabeth to accommodate the visiting priest. "He'll come on Saturday and leave on Monday", he said. "It'll be good for your father to have a fellow clergyman to talk to." When Elizabeth expressed her gratitude and told him she'd been hoping for such an arrangement, Squire Thomas assured her they'd have her father back in the pulpit before long and rousing the village with one of his sermons. Yet his face had told her plainly he didn't believe what he'd said any more than she!

Picking daffodils in the garden the following Saturday she saw a lone horseman approaching. It was David come to read Matins on the morrow. He was almost a stranger now. She hadn't seen him for months, not since she had told him for the second time, she'd not marry him. He doffed his hat and dismounted. "Elizabeth. I'm so glad to see you. It's been a long time!"

She welcomed him to Hanbury and thanked him for coming.

"It's my pleasure Elizabeth. I was so sorry to hear about your father. How is he?" She told him he was making slow progress and asked if the Reverend Parker was well. When David assured her he was, she couldn't help feeling irritated. If the Vicar was well, why hadn't he come, instead of David? One might have expected the Vicar himself to come on the first occasion! She hoped it didn't mean that David would come every time! She was certain he'd start pestering her again with pleas to marry him!

As they neared the stables, Turnip whinnied.

"Hello boy." David fondled his nose. "You must persuade your mistress to come riding again with Flyer and me." Turnip's head went up and down as if he agreed! "We enjoyed those rides together didn't we?" He turned to Elizabeth. "I miss those happy days, Elizabeth. Couldn't we ride together again?" He laughed. "Turnip seems to be keen!"

"David, I can't leave Father. He's far too ill!"

"Yes, of course," he paused. "But maybe when he's better?"

Elizabeth sighed. "David you must excuse me. I can think of nothing but my father's afflictions at the moment. Pray let me show you your room." As she led him into the house Martha appeared. "Martha dear. Please take the Reverend Hart's bag up to his room."

Then putting a finger to her lips she whispered "Shhhh" and led him into the drawing room. Happily her father was awake and appeared to be comfortable. "Father dear." She kissed him lightly on the forehead. "We have a visitor. David's come to say Matins tomorrow." Her father gave one of his twisted smiles, lifted his right hand in greeting and welcomed David in the faltering, stuttering speech, which Elizabeth had come to accept. David plainly shaken by his appearance appeared not to understand what her father had been trying to say.

"He says he's very pleased to see you," Elizabeth explained.

Unsure how to respond, David turned to Elizabeth. "Tell him I'm pleased to see him too!"

Seeing her father looking a little hurt Elizabeth whispered, "He can hear you perfectly well he just finds speaking difficult!"

David looked disconcerted and mumbled his apologies. He was clearly uneasy in her father's presence, but she thought it best to leave them together. Only in that way could David adjust to her father's condition. She excused herself. "I'll ask Mrs Jackson to bring some tea."

When she spoke to Mrs Jackson she saw Alice. "Are you going to see Gampy?"

Alice nodded. "Yes. I want to tell him a story."

"Is it one of your funny ones?" Elizabeth smiled. "One that'll make him laugh?"

"Yes," Alice replied as she slipped past.

When Elizabeth returned to the drawing room, she saw her father captivated by Alice, who perched on his lap, was telling him her story. She had the natural talent of a mimic and accompanied her tale with exaggerated actions interspersed with peals of laughter. Her father appeared to hang on her every word. Whether or not he understood Alice's garbled story it was clear he was enjoying every minute! She glanced at David. She knew the sight of her poor handicapped father had shocked him, but the undisguised look of horror on his face as he watched this black child beguile her father, quite took her aback. It was clear he deplored the way Alice had been accepted in the Rectory. It made her wonder how real was the hatred of slavery he'd proclaimed with such fervour when they first met. Had he really meant what he'd said? She was beginning to have her doubts. How would he react she asked herself, if she were to tell him that Martha's father, like his, was a rich plantation owner in Barbados? Indeed it was not beyond the bounds of possibility that he and Martha actually shared the same father! How she wanted to challenge him, but her indignation waned at the approach of Mrs Jackson laden with a tray and she busied herself opening the tea caddy and spooning the leaf into the pot. While Alice chattered away happily and they drank their tea, conversation between Elizabeth and David was strained and laboured. After a period of silence David asked if he could see the church. "I'd like to acquaint myself with it again before tomorrow." As she walked him to the church, David told her he'd had no idea her father was so ill. "It's really painful to see him struggling with his speech. Does the Doctor think he'll ever get better?"

The inferred doubt upset her. Could he not have said something encouraging? "He's made some progress," she said defiantly. "He's certainly better that he was. At first he couldn't talk at all or even walk! Now he can manage a few words and you'll see he can walk a little." She explained how she'd found him on that never to be forgotten morning. David listened patiently, then he frowned. "He seems excessively fond of that black child. She's Martha's, isn't she?"

"Yes, David." She smiled. "He's very taken with her and you can tell she loves him too. Y'know I'm sure she's done more to help him talk again than any of us!"

"Mm, that's as may be. But Elizabeth do you think it's a good thing for him to spoil her so, to treat her as if she were his grandchild?"

"Why shouldn't he?" She found his pettifogging question irritating. "Alice is a very affectionate child and she helps him with his talking. I don't understand what you mean, David."

He shook his head but made no reply until they reached the church door. "Well, she is black, Elizabeth and say what you will the black race is different. Of course we should respect them, but it's no good fooling ourselves, they aren't the same as us and it's a mistake to make them feel they are!"

A flush of anger surged through her. "What nonsense, David. Did you think poor Tilly was so different when you took her to your hay loft? And what about Zebedee? Doesn't he have your blood coursing through his veins?"

He said nothing for a moment, her taunt had struck home. Then in a quiet voice he said "I seem to have made you angry. I'm sorry."

He opened the door and they walked slowly down the nave.

"Elizabeth, this is a beautiful church. It must be one of the finest in the deanery. I've always admired it."

"Then I'll leave you to enjoy it, David." She felt so cross with David. Clearly she had seen him in his true colours. All along it seemed he'd paid lip service to her feelings about slavery. She needed to get away from him. She had talk to someone, anyone who'd make her forget that he'd said Martha and Alice were different! She strode purposely to the house and reached the kitchen, but at the door she stopped. Mrs Jackson and Molly were talking, talking about David. "He's such a nice young man, that Reverend. He'd make a good husband for Mrs Lugger! That Captain Youle's nice enough, but he's not so refined and well mannered! I suppose he's just not a gentleman, not like that Reverend. No, Molly my girl, she don't want to get stuck with that Captain Youle. He'll always be at sea, just like her last husband. She never saw much of him!"

Elizabeth's anger returned. Why does everyone think I should marry David? Didn't they know he's a sham? She stopped to let her anger abate, then she walked in.

"Mrs Jackson, about lunch tomorrow, has Miles killed the cockerel?"

"Yes ma'am." Mrs Jackson was busy at the range. "I've drawn and plucked him and Martha's been helping with the stuffing."

They discussed preparations for the next day and briefly about supper that night. When all was to her liking and she was about to go, Alice came in. She wore a puzzled look on her face and running to her mother pulled at her skirt. "Gampy's stopped talking!"

"I expect he's had enough of you," Martha replied as she lifted Alice off her feet. "You always wriggle so much when you're on his lap. How he puts up with it, I just don't know. I expect he's tired and wants to have a little sleep."

"But Mummy," Alice shook her head. "He's not asleep, his eyes are open."

"Oh! Dear God," Elizabeth whispered as she ran to the drawing-room.

"Father dear, are you all right?" He was slumped in the chair, his eyes open and his head hanging on one side. A stream of saliva ran from his mouth! She shook him gently at first, then more roughly, but he wouldn't wake up. She couldn't hear any breathing and his chest was still! In her heart she knew he was dead, but she couldn't accept it! When Martha and David had come into the room, she had opened his waistcoat and with an ear to his chest was listening and praying for a heartbeat.

She straightened up. "I think he's gone." As she crossed herself she heard a cough. "Should we get the doctor, ma'am?" Mrs Jackson was standing at her elbow with tears in her eyes.

"Yes, Mrs Jackson. Ask Miles to go."

At last Doctor Wilkinson had come and her father had been pronounced dead. Everyone was in a state of shock. It had seemed he had been recovering, albeit slowly! No one had thought he was near death! Everyone came to console Elizabeth. A tearful Martha and Mrs Jackson dabbing tears from her eyes, Doris very quiet and Molly almost hysterical! Even Miles, long thought to be insensible to affection, seemed distressed! Only David appeared to be unmoved. He made the sign of the cross on her father's forehead and spoke in a reverential tone. "God in his mercy has given him relief from his suffering and he will surely receive a rich reward from our Heavenly Father!" Though Elizabeth agreed with what David had said, the lack of emotion in his voice upset her. Couldn't he have expressed some sadness at the loss of the man she thought he admired?

The following day David led the parish in prayers for the soul of their departed priest. When the service ended, the congregation led by the Squire and the church wardens, filed slowly past her to offer their condolences and so many expressed their love and admiration for her beloved father. It was a moving experience but she fought off her tears, determined not to seek sympathy for herself.

At luncheon they sat in sombre mood and it was not long before they began to discuss arrangements for her father's funeral. David said it would be a privilege to officiate and sought Elizabeth's permission, provided, he said, "that the Reverend Parker does not wish to do so himself. As you know Elizabeth, I held your father in the greatest esteem. He was a wise and compassionate priest and I pray for the strength, ability and dedication to follow in his footsteps." The following days passed quickly, there was much to do. Keeping busy, Elizabeth discovered, helped her to accept her loss. But on the night before the funeral, as she was making a wreath in the quietness of the scullery, a frightening emptiness overtook her. Never before had she felt so utterly alone. The loss of her mother, just three short years ago, had been hard to bear, but her father had been with her then and they had comforted and supported each other. Now who could she turn to? She was on her own, without family or friends. Only two people could support and comfort her, but for all she knew they were on the other side of the world! Her fingers worked automatically weaving flowers into the wreath as the finality of it all and worries about her future filled her thoughts. The future looked bleak. When the new incumbent arrived, her tenure of the Rectory would end. The house that had been her home since before she could remember, would be hers no more! It was an alarming thought! Where would she live? How could she give shelter to Martha and Alice? She caught her breath, and what would she do for money? While she would be the main, if not the only beneficiary of her father's will, he had little to leave. What would she, could she do? She tried to reassure herself. The new Rector might ask her to stay as his housekeeper. But what if he had a wife? She wove the last flowers into the wreath and silently asked God to watch over her. She had to believe He wouldn't fail her!

David arrived on the day before the funeral. He told her proudly that he would be officiating and the Rural Dean would be representing the Bishop. By four o'clock he had arrived too and both had been welcomed, given tea and settled in their rooms. As she helped Mrs Jackson prepare the evening meal, Elizabeth was sure it would be a cheerless dismal affair and indeed it was. The two clergymen seemed bent on outdoing the other's lavish praise for her father's ministry. But she had been flabbergasted when David asked the Rural Dean even before they had sat down to dinner, to propose him as a suitable successor for her father. Stopping momentarily outside the door she had heard David extolling the beauty of the Rectory. Then he went on "I do hope sir, that you'll be putting my name forward for this parish. I knew the Reverend Lunt very well and I'm sure he would have recommended me. I've preached in St Peter's a number of times now and I shall be holding the fort until the new incumbent is appointed. So you see, sir, I feel part of the parish already and it seems I am liked! And I can tell you that Squire Thomas has hinted on more than one occasion that he'd be happy to give me the living." She found it scarcely creditable that David would advance himself with such unseemly haste to profit from her father's death!

The weather was kind for the funeral and it seemed the whole village came to pay tribute to her father. The congregation stood as the two clergymen led the coffin to the chancel steps, with David intoning "I am the resurrection and the life, saith the Lord: he that believeth in me, though he were dead, yet shall he live: and whosoever liveth and believeth in me shall never die." Try as she might to concentrate on the service, her mind kept wandering as memories of her father and mother flooded back. But the sight of the Rural Dean climbing into the pulpit made her cast memories aside and she listened to his fulsome praise of her father. Such appreciation gave her some solace, but when they stood around the freshly dug grave, the reality of it all struck home without mercy. "Man that is born of woman, hath but a short time to live and is full of misery. He cometh up and is cut down, like a flower," David's monotone articulating the moment of finality was carried away by the breeze. She took one last long look at the coffin and tried to visualise him looking as peaceful as he'd seemed before the lid had been nailed in place. "Earth to earth, ashes to ashes, dust to dust," David was saying and she stepped forward to throw her handful of earth into the grave.

When the burial was done she returned to the Rectory with David, the Rural Dean and Squire Thomas to offer them tea. As she did so David bent and kissed her on the cheek. "He was a good man, Elizabeth. Be content, he is alive with Christ."

"Yes, David. I pray that he is." His air of saintly conviction disturbed her. Wasn't he human? In moments of remorseless grief like this, didn't he like her, have any doubts? She'd always thought her faith was steadfast and unquestioning, but now when she needed it most, it had begun to falter! She needed help to understand the mysteries of death and resurrection, not dogma! But David seemed unaware of her plight.

She spoke to the Rural Dean and thanked him for representing the Bishop and to Squire Thomas she said, "And I must thank you, Squire for the many kindnesses you have shown my father and me during his long ministry. We have been so very happy here. I'm certain the next incumbent, whoever he may be, will be too. It's such a happy village and the church and rectory are so beautiful."

Squire Thomas smiled. "We've been very fortunate to have your father as our Rector. The tributes paid to him today were most pertinent and reflect the great loss we all feel. I'm glad to hear you have been happy here." He paused as if unsure what to say next. Then he continued. "Well, my dear, I feel I should be leaving. It's been a long sad day for you." He half-turned as if to go then took her two hands in his. "Mrs Lugger I know you'll find it a great wrench to leave this house, but there's no hurry for you to go. We'll not be finding a new Rector for a while. You'll be able to stay on for some time." She thanked him. "I'll give you as much notice as I can," he said as he left.

Chapter 36

The apple trees were in full blossom and the hedgerows white with May. Summer was near. Her father had been buried for nearly three months now, but still there was no news of his successor. Was the Bishop finding it difficult to select a suitable cleric? Had he like her rejected David? Was he now casting his net wider? And might she be able to stay a few months longer?

Where she would live when finally she had to leave the Rectory made her sick with worry. She had to find shelter for the three of them for she would never be parted from Martha and Alice. Now she was a slave-owner [the very idea filled her with shame!] she had a duty to look after them. Squire Thomas had asked about her intentions after church only last Sunday. He'd been sympathetic and had said her plight was in the forefront of his mind. He'd like to find her a little cottage somewhere, but where would he find one? Had she thought of approaching Miss Dandry, the previous Rector's daughter? "She lives alone, perhaps she could offer shelter. But of course," he'd admitted. "Hers is the tiniest of cottages!" Then he'd smiled. "Elizabeth, my dear, you are aware I'm certain, that my dear wife Mrs Thomas has been unwell for many a month. She bears her afflictions bravely and endeavours to carry out her wifely duties, but of late I've been wondering whether a good housekeeper wouldn't be a great blessing. Might it be that you would consider coming to keep house for me? It could be a happy solution for both of us! There's a nice room you could have." He eyed her closely. "I've been thinking of you a great deal recently my dear. You're a good-looking woman and I do worry what may happen to you if you've nowhere to go!" She'd thanked him for his kindness and had asked for time to consider his offer.

"Well, think about it, my dear. I'd make you very welcome." The offer had caught her unawares; perhaps it could be a happy solution, but what about Martha and Alice?

"Before you go Squire, I presume I may bring Martha and Alice?"

"Martha and Alice?" He'd looked puzzled for a moment. "Oh, you mean those two niggers?" He'd shaken his head. "That would be difficult. Mrs Thomas wouldn't have them in the house, I'm afraid!"

Elizabeth had felt deeply hurt. "I couldn't leave them."

"Well, my dear," he'd smiled and had adopted a more benevolent air. "Perhaps they could live over the stables. There's a little room they could have there. I might be able to persuade Mrs Thomas to agree to that." Then, as if he'd found a happy solution, he'd smiled. "I don't suppose the horses would mind!"

With an effort she'd controlled her anger. "I need time sir, to consider your offer. May I give you my answer next Sunday?"

For the rest of that day she had fumed over his offer! How she kept asking herself could she keep house for someone like him, a man who thought Martha and Alice little better than animals? Did he not profess to be a Christian? Was he not the patron of the church, the one who gave the living to the Rector? How could he of all people not see that despite the colour of their skin, Martha and Alice were human beings? Yet a quiet voice within her kept asking, "Where else will you find shelter?" And when she found no answer it persisted "And he has offered to house Martha and Alice too!" But what, she wondered would Squire Thomas expect of Martha for giving her and Alice a room? He wasn't a Good Samaritan, she was sure of that! He'd require some recompense! What if Martha was debarred from the house? Would he require her to work in the stables? Then a terrible possibility struck her. Would he be another Gordon Crosbie? Would he look to Martha to satisfy his carnal desires? And he'd said she herself was a good-looking woman! What had he meant by that? What she asked herself angrily had good looks to do with being a competent housekeeper? Worries about his motives reinforced her earlier decision. She would never keep house for the Squire. Yet concern for the future returned to haunt her. Where would she live? Perhaps, she thought hopefully, the new incumbent would want her to manage house for him. She would tell him she had kept house for her father and she could help him settle into the village too. "Oh Dear Lord! That would be such a happy solution!"

During the ensuing days she agonised how best to refuse the Squire. She had no wish to upset him. Friday came without any suitable turn of phrase and putting her problem aside, she began to prepare for David's arrival. He came at two o'clock, earlier than expected! He seemed unusually pleased, almost ecstatic with his blue eyes shining with obvious delight. "Elizabeth, I've wonderful news!" He took her hand and led her to the bench under the chestnut tree. "You don't look at all excited," he chided her. "Don't you want to hear about my good fortune?"

"Yes, of course, David. I'm sorry. It's just that I've a headache." She'd lied, she was certain she'd not like his news. He made no reply, but gazed at her with sparkling eyes.

"Tell me your news then, David." She managed a little laugh, she hoped it didn't sound forced. "Don't keep me in suspense." She dreaded his answer; she knew what he was about to say.

David was watching her attentively. "Yesterday a messenger brought me this." He held out a letter bearing a large red seal. "It's from Bishop Timothy. He wants me to be the new Rector of Hanbury. Isn't that wonderful?"

All along she'd feared this would happen and now her fears had come true!

"Aren't you pleased, Elizabeth?"

"David, of course I am." She lied a second time! "You'll have your own parish at last!"

"Yes, Elizabeth. I've been a curate long enough. Playing second fiddle may be good for the soul, but I've longed to have a parish of my own. And I must confess I've always coveted Hanbury."

"And, David, I hope you'll do well for Hanbury." As she heard what she was saying she felt mean and uncharitable. He'd been so excited, so pleased with himself and she knew her father would have been delighted. Hastily she added "Father would be pleased."

David smiled. He looked more at ease. "Thank you, Elizabeth. It'll be difficult to follow your father, I know. He was greatly loved by all, but the spiritual health and wellbeing of the parish will be my prime concern and with God's help and guidance I hope I will prove a worthy successor."

His pomposity annoyed her. How very trite, she thought dismissively. Was that how he'd presented himself to the Squire and the Rural Dean?

"Well, David", she rose to go. "You'd better come to your Rectory and have some tea."

He laughed and followed her, his eyes admiring the hall and its graceful stairway. "It is a fine house," he sighed.

She led him into the drawing room. "It's so elegant," he murmured as with evident pride of ownership he surveyed the room. As he strode masterfully to the window he seemed too taken with the view to notice she'd slipped away. She had to escape! She needed time to digest the news he'd brought! To learn that this young ambitious, complacent man would indeed replace her wise, compassionate, understanding father hurt her dreadfully! She hid herself in the kitchen to regain her composure.

Mrs Jackson appeared. "The Rector would like his tea," Elizabeth said.

"The Rector, ma'am?" Mrs Jackson gave a startled look. Elizabeth managed another forced laugh. "It's the new Rector, Mrs Jackson. It's the Reverend David Hart who wants his tea!"

Having accepted the unwelcome news Elizabeth returned to the drawing room to find David sitting in her father's chair, apparently at home already!

"David, I hope I've done the right thing. I don't know when your appointment will be announced, but I'm afraid I've told Mrs Jackson and Martha already!"

"That's fine, Elizabeth. The Squire will tell the congregation tomorrow and then the whole village will know."

Mrs Jackson entered tray in hand and genuflected, "Congratulations, your Reverence."

"Bless you, Mrs Jackson." David looked at Martha. "Well, Martha, what d'you think of my news?" He laughed. "Will you still want to come to church?"

"Oh yes, sir, of course. I hope you'll be very happy here."

"Thank you, Martha, I'm sure I will." He smiled at Alice standing at Martha's feet. "And I hope you'll be pleased too." Alice examined this man with her large brown eyes. "Will you tell me stories?" she asked.

David, clearly embarrassed by this precocious child, seemed lost for words. Then inspiration came. "Yes Alice, come to church, that's where I tell my stories!"

Elizabeth stifled a laugh, while Martha, sternly telling Alice she must be more respectful to the new Rector, took her from the room.

Elizabeth apologised. David's discomfort was all too plain. "I'm sorry, David. I can see you're not used to children. Alice is a very sweet child and she and father were always telling stories to each other. He did love her, you know!"

David nodded. "I remember your father making a fuss of her, but I'm sorry to say I always thought it wasn't appropriate and I must say I hope she'll stay in the servants' quarters when I'm living here."

The incident had unsettled him and for a while he didn't speak. It was Elizabeth who broke the silence. She could wait no longer for an answer to the question that had plagued her for so long.

"David, when do you intend to move in?"

"It's too early to say Elizabeth. Naturally I want to move in as soon as possible. I'd like to be settled before my induction. I hope it'll be before the end of the month."

"Well David, I'll move out in good time, but I'd like as much notice as possible please."

He stopped and took her hand. "Elizabeth dear, I don't want you to leave. I want you stay and look after me. How can I live in this rambling house on my own? Please don't go!"

Stay as his housekeeper, is that what he meant? He saw her hesitating. "Elizabeth, I'd hoped you'd be pleased."

"It's a generous offer, David, but I need to think about it. I have to consider Martha and Alice."

"They can stay too, if you wish. Though I shan't want Alice having a free run of the house!" He smiled; he had no wish to upset her. "But we can discuss that later, when you've made up your mind. Do stay, Elizabeth, stay as my housekeeper."

"As your housekeeper?"

"Yes, as my housekeeper. Elizabeth I want you to stay and look after me, then perhaps…" His voice tailed off.

"Perhaps?" She studied him intently. "Perhaps what, David?"

For a moment he seemed lost for words. Then he took a deep breath "Elizabeth my dear have you forgotten that day I first preached in St Peter's?"

"No, David, I remember we all congratulated you on your powerful sermon and I suggested you should preach about the evils of slavery."

He sighed. "You were angry with me when I declined, weren't you Elizabeth?" He saw her nod. "But maybe I should, now that Martha and Alice are here."

"David, why are you telling me all this?"

"Elizabeth, I was hoping you'd recall what I said to you before I left."
She said nothing but withdrew her hand.

Doggedly he continued. "I told you that my respect and admiration for you had grown into devotion and love. I remember saying that when I had a living of my own I should need a wife to help me with my ministry. Elizabeth dear, don't you remember? I asked you to marry me!"

"Yes, David, I do remember!"

"Elizabeth, you refused me then, but could it be that if you were my housekeeper for a while, you might change your mind?"

To her surprise his downcast look troubled her. How could she tell him she would never, ever marry him? "David, I must have time to think." That was all she could say!

She saw him smile. "There's no hurry, Elizabeth. I do hope you'll accept my offer".

"Yes, David."

Her unenthusiastic reply clearly had him thinking. "Have you any other plans, Elizabeth?"

"Yes, I do." The defiant note that had crept into her voice gave her confidence. "Yes. Squire Thomas has asked me to keep house for him."

David looked shocked. "You can't work for him, Elizabeth!"

"Why, Why not David"'"

"It's evident you don't know him. Haven't you heard he's a womaniser?" He saw her shake her head. "Why else do you suppose Mrs Thomas is always so unwell? Even in Olverton folk have heard of the many young girls he's seduced."

"David I think you're exaggerating. In any case I'm a mature woman. I can assure you I'd stand no such truck from him."

"Perhaps you might not, but what about Martha?" She didn't answer. "What about Martha, Elizabeth?"

"I think you have a vivid imagination David. Squire Thomas is a pillar of the church. He's held in high regard by everyone."

"Elizabeth, I'd hate to see you hurt. Please don't work for him. Please don't reject my offer, please consider it carefully."

She had to escape, she had to disentangle herself from this argument she was in danger of losing. "Thank you for your concern, David." She smiled at him. "And for your offer. Give me time, let me sleep on it."

The die was cast, Elizabeth muttered angrily as she fled. David was to be the new Rector and she would have to go. It was so ironical. She had hoped to be the new Rector's housekeeper, but never had she accepted that it would be David! How could she keep house for him, when he so clearly expected it to be but a stepping stone to marriage? For the next few hours she managed to keep him at a distance, but that evening she was obliged to dine with him. It was a difficult occasion, with conversation restricted to trivial matters! At last she could excuse herself and retire to her chamber. A good night's sleep had become a precious rarity and that night she hardly slept at all. Next morning was strained, he pressing her by innuendo to accept his offer and she politely avoiding an answer. When he'd left for St Peter's, she'd followed with a heavy heart and on entering the church with Martha and Alice had begged the Good Lord for his mercy and help.

As David had foretold, Squire Thomas had indeed announced David was to be the new Rector. David had graciously accepted his appointment and the service had begun. "Dearly beloved brethren," she heard David reciting, "The Scripture moveth us in sundry places to acknowledge and bewail our manifold sins." Elizabeth followed the service mechanically; it was the beginning of the end. Her bond with St Peter's was slipping away!

When she emerged once more into the spring sunshine, Alison was waiting for her. "So David's to be our new Rector, I suppose we all knew it would he him!"

"Yes, Alison." Elizabeth couldn't hide the bitter note in her voice. "You could say it was inevitable."

"You don't seem pleased, Elizabeth!"

"Don't I? It's just that......, Oh! I don't know Alison. Suddenly I feel I don't belong here anymore!"

Alison touched her arm. "What nonsense Elizabeth my dear! Of course you do! Surely if you're going to be his housekeeper you'll still be involved with the life of the church!"

"Housekeeper?" Astonished, Elizabeth repeated "Housekeeper? Whatever makes you think I shall be keeping house for David?"

"Well Elizabeth, the whole village has always thought you'd be keeping house for the new Rector!"

"Well, Alison, you're wrong. You're all wrong. I'm not staying!" It was the first time she'd voiced the decision she knew she had to make.

"Doesn't he want you to stay?"

"Yes, Alison, of course he does. But I really can't."

"You can't? Why ever not, Elizabeth? Surely he'd provide for you and you'd stay in the house you love!"

"Yes, Alison. Everything you say is perfectly true!"

"Well, Elizabeth dear, tell me why can't you stay?"

Elizabeth seemed reluctant to answer, but then she spoke. "You may not be aware Alison that David has asked me to be his wife."

Alison looked surprised, but said nothing.

"I have refused him twice, but he'll not be thwarted! Now he plans to employ me as housekeeper in the hope that I shall succumb. But I never will!"

"Elizabeth, would he not make you a fine husband?"

"Oh, Alison, you remind me of my poor dear father. He was always wanted me to marry David!"

"But Elizabeth dear, if you won't keep house at the Rectory, where will you live?"

"That I don't know, Alison. Something will turn up. I just have to put my trust in God."

Chapter 37

At last, the Mary Anne was nearing the end of the middle passage. Landfall had been made on the North Carolina coast and with a moderate wind good progress was being made towards Chesapeake Bay. It had been a slow passage with storms followed by light fickle winds, but thankfully only nine slaves had succumbed to the dreaded flux and he had lost but two of the crew.

Having entered the landfall in the log, Jim had retired to the privacy of his cabin to read again the instructions issued by the Partners. *"In the event that you consider prices at Montego Bay to be too low you are to proceed to Annapolis in the colony of Maryland. There you are to call upon Mr Jeremiah Healey of Healey, Durnmock and Partners, who will advise you concerning the sale of your slaves".*

He recalled the Partners' meeting. Gordon Crosbie had been convinced that the best prices for slaves were to be got in the American Colonies and had proposed selling them in Annapolis. As usual the other partners had nodded respectfully, but Jim had suggested landing them at Norfolk, Virginia. Norfolk, at the entrance to Chesapeake Bay, would be easier to reach, whereas Annapolis lay on the River Severn, a hundred miles or so up the narrow inlet which calls itself Chesapeake Bay. Gordon however wouldn't hear of it. Annapolis was his choice and he'd brook no argument. So here was the "Mary Anne" heading past Norfolk with Cape Charles on the starboard bow and soon to be confined in the bay where the tides would be strong and the rocks waiting for the inattentive navigator. Jim shook his head in despair. Landlubbers like Gordon Crosbie never understood that the final leg of a voyage close inshore could often be more hazardous than the ocean crossing. Many a well found ship had come to grief close to its destination! He sighed, his worries weren't over yet, but the weather was fine, the wind fair and good speed was being made towards Newport News where he hoped to anchor that evening.

Nathaniel was intrigued by this new and exciting land and was up early next day surveying this strange land. In the distance he could make out the town, marked by column after column of smoke rising into the morning sky. He could see the sharply etched spire of the church and to his right a forest of masts. Close inshore, where the gulls were wheeling and screeching, he spotted a boat. He counted four men at the oars, and in the sternsheets sat a passenger. Could he be the pilot he wondered. With growing impatience he watched the boat draw slowly nearer, then it shaped up to come alongside.

"Good morning, sir. Are you by any chance the Pilot?"

"Sure am." A lean, weather beaten man scrambled up the chains. "Goin' to 'Napolis I presume."

"Yes, that's right, sir. I'll tell the Captain you're here." But he was too late; the Captain was just appearing.

"Howdee, Cap'n." The Pilot doffed his tricorn. "Guess you're from the Slave Coast. We can smell you 'slavers a mile away!"

"Morning, Pilot." Jim ignored his comment. All Pilots seemed to make the same hackneyed remark; it always irritated him. "We're headed for Annapolis. I'm told slaves fetch a good price there."

"Well." The Pilot laughed. "Can't say for sure, ain't sold any lately, but if you'll weigh anchor Cap'n we'll soon find out."

Once the ship was safely under way, the two men began to chat. Formerly a ship's master, the Pilot had tired of the sea and having studied the shallows and currents in the bay and learnt the leading marks he now guided ships up and down its narrow waters.

"Ain't a bad job," he admitted. "And you see more of the family." He grinned, "If that's what you want!"

Nathaniel was fascinated by this American and listened avidly as the two men talked. He heard the Pilot tell of life in Virginia, of the price of tobacco and the state of the plantations. How they'd founder if it weren't for the slaves. "Reckon there must be twenty or thirty of them niggers to one of us whites hereabouts. Sometimes," the Pilot eased his tricorn onto the back of his head. "It feels as if we're sittin' on a powder keg. God help us, Cap'n, if those damned niggers ever find some guns and get organised. If that ever happens and there's a fight it'll be the planters who'll get it first and they know it. Yeah, they know it all right and when there's trouble on one of the plantations nearby, they get edgy, mighty edgy! That's when the whips really come out, that's when the owners'll have any slave flogged for just lookin'." He stuffed a plug of tobacco into his mouth and began to chew. "And any dumb slave who does manage to escape, won't be free for long, you can take my word for that! The poor whites, those who can't find a job will see to that, Cap'n." He strode to the gunwale and spat a globule of amber spittle over the side. "They hate the slaves. They say the niggers are doing their work. But then, Cap'n, he shrugged his shoulders. "Why should a Planter pay wages to a white man when he can use a nigger to do the job for a plate of corn mash?" Nathaniel saw Jim nod. "But I tell you the whites who can't find work to feed themselves and their family, don't see it that way. They really hate the slaves. If they ever find a nigger actin' suspicious, they grab 'im and 'and 'im over for the reward. No, Cap'n," he pulled a wry face. "It's damned nigh impossible for the slaves to escape." He spat another globule into the sea. Some try though and hope to get across the border to Ohio."

"Ohio?" Jim broke in. "Why Ohio?"

"Well, Cap'n, Ohio's a Yankee state and for reasons we can't fathom here in the south, the Yankees don't hold with slavery. But give 'em their due; they'll not stand in the way of a Southerner trying to recover a runaway, except the Quakers, that is." He'd resumed his methodical chewing, then he stopped and shook his head. "Can't figure them Quakers out, Cap'n. They're a tight knit lot who go their own way." He spat again. "They won't admit it of course, but I've heard tell they've got a safe route that gets a nigger all the way to Canada and once he's there, he's a free man!"

As Nathaniel heard the two men discussing life in the American Colonies he became aware that this was a huge vibrant land, which made Montego Bay seem but a sleepy village. The Pilot spoke with obvious pride of a land of opportunity, where initiative and new ideas blossomed, where folk were no longer constrained by the conventions they hated so much in England. "This is a land with all the trappings of a nation state," the Pilot had said proudly. "But we still look to King George to protect us against the Indians and the French." Yet later he was to voice his countrymen's anger at the taxes levied on them by the King.

In Annapolis, Nathaniel was mesmerised by the hustle and bustle of the port. A never ending procession of carts and wagons loaded with tobacco, huge bales of cotton, sacks of sugar and great barrels of rum made their way along the quay to ships loading for the homeward run. Everywhere bare-footed slaves in ragged shirts and trousers, their ebony faces topped with battered straw hats, struggled with great loads, while a handful of white men stood idly by.

For the first two days the Mary Anne was busy landing her slaves. A few finding new strength struggled and spat at their captors as they were taken ashore, but most, thankful to be free from their evil smelling prison, caused little trouble. Once the last slave had left, the ship's company began scrubbing the decks and cleaning the slave decks and readying them for the cargo they'd take home. For Nathaniel this was a defining moment. Two voyages in a slaver had been more than enough and he'd promised himself they would be his last. He had tried not to show the others that he'd become more and more sickened by this inhuman trade, but he knew, from the way the Chief Mate baited him, that he'd failed. So when the Chief Mate, a man he'd never taken to, an overbearing man who seemed oblivious to the suffering of the slaves, had said, "The niggers are to be auctioned on Wednesday at ten o'clock. You should be there, Mr Lugger, to see our cargo sold and discover what we've earned for our labours," he'd meekly complied.

The saleroom was in one if the warehouses nearby. The auctioneer's desk stood at one end alongside a small podium. When Nathaniel arrived the room was already full of planters waiting for the sale to begin. They looked decent enough men, smartly dressed in tailcoats and breeches and wearing those wide brimmed hats that everyone of importance seemed to favour. These slave owners intrigued Nathaniel for, but for their style of dress, they were not unlike the people he knew at home. Perhaps they were better dressed and had an air of affluence and privilege, but they didn't look evil. They weren't the ogres one might have expected! Even the auctioneer looked harmless, a man of no consequence, yet with the tap of his gavel he could decide the fate of every wretched slave who passed through his auction room! Nathaniel studied him standing at his desk waiting to start the sale. When at last the time came he picked up his gavel and with a respectful tap addressed the assembled company. "Gentlemen with your kind permission, I'll make a start." Suddenly a change came over him. He seemed to revel in his new found importance. "We've some fine slaves for you this morning, gentlemen. They've just arrived in the slaver, the "Mary Anne" and they're all in good health thanks to the most considerate treatment of Captain Youle and his crew." He turned to his assistant. "Bring in the first lot, Joe."

All eyes turned to the doorway. Nathaniel heard cursing and swearing and three slaves bound by chains were dragged onto the podium. All three looked terrified with their big round eyes exploring the scene before them. He heard the auctioneer's voice. "Three young bucks. They'll work well, once they're broken in. Who'll start me at a hundred? You sir?" Then the chanting began. "At one hundred then, one hundred and ten, one twenty over there, one thirty, one forty, do I see one fifty. Yes, one fifty, one fifty. Come along gentlemen, who'll give me one hundred and sixty guineas for these three strong bucks? You, sir?" And so it went on until the gavel came down at one hundred and seventy guineas and the slaves were dragged away. Their future had been decided. They might be lucky and find a tolerant master, or more likely they were now the property of a cruel and selfish one, a planter who would abuse them and work them into an early grave, to be replaced by younger, fitter slaves bought at a trifling price.

Another lot had been announced and three more black men were propelled onto the platform. The auctioneer was shouting "Look at those muscles, as strong as an ox." Then the bidding began again. Finally it was time for the women. Unlike the men, they were put up one by one, the first being heavily pregnant. "Two for the price of one," the auctioneer cried. The next was a young girl no more than thirteen years old. She looked frightened and sobbed quietly, but the auctioneer was untouched. "Very gentle, this one", he exclaimed. "She'll be a comfort to her owner, mark my words. She'll fetch a good price, gentlemen. Now who'll start me at ninety guineas?" The auctioneer knew his market well, for the price reached one hundred and twenty guineas before the hammer fell. The bidding for the older women was slower and the last was sold for what the auctioneer called a "give away price."

As the buyers were settling their account, Nathaniel slipped out. He needed to escape from that awful human market and fill his lungs with fresh clean air. Now the sale was over he wanted to forget this hideous trade. Yet, as he watched the slaves being crammed into wagons to take them into a life of bondage, he asked himself, how could he ever?

With the auction over, Jim felt that a great weight had been lifted from his shoulders. He'd promised Elizabeth this would be his last slaving voyage and now that all the slaves had gone he was a slaver no more. Now she had to marry him! In high spirits, Jim sent for the Chief Mate. "Mr Murray, I'd like you and the mates to join me for supper tonight at the Shamrock Tavern. I'd like to celebrate the sale of the slaves and our forthcoming return to England. Oh! And tell young Lugger he's to come as well."

Jim had booked a room which overlooked the quay with a fine view of the river. Nathaniel and the others waited for the Captain to take his seat at the head of the table and then for the Chief Mate to take his at the opposite end. Then as the others sat down, he'd respectfully held back and had had to take the chair next to the Chief Mate. He cursed his luck and prayed he'd be allowed to enjoy the evening without being taunted. The food soon appeared, lobster, fresh Chesapeake lobster the landlady called it. Nathaniel had never eaten lobster before with its huge claws and spindly legs. It reminded him of the fresh water shrimps he used to find in the village pond, but they were grey, almost transparent. The lobster was bright red and when at last he'd managed to crack its armour he savoured the firm white flesh. The rum was beginning to flow now and everyone was in party mood, telling jokes and recounting memories of earlier voyages. Even the Chief Mate seemed friendly but when the turkey was brought in, he started making lewd suggestions to one of the black serving girls. The others laughed and Nathaniel thought it wise to follow suit. Then as they tackled the American food piled high on their plates the conversation fell away. Great piles of fruit followed; it was a rare feast! When all had eaten their full and were toying with the last pieces of fruit the Captain rose and tapped on the table. "Gentlemen," he said. "Well, that's another slaving voyage behind us and by all accounts a profitable one too. And I'm certain our cargo of cotton and tobacco will fetch a good price in Bristol. If it's half as good as this rum gentlemen, there'll be no question about that! He let the titter of laughter subside before he went on to review the voyage so far and his plans for the homeward passage. Finally he thanked them for their loyalty and hard work and raising his glass announced a toast, "The 'Mary Anne', God bless her and grant us a safe passage home."

As they savoured their rum, the landlady and her serving girls arrived to clear the table. "I hope the meal was to your taste, gentlemen." There was a chorus of approval and much nodding of heads.

"Well now, gentlemen," the landlady continued. "What about something a little more personal? I've some real pretty nigger girls I keep for my special customers. There's Linda and Maggie here and some more." She glared at Maggie. "Don't stand there sulkin', Maggie. Make yourself look interestin'."

Maggie obediently wiggled her hips and the Chief Mate got unsteadily to his feet. "She'll do for me. Come on lads, let's have a bit of fun. You too, Lugger, let's see if you're a man! S'pose you know what wenches are for!" The rum was beginning to have its effect and the Mates eagerly followed the Chief Mate to the door. Nathaniel hesitated. The Chief Mate was bad enough sober, but now he was drunk he knew he'd bate him endlessly. Reluctantly he turned to follow them. Then he heard the sharp, disapproving voice of the Captain. "Mr Lugger, you're too young. While you're an Apprentice in my ship you'll leave wenches alone. D'you hear? When you're a Mate you can do as you please, but not now. So sit down."

Nathaniel sat down. Knowing the others would laugh at him, he tried to look disappointed, but it was with relief that he watched the others disappear. "Thank you, sir," he said when they were alone. "I didn't want to go anyway."

"Yes, Mr Lugger, I thought you needed a good excuse. I've seen the Chief Mate giving you a rough time of late. He thinks you're too soft with the slaves."

"D'you think so too, sir?"

"No, Nathaniel. It's a pretty bloody trade. You don't mind me calling you Nathaniel, do you?"

"No, sir. Of course not. You've called me Nathaniel before."

"Yes, you're right! But only in the presence of your mother."

In the silence that followed, Nathaniel wondered why the Captain suddenly wanted to call him by his Christian name.

"Nathaniel." Jim cleared his throat. "I want you to know that I'm hoping to marry your mother." He eyed the boy carefully, but there seemed little reaction. Though he didn't show it, Nathaniel was dumfounded. He couldn't believe what he was hearing! After a moment he asked him. "Did you say you wanted to marry my mother?"

The Captain began to look uneasy. "No, no, not exactly, Nathaniel. I said I am hoping to marry your mother. But you're quite right I do very much want her to be my wife."

For a moment Nathaniel couldn't speak. It had never crossed his mind that his mother would ever marry again. He'd presumed she'd accepted her lot as a widow. She'd always seemed happy to devote herself to her father and him. She was the only person he really loved and the thought of sharing her love with some other man upset him. He'd supposed some day in the distant future he himself might find a wife, but never had he thought she might find another husband! It was all very disturbing. He saw the Captain waiting for an answer. What could he say? Then he heard himself saying, "Does she want to marry you?"

"Yes, I believe so," came the reply! "But she's quite adamant. She won't marry me unless I give up the slave trade. Your mother's a woman of principle." He saw Nathaniel nod and added "And I admire her for it. So Nathaniel this will be my last voyage in a slaver, and I'm hoping she'll agree to be my wife!"

Jim was looking confident again. "You'll not believe me, Nathaniel, but I've been captivated by your mother ever since I first saw her when she brought you on board the "Mary Anne"." He chuckled and shook his head. "Nathaniel, I never had any intention to have apprentices onboard my ship, but y'know with her being so damned insistent and," he chuckled. "So close, I just couldn't think straight and before I knew it I'd signed you on!" He paused a while as he recalled that first meeting. Then he gave the boy a searching look. "Does the thought of us being wed shock you?"

"Well, no, sir, no, I don't think so." Nathaniel spoke hesitatingly. "Though I have to admit it's come as a surprise. But, if she really wants to marry you, well, I'll support her."

Chapter 38

The happy day had come and the "Mary Anne" was finally secured alongside in Bristol, but hardly had the last mooring rope been made fast when Gordon Crosbie appeared.

"Welcome home." He shook Jim's hand. "You're earlier than expected! Y'must have had a good passage."

"Aye, we had fair winds."

"So what about the slaves? You lost seventeen last time I recall. I hope you did better this time."

Jim fought back his irritation. "You'll get the details in my report Gordon, but I'm pleased to tell you the flux only took nine."

"Disappointing, Jim. I'd hoped it'd be fewer than that. What's that damned surgeon of yours been doing eh?"

"He did his best, Gordon. No one knows what causes the bloody flux. When we know that, maybe we can stop it!"

Gordon seemed unimpressed. "Tell me. Did you get a good price at Annapolis?"

Jim groaned inwardly. Gordon wouldn't let him rest till the profit had been calculated. "Depends what you mean by a good price, Gordon."

"Mm, that don't sound too promising. I'll get the clerk to check your papers. Then we'll see how you've done. Ah! Here is Mr Weller. I'll leave you in his good hands."

Jim sighed, what a despicable man Gordon was! The loss of slaves upset him, but only because it meant less profit. But, what of the crew? He didn't seem to care how many of them had died! He led the clerk down to his cabin, gave him all his papers and left him to it. He wanted to see the cargo being unloaded. He would enjoy that. That was a tangible result of the voyage, though it would have to be expressed in terms of a profit or heaven forbid a loss! That's what the clerk would be doing; calculating the profit. The difference between cost and selling price of the slaves and cargo would be calculated to give the Gross Profit, from which the use of the ship and its repairs and the cost of the crew would be deducted to give the Nett Profit. Nett Profit that was the only yardstick Gordon used to measure the success of the venture!

Two days later he called on Gordon to deliver his written report. To his surprise he had found him not too displeased! But he had a much more important reason for seeing him! It was to tell him of his decision not to sail again as Master of the "Mary Anne". Gordon appeared greatly shocked and with disbelief in his voice asked if he had heard him aright? Jim assured him he had. For a moment Gordon seemed lost for words, then in a fatherly way he put an arm around Jim's shoulders.

"Jim, Jim my dear fellow, I'd be very, very sorry to lose you. I remember we made a respectable profit on your previous voyage and by all accounts we'll make a handsome one this time." He shook his head gently as if it was all too difficult to believe. "Jim you must know that the partners and I hold you in high esteem. We have great faith in you as Master of our ship and with you in command we're all looking for good profits in the years ahead." He gave Jim a searching look as if trying to discover what lay behind this ridiculous decision of his. "James, my dear fellow, I must ask you to think again."

Jim however told him that he was adamant, that his mind was made up and to emphasise his resolve he thanked him for hearing him and turned to go. But Gordon begged him not to be hasty. "Could it be, my dear fellow", he adopted an obsequious manner. "That a greater share of the profits would persuade you to change your mind?" The temptation to drive the hardest possible bargain and see Gordon Crosbie squirm proved too much for Jim. He put down his hat and asked Gordon what he had in mind.

"Well," Gordon was affable now. "We might increase your share of the profits by a half." He stood back to observe the other's reaction, then clearing his throat he added. "Mind you I'd have to ask the partners to agree such a generous offer." Jim remained silent, but when pressed for a reply, said that the offer was quite insufficient and his original decision must stand. Gordon had looked surprised, even hurt, but when it was clear that Jim would not be moved, he asked in a tetchy voice "What inducement, sir, do you expect?"

Jim had been struggling to keep a straight face and told him he had no wish to be greedy, but other masters received a far greater share than he did! Gordon had scowled, but undeterred Jim continued. "I want to be fair with you Gordon. I might stay as Master if you were to treble my share."

Gordon looked aghast. "Treble your share?" For a moment Jim thought he might strike him, he appeared so irate! But instead he strode to the window as if to cool his temper. Then turning, he barked, "Have you taken leave of your senses?" When Jim made no response, he adopted a friendlier manner. "Jim my dear fellow, you must know how fond I am of you! Indeed 'tis my fondness for you that makes me rue your goin'. Aye, 'tis my affection for you that makes my benevolence know no bounds!" He shook his head slowly and with outstretched hand came towards him. "James, I'll settle for a doubling of your share!"

But Jim withheld his hand. "I can't accept that, Gordon. My decision to part company with you must stand."

In his rage Gordon swore, called him an ungrateful knave and reminded him of his scant experience of the trade. "You've an inflated opinion of yourself James. You'll not find another owner in this port to meet your monstrous demands, so don't come begging me to take you back." Then he snarled. "I suppose it's your future wife we must blame for your grand ideas!"

Jim ignored his vilification and his remarks about Elizabeth and bid him "G'day." Though now he too was angry, he had to admit he'd enjoyed baiting his miserly former partner. Then the realisation that he was no longer a slaver struck him! It brought immediate cheer and relief. Now she'd have to marry him!

He returned to the ship with a new-found spring in his step and sent for Nathaniel. "Mr Lugger, now that your second voyage is over, it's time we discussed your performance as an Apprentice. Sit down, please." Nathaniel drew up a chair and watched Jim sign and date his journal. He remembered the day he'd been given it. How pristine it had looked then, its leather binding unblemished, its pages un-creased. Now with its binding damaged, water marks on the cover and its pages dog-eared, it had a story of its own to tell!

"That's a well-kept journal," Jim interrupted Nathaniel's thoughts. "I've enjoyed reading it!" Then he'd talked about his performance pointing out where Nathaniel had done well and where improvements could be made and after answering his questions had reached for the quill to sign the certificate. "Congratulations, Mr Lugger! Here's your Third Mate's Certificate. And I want you to know that I'd be happy to have you sail with me as Third Mate in my next ship. Or if you prefer, I'll recommend you to some other Master."

"Thank you, sir." It was the moment Nathaniel had waited for so long. He wanted to rush on deck and shout for joy. He got up to go. "Thank you sir, thank you. I'd very much like to sail with you as Third Mate sir! I'll sign on whenever you want."

"Good, Nathaniel, but don't go. It's Sunday tomorrow."

"Yes?" A puzzled Nathaniel replied.

"Well, Nathaniel, I've hired a couple of horses. I thought tomorrow we might go to Hanbury. You'll want to see your mother as much as I do, I'm sure. Will you come?"

Of course he'd agreed. He hadn't thought he would see his mother so soon!

"Good, Nathaniel. I've asked for the horses to be ready by seven tomorrow morning. It'll be getting light then and with luck we'll be in Hanbury by ten."

The following day they were up early and at the stables by seven. They could hear the horses snuffling and snorting, but there was no sign of the ostler. Jim cursed. "Probably sleeping off a skinful of ale!" They searched the stables and alleyways for him until when their patience was exhausted, a dishevelled figure appeared. "You're late, Mr Reed!" Jim's face showed his anger. "I wanted to be on the road by now, damn you."

"Sorry sir." 'Fraid I overslept. Couldn't settle the bairn. Kep' us awake 'alf the night. I'll 'ave the 'orses ready in no time."

"Damn, damn, damn." Jim could contain his pent-up anger no longer. "We'll probably find your mother's in church by the time we get there! What time does it start?"

"Ten o'clock, sir. It's always been ten o'clock, ever since I can remember."

It was almost eight o'clock when they eventually set off. Neither had sat on a horse for nearly a year and though Nathaniel was soon confident enough to trot Jim, never a horseman, could only walk his horse. Only when clear of the town and dismayed by their woefully slow progress did he pluck up courage to try. Soon they were making better speed and eventually after what seemed an age the church spire came into sight and they heard the church bells. But the bells had fallen silent before they'd reached the church and it was clear the service was about to start. Dismounting, they quickly tethered the horses and ran to the door.

The church was full and they had to stand at the back, Jim looking anxiously at the front pew where he knew Elizabeth would sit. It was empty! He scanned the other pews but could not see her. "Could she be late?" He whispered. Nathaniel shook his head. "No, Mama is always early."

The congregation stood as the priest appeared. "That's not your Grandfather Nathaniel. Who is it?"

"I don't know. Perhaps he's a visiting priest."

"Well, Nathaniel, where's your grandfather?"

"I don't know. Maybe he's ill. Mama could be with him!"

"Oh!" Nathaniel could hear the disappointment in Jim's voice.

Jim hardly heard a word of the service as he wondered where she was. Her absence was a bitter blow. He wanted to rush out and hammer on the Rectory door, but he knew he couldn't do that. He had to endure this wretched priest droning on from the pulpit. It seemed interminable, but finally the priest blessed the congregation, genuflected before the altar and disappeared through a doorway in the chancel. As the villagers respectfully made way for their betters to leave, Jim continued to search desperately for Elizabeth. Then in an instant he saw her! It wasn't an illusion! It really was Elizabeth! His Elizabeth looking as trim and graceful as he'd remembered. Nathaniel was the first to speak.

"Mama!" His voice rang with joy. "We didn't see you!"

She stopped. She saw them in the half light.

"Nathaniel! Nathaniel dear, it's you! And you too, James! Thank God you're home safe! How wonderful it is to see you!" She took them by the hand and led them out into the sunlight. Nathaniel told her excitedly about their early morning ride, while Jim's eyes devoured her lovingly. It seemed an eternity since he'd last seen her waving bravely as he'd ridden back to the ship so long ago! He'd been badly shaken when he couldn't find her in church and now he could scarcely believe it really was her. But it was Elizabeth, Elizabeth radiating love and joy! Like her he was laughing now and fighting back the tears. He longed to hold her in his arms and kiss her and tell her he'd given up slaving. Then he could ask her the question he'd wanted to ask for so long! But not now, the villagers were everywhere and Martha and Alice were looking awkward and uncomfortable. He turned to acknowledge them and they welcomed him too. Though he couldn't ask the question he longed to, her very proximity sent his heart racing and he knew he had to content himself just looking at her and hearing her talk and laugh! But what was she telling them? Grandpa had departed this life and she no longer lived at the Rectory? She took them to the grave now shared by her mother and her father. She told them how he'd died, about David and how hurt her she was to learn that this self-satisfied man had been given her father's living. As they walked through the village, Elizabeth explained that David had asked her to stay as his housekeeper, but she'd refused. She spoke of the difficulties in finding somewhere to live with Martha and Alice. "But dear Alison came to our rescue. She found me a little cottage on her husband's land." She paused awhile, then laughed. "It's tiny, isn't it Martha? But it's a roof over our heads! Well," she laughed again. "It keeps most of the rain out, doesn't it Martha?"

They had reached the edge of the village now and, turning off the road, she led them along a pathway winding through the trees. "Mind the puddles," she cried. "And the mud too, Alice please!" The sunlight beckoned them and when they felt its warmth again, she stopped and pointed to a ramshackle structure in the distance. "There's our little home. We're nearly there aren't we Alice?"

"Yes, Miss Elizabeth, nearly home," Alice replied as she skipped ahead.

Jim's first glimpse of her "little home" shocked him greatly. The more he surveyed it the more horrified he became. It looked derelict! It looked as if it had been abandoned! Its thatch was worn and patchy and though attempts had apparently been made to plaster up the cracked walls, they looked as if they might collapse at any moment. Only the timbers seemed sound enough!

"You haven't been living there, Elizabeth?" She could hear the disbelief and concern in his voice.

"Yes, James. This has been our home for many a month. It may look a little worse for wear, but we've really been quite comfortable, haven't we, Martha?"

Martha giggled. "Yes, ma'am. We've been happy enough, except when it's rained!"

"But, Martha dear, the roof's really quite sound and," she hesitated, "we'd have been very unhappy if I'd agreed to keep house for the Squire!"

Jim saw Martha shudder. "Yes, ma'am. That would have been awful!"

On reaching her little home, Elizabeth pushed the door open and bade them enter. In the half-light James could see two simple chairs on either side of the hearth and a doorway leading to another room. As his eyes became accustomed to the gloom he saw a few blackened pots standing near the fireplace, a table by the wall and found he was standing on a rush mat laid on the bare mud floor. After the grandeur of the Rectory he couldn't believe she had survived in such appalling surroundings. To him her little cottage seemed no better than the native shacks he'd seen on the Bonny River!

"Elizabeth." The horror in his voice was unmistakable. "How have you managed to live in this dreadful place?"

The sparkle in those blue eyes of hers answered his fears! "James dearest, it was all we could find and it's really quite cosy once the fire is burning. Many villagers live like this, so how can I complain? Especially as I have Martha and Alice!"

"But after the Rectory." Jim began, but Elizabeth broke in. "James dearest, I've left the Rectory, my home is here now."

While they'd been talking, Martha had been busy blowing on the ashes and the twigs she'd placed on the glowing embers. Soon she was rewarded with flames licking the great black pot above, which she began to fill. Meanwhile Elizabeth was busy finding bowls, plates, and utensils to set upon the table. She talked as she worked. "Dear Alison wouldn't take a penny for rent James! But I did so want to pay her and when I insisted, she suggested I might teach her children to read and write. It was a wonderful offer and now I teach four other children as well. And of course there's Alice to be taught too." She reached fondly for the little black girl. "You know I think she's the brightest of them all!" And before Jim could express his admiration she went on. "And Martha is very good with her needle and is making clothes for some of the villagers, so we've managed, haven't we, Martha dear?"

As they sat to eat, James gazed proudly at this resourceful, competent woman who had overcome her setbacks with such equanimity. While he'd been gone it had never occurred to him that she might be forced to leave the Rectory, find shelter and earn her own livelihood. But she had. She was indeed a remarkable woman!

When they had finished eating, Jim could contain himself no longer. He caught her eye.

"Elizabeth," he whispered. "I've something important to tell you, something I want you and only you to hear." She made no reply, but giving him a smile she turned to Nathaniel. "I must show James the rest of our estate!" And as Martha laughed she led James through the door into the tiny garden that bordered the path. Now at last alone, Jim's heart began to race as holding her hands he began. "Elizabeth dearest, take a good look at me. Do I seem different?" For a moment she surveyed him intently. Then she smiled. "No, James dearest, you look just like the man I've been longing to see for the past year. Tell me, tell me how are you different?"

Drawing himself up to his full height he tried to look dignified, but Elizabeth began to laugh! Then he was laughing too and before he knew it he was holding her close and they were kissing. But quickly she broke away.

"James, we must stop. I shouldn't be kissing a slaver!"

He smiled and shook his head. "Elizabeth, I've loved you since the first time I ever saw you. Your integrity and determination bewitched me then and," he chuckled. "So did your beautiful eyes!"

She took his hand again. "James, what are you trying to tell me?"

"What am I trying to tell you? Dearest, ever since I saw you again this morning, I've been longing to tell you I'm no longer a slaver! I've told my partners I'll not sail as Master of the "Mary Anne" again. Elizabeth my dear, I'll never, ever trade in slaves again!"

"Oh! James. James dearest, how wonderful! I knew you'd keep your promise!" She held him at arms length and he felt her eyes caress him. Then laughing she exclaimed. "James dear you're so right, you do look different! Yes, I can see it now. I can see what's changed you, it's your lovely shining halo!" She kissed him on the cheek. "James dearest, it suits you so well!"

Jim laughed as he gazed at her. He wanted to savour this moment for ever. "Elizabeth, dearest Elizabeth, I've wanted to have you as my wife from the first day we met. Please, don't make me wait any longer. Please, I beg you, tell me you'll many me."

"James my love, now you're no longer a slaver, of course I'll marry you. Did you have any doubts?"

He kissed her and laughed and kissed her again. "Did I have any doubts? I kept telling myself you'd say yes, but then a voice within me would ask why should a beautiful, talented, resourceful woman like you want to marry a man like me?"

"Well tell that voice I want to marry him because he's kind, gentle, and honourable and because I love him."

"Oh! Elizabeth my love, you've made me so happy." He kissed her again, then holding her at arm's length he reached inside his shirt collar. "Look", he whispered as he pulled on a string. "It's a ring, a wedding ring. I had it made for you in Jamaica."

He undid the knot and gave it to her. "D'you see the letters the inside? They're our initials JY and EL. It's our wedding ring, dearest."

Elizabeth examined the ring closely. "James, it's beautiful!"

"Try it, Elizabeth. I'm longing to know if it fits!"

"Do you think I ought? Should I not wait until I'm your wife, dear husband to be?" Oh! But how can I resist the temptation?" She slid the ring onto her finger. "James dearest, look. It's a perfect fit! I can't believe it! The Good Lord must have made it! He must surely want us to wed!"

Epilogue

As His Britannic Majesty's frigate "Curlew" sails in the Gulf of Guinea on anti-slavery patrol, her Captain, Lieutenant Nathaniel Lugger is sitting on his chair on the quarterdeck. It is one of those rare afternoons when the wind is light, the sea calm, the sun warm and the ship sails herself with only the lightest touch on the wheel to guide her. Nathaniel is humming quietly. It's a tune that's been with him all day, a tune he'll never forget, though he struggles to recall the words. How do they go? Ah! Yes:

> Glorious things of thee are spoken
> Zion, city of our God;
> He whose word cannot be broken
> Formed thee for his own abode.
> On the rock of ages founded
> Who can shake thy sure repose?
> With salvation's walls surrounded
> Thou may'st smile at all thy foes.

When he'd made his first entry in the ship's log that morning, the seventh day of May, eighteen hundred and ten, he'd remembered it was the anniversary of his mother's wedding to James Youle and the hymn they'd sung on that happy day had come back to him. He recalled his mother saying that the Rector, the Reverend David Hart, had been greatly shocked when she'd told him of her intention to marry James and had been difficult, even unpleasant! David had wanted her to marry him and had twice proposed marriage. On the day she and James had seen him to discuss their wedding he had taken her into the sitting room, leaving James in his study. When they were alone he had advised her to reconsider her decision to marry such an uncultured man of the sea and had reaffirmed his wish to make her his wife. Mother had been infuriated, but had controlled her anger and told him she would never marry him and that she considered herself truly blessed to have James as her suitor. James, she'd told David, was a kind, generous and honest man, who had shown her nothing but love and respect. She was sure the Good Lord would look kindly on their union, which she believed had been preordained. Even then David had persisted, saying her Father had always hoped she would marry him, but she had been adamant; she would never forsake James for him!

David had looked resentful as he led her back to his study. Then it was James' turn to be taken away to be asked whether he really considered himself good enough to marry such a graceful, cultured and elegant woman as Elizabeth? Was he sure that a man of his repute, a slave ship master, a man without the benefit of a proper education, a man such as he could make Elizabeth happy after the first flush of bodily love? Nathaniel recalled the anger in Jim's voice as he'd told him. "What an arrogant dog he is! How I managed to control my temper I'll never know! But I did, though I could scarcely speak! "Mr Hart," I said, "everything you say about Elizabeth is true. She is cultured, graceful and charming and I admire and respect her and applaud her resolute integrity. I am indeed the most fortunate of men that she should consent to be my wife and nothing will prevent me from becoming her faithful and devoted husband! Now sir, let us get down to the business of arranging our wedding." They had then returned to Elizabeth and at last had begun to plan the wedding. Mother had wanted Psalm 128 to be sung and had said that James wished to choose one of the hymns.

"What hymn is that?" David had asked.

"It's a new one. It's called "The City of God," James had replied. "Do you know it?"

"Yes, I have heard of it. But remind me how it goes."

"I can't sing it, sadly I don't have much of an ear for a tune," James had said. "But it starts "Glorious things of thee are spoken, Zion, city of our God."

David had nodded. "That was written by John Newton."

Jim had agreed and told him he had great respect for John Newton and that they had something in common.

David had found his assertion difficult to believe and had asked, in a supercilious tone, whatever did he have in common with John Newton. "He's the curate of Olney!" He'd exclaimed.

James had given a knowing smile. "Aye, he maybe a curate now, but when I was an Apprentice in the "Maid of Fowey", he was Master of the "Duke of Argyle" and later Master of the "African!"

David was looking mystified, so he'd continued. "Maybe you don't know, but both the "Duke of Argyle" and the "African" were slavers, the same as my ship the "Mary Anne!"

Astonished, David had shaken his head. "I can't believe that!"

"'Tis true, I tell you. I met him once when he came aboard the "Maid of Fowey."

"Well, Captain Youle", David had composed himself. "It's clear he listened to God when he gave up that evil trade."

Whenever James reached this point in the story his mother would always interrupt him and say "Then James looked tenderly at me and said 'Elizabeth my love, God must have sent you to make me give it up too!'"

And Jim had been as good as his word for he had never sailed again in a slaver. Instead he'd sought employment as a pilot in the estuary, but there had been no vacancies. After a few months he'd been offered the command of the "Fulmar" a barque working the wine trade. Nathaniel had joined him as Third Mate and together they had made several voyages to and from Bordeaux. The voyages were short compared with those in the slave trade, but even so both James and his mother had hated the separation and when one of the estuary pilots died James had been appointed in his place.

When James had given up command of the "Fulmar" he, Nathaniel, had decided to stay with the new Master, but had quickly regretted it. A pernickety man with little patience, Captain Oakley was always breathing down the neck of the mates and what had formerly been a happy, well ordered ship soon became full of discord, with everyone blaming the other when things went wrong, as they so often did with Captain Oakley as Master.

Nathaniel stood up to ease his ageing limbs. He glanced astern; he'd always kept a good lookout astern ever since that time the Moors had so nearly boarded the "Mary Anne"! Jim had been right to have been so angry!

He called the Officer of the Watch. "Bring her about, Mr Barrett. We don't want to lose the coast!" He watched the hands bring her smoothly onto the other tack, then he sat in his chair and was soon lost in his memories. He recalled how radiant his mother had looked when she told him that Parliament had abolished the slave trade. To enforce this the

Government had wanted a naval squadron to patrol the Slave Coast, but the war with France had made the assembly of such a squadron impracticable. Unhappily accepting the Admiralty's reluctance, the Government had however insisted that a naval presence on the coast must be provided. After much argument the Admiralty had agreed to send a token force to the coast and the frigate "Curlew" had been sent. Finding a ship and its crew had been hard enough, but appointing a Captain had proved almost impossible. No self-respecting Captain wished to be marginalised in a little ship off the West Coast of Africa, where the chances of action were slim and he'd soon be forgotten. Every Captain worth his salt wanted to command a ship of the line or if not at least a frigate attached to the main fleet. Only in such a ship would there be the opportunity to distinguish himself and catch the Admiral's eye. In the impasse which had resulted Captain Lloyd, who knew of Nathaniel's service in the slaver "Mary Anne" had called on Admiral Collingwood and had suggested that Nathaniel could be a suitable choice and so after an interview with the Admiral, he had been promoted Lieutenant and had been given command of the "Curlew".

Now here he was in the Gulf of Guinea with orders to arrest any English ship found carrying slaves. On a coastline some two thousand miles long it seemed an impossible task as all those Captains who'd refused the job had clearly foreseen! But despite that he was happy. He had his own command and who knew, he might have the chance to make amends for all the cruelty the slaves had suffered in the "Mary Anne".

His first chance to arrest a slaver had come a week ago. They'd spotted a ship leaving the Bonny River. Thinking it could be English, he had given chase and was overhauling her nicely when he'd seen barrels being thrown over the side. Mystified, he'd stopped to pick one up and had found a terrified, half drowned Negro inside. He couldn't believe anyone could treat another human being with such appalling cruelty, but he realised it had been a ploy to put him off the chase. And how successful it had been! By the time all five barrels had been recovered with two live and three dead men inside, the slaver was almost over the horizon! As he remembered how angry and frustrated he'd been, the Officer of the Watch pointed out a vessel up ahead. "Can you see her, sir? She's close inshore. Looks as if she could be on fire!"

Whatever it was, it was about five miles upwind. He studied it carefully. It did look like a ship and it did look as if she was on fire. He sent for the First Lieutenant. "Mr Fraser it looks as if those poor devils up there are on fire. Lower the pinnace and send young Smithers with the Bo's'un and a dozen hands to see what they can do. They'd better be armed. Meanwhile we'll continue to work the ship upwind and be ready to lend a hand."

As the pinnace set off, the fire began to show up well in the fading light. "Poor devils," he muttered. "We'll probably be too late!" Then as if in answer to his prayer the wind backed and the ship began to pick up speed. He told the Officer of the Watch to put the Leadsman into the chains. "I want constant soundings," he said.

It had been a cloudy, moonless night and he'd been on deck since the first sighting of that fire with his eyes searching for the shoreline and his ears straining to catch the monotonous call of the Leadsman as the "Curlew" beat to windward in the shallow uncharted bay. But despite the chill and his worries about the safety of his ship, he assured himself he'd done the right thing joining the King's Navy."

With Captain Oakley making life intolerable for him in the "Fulmar" he'd decided to find himself another ship. Then he'd heard that the trouble in the American colonies had erupted into full scale rebellion and outright war seemed a distinct possibility. Wanting to see some action he'd decided instead to volunteer for the King's Navy. When he'd told his mother she'd been horrified, but he'd said the Admiralty would need men for the fleet and anyway he could be taken by the press gangs, which were scouring the ports. He'd heard they'd even begun boarding ships in the channel and pressing some of their crews! So he'd decided to offer his services to the King's Navy as a volunteer and so might be able to make use of his experience as a Mate. James had supported him and when his mother had been convinced, she had sought help and advice from Captain Wells. Captain Wells had commanded the "Warspite" in which his father had been killed in the Battle of Quiberon Bay. He had asked his young cousin, Christopher Lloyd, then Captain of a ship of the line, whether he could help and shortly afterwards he, Nathaniel, had received an invitation to present himself aboard the "Marlborough", fitting out at Portsmouth. On arrival he'd been ushered into the great cabin and had taken an instant liking to Captain Lloyd, who'd seemed impressed with him. "With your knowledge and experience, Mr, Lugger he'd said. "I'll be pleased to have you aboard as Master's Mate". He'd had been overjoyed and had accepted his welcome offer immediately. After his years at sea, he'd had no wish to join the Gunroom as a Midshipman and was delighted to be made an assistant to the Master, who was charged with the sailing and navigation of the vessel.

It was getting lighter now and the horizon was becoming visible again and on the port bow the coastline was beginning to show. Feeling happier, he was further pleased by the appearance of his steward with his morning tea. As the drink warmed him, memories of the "Marlborough" returned. She was an impressive battleship and had formed part of Admiral Rodney's fleet, which had covered itself with glory during the war. He heard again the roar of the cannon and the din and clamour of battle as he remembered the capture of that Spanish convoy off Cape Finisterre and later catching and defeating the Spanish Fleet off Cape St Vincent. Then there'd been the Battle of the Saints. That was a fight he'd never forget! They'd met the French in the channel between Guadeloupe and Dominica and, when they'd finished with them, the Frogs had known their plans to invade Jamaica had been well and truly scuppered. He recalled the long chase in light, fickle winds when the Master and he had tried to coax every ounce of speed from the sails; how two French ships had begun to lag behind and when Admiral de Grasse had turned about to protect the two stragglers, they had at last caught up with them. What a battle it had been! The "Marlborough" leading the van, was the first in action and what terrible punishment she took! Never would he forget those scenes of death and carnage. After hours of fighting a change in the wind caused a French ship, the "Diadem" to be taken aback allowing a gap to open between the French centre and rear divisions; a gap which Admiral Rodney had been quick to exploit. The first to surrender had been the "Glorieux", and at last the French flagship the "Ville de Paris" had been taken and the battle was finally over. Five of the French had been captured, a sixth sunk and the rest had cut and run. Over a thousand Englishmen perished in the fighting that day and in the "Marlborough", one of the many wounded was the Master. As they'd limped from the battlefield he'd held the Master in his arms, trying to comfort him as another bound the wound where his arm had been. But it was of no avail and like so many others the Master had died. When he'd told the Captain of his death, Captain Lloyd had said he was to navigate the ship to Castries and when they'd anchored he'd made him Master!

The freshening wind broke his musing. He studied the foreshore again, searching for his mark. Then he saw it, a low spit of land a mile or two off. The fire up ahead was burning as strongly as ever, but now he could see it wasn't the ship that was burning. The flames came from the headland. Thankful that it was a false alarm, he examined the ship they had set out to help. She was a brig rolling gently in the swell as she lay at anchor. But of the crew he could see no sign. Closer inshore, but to seaward of the breakers he saw two strange objects. Neither he, the First Lieutenant, nor the Officer of the Watch could fathom out what they were! Could they be wrecks? If they were it was odd that they looked so similar, and why were they so close together? And he thought he saw people on them! Mystified he searched the shoreline for the pinnace. It worried him. They'd not seen it since the previous evening. Then to his relief he saw it, its sails furled and the crew pulling hard towards the "Curlew" now about to anchor south of the mysterious brig. When he was sure the anchor was holding he ordered the First Lieutenant to get the longboat ready for lowering and to prepare a boarding party. "I'm beginning to smell a rat. I can't see any crew on that ship and look, those two strange objects do have people on them!"

The pinnace was now alongside and Smithers was telling him that when he saw that the flames were on the headland and that it was clearly a false alarm, he had planned to approach the brig and ask to lie alongside for the night. But as he got near he got a whiff of her and straight away he knew she was a slaver! "So I decided to anchor nearby until first light. Then I moved closer and hailed her. She gave no reply so I hailed her again. Still there came no reply, so I fired three muskets at her side and we managed to scramble aboard."

"You did well, Mr Smithers."

Henry Smithers smiled. He thought he had too. But there was more to tell. "Well, sir, we had our cutlasses at the ready expecting a fight, but the decks were empty! There wasn't a soul about! Then we looked over the other side of the brig we saw two boats pulling for the beach. Then I realised that the Master and most of the crew had given us the slip. Later I found the ship's log, sir. She's the "Severn Lady" from Bristol and her Master is Captain John Trafford. Then I saw you coming to anchor, sir, so I left eight hands behind with the Bo's'un in charge and came to tell you what's happened."

"Thank you Mr Smithers it seems we've got a prize! Now get back to the "Severn Lady" and make a thorough search of the vessel. Some of the crew may be hiding down below. In the meantime I want to find out more about those two wrecks. Have you any idea what they can be, Mr Smithers?"

Mr Smithers shook his head. "They looked like pontoons to me when I saw them at sunrise and I swear I saw people on them, but I didn't take a closer look. I felt the brig was more important".

"You made the right decision, Mr Smithers." He turned to the First Lieutenant. "Mr Fraser once the pinnace has put Mr Smithers back on the slaver, take the pinnace and the longboat and have a good look at those two pontoons and do what you think is necessary. Put Mr Hamilton in charge of the longboat and I want everyone armed with cutlasses."

He watched the two boats leave. All he could do now was to wait for Mr Fraser's report and consider his options ready to form some plan of action. He didn't have to wait long. Almost immediately he saw the pinnace leaving one of the pontoons. It looked well loaded with the crew pulling hard against the wind. It headed for the slaver. There he counted six black men being hauled aboard. Then the pinnace set out for the "Curlew".

"They're not wrecks, sir", Mr Fraser shouted through cupped hands. "They're rafts anchored off the beach. They've been made with water casks and there are slaves on each. They're in a dreadful state, cold, frightened and seasick. At the moment they're causing no trouble. They just seem to be thankful to be alive!"

For the rest of the day the two boats shuttled between the rafts and the slaver and when at last the rafts had been cleared they were cut free of their anchors and towed to the "Curlew" to be dismantled. It had been slow hard work, but it had given him time to prepare his plan. He would leave a prize crew aboard the "Severn Lady", put Fraser in command with Smithers and the Bo's'un to help him and the two ships would sail in company to the Gambia, where he'd been instructed to land any slaves he'd rescued. Later he went onboard the "Severn Lady" to see what was happening for himself and to check that she was ready for sea. Mr Smithers showed him round the ship. "We found eight of the crew, including the Sailmaker hiding up for'ard. They're scared and very keen to please!"

"Mm," he grunted. "I bet they are. They're worried about their own skins now. Have you put them to work?"

"Yes sir. They've found water and food for the slaves and helped us get them down below."

"How many slaves are there?"

"The log shows fifty-two slaves had already been embarked, so with another sixty-three from the rafts, there'll be one hundred and fifteen!"

Going for'ard they passed the gratings over the slave deck and the long forgotten, yet familiar smell struck Nathaniel's nostrils. For a moment he fancied he heard Mr Braithwaite's voice; "Laddie, it's time we got them up". He struggled to control his emotions; Fred's death at the hands of the bloody flux had always upset him! He shook himself free of his memories. He had to concentrate! The magnitude of his problem bore heavily on him. How was he going to win the cooperation of these poor creatures and convince them that they were now in safe hands? How could he persuade them to believe that they were not about to be shipped over the ocean, that soon they would be set free? How could he tell them? If only one of them could understand a few words of English.

"Mr Smithers, can any of these people understand English?"

Henry Smithers nodded. "I think there's one that might."

"Well find him please and bring him to me." He turned to the Bo's'n. "Mr Murfitt, do you know the rig and can you work the sails?"

"Aye sir. 'Taint much different to the "Curlew" and one of the men we caught is the Bo's'un's Mate. 'E knows the rig and where everythin's stowed, so we'll be alright. Just let us start slow without too much canvas and we'll 'ave the 'ang of it in no time!"

"Right, Mr Murfitt, I'll remember that. You've done a good job today."

Now he was beginning to have more confidence in his plan, yet would his scratch crew be able to handle so many slaves and still work the sails? He knew he had to get the slaves on his side! Young Smithers was approaching with two hands and a black man bound at the wrists. He studied him carefully. He was a giant of a man!

Mr Smithers pushed the man forward. "Here he is sir. He's the one who seems to understand what we say to him."

With his powerful frame and quick darting eyes, he looked a fearsome figure. "Undo his bindings and bring him onto the quarterdeck," Nathaniel said as he led the way. Then with he and the Negro standing on opposite sides of the deck, he told the First Lieutenant and others to stand back. As Nathaniel approached the slave with outstretched hand, the men drew back and fell silent, while the black man eyed him warily and made no move to reciprocate.

"I come in peace," Nathaniel spoke slowly and deliberately. "I come to rescue you." It seemed the black man neither heard nor understood him! He stood there frowning, his dark mistrustful eyes watching Nathaniel's every move.

Nathaniel tried again. "I come in peace." He paused. "I come as a friend, do you understand?"

A long silence followed then Nathaniel heard a hesitant reply. "Me no sure!"

Nathaniel offered his hand again and took a step closer. He'd half expected the man to back away, but he was mistaken! The man seemed rooted to the spot. He'd begun to despair. He was making no progress! As he thought what else he could do, the black man extended his hand. With rising expectations Nathaniel held out his own. To his great joy the slave reached out slowly and took it! Then his hand was being gripped tightly, so tightly it made him wince and with a mighty heave the black man threw him onto the deck. The fall jarred his bones and he went sliding to the bulwark. His head was spinning and as he touched his temple he felt warm sticky blood! As his vision cleared he saw the First Lieutenant and the hands grappling with the man, pinning him to the deck. Others came to help him to his feet, but he shook them off.

"Leave him," he shouted. "Leave him. I must make him trust me!"

Fraser and the men looked at him in disbelief. "Let him go," he said quietly. Reluctantly they released the black man. Once again Nathaniel faced him alone.

"I come in peace, I come as a friend," he said again. "I want to save you and your people. Do you understand?"

The black man eyed him suspiciously. Then for a second time he said "Me no sure!"

Nathaniel kept his distance, studying him carefully while he thought frantically how he could persuade this black man that he was not a slaver; that he really wanted to be his friend. Then on impulse he took off his tailcoat, its gold lace glinting in the sun and held it out to the Negro. "This is a gift from me," he said.

His black adversary seemed puzzled.

"Take it, take it. It's for you!" Nathaniel shouted as he held the coat up. The black man hesitated. Then gently Nathaniel took one black arm and put it into the sleeve. Then almost before either knew it, the slave was wearing the uniform tailcoat of a Lieutenant of the King's Navy!

The slave looked baffled. He raised one arm to examine the fine cloth and finger the gold decoration. Then a huge grin spread over his face and he began to laugh, to laugh until the tears were running down his face. Nathaniel found he was laughing too and then so was everybody! The ice had at last been broken and while the black man pranced around in his gold bedecked jacket Nathaniel prayed that he had gained a friend who would trust him and translate his message to the others.

When the laughing had died away, the black man held out his hand. "Me like coat."

Nathaniel grasped the black hand and shook it. "You speak good English. How you learn?"

"I work for Englishman. He dead. Now they take me as slave."

"Well, tell the others, I have come to set you free."

The black man looked mystified.

"I have big war canoe over there." Nathaniel pointed to the "Curlew". We capture this slave canoe and take you to big river near here and set you free. Do you understand?"

"You not take us across big water?"

Nathaniel shook his head. "No. We take you back to Africa. We take you to big river called Gambia and set you free."

"You set us free?" The black man remained unconvinced.

"Yes. We set you free. We set you free, where you'll be safe. Do you understand?"

The black man shook his head in disbelief; then a huge smile spread over his face. "You set us free?" "Yes." Nathaniel was grinning now. "That's what I said and that's what I'll do. I'll set you free. Now will you tell all your people and say we mean them no harm?"

"Yes, Massa. I tell people you take us to big river and set us free."

"That's right. Make sure they understand. But tell me what is your name?"

"Me called Boto."

"Well Boto, thank you. I must leave you now. You help Mr Fraser here to get your people to big river. I will come with you in my war canoe."

At sunrise the following day the two ships weighed anchor and set sail for the Gambia. During the passage Nathaniel laboured over his report to the Lord Commissioners of the Admiralty. When he had finished he sat back and relished the fact that under his command His Britannic Majesty's frigate "Curlew" had rescued one hundred and fifteen natives from a life of bondage in the New World. Then he began to write to his beloved Mother. When she would get his letter he could not tell, but he had to tell her that at last he had done something to atone for his service in the slaver the "Mary

Anne". This he hoped would help assuage the guilt she felt for allowing him to sign indentures in a slaver.

As for himself he had no doubts that God's hand had been behind the fire that had guided him to the "Severn Lady" and he was thankful to have been able to make some recompense for his time as a slaver.

THE END

Lightning Source UK Ltd.
Milton Keynes UK
UKOW02n0508121115

262527UK00002B/16/P